Midnight Blue

Midnight Blue

If you believe in someone, will they come back for you no matter what? Even after they die?

A Novel

gregory r. schussele

iUniverse, Inc.
New York Lincoln Shanghai

Midnight Blue

If you believe in someone, will they come back for you no matter what? Even after they die?

Copyright © 2007 by gregory r. schussele

All rights reserved. No part of this book may be used or reproduced by any means, graphic, electronic, or mechanical, including photocopying, recording, taping or by any information storage retrieval system without the written permission of the publisher except in the case of brief quotations embodied in critical articles and reviews.

iUniverse books may be ordered through booksellers or by contacting:

iUniverse
2021 Pine Lake Road, Suite 100
Lincoln, NE 68512
www.iuniverse.com
1-800-Authors (1-800-288-4677)

This is a work of fiction. All of the characters, names, incidents, organizations, and dialogue in this novel are either the products of the author's imagination or are used fictitiously.

ISBN-13: 978-0-595-41675-2 (pbk)
ISBN-13: 978-0-595-86019-7 (ebk)
ISBN-10: 0-595-41675-6 (pbk)
ISBN-10: 0-595-86019-2 (ebk)

Printed in the United States of America

For Rosita, who said she'd never leave her "home"

Meet Gordon Schell

The sun blazes brilliantly over a trailer park in Clayville, North Carolina as it crowns a tree line in the distance. This morning, on the main drag several lots from the park entrance, the screen door at the side of a trailer flings back and a skinny little white man explodes through the opening, dashing across the porch. Clean shaven and with short, thin brown hair, Gordon Schell hurtles off the porch, late as always for work and clutching tightly his usual stack of CDs in their jewel cases in his left hand while swinging a small bag containing his laptop from his right.

From his right pants pocket he yanks out his keys and presses the button on the fob to open his blue, uniquely painted, 4 by 4 truck. Swinging the door open, he flicks the driver's seat forward, sets the bag on the floor behind it and flicks the seat back. Tossing the CDs on the passenger seat, he climbs in.

After firing up the truck parked next to a beat-up, rusty white Chevy Malibu, which is his wife's temperamental mode of transportation, he flips open the top jewel case and removes the first of two CDs that he's labeled "Rokn78 Feel It" with a felt-tip marker. He slips the CD into the player on the dash, shifts the truck into reverse gear, backs out of his tiny driveway, shifts into Drive and takes off down the main drag.

As the music from the CD, *Feel It Inside* from Trapeze, permeates the atmosphere of the truck's interior, a calm and carefree expression replaces the harried look of concern on Gordon Schell's face. Quickly approaching the entrance to the trailer park, Gordon stops to check traffic to his left; the sign to his right reads

"Stonewall Jackson Mobile Home Park" and underneath, "42 Lincoln Way." Seeing the traffic open to his left, he stomps the accelerator and turns right.

Cruising now, Gordon lets his mind slip to what he does best, dream. Mornings are the worst, when he and his wife, Rosita, invariably argue about this and that, and the battle never reaches a conclusion. Instead, he will notice that he is late for work, again, and they simply postpone the engagement until the following morning.

Gordon, however, never contemplates the argument. It is forgotten, as though he can flip his brain into cruise control and just drift into dream world, partly here, partly somewhere else, where it's calm and peaceful and co-operative. In his dream world, form is non-existent but recognition is pervasive. He can't tell anyone exactly who or what exists there but he doesn't care. When he dreams about here, it serves no purpose or function other than respite. He never follows through on his dreams so they never come true. His dreams for this world, the big blue spaceship, will always remain only dreams.

Fighting the traffic and able to see above most of the cars and around the SUVs, Gordon tries to anticipate the traffic flow, darting in and out of the two lanes running in his direction. Seeing the impending slowdown, he darts off the thoroughfare and takes a shortcut through residential streets, accelerating too fast through the quiet, tidy neighborhoods and barely slowing down at stop signs as he spies for vehicles with multi-colored lights mounted on top, the police.

Flying down another residential lane, two women walking to a parked car snag his attention, and he smiles as he glances to his right and in their direction. The house behind them is distinguishable by the laid, irregular rocks serving as steps to the porch. Gordon's smile is one of recognition but the two women barely notice him. Instead, they frown at the blue blur that speeds by.

A few minutes later, the neighborhoods give way to a collection of business and industrial parks which have been springing up in the area. Veering into a left turn lane, Gordon impatiently waits for the opposing traffic to clear just enough for him to jut across the road and into the parking lot of one of these complexes, where most of the offices house software and technical service companies, like the one where he works.

Gordon steps quickly toward a four-story, gray stone structure with considerable, dark glass exposure. He steps through the main entrance with many others, some of whom greet him and he nods back. Reaching the main hall cut through the middle, he turns right and walks nearly the length of it, suddenly spinning to his left to open the door to the stairwell. He jogs the two flights, skipping every other stair, and exits the stairwell to the third floor hallway, immediately turning to his right. With a door on either side, he heads straight for the door at the end of the hall. Pulling his wallet from his rear pants pocket as he approaches the solid door at the end, he places his wallet against a box with numbered buttons to the right of the door. When he hears the lock click on the door, he pulls the handle and opens the door to step inside, but glances back in the hall and sees the stairwell door fling open and a young man emerge into the hall. Gordon waits, holding the door open as the young man briskly walks toward him and reaches for the open door.

"Thanks," the young man says.

"You're welcome," Gordon replies, and spins around to step into a walkway convergence where he can choose any of three directions. Turning right, he walks past a lounge to his left and a solid wall to his right for thirty feet with the young man following closely behind. He reaches a huge open room littered with movable, carpet-covered cubicle walls arranged three or four deep to the outer windows, aisle after aisle stopping short of the inner wall to create an open walkway.

While the young man darts to his right, Gordon strolls to his left along the walkway next to the inner wall crammed with small, enclosed offices. He greets colleagues as he makes his way to the aisle where his cubicle is located, halfway along the walkway. He curves into the aisle and walks past the first two cubicles, both of which are empty.

Looking to his left he passes the next set of cubicles and spies Barry, a young man of Asian descent with short, neatly trimmed hair, clean-shaven, and sitting at his desk perpendicular to the aisle. While looking at his computer screen, Barry notices the blur of motion in the aisle, and looks up to smile at Gordon. Gordon smiles as he passes and they both quickly extend their left arms and slap hands.

Seconds later Gordon drops his bag on the desktop of the cubicle next to Barry and glances out the window to admire the sunny day and the rolling hills far away. He steps back to the desk to remove the laptop inside the bag, and places it to the right. Grabbing the cable in the back corner of the desktop, he plugs it into the side of the laptop while he flips it open and presses a button above the keyboard to bring it to life …

With the time on the laptop displaying "8:32," Gordon holds a phone receiver to his ear and says, "Hi, Marilyn, I got your message from late yesterday but didn't have a chance to call until this morning." He listens for a moment and asks, "So, those claims did get paid on the check from yesterday?" He listens for a few more moments, smiles, and pumps his fist. He exclaims, "Cool!" Silent for a moment, he asks, "Then, you're satisfied that the fix I put in place has finally resolved the lab group's claims problem?" He listens for another moment and says, "Money talks and bullshit walks. Couldn't uh said it better. Well, I'll submit the fix upstairs for review and formal support, but you just keep doin' what you're doin'. Give me a ring if there's anything else that you need my help with, okay?" Listening for a few moments, he returns the receiver to the phone.

Pushing his chair away from the desktop past the cubicle wall to look at Barry, Gordon declares, "One down, forty-seven million to go. Think I can slam forty-seven million by lunch, Barry?"

Barry turns around to face his colleague and friend and says dryly, somewhat effeminately, "If anybody can slam forty-seven million, Gordon, it's gonna be you."

Gordon stands up from the chair, pushing it to his right, and steps to the desk to lift a folder. He turns to his left to walk into the cubicle aisle, but steps up to Barry, pats him on the left shoulder, and states, "Slammin's the easy part. *Now comes the impossible* ..."

A tall, heavy and imposing male sits behind a desk in a small office with the door closed, glancing at pages which he flips over frequently from a folder laying on the desk. His short hair glistens from some secret compound massaged through its strands, and he occasionally rubs his clean-shaven right cheek and chin with his perfectly manicured right hand.

Silence saturates the office as Gordon sits in a chair opposite the desk from his boss, comfortable in his slouch, casually glancing about. The boss suddenly closes the folder and looks up at Gordon. With the demeanor of overly dramatic seriousness, he utters, "This is very good documentation, Gordon, but it shouldn't take three months to complete."

Gordon replies calmly, his expression betraying frustration, "You may recall that this is now the third time I have implemented this fix, since Sales and Support seem to be bent on screwing it up."

The boss is unfazed and responds, "And whose fault is that?"

Gordon, smiling with obvious mockery, replies, "Well, considering that our Support software had no alert function until three weeks ago and both the division's Sales and Support managers have been replaced since I started this project, must be me, huh?"

The boss frowns with great displeasure, and stands up from his chair, quickly and unconsciously fingering the tie adorning his impeccably ironed shirt. He slowly states, "There's no need to be sarcastic, Gordon. Everything changes, as you should know." He pauses and shakes his head, adding, "And, you should have submitted a patch proposal."

Gordon smiles, having secured the boss' lack of familiarity with the issue and, perhaps, with the entire company process and Gordon's function as a whole. With unbounded confidence, he asserts, "Done, as the back of that folder amply documents. Your predecessor shot that down. I think the response was, 'That's scheduled for inclusion three versions on the horizon.'" Gordon nods his head and adds, "That, of course, means two years down the road, assuming it's not yanked before release. You know what they say about 'assume', don't you?"

The boss appears upset and his tone is more demanding as he responds, "The company has undergone significant change lately and you're not the only one affected. Your attitude needs to change with it, Gordon, and you'll need to write up the patch proposal, again."

Shaking his head, holding his anger back somewhat unsuccessfully, Gordon spits, "I'm tired of doing the same things over and over." He points at the folder on the desk. "There's the formal documentation for the fix already installed on the client's system." He pauses while pointing at the boss. "There's one thing that never changes here," he adds, "and that's the Sales department and their ability to close sales with undeliverable promises, which, may I remind you, I have fixed time and time again."

The boss, growing impatient, snaps, "There will be no junior fixes in the field, Gordon. Period."

Gordon glances at the wall next to the door to read the sign hung by the boss, reading "Our Customers are No. 1". Gordon remarks, "You know, the only way to read that sign around here is 'our customers are no one.' Normally, I would give a two week notice, but I reserve that for those who deserve respect. I'll require fifteen minutes to clean out my personal items and I'll wait for security."

Taken totally by surprise, the boss displays consternation briefly, followed by an accepting disappointment. Softly, as he looks down at his desk, he says, "That won't be necessary." The boss lifts his head and the two men look at each other for a moment until the boss looks down at his chair and sits down. Gordon stands up and quickly exits the office.

Returning to his cubicle, he lifts a box of company propaganda and dumps it on the floor. He goes through all the drawers and shelves, throwing his personal effects in the box. Barry peeks around the cubicle wall and asks, "What are you doing, Gordon?"

Gordon stops to look at Barry and says, "Outta here, Bud."

Dejected, Barry pleads, "You can't be serious."

"Watch me," Gordon calmly replies, turning his attention back to packing the box.

Barry asks, "What are we gonna do without you here? What about your wife and kids?"

Emotionless, Gordon states, "You'll manage. They'll manage. I've got prospects." He lifts the box and walks past Barry, but stops and adds, "Listen, I'll be in touch. We're still friends, aren't we?" Gordon extends his right hand and Barry grabs it and lets his fingers slide off Gordon's hand.

Barry manages a smile as he struggles to speak loud and strong, saying, "Always. Don't be a stranger."

Gordon turns to walk away and sticks out his right hand with the thumb up.

Instead of driving home, though, he drives around in his truck aimlessly the rest of the morning and early afternoon, stopping at a park, at a convenience store, glancing occasionally at his watch while he drives. He passes a bar sign which reads "Cogent Coxswain Restaurant and Bar" and pulls into the parking lot.

Remorse, Recovery and Reconciliation

In the kitchen of the Schell trailer, which is an open area shared with the living room separated by a wall across half of each room opposite the side door, Rosita Schell is busy preparing dinner for the family of five. Diminutive in stature but full bodied, she carries her endowments with grace and ease as she bends down to check the chicken baking in the oven, her white T-shirt open at the front and displaying her ample cleavage. As she closes the oven door, she unconsciously slides her left hand through her short, jet black, curly hair on her left side.

The front door swings open and Gordon steps slowly, carefully, into the trailer, closing the door behind him softly. Hearing him enter, Rosita turns to the door, her beautifully angled face showing disdain, her thick and bushy black eyebrows raised to the top of her forehead, her eyes wide and piercing. She gathers herself to control her tone as she calmly asks, "Where's your computer case?"

Equally as calm, but avoiding her gaze, Gordon admires her full hips covered by her shorts and moves his ogle down her bronzed, smooth and thick thighs, past her knees and calves to her ankles. He replies, "I left it at work."

Undeterred and unsatisfied with his answer, her appearance unchanged, Rosita demands, "Where have you been?" When she senses that an immediate answer is not forthcoming, she adds a moment later, "Or didn't you think Barry would call me worried about you?"

Instead of confronting Rosita in the kitchen, he moves to his left through the living room to the sliding door leading outside. With a rapid delivery he says, "I want to play with the kids first." He gropes for the handle and yanks the door open, steps hurriedly through the door, and escapes to the back yard of the run-down trailer once he slides the door shut.

"We need to talk, muchacho!" Rosita shouts after him, turning back to look out the window above the sink. She slaps her right hand hard on the counter and grits her teeth in anger.

"Daddy!" yells a darting, little three-year-old girl, her long, sun-bleached blond hair swirling around her face and shoulders. She reaches Gordon as he dances down the four steps of the back porch and swoops her from the ground to hug her tightly against him. Twirling around in his arms, she smiles broadly and giggles several times as they walk to the back.

Approaching the two twirling together is Melanie, whose maturity is advanced far beyond her eleven years. When her father's eyes meet hers, she says, calmly, "Hi, Dad." Her expression is blank, reserved, waiting, and Gordon is reminded, once again, just how much this girl resembles her mother with the jet-black, curly hair, the thick dark eyebrows. At the same time he is always struck with their differences, for he knows that the girl before him exudes the supreme confidence and self-esteem which his wife struggles to secure, and, if she continues growing as she has, she will certainly be taller than her mother.

"Hey, Pops," comes a familiar greeting from Gordon's left and he turns to look at his seven-year-old son, Mark. Mark smiles briefly when Gordon sees him and brushes his brown locks self-consciously from his forehead to his right, away from the part on his left side.

"Mom's really mad at you," warns Melanie, her face still emotionless.

The little blond girl puts her right hand to his left cheek. "Mom kept saying, 'I don't know what's wrong with your father,'" she says. She wriggles back to look at him quizzically and asks, "What's wrong with you?"

He settles the little one in his arms and lowers her so she can lean back, and she smiles at the attention. Gordon replies, "I quit my job, today, Melinda, so I could spend more time with *you*!"

"That ain't flyin' with Mom, Dad," Mark responds, shaking his head with his brown eyes wide and disbelieving. "She was talkin' about packin' up and leavin' you."

Melanie's expression now softens as she adds, "But she decided to give you one more chance, and if you blow that one, we're leavin'."

Gordon sets Melinda down on her feet and she immediately wraps her arms around his left thigh, glancing around his leg from one to the other of her siblings. Gordon brushes her hair to either side from the middle momentarily, smiling gently, and waves his arms for all of them to gather around. While he sits down on the ground, as Melinda releases him and sits down next to him, he crosses his legs, and the older kids sit down around him and cross their legs, too.

"Pow-Wow," Gordon says, in a mock serious tone. "Little braves need to speak! Need answer to this question. Is Big Chief blowin' it? Speak first, Delicate Swan Who Moves with Grace." He looks at Melanie.

"Dad, you're not thinking of us when you do that," Melanie states, frowning. "Mom says you just think about yourself. She said this is the fourth time you've quit your job in the last six years! And every time you quit your job, we fall farther and farther behind! You've got to stick with it!"

"Well put, Delicate Swan," Gordon agrees, turning to look at Mark. "What say you, Bear Who Stands Tall and Proud?" Mark smiles at the name, his short stature temporarily forgotten.

"Melanie's right, Dad," he agrees, nodding at his older sister. "Every time you do this, it tears Mom up. She's like a nervous wreck."

"Nervous wreck?" Gordon interrupts. "Where did you come up with that phrase?"

"*Dad!*" Mark admonishes his Father. "She broke a glass after our snack and started crying. I had to hold her until she stopped. That's *your* job, ya know, but you're the one making her cry!"

"There is much truth in what you say, Bear Who Stands Tall and Proud," Gordon says, bowing his head. "And you, Little Doe of Everlasting Beauty, are you in agreement with your fellow braves?"

"Uh-huh," Melinda says, nodding, "you're not doin' too good, are you?"

"No, I'm not." Gordon looks over his children. "The tribe of Schell has spoken, all wise words, indeed. Big Chief needs to *be* big, act big, work out problems instead of quitting. Big Chief must protect his tribe. I will not quit my job ever again, unless I speak first with Squaw of Great Strength and Vigor, and she gives me her blessing, of course. This I pledge to you, my valiant braves, never again will I quit without seeking our mighty squaw's approval. Does that meet with the tribe's approval?"

"Yeah, just don't do it again," Mark says, unimpressed, looking away.

Melanie adds, "You're on notice, Dad, and Mom expects you to find a job *really* soon."

Gordon waves his right arm and announces, "I now declare Pow-Wow complete."

The older kids get up and go back to their play, but Melinda gets up and lunges at her Father to hug him. "I still love you, Dad," she says.

Closing his eyes with a rush of emotion, he softly moans, "I don't know if I could live without it, little girl." He hugs her back, sets her down, and stands up.

Melinda asks, "Daddy, will you do your thing with me?"

"My thing?" he asks. While Melinda nods her head in anticipation, he drops to his knees in front of her and the older kids stop to watch. He puts his right index finger to his heart, then to his nose, then to Melinda's nose, then to her heart. "The nose knows *all!* The wisest sense of all senses is the nose!"

Melinda chimes in to add, "And it knows *ev'rything!*"

"The nose knows all," Gordon repeats.

Sounding a little hurt, Melanie asks, "Why don't you do that with us anymore?"

Still on his knees, he turns to Melanie and explains, "Because you've both gotten so big and smart and you know everything. You've become," and he says it mockingly, "jaded and cynical. Why, you don't even believe in magic anymore!"

"I know, Daddy," Melinda agrees, shaking her head. "And there's magic ev'rywhere!"

"What did you tell me the other day about Santa Claus?" Gordon asks, looking from one to the other of the older kids. He cups his hands over Melinda's ears. Though she can't hear him, he says as he looks at her, "Sorry, little girl, but I must protect you from what will surely follow."

The older ones speak in unison. "There is *no* Santa Claus! *Mom* is Santa Claus!"

When they're silent, Gordon lifts his hands from Melinda's ears and she asks, "What did they say, Daddy? What did they say?"

"I can't repeat it!" Gordon exclaims with mock hurt, his head shaking and his mouth forming a deep frown. "They said terrible things about Santa Claus!"

Melinda puts her right fist against her right side in a stand-offish manner and exclaims, incredulously, "Is *nothing* sacred?"

Gordon laughs. "All things are possible," he replies softly. He looks to Melanie and says, "Come here, please."

Melanie steps toward her father cautiously, carefully, but stops just out of reach.

"You're gettin' so big I can't get on my knees unless you get on your knees, too," he says, pausing to add, "if I'm gonna do my thing."

Melanie takes one step closer and gets on her knees. Gordon touches his heart, then his nose, then touches Melanie's nose, then her heart. He says, "The nose knows," and he leans to her, "all." It's quiet for a moment until he asks her, "What's the rest?"

Melanie replies shyly, "The wisest sense of all senses is the nose."

"May I have a kiss, please?" he asks and Melanie wraps her arms around his neck and kisses her father on the lips. "Thank you," he says softly, gratefully, his expression one of appreciation. He quickly glances at Mark, and asks, "How about you, big man?"

"I'm cool," the boy replies, proudly adding, "and I know what jade means."

"You've been holding onto that all this time, haven't you?" Gordon asks, shaking his head.

"Yep, and I know what it means, too," Mark says confidently.

"Hit me, dude!" Gordon shouts.

"It means green," he replies, stopping to think a moment, and adding, "with envy."

"Where did you hear that?" Gordon asks, lifting his eyebrows skeptically.

"Didn't *hear* it!" Mark proclaims. "I read it. I read a *lot*!"

Gordon asks, "How come I don't see you read much when I'm around?"

Mark lifts his eyebrows as he replies, "Maybe you're not payin' attention."

"Maybe if I was around all the time I would see you read, how's that?" Gordon counters.

"Don't start, Dad," advises Melanie.

Mark volunteers, "I read jade is green."

"Okay," Gordon replies, asking, "and where did the envy part come from?"

"Wouldn't you like to know?" Mark counters.

Gordon glances to all three of his children as he says, "What I'd like to know is if dinner's ready. How 'bout you guys?"

"Yeah" comes the unanimous chant and Gordon stands up and walks to his son, extending his right hand, palm up. "Gimme five, kiddo," he says, and Mark slaps his hand hard, which Gordon draws back, shaking it while wearing a pained expression.

Gordon puts his arm around his son's neck and they start to walk to the trailer's sliding door, the girls in tow. Looking down at Mark, he says, "You know, son, there are days when you just amaze me. If there's ever a first person to clone a human being, it's gonna be you. But you won't share it with anybody. Instead, you'll clone your wife so that twenty years later, you've got a woman just like the woman you married, and everybody will be saying, 'Why, your wife hasn't aged a bit!'"

Gordon shakes his head as they enter the trailer and Mark's face is beaming. Melanie rolls her eyes as they step inside and Melinda squeezes past everybody to race into the kitchen …

In the kitchen Rosita removes the baked chicken from the oven and turns her head to the living room, hearing everyone enter the trailer. She sets the pan on a warmer on the counter, and flaps her T-shirt above her breasts in a futile effort to cool her chest. She steps to the other side of the sink to lift a towel from the counter and wipe her glistening face, stunningly gorgeous despite a lack of make-up.

"Mom," Melanie yells from the living room, "is dinner ready?"

Melinda scoots into the kitchen and quietly wraps her arms around her Mother's hips. "Yes," Rosita replies, gently rubbing Melinda's head, "and you kids need to set the table."

Mark and Melanie rush into the kitchen and Melinda climbs up into her chair and onto the booster. Melanie lifts plates from a cabinet shelf on the left and hands them to Mark and he distributes them on the table over the placemats. Melanie hands two glasses to Mark when he returns and he places them on two placemats next to their plates. He steps to the top drawer to the left of the sink and opens it, while Melanie sets three more glasses on the table in their appropriate places. Turning to Mark behind her, she receives the knives and forks he has removed from the open drawer. She sets one of each on each placemat as she moves around the table, followed by Mark, having pushed the drawer closed with his body, who sets a spoon at each placemat. As Mark takes a seat, Melanie tears off five sheets of paper towels from the holder dangling under the cabinets and sets one near each placemat.

Gordon leans against the wall between the kitchen and living room and watches the two in action. Rosita turns to Gordon and says, "Come and cut some chicken for the kids," nodding to her right. Gordon steps up next to his wife, grabs a knife and fork from the drawer, slips around her to the pan on the counter and begins cutting the chicken into small pieces, setting them on a separate plate.

"Mom, can I have something to drink, please?" Melinda asks.

Rosita steps to the refrigerator to her right, opens it and withdraws a plastic jug of milk. With the jug in her right hand, she moves around the table to fill the three glasses before her children, always brushing the cheek of each with her left hand as she finishes. Melinda takes a long gulp from hers.

Rosita returns the jug to the refrigerator, steps back to the counter, grabs two bowls, one with green beans and the other with noodles and sauce, and sets them in the middle of the table. Gracefully, she sits down between Melinda and Melanie.

"Waitin' on you, Daddy," Melinda says, turning to smile at her mother.

Gordon spins around holding the plate and steps between Mark and Melanie, scooping some of the pieces on Melanie's plate. He turns to scoop some on Mark's plate and scoots around the table to Melinda to deposit the last of the chicken on her plate. As he swings to the counter to lay down the empty plate and grab the pan holding the rest of the chicken, he says, "There's more chicken, so if you want more, I'll cut you some at the table, okay?" The children nod their heads while they fill their plates and begin eating.

Gordon slides next to Rosita and offers the pan, saying, "Take what you want, babe." She picks a breast piece and sets it on her plate. Before he steps away, he kisses her on her right cheek, but she ignores it.

"We had a pow-wow, Mom," Melinda says.

"I saw that," Rosita replies, smiling at her daughter.

Gordon walks around Melinda, sets the pan of chicken on the table and sits down, reaching over to Mark to pinch his side. Mark flinches and smiles at his father briefly before he continues eating.

Melanie says, "Dad promised that he wouldn't quit his job ever again without your okay first."

"He didn't say it like that, though," Mark offered.

"Oh?" Rosita exclaims, curious.

Melanie explained, "He said something like, 'I will never again quit my job without the mighty squaw's approval.'"

Rosita smiles at her oldest daughter as Gordon looks at his wife for her reaction. "Did you like that?" Gordon asks his wife, adding, "I saw you smiling."

"I was smiling at my daughter, if you don't mind," is Rosita's terse reply, refusing to look at him.

"I'm in deep shit, aren't I?" Gordon offers.

She turns to glare at him, replying calmly, "The deepest."

"I'll be diggin' out of it for a while, won't I?" he further offers.

"Longer than you can imagine," Rosita calmly answers.

After a moment of silence, Mark asks, "Dad, we don't have a shovel that *big*, do we?"

Everyone laughs, while Mark wears a huge grin. Gordon smiles as he looks at his son and remarks, "They make some pretty big shovels, but none as big as I'll need. I'll be diggin' for years."

"Count on it," Rosita remarks, but she smiles as she glances at her husband …

Gordon washes the dishes, placing the cleaned ones in the second sink for rinsing. Melinda stands beside him, watching with great interest. "Okay, Mark," he shouts, "rinse time, buddy."

Melinda steps to his right side and puts her arms around his right thigh, pushing the left side of her face against his leg. Gordon looks down at her, brushes her hair with his right hand, until he slides his hand around her head and pushes her head tight against him and holds her there. Silently, she squeezes his leg tighter.

Mark runs in from the living room and climbs to stand on the chair before the sink. Gordon turns on the cold water to a medium flow, pulls Melinda's left arm from his leg, and, holding her left hand, he steps around the chair next to the strainer. Melinda crosses to his left side and they both repeat the same actions as before but on the opposite side. Mark rinses the cleaned dishes, hands each to his father, who places them in the strainer with his right hand until they're all done.

"Call me for round two," Mark says as he jumps down from the chair and runs back to the living room.

"Will do," says Gordon and he steps around to the wash sink as Melinda takes a step away and watches.

Gordon scrubs the bigger pans and bowls clean, sets them in the second sink and calls for Mark when he finishes the last item. Melinda grabs his right leg and the two squeeze each other as before until Mark arrives from the living room. Gordon takes his daughter's arm and slides his hand to hers and they step around the chair to the strainer. Just as before, Melinda hugs her father's left leg and he buries her face against it and holds her like that while he places each dish that Mark hands him in the strainer.

Mark jumps down from the chair when he's done and Melinda lets go of Gordon's left leg and runs into the living room. Gordon slides the chair back to the table and announces, "Everybody got their homework done? Who needs help?"

Gordon steps into the living room and glances at each of the occupants in rapid succession. Melanie sits in the lazy boy against the wall on the right, Rosita and Melinda sit on the sofa engaged with a talking book, and Mark sits in a chair at the left, his head down, engrossed with reading a primer from his second grade class.

Melanie looks up at her father and says, "My homework's all done."

Without looking up from his book, Mark says, "I don't have any."

"I see you're reading," Gordon says. He stops to lean against the wall, staring at his son.

"Told ya," Mark says, head still buried in his book. He adds, "third time."

"That's the third time you've read that primer?" Gordon asks incredulously.

"Yep," Mark replies. He looks up and adds, "Dad, I want to read something a little harder. Can I read one of your books?"

Remorse, Recovery and Reconciliation 15

"Sure," Gordon says, as he steps across the living room to stop before his son. He sits down on the floor with his legs crossed, looking up at Mark.

"How about Teropik of Kanker?" his son asks, struggling somewhat with the words.

"Cancer," corrects Gordon, "and, uh, I don't think so."

Rosita had been listening intently, and she frowns as she stares at Gordon. "Why not?" she demands, her eyes narrow. "You said it was all right, but the first one he asks for, you say, 'no.'"

"Not that one, dear," Gordon calmly replies, turning his head to meet her scolding countenance, "unless you want to explain all the references to pleasures of the flesh, which is just about the whole book."

"Oh!" Rosita exclaims, her anger suddenly changing to surprise. She looks at Mark who returns her surprise with one of displeasure. Rosita gathers her composure and calmly advises, "No, Mark, that one won't do, but your father will help you pick one."

"Okay," Mark says, satisfied with his mother's response, but asks, "what's 'pleasures of the flesh?'"

Melanie laughs, glancing at her mother and her father to gauge the reactions. Rosita sighs as she says, "When you're a little older, your father will tell you all about it." She looks at her husband, frowning, and scolds, "Why do we even have that book here?"

"Barry gave it to me," Gordon explains, innocently.

"Barry!?" Rosita exclaims in disbelief, quickly adding, "Give it back."

Gordon frowns at his wife and says, "Son, one day I'll tell you all about it. Or maybe I won't and just let you fend for yourself like I had to." Mark frowns at his father and Gordon smiles devilishly, his gaze still locked on Rosita, as he adds, "In fact, you should ask your mother, since she taught me everything I know about that stuff." Finished, Gordon's smile grows wider.

Mark lowers his eyelids, appearing to have guessed the topic in question. Smiling, he offers, "You guys are talking about sex, aren't you?"

Melanie cannot contain her laughter as she stares at her mother. Melinda looks up from her book and glances back and forth at each parent.

Gordon's face flinches for a moment. Carefully, he asks, "Does that interest you?"

"Does it have anything to do with girls?" Mark asks back.

"Possibly," Gordon replies, even more carefully.

Mark's face suddenly contorts with a pained expression. "Because if it has anything to do with girls," he states, "yuk!"

"Good answer," Gordon says with a smile of relief, and puts up his right hand. Mark immediately slaps it gleefully.

"It doesn't always have to be with girls," Melanie advises, looking at her father with a strong sense of knowing.

"New subject!" exclaims Gordon.

"You started it," Rosita admonishes.

"And I end it," Gordon counters.

"I wanna hear about sex," Melinda says.

"Yeah, you end it, all right," Rosita remarks, sarcastically.

Gordon gets up, jumps over to Melinda, and whips her off the sofa, over his right shoulder and lets her dangle upside down, while she squeals throughout. He swings her around for a little bit as she laughs. Pulling her back over his shoulder and holding her up so their heads are level, he asks, "Can I have a kiss?" She throws her arms around his neck and kisses his lips.

Sitting her down on the sofa, he looks into her twinkling eyes and says, "I could tell you about it, little girl, but I can't remember anything. I think I have amnesia, our new subject." Instantly, he turns to Melanie, and asks, "Melanie, what is amnesia?"

Confidently, Melanie states, "Amnesia is about forgetting things."

"Yeah, but everybody forgets things," Gordon says. "Amnesia is more about forgetting important things, like," and he turns to Melinda, "who are you?"

"Melinda," she says.

Gordon looks at Rosita and, using a pick-up voice, says, "Say, who are you, little girl?"

"Your worst nightmare," Rosita replies calmly, raising her left eyebrow.

Mark advises, "She's still mad at you, Dad."

Gordon spins toward Mark and proclaims, "She'll feel better after I give her a back rub tonight."

"And every night while I'm waitin' tables," Rosita promises him.

"I hear ya," says Gordon, turning back to the sofa. He lifts Melinda to sit down next to Rosita and sets Melinda on his lap. Gordon whispers in Melinda's ear but loudly so all can hear, "I'm going for shameless, now, so I'm gonna use you, okay?"

"Okay," Melinda shouts.

Gordon hides behind his daughter and, speaking in a little girl's voice, says, "Mom, remember how you always say that I look like you when you were a little girl but I have Dad's personality and smile? And that I walk and talk like you, but you always see something in me that reminds you of Dad, and that it took both of you to make me, and that Dad knows he really messed up this time, but all he wants, no, he needs, is just one little kiss from the only woman he's ever loved." Gordon peeks around the far side of Melinda's head and Melinda laughs. He adds, "So would you give him just one little kiss for me, please?" He looks at Rosita with a mock forlorn, sad expression.

Rosita stares at Gordon's mock sadness and shakes her head softly a few times. In resignation, she says, "Come around the other side, silly boy."

Gordon moves to the other side of Melinda's head, and Rosita strokes his right cheek with her left hand. Gordon closes his eyes. She moves her hand close to his mouth and touches his lips with her thumb, leans forward and kisses him softly for several seconds. When she pulls away, she asks, softly, "What are we gonna do?"

Gordon opens his eyes and gazes into his wife's eyes with a serious expression. He replies, softly, "I'll have another job soon. I have some prospects, some old clients who like me and my work. You'll see." Nodding his head once, lifting one side of his mouth in a half-smile, he adds confidently, "We'll be all right."

Rosita's not convinced, but quite calmly asks, "How can you be so sure?"

"Because I'm good at what I do," Gordon responds with bravado, adding, "very good …"

Rosita stands in the kitchen drying the dishes and putting them away in the shelf above her with its doors open. In the living room it's quiet, except for the sound from the television. When the show ends a few minutes later, Gordon announces, "Okay, bed time for you, little one."

When he looks over at Melinda, she pleads, "Oh, I want to stay up a little longer, please?"

Gordon ponders, "Well, we haven't done it in a while." He stands up from the sofa and walks across the living room to the audio gear on the entertainment center, against the wall opposite the kitchen. He turns to face the kids and asks, a gleaming mischief in his eyes, "Do you think it's bedtime in Belgium?"

Together, all three shout, "Yeh! Bedtime for sure!"

From the kitchen Rosita shouts, "No, Gordon, not now! I'll never get those kids to sleep."

"I'll put them to bed at the usual times and they'll be all right," Gordon assures her. "Besides, the crowd is growing anxious." He pulls open a drawer in the middle, removes a jewel case and opens it. He lifts the top CD, presses a button on the player and a tray opens. Laying the CD on the opened tray, he presses the same button and the tray disappears inside the player. Below the player, he pushes the power button on the amplifier and solemnly states, "And, now, let us bow our heads and observe a moment of silence for rock n roll."

All three children immediately bow their heads with complete silence. Gordon presses the play button on the CD player, turns the volume knob on the amplifier several clicks clockwise, and turns around with eyes wide and crazed, his face displaying a deviant grin. A guitar struggles to find a beginning, the high-hat slips in to set the beat, the guitar finds its place, and in four bars the whole house is shaking to *Bedlam in Belgium* from ACDC.

With the living room a total madhouse, Rosita stops to shake her head in surrender, and continues drying the dishes and setting them in the shelf above. One by one, each member of her family enters the kitchen, jumping, dancing, skipping, only to stop momentarily to give her a hug. Gordon hops up on the counter to Rosita's left before the next chorus and mouths "it was bedtime in Belgium" with the chorus, while she tries to stare at him sternly, without success. Gordon hops down, grabs her around the waist from behind, holding her tight while he wiggles his hips. He suddenly lifts her off the floor and swings her completely around while she attempts to dry another dish, surprised but smiling. He kisses her on her right cheek, and moves back to the living room doing the "angus stomp."

When the song concludes in a rush of musical instruments colliding, Gordon stops the CD, steps over to Melinda and sweeps her up from the floor as she jumps into his arms. He carries her into the kitchen to Rosita, saying, "Give your mother a kiss good night."

She leans forward as Rosita leans to her and they kiss. Melinda says, "Good night, Mom."

"Good night, my little lovebug," Rosita says, smiling.

"Next stop, beddy bye," Gordon promises, as he turns around and carries her out of the kitchen and through the living room. A moment later they disappear down the hall to the bedrooms ...

In the master bedroom at the end of the hall, the only bedroom with the full width of the double-wide trailer, the clock on the headstand next to the bed displays "10:15." Rosita lies naked on her back, the curves and dimensions of her body perfectly framed by the sheet covering her body to her neck. To her right, his back to the bed, Gordon drops a CD labeled "Rokn69 Sensation" into the top of a small sound system on the dresser, flips the door down, and starts the player. The opening thumps of a drum beat cascade around the room as *Sensation* by Brian Ferry plays through the tiny sound system.

Gordon spins to his right, steps to the bed in the middle of the room and drops his pants. He lifts his right leg to pull his pants leg over his foot, repeats the procedure with his left leg and tosses the pants to the floor a few feet away. He pushes his white cotton briefs to his knees and they fall to the floor. Stepping out of them, first with his left leg followed by his right, he flicks them on top of his pants with his right foot. Leaning over the bed to a couple feet from Rosita's head, which is turned away from him, he says softly, "Turn over." Obediently, quietly, she turns over slowly, laying her head on her arms, and he pulls back the sheet, dropping it over her mid-calf.

Surveying her naked body with long appreciation, Gordon climbs onto the bed, lifting his right knee over her to place it on the opposite side. He straddles her as he settles his left knee against her left thigh. Stretching to the headstand, he grabs a bottle of lotion, flips the cap up, and squeezes some into his right hand. Returning the bottle to the headstand with his left, he massages the lotion in both hands before he drops his hands on her back, slowly spreading the lotion over all of her soft and sensual dark skin.

"We're never gonna get ahead this way," Rosita complains softly. "You've *got* to know that by now."

Gordon frowns and looks away to his left as he rubs her neck and shoulders as hard and deep as he can, his fingers straining. He responds in a slow, measured, soft tone. "I got pissed off at all the work I did for this client and that swine of a manager shot it all down." He pauses to turn and look at the back of her head, but his delivery starts to pick up in speed. "When he told me I would have to go through all the formalities that I had already done previously to no avail, coupled with all the management and structure changes and the frustration at having to re-do everything three times, I just lost it." With a slight hesitation, he bends forward to get closer to her, and whispers, "I was quite civil. I didn't even tell him to fuck off." He sits up straight wearing a slight smile.

Rosita's body remains unmoving as she protests, "Civil or not, we're the ones who suffer. You don't even think about us when you do that."

"True," Gordon agrees, and he knows that she's right. "I didn't." There's a moment of silence, and he adds, "I think I'm getting too old for this job-hopping. I'll find a job and stick with it."

"You'll have to," Rosita replies immediately. "We can't take this anymore." She turns her head up slightly, though she does not look at him when she adds, calmly as though stating a fact, "One more thing, hon. I always appreciate it when you get hard just because I'm lying in bed naked with you, but your wee willie winkie is thumping my ass right now and it's annoying me."

He leans far over on her right side where her head is turned so that he can look at her face to face from inches away. He says, "It never annoyed you before. Why, when the wee one would be thumping that fine mound of yours, you'd be so turned on when I finished, you'd tell me *two* words."

"Not tonight," she interrupts him.

"That's not the two words," he says, trying to make light of her interruption, but her glare convinces him to drop it. Instead, he sits up, puts his hands lightly on her back to steady himself, lifts his right knee and swings it over her and hops off the bed. He steps to his discarded clothes, and lifts his briefs from the floor. Glancing down at his erection, he announces, "Sorry, Winkster, but the boss says you have to be put in restraints."

As he lifts his right leg and pushes his right foot through the brief opening, he protests, using a little boy's voice, "No, no, not the restraints, don't do that to me. I have to be free, run wild." Bending over with his right foot on the floor, he lifts his left leg and pushes his left foot through the opening, draws the briefs over his legs to his hips, and continues, "Think of all the success we've had. No, not the underwear!" He puts his left hand over his mouth like a muffler, and protests, "Let me out, please. I promise I'll behave."

Gordon bends down to lift his pants from the floor, and holds the waist open with both hands. Shoving his right leg through its opening until his foot touches the floor, he holds that position momentarily, returning his left hand to his mouth, and, still using the little boy's voice, protests, "No, not, the pants, too. That hurts. That's too much. I won't be able to breathe. You'll stifle me. Let me out. Let me out." He quickly shoves his left leg through its opening until that foot hits the floor, yanks the pants to his waist, buttons and zips them shut.

Climbing back on the bed, he swings his right knee over her and straddles her again, protesting, his left hand over his mouth, "Let me out." Dropping both hands to swirl over her back, he concludes, using a calm announcer's voice, "I have shackled the junior faculty member, per your request."

She never moves, but smiles as she listens to him, and says, "That was dramatic."

"For one of us, it was trau-matic," he says, reaching for the lotion, pouring some into his right hand and returning the bottle with his left. He rubs the lotion in his hands first before he applies it to her back.

"I'll never understand you men," she says, "and your preoccupation with—"

"Personifying our sex organs?" Gordon interrupts. "Yep, it *is* stupid." He shakes his head, smiling, and adds, "Sometimes, though, it *does* seem like it has a mind of its own. There I'll be, tending to my own business, when I'll be confronted with your wonderful nakedness and a chain of events occurs which results in—boing!"

"I know I'm going to regret this," she sighs, "but what chain of events?"

Sitting up straight, he rubs both hands hard into the small of her back just above her bare ass and smiles as he enters his element, total silliness. Slowly, he explains, "First, the vision center of our brains sends a message to the sexual impulse center. The guys in the sexual impulse center—who, by the way, are all Scottish refugees—read the message—'naked woman!'—and spring into action." He stops rubbing her back and his voice sounds strangely Scottish, the first deep, and the second higher, more like a boy. "*Alright, boys, everyone to your stations. We need to open the blood valve to the penis. But, Cap'n, how much pressure can it take? Full bore, boys, and don't waste a drop!*" He starts rubbing her back again and his voice returns to normal. "Seconds later, that thing is hard."

Rosita lifts and turns her head around to look at him and says, "I see. Well, that would explain why you men are so confused and strange when it comes to sex."

"That's only half of it," Gordon says, looking down at her face with a smile. "After junior salutes, every guy thinks the same thing. 'Get down! It's too early!'"

"Yeah, that's pretty early," she says, settling her head back down on its side. "You men are sexual messes if all we have to do is parade around naked."

"I have never said you weren't in control," he says. "You're the boss."

Both are quiet for a while as he vigorously rubs her back from top to bottom.

"Does that feel good?" he asks.

"Uh-hum," she mumbles. It's quiet again, until Rosita asks, "Gordon, would you ever leave us?"

"What brought that on?"

"I'm asking," she continues, "*would* you?"

"You mean for another woman?"

"Would you?"

"Never," Gordon scoffs, wearing an irritated expression. He lifts his hands from her back, leans forward to the table for the lotion.

Rosita stares at the wall uncertainly. She asks, "Would you leave us for any reason?"

Gordon opens the lotion and pours some into his right hand. "Any reason?" he asks, a liitle confused. "How many possible reasons are there? How can I answer that?" He closes the top on the bottle, returns it to the table and rubs the lotion between his hands.

"So you *would* leave us," she sighs, and buries her head in the bed, fearing an answer she has already considered many times.

"I didn't say that," he protests, leaning toward her, placing his hands on her back just below her shoulders. "Look at me." She turns her head around and looks at him, a pained expression on her face. Gone is the goofy smile, replaced with a stern expression, as he explains, "That's a lot of reasons, reasons neither of us can even think of. But you want me to give you a simple answer, so I will. If it's a reason I can control, it'll never happen. I love you. I can't live without you. I love our kids, and they're our kids, not your kids. *Our* kids."

Still unconvinced, she asks, "What reason could you not control?"

"I could be drafted," he replies with deadpan seriousness.

Suddenly her fear disappears and she laughs as she turns her head back to the bed. She scoffs, "You're too old to be drafted."

"That's just one example," he counters.

Rosita looks up at him and demands, "Give me another one."

Gordon thinks for a moment and replies, "What if we were invaded by outraged Canadians who separate the men and take the women and children back to Canada to take advantage of their extra government benefits for instant dependents, not to mention a reduction in their withholding?"

She closes her eyes, shaking her head in disbelief, and asks "Canadians?"

Acknowledging the complete lack of probability, he explains in a more serious tone, "Well, I could say Mexicans, but as soon as they cross the border, they never go back."

"Ha-ha, very funny," she says.

"Something is bothering you," Gordon observes, briefly stopping the rub. "Spill it." His hands move over her back again.

She sighs before she begins. "You quit your job today, which is now the fourth job you've quit in six years. You can't get ahead like that unless you're moving to another job with more pay and a higher position. That's *never* been the case, though." Gordon stops rubbing her back and Rosita lifts up on her arms, so Gordon leans back and sits up on his knees. She turns around on her back and lifts her right arm to stroke his cheek as she continues, "You're not single, but that's what a single person would do. You're a married man with children. You have a wife that loves you madly, and your children love to be around you. You make them laugh and feel good, and I know they make you feel younger, but you do something like you did today, and I think that, maybe, you feel trapped, that you want to be single again. So, I'm asking you, are you going to leave us?"

"No," he says, calmly, looking into her jet-black eyes, "but just saying that won't make any difference to you or me. You have to trust me."

"But when you do what you did today, I lose trust in you," she argues. "It shows you'll ignore your responsibilities and your obligations to me, to us."

"Okay," he agrees. "I was only thinking of myself." He pauses for a moment. "But, you've put me on notice, that if I do it again, you'll take the kids and leave *me*. I can't have that. I can't live without you. I can't live without the kids." His voice is trembling slightly and his face displays deep worry. Softly, with his head bent low, he says, "That would kill me."

Rosita lifts her left hand and cradles his face with both hands, looking deep into Gordon's eyes. She shakes her head as she softly says, "Silly boy, I would never leave you."

He lifts his head to look at her skeptically as he replies, "So, you didn't mean any of that?"

She raises her eyebrows as she replies, "You made me very mad when I heard about it. I wanted you to know how angry I was."

Gordon takes her hands from his face and kisses them. He says, "You should never take back anything like that. You need to be clear with me, that when I don't take care of us, all of us, and do what's best at all times for all of us, you're going to take action to protect you and the kids." He looks away as he adds, "Sometimes, I don't think about everyone else, I'm just thinking about me, and you need to make me stop doing that. It's harder for me to do what you do naturally." He turns back to look into her eyes. "You would sacrifice yourself for any one of us at any time, because you always think of all of us before you think of yourself." He stops for a moment before he adds, "And that's why I love you so much, because you're so much better than I am."

Rosita pulls him down to her and kisses him long and sensually. When their lips separate, she says, "I still would never leave you, but I know what I *can* do." She pauses as she slides her hand underneath him and rubs his crotch. He slides his legs down to lie on top of her, and she pulls her legs out from under him to put them outside his. Lifting her right leg to lay it on top of his leg, she gently rubs her leg over his, while undoing his pants. With a serious expression, she says, "I can cut you off, because I know you'll miss this, what I'm going to give you."

While she pushes his pants down to mid-thigh, Gordon asks, in mock tone, "You have a gift for me? Is it hidden in this room? What is it?" She swats his ass before she pushes his briefs down, but he stops her and says, "Wait! It doesn't bend that way." He lifts up to clear the front of his briefs from the obstruction and adds, "There." She pushes his briefs down to his pants and slides her right hand back underneath him and around his growing erection. He asks, innocently, "No, seriously, what did you get me?"

Rosita moves her head to his side, kisses his left ear and whispers, "Shut up and fuck me."

"*Those* are the *two words*—" he remarks but cannot finish, because she gently places her left finger over his mouth, kisses him long and hard, and begins to moan softly.

Scene of the Crime

The following morning a number of police cars with lights flashing congregate before a small house, distinguishable by the laid, irregular rocks serving as steps to the porch. Inside the house, two plainclothes detectives approach one of the officers who answered the initial call. The uniformed officer wears a serious expression and draws up his medium height as the two detectives grab his attention.

The taller detective, a well-built black man with short hair and wearing an expensive charcoal gray, three-piece suit, says, poking his own chest, "Detective Lewis and this is my partner, Detective Schneider. Who discovered the victim?"

The uniformed officer replies, with a slight, Latino accent, "Apparently, she's the victim's carpool friend, Betty. She was so shook up when we arrived that we had to call an ambulance, so she's at the hospital now. She showed up to take them both to work, but there was no answer when she knocked, so she got the spare key the victim leaves outside and found this." The uniformed officer nods in the direction of a hallway off the living room where all three stand. "Bedroom's the first door on the left," he adds.

The other detective, a shorter than average man wearing a severely wrinkled brown suit lacking any distinction, asks, "Has anyone compromised the crime scene?" He frowns as he hunches forward while jotting something in the mini-notebook he holds in his left hand.

The uniformed officer calmly answers, "No, sir. I was first to see it and I've kept everyone out of the bedroom until Forensics arrives. I know how important it is, sir."

"Good job, Officer," Detective Lewis commends, searching for a name.

"Dominguez, sir," the uniformed officer advises.

Detective Lewis nods his head in acknowledgement toward the officer and turns to walk down the hallway. Detective Schneider raises up his full height to look at eye-level with the officer and says, "That was good thinking, Dominguez. It makes our job easier. Thanks." Schneider quickly turns to follow the senior detective down the hallway while the uniformed officer nods once.

The two detectives gingerly step into the bedroom. Detective Lewis briefly glances at the lifeless female on the floor, holds out his right arm to stop his partner and gazes all around the room. Detective Schneider stares helplessly at the body on the floor for a few seconds, spins around to leave the bedroom, scrambling past the uniformed officer standing at the hallway entrance. The officer watches Schneider put his hand tightly over his mouth and rush out of the house. The officer turns back to the bedroom entrance and calmly says, "Sorry. Forgot to tell you it's a gruesome sight, one of the worst I've ever seen."

Detective Lewis looks down at the fully clothed body and says, "Gruesome ain't the word I'd use. This is barbaric, depraved, beyond redemption. This woman was obviously tortured mercilessly before she was killed. Whoever did this is one sick bastard." He looks to his right and to the right of the body, and asks, "What's that? The killer's calling card?"

The officer steps to the bedroom door and looks inside. "Don't know," he replies. "I suppose it could be."

"Is that her blood?" Lewis asks.

The officer says, "It appears that way, sir. Yes."

"I sure hope that's where she's at now," says the detective, looking to the right of the body and reading the message written in the victim's own blood. "Goddamn, the horror she must have endured."

The officer advises, "Forensics is due anytime. I'll wait outside for them."

Lewis turns to the officer and nods. Turning to leave, the officer twists his body along the hallway to allow passage of the police department photographer. When Lewis sees the photographer, he advises, "Hold on, Dominguez." The officer freezes and slowly turns around to step back into the doorway of the bedroom next to the photographer. Lewis continues when he sees the officer. "Okay, we want photos of the entire scene, including the writing, followed by close-ups of the body and the writing, being careful to keep them separated. We're going to keep the writing under wraps, so is that understood by both of you?" Both the photographer and the officer nod. Lewis glances to the officer and asks, "Who else has seen this?"

"Only my partner," the officer advises.

"No discussion of the writing, period," Lewis warns. "Make sure your partner understands that."

"Will do," nods the officer and he turns around and walks out of the hallway and through the open front door onto the porch. The photographer carefully places his feet into the bedroom and begins snapping pictures.

Detective Lewis turns around, exits the bedroom, through the living room, and walks out of the house to the porch. Yanking out a pack of cigarettes from his shirt pocket, he removes one while retrieving the lighter from the same pocket, lights the cigarette and takes a long, first drag. He surveys the neighborhood, just a quiet, residential street, with nothing to leave the impression that it harbored a butcher with no compassion.

Detective Schneider crosses the street to return to the house of the crime scene while a balding, portly man walks back to his house. The two had been talking and Schneider briskly steps up to the porch and says, "The neighbor across the street over there," and he pauses to turn to his right and point to the house next to the corner house, "thinks he may have seen the killer up close last night, about ten-forty-five. Got as close as directly across the street from a man that he watched leave the house, so he came out to the street to pretend like he was checking his garbage cans—they picked up this morning—and the man walked right by him on the sidewalk across from his house, went to the corner, turned left and disappeared down this opposite street. He says the man looked right at him for about ten seconds or so. He didn't seem to be hiding himself, so he didn't pay it much mind at the time, other than the woman almost never has visitors and never that late."

Detective Lewis rubs his fu-manchu-styled facial hair and asks, "Does he think he got a good enough look to ID him from a photo?"

"He thinks he did, yeah," Schneider confirms.

"We'll want him down at the station to go through the photo books as soon as possible," Lewis advises, looking at his partner with a bit of concern. "See when he can meet us down there."

"Right," Schneider agrees, and steps from the porch to talk to the witness across the street.

"You all right?" Lewis asks, raising his voice.

Schneider stops and turns quickly to face his partner. "Sorry," he explains, dropping his head momentarily. "I just have never seen anything like that in person before."

Lewis nods his head in agreement. "Okay," he consoles Schneider. "You'll see the worst that people can do to each other in this job. Anyway, let's get that witness downtown."

A man and a woman, both carrying bags, step up to the porch from the car they just parked on the street before the house next door. The man is younger with brown hair to his shoulders and he walks slightly behind the woman, towering over her, but his position signals that he is the helper while she is the lead. As they near the porch, he looks down and runs his right hand through his long hair self-consciously.

Detective Lewis watches the short, slight but attractive woman, her black hair tied back in a pony tail and bobbing back and forth as she walks toward him. When she meets his gaze, he advises, as he draws another puff from his cigarette, "You bring your barf bags?"

The woman answers confidently, almost as though she had been insulted, "Don't need 'em. We've seen everything." She never slows her stride as she meets and passes Lewis, looking away from him only after he's behind her.

Lewis turns with her as she passes, his eyes narrowing, and says with dead seriousness, "You ain't seen anything like this."

After School

Gordon drives his truck down the main drag at the trailer park, turns left into the small drive before the trailer and shifts the truck into the park position. With the truck stopped, Melanie throws the passenger door open from her seat in the front and jumps out to the concrete drive. Mark flips the passenger seat forward and squeezes through the opening to jump out and run after Melanie. Gordon steps out of the truck, turns around to pull the seat back and remove the straps holding Melinda in her car seat. He pulls her out of the seat and truck and sets her feet on the concrete drive and she scoots up the porch to wait with the other two.

An attractive woman with short but smartly styled brown hair sits behind the wheel of a vintage early eighties' Ford sedan next door, frustrated and worried. She watched the Schell family pull up and get out. Now that Gordon is out of the truck and walking to the side of the trailer, she yells over to him, "Gordon!"

Gordon stops and looks over to the woman as she looks anxiously at him. He yells back, "Yeah, Penny."

"Can you help me with this piece uh crap?" Penny asks, desperate, rubbing her left hand over her face. "I can't get it started and I'm late for work as it is."

Gordon looks over at the kids, pulls his keys from his right pants pocket, sets them on the hood of the truck, and says, "Melanie, here's the keys to the trailer. Please take the kids inside. I'm gonna see what's wrong with Penny's car."

"Okay, Dad," Melanie responds, and runs down the stairs to get his keys.

Gordon walks the twenty feet to his neighbor's drive and stops to stand next to the hood. He says, "Okay, Penny, let's hear it." Smiling, she flips the curl of her forehead locks with her left hand and turns the key to try to start the car.

From under the hood Gordon can hear a series of clicks and nothing more. He looks at Penny through the windshield, puts his right arm up in a halting signal, and says, "Okay, Penny, pop the hood."

Penny pulls the hood lever under the dashboard and, when the hood unlatches and pops up a few inches, Gordon steps to the front of the car, searches for the hood release lever, pushes it open, lifts the hood and sets the rod in its holder to rest the hood up. He yells, "Try it again." The same clicks are heard, a little louder, and he looks at the battery and yells, "Okay."

When he steps to the left side of the car next to the battery, Penny asks, "Think you know what's wrong, Gordon?"

"Maybe," he says, looking up at her through the windshield. "Good thing you've got an *old* piece uh crap instead of a *new* piece uh crap."

"Why?"

"Because I might be able to fix it with a screwdriver," Gordon replies, leaning over the left side of the car, scrutinizing the red, positive cable from the battery and where it's connected. He glances up at Penny to ask, "Got one?"

"I think Alan keeps a screwdriver in the glove compartment," she replies. She leans over, opens the glove compartment, and adds, "Does it matter what kind?"

"Philips. Flathead. Don't matter," he replies, adding, "It's gotta be about six inches long, though."

"How's this?" she asks, sticking out a flathead screwdriver with a blade about six inches long, while he steps over to the window.

"That should do," he says, taking it from her left hand. "Put the ignition switch in the 'on' position and get ready to pump the gas in case it needs it."

"Okay," Penny says, and sets the ignition switch in the "on" position and readies her right foot over the accelerator pedal.

Gordon steps back to the left side of the car and looks at the battery cables, following the red positive cable to a small component mounted to the sidewall with cables running from terminals down to the engine block. Using the screwdriver blade, he connects the terminal where the positive cable from the battery connects at the top to a terminal at the side that has a cable attached running to another component attached to the engine block. Instead of clicks, the engine starts to turn over and Penny gives it some gas for a few seconds, lets up on the accelerator, and the engine continues to run.

Penny smiles broadly as Gordon steps over to the window, holding the screwdriver. She gushes, "Gordon, you're a lifesaver. How can I ever thank you?"

He returns her smile and says, "You're just lucky I quit work yesterday. Otherwise, I wouldn't be home and you'd be SOL."

"Rosita told me that," she says, her smile fading. "How's she taking it?"

"She wasn't too happy, but I've got an interview scheduled tomorrow," Gordon assures her, shrugging his shoulders. "I'll be working soon."

Penny squints at him severely, saying, "You know, you shouldn't have quit. You've got a family to support. If Alan did that, I'd kick his ass."

"Yeah, I know, I know," Gordon responds, sheepishly. He brightens, though, and asks, "Well, listen, have you been having problems starting it recently?"

"Yes, the damn thing sometimes won't start, and I have to let it sit, and finally it kicks over."

"All right," Gordon explains, "you've basically burned up the solenoid. On older cars, the solenoid kinda acts like the regulator between the battery and the starter. Anything with electronic ignition, and some before that, don't have solenoids." Penny gets out of the car to look at what Gordon is talking about. Gordon steps backwards to the front of the left side of the car to make room for Penny and continues. "The nice thing about a solenoid is, even if you burn it up, you can usually start the car by connecting the positive terminals on it." He points to the solenoid, then to the positive terminal from the battery. "Here's where the positive cable from the battery connects and on the side here is the positive cable to the starter. Connect these two terminals with the blade of the screwdriver while someone is behind the wheel with the ignition 'on' and it should fire right up."

Penny gives him a hug, her frame almost as tall as his, saying, "God, you are good!"

When she releases him, he salutes her, and says, "Just doin' my duty, ma'm. Sergeant Rock, at your service."

Penny smiles and says, "Well, we like country music."

"You're a little bit country," he says, "I'm a little bit rock n roll. Takes all kinds. Anyway, you'll need this," he hands her the screwdriver, "and tell Alan he needs to find a replacement solenoid for this old piece uh crap." He steps to the front of the car, lifts the support rod and sets it in place on the front panel while holding the hood. He lowers the hood to a foot from its resting position and lets it fall with a bang. He steps back to Penny.

"Thank you, Gordon," Penny says gratefully. She turns to the car door, steps around it and sits down behind the wheel. "If I don't see you before, good luck on your interview."

"Thanks," he replies, pausing to glance at her while he walks to his trailer. "Be careful and don't let it die."

"Bye," she says as she backs away, and they wave to each other.

When Gordon steps into the trailer, the kids sit in the living room, surrounding a game of *Sorry*. Mark flips over a card on the board and moves one of his pieces while the girls chide and tease him. Before looking inside, Gordon shouts when he closes the door, "Who's got homework to do?"

"I didn't have any, Dad," replies Mark, calmly, and Gordon spins to look at his son in the living room.

"Mine's already done," replies Melanie, looking up at her father briefly, before turning her attention back to the game.

Gordon strolls into the living room, looking at the face of his oldest daughter. He asks, "Want me to check it for you?"

Melanie glances up at her father and shakes her head, saying, "No, it was easy."

Gordon replies, "Okay." He looks at the game on the floor and says, "Oh, you guys started the game without me."

Little Melinda looks up at him, puts out her arms and hunches her shoulders, and says, with absolutely no hint of regret, "Sorry."

"You can play next one, Dad," Mark says.

"We'll see," says Gordon, stepping away from the game toward the kitchen. "I've got to clean up the kitchen before your mother gets home. Jose and Maria are coming over tonight," he adds, referring to Rosita's long-time friends who were once his neighbors.

Mark looks up from the board and asks, "What was wrong with Penny's car?"

Gordon stops and turns to face his son. "She has a problem with a piece in it that won't let it start," he replies, smiling, "but you can get around it with a screwdriver, so I showed her how. No biggie."

Mark puts up his right arm with his palm outward, so Gordon quickly steps back and swats it as Mark says, "Good job, Dad. You're pretty handy, ya know?"

"For some things, maybe," Gordon says, wearing an uncertain expression and flipping his shoulders up. "I try. That's all you can do."

Melanie looks up at Gordon. "Dad," she says, "I know the reason is not so good but it's nice to have you home when we get out of school. We love having you around more."

"I got to be with him all day," smiles Melinda.

Gordon steps around the two girls and sits down between them, puts his arms around both, and pulls both to him. He kisses Melanie, and turns to Melinda to kiss her, too. "Maybe I don't tell you girls enough how much you mean to me, but I love you both so much, and you always make me proud."

After a moment of silence, without looking up from the game board, Mark asks, "What about me?"

"Oh, you're a man," Gordon replies, "be a man."

"I'm a boy, not a man," counters Mark, looking up at his father with minor disappointment.

"You're a little man," Gordon insists, as he gets up from the floor to step around to Mark.

"No, I'm a little boy," Mark says, watching Gordon's every move. His father now stands directly above him.

"Stand up, little man," Gordon demands. When Mark is slow to respond, Gordon adds, "please."

Mark gets up from the floor and, once standing, turns to face his father. Gordon immediately wraps his arms around Mark's waist, lifts him off the floor, and swings him around four times. When he stops, he looks at Mark and kisses him on the lips. Smiling, he looks in Mark's eyes and says, "*Now*, you don't feel left out, do ya?"

Mark smiles as he replies, "No."

Gordon sets Mark back on his feet, but admonishes, "Just don't tell your friends that your Dad swings you around and kisses you like a girl." He narrows his eyes at Mark and adds, "Don't think they'd get it. Whadda *you* think?"

Mark is still smiling broadly as he sits back down and says, "Never goes past me, Pop."

Gordon turns and steps back to the kitchen, announcing, "I'd love to be able to spend time with you like this all the time, but I've gotta work, and tomorrow, I may be back at it. I've got an interview that's right up my alley."

"We know, Dad," Melanie says. "You gotta take care of us. I hope you get the job."

"Thank you, dear," Gordon says, already in the kitchen, picking up the dishware still on the table from lunch.

Outside, a man about the same height and build as Gordon, wearing a scruffy T-shirt tucked into a pair of jeans with long, straggly, thin hair, a thin mustache and long sideburns, walks in the street next to the curb. Approaching the Schell trailer unheeded, his hands are tucked tightly into his jeans pockets. Casually, he leaves the street to walk along the passenger side of Gordon's truck. Wearing a pair of tight leather driver's gloves, he tests the door handle and when it offers no resistance, he holds the door steady as he opens it silently. Leaning into the cab, he pulls his T-shirt from his jeans and some items tumble onto the passenger seat. Calmly, he scoops the items and shoves them carefully under the passenger seat and glances at the truck floor from the front and rear. Satisfied that the items are hidden from easy view, he steps back and silently closes the passenger door shut. Continuing his leisurely pace, he steps around the truck and back into the street in the direction from which he came, his hands tucked tightly into his jeans pockets.

The Police Station

In a small interrogation room at the police station, Detective Lewis sits across a table from the witness, Bill, who is a bit bewildered and nervous, his eyes darting around the room but never focusing on anything. Detective Schneider stands next to Bill on Bill's left side, holding a police photo book, which he has picked up from the stack of photo books in the middle of the table. Schneider places the book on the table before the witness and flips open the cover to the first page. Lewis holds up his hand, glancing at his partner, turns his head to Bill, and says, "Before we have you go through our books, tell me again what you saw last night."

As Schneider removes a small notebook from inside his jacket and prepares to take notes, Bill begins, "I was standing on my porch just looking around the neighborhood, getting a breath of fresh air, if you will, when I was looking over at the victim's house and watched the door open. Usually, no one is going in or out of her house that late at night, so I watched closely, and this man—"

"What was he wearing again?" Lewis interrupts.

"Well, he was wearing blue jeans, and some type of white, half-top sneakers," Bill recalls. "He was wearing a dark-colored T-shirt with sleeves, no collar, and it had some design on the front, but I never could tell what it was." Bill is looking back and forth between both detectives as he recounts what he saw the night before, but he pauses to lift the styrofoam cup of water and take a sip. As he sets the cup on the table, he continues. "When he had walked past me, there was nothing on the back. He had a necklace, looked like silver or that color, a dark colored band around his left wrist that I assumed was a watch, and I don't remember seeing any rings, earrings, anything like that."

"Good," Lewis comments. "Go on."

Bill continues, anxious to get it out. "So the man steps out of the house and closes the door behind him and I knew this was unusual, so I wanted to get a closer look and I walked out to the street and played like I was trying to secure the lid on my garbage cans, but I was looking at him the whole time. When he gets to the sidewalk and turns to come down it across from me, I'm almost out to the street, and that's when he looks over at me. We look at each other for, it seemed like about ten seconds or so, until he got directly across from me, then he looked straight ahead, turned left at the corner and disappeared behind the houses on that street."

"He wasn't wearing a hat or anything on his head?" Schneider asks.

"No hat," Bill replies, turning to Schneider. "Nothing."

"Describe what he looked like," Lewis encourages Bill.

Bill pauses, narrowing his eyes and looking away from both detectives, staring at the wall. He replies, "First, he was a white man, and probably average height, and he was skinny, not muscular at all."

"Approximately how tall would you say?" Lewis asks.

"Maybe around five eight, five ten, right around there."

"Good," Lewis says. "Continue, please."

Bill looks directly at Lewis and, using his hands, animates what he is saying. "He parted his hair in the middle and it was long, down below his shoulders, and it was kinda stringy, straggly. The wind would blow it and I could see light through it. What I mean is, it wasn't thick hair. It was thin."

"How far did his hair hang below his shoulders did you say?" interrupts Schneider.

"I don't think I did," Bill apologizes, turning to Schneider. "Not very far, maybe an inch or so."

"Thanks," Schneider says, motioning with the hand holding his pen for Bill to continue, and he writes something in his notebook.

Lewis asks, "How old did this man look?"

Bill turns to Detective Lewis and replies, "I would say he looked like he was in his mid-twenties, but I've seen guys like that that just look young for their age. I would bet that he's actually in his early thirties. He just kinda looked young for his age."

"Okay, good," Lewis comments. "Anything else?"

"He had a fairly high forehead, against the rest of his face," Bill adds. "His eyes were close-set. His nose was a little big, kinda wide for his face." He pauses to drink from the cup of water before him, thinking about the face he saw. Returning the cup to the table, he continues, "His face was mostly square. His chin was weak, kinda lumpy. I couldn't see his ears well, because his hair was so long, but they didn't stick out in any way. He was clean-shaven, except for a mustache and long sideburns, which came to an end about halfway down each cheek."

"Any distinguishing marks? Tattoos?" Schneider asks, leaning forward writing in his notebook.

Bill responds, "Nothing on his face nor on his arms below his sleeves. No tattoos or anything like that, no."

"Anything that we might be overlooking?" Lewis asks. "Did his clothes look torn, or dirty, or anything else that might have stood out?"

"I didn't see where his clothes were torn or dirty, no," Bill replies. "They just looked like normal jeans, nothing special about his sneakers, but his shirt had some writing on it and a design, like a scene of some kind, but I couldn't make it out at all."

"Okay, that's good," Lewis encourages. "We appreciate your patience in coming down and answering our questions and helping us out."

"It's the least I can do," Bill offers, adding, "Was she really tortured like they've said in the papers?"

"We can't comment on that, right now, Bill," Lewis responds, "but I will say, I've never seen anything like it in almost twenty years on the force."

Schneider points to the first photo book that he had placed before Bill. He says, "Now, Bill, what we'd like you to do is go through these books. Concentrate on that man you saw last night and see if you can find anyone that resembles that man. Take your time and we'll check on you periodically." The two detectives get up to leave Bill alone.

Lewis says, "If you find him while we're out of the room, just go to the door and tell any of the officers in this room out here that you think you found him. Okay?"

Bill says, "Got it." He begins to look at the pictures in the book as the detectives step to the door. Schneider opens it and both leave the room with Lewis closing the door behind him.

Schneider pauses to turn to Lewis and ask, "Why did you ask him to describe the suspect? The books were right there."

Lewis looks at his partner unfazed and says, "We need him to be consistent, for our case and when this goes to trial. We can't ignore anything. There's a lot of pressure on us to find this guy, soon."

The two detectives maneuver through a large room full of desks and people, some officers in uniform or plainclothes, some citizens and criminals in various attire, and the overall appearance is busy. They walk around several desks to a more open area before a wall blanketed by filing cabinets seemingly placed haphazardly and absent of any matching characteristics. Once they reach the end of the cabinets, Schneider settles behind a desk in the corner while Lewis takes a seat across the desk from his partner. Lewis says, "Records did a legal search on the victim, Darcy Rowland."

"Yeah," Schneider comments.

"There was a final judgment on her divorce from her husband six months ago," Lewis continues. "Apparently, she came out of it in pretty good shape."

"Wouldn't that make the ex-husband a prime suspect?" Schneider asks.

"You would think so," Lewis comments, looking away. "They're running inquiries on the ex with insurance companies for life insurance policies." He looks back to Schneider and adds, "We'll need to find her lawyer for her will, if she had one."

"Okay," Schneider replies, pulling his notebook out and jotting something on it.

The door from which the two detectives emerged into the larger room opens and Bill steps out. Before he can get anyone's attention, Schneider rises from the desk in the corner, and yells across the room, "You found him already?"

Bill looks over where he heard the question, recognizes Detective Schneider standing behind the desk in the corner and nods his head, saying, "Yes."

Schneider looks down to his partner still seated, opens his eyes wide and drops his head once. Lewis says to Schneider in a lower tone, "Let's go." He rises from his seat and follows Schneider back to the interrogation room.

Bill sees the detectives move toward him, so he re-enters the room and sits down where he had sat previously. A photo book is open with a third of the pages on the left side and the rest on the right; four more photo books are stacked to Bill's right and one remains in the middle of the table. Once the two detectives enter the room, Schneider stops to stand to Bill's right and Lewis flanks him to his left.

Bill glances at Schneider first, then to Lewis. He turns his head and gazes to the book and puts his finger on one of the photos on the right side of the book. Confidently, he states, "That's the man right there. His hair is shorter, there are no sideburns or mustache, but his face is the same one I saw last night. Fits him to a T." Bill glances up at both detectives.

Lewis says, "Cory, hold that side of the book up so I can read the name." Lewis squats down level with the table while Schneider holds up the right side of the book. Bill points to the photo again, saying, "That one." Lewis writes down the name in his notebook and says, "Gordon Schell." He stands up full, looks at Bill and adds, "You're sure about this one?"

"That's him, no question," Bill says with complete confidence. "I'd swear to it, if I had to."

"You just may have to," Lewis assures him.

Schneider loses his grip holding back the pages and a few fall to the left side. One of the photos on the new page on the right side looks very similar to the photo with the name "Gordon Schell," but none of the three men in the room notice the resemblance or even glance at the page. While the photo looks almost exactly like the first, the man's hair in the photo is longer, and he has sideburns and a mustache. The name reads "Gunther Rankin."

Lewis says, "Let's go back to that photo and take a closer look."

Schneider quickly lifts the pages on the left side back to the first photo. He asks, "Think we should pull it? Check him out?"

"I don't think we have a choice," Lewis advises.

"That's definitely him," Bill says.

The Future Past

That evening, in the kitchen of Gordon and Rosita's trailer, all the Schells sit around the table, longer than usual with the extra leaf, accompanied by a slightly older couple sitting at one end with Rosita. Across the table from Gordon sits an attractive man, Jose Montanez, a short, complacent, always smiling man with thick, dark hair, brushed back on his head, his face smooth and shaven. Seated to Jose's left is Rosita, and Jose lifts a bottle of Corona before him, takes a sip and sets it down, listening intently to the spirited conversation in Spanish between Rosita and the heavy-set woman sitting to his right, an attractive woman of average height with short, dark hair parted in the middle, Jose's wife, Maria.

On the kitchen counter are four mostly empty pizza boxes as everyone has finished eating. Jose says something in Spanish and Maria nods while Rosita spins her head to face Jose. Gordon smiles as he watches the expressions on the others' faces as they speak about nothing he can understand. He lifts a half-full Corona bottle with his right hand and gulps a swallow and sets the bottle back on the table in front of him.

In the living room, music is playing from a CD at a comfortable volume. A single guitar's chords can be heard as the song *Look into the Future* by Journey begins.

Melanie sits to Gordon's right and asks, "Dad, why do you always smile when Mom, Jose and Maria talk in Spanish in front of you?"

Gordon smiles even more at his daughter, replying, "I just love watching them spew conversation I can't understand, mostly because they're talking about me."

Jose, Maria, and Rosita stop speaking momentarily and glance at Gordon and Melanie.

"They're not talking about you, though," Melanie confides.

"Now you're spoiling it," teases Dad, displaying a mock frown, which instantly turns back into an easy smile.

"They're talking about Jose's back and how it's been hurting him lately," she translates. "Maria thinks his back is never gonna get better as long as he's standing all day cooking at the restaurant where he works."

To Melanie, Gordon comments, "Jose needs to get out of the physical labor business."

Rosita speaks to the others in Spanish, again, and Melanie translates, saying, "Mom says you're one to talk, since you left her no choice but to go back to her waitress job, which is, she wants to remind you, physical labor."

Rosita flashes her husband a hollow smile when he looks at her.

"Good point," Gordon says, looking at Rosita. "Kinda makes me a hypocrite, doesn't it?"

"You said it, not me," she replies, her smile a little more sincere.

"It still doesn't address Jose's predicament, though," Gordon says, smiling back.

Jose asks, "What would you do, Gordon?"

"I'd take steps to better myself, Jose," Gordon says, turning to Jose.

"Like what?" Maria asks.

"Where we live in North Carolina, mi bueno amigo," Gordon says, "everywhere you go, there's a university, a college, a community college. You're a U.S. citizen."

"Yes," Jose replies.

"So you qualify for scholarships, grants, loans to go to school, Jose," Gordon advises. "With your income, they may even *pay* you to go to school, especially when they include your whole family."

"I'm too old to go to school, my good friend," Jose protests.

"Are you breathing?" Gordon asks him.

"Yes," Jose chuckles.

"Then, you ain't too old to learn," Gordon insists.

"That is all a," Jose struggles for the word, adding, "dream. My English is not so good."

"So take English," Gordon counters.

Jose looks at him, thinking, but Maria says, "We're not those kind of people, Paco. We're just working people. We work."

Gordon smiles as he says, "And, you should go to school, too, Maria. You can go part-time, when the kids are in school. You could get an Education degree, take your teacher's certification test, teach Spanish, and still be home before the kids get back from school."

Maria smiles but shakes her head.

Rosita laments, "That's fine for you, but we're not as smart as you."

"Who told me she couldn't balance a checkbook, so she never put her money in the bank?" Gordon asks.

"I did," Rosita replies.

"Who balances our checkbook now?"

"I do," she says.

"Good job, Mom!" Mark exclaims.

"That's because you showed me how," she continues, "and you spent a lot of time explaining it, and helping me understand it. You were very patient with me. Are you going to do that with all of us when we go to school, too?"

"No," Gordon replies, "but I don't have to. There's help for your courses everywhere, people who will take the time to show you what this means and why. There are counselors to help you plan your coursework, self-help groups, groups in your area of study, professors, other teachers, adult education groups. If you're not too proud to ask for help, people will help you."

He takes a last gulp of beer, rises from the table to place the bottle on the counter, opens the refrigerator and draws two, grabs the bottle opener and flips open both, sits back down and slides one over to Jose, all the while saying, "All of these educational institutions have Spanish-speaking groups of students, some even have faculty members that work with the groups, and they will definitely help you. And who knows? You might meet a Spanish-speaking student who's smarter than me. In fact, I guarantee it, though they won't be as funny as me." He glances at Maria and Rosita, and adds, "Could easily be a woman," and he glances to Jose, and tips his bottle to him, "or a man, in your case, Jose." He lifts the bottle to his mouth and takes a gulp.

"I'll think about it," Jose promises.

"Then include this," Gordon says, sitting back down in his chair, "the only thing that holds you back is you. If you really want to, you can overcome anything." He taps his right index finger to the side of his head, adding, "It's all in here." He pauses momentarily, adding, "Or you can have chronic back problems all your life, which will get really bad when you're old."

After a brief silence, Melinda speaks up. "Maria, will you tell me the story about Mommy and Daddy, please?"

"Not again!" Mark says, shaking his head vigorously.

"Maria told you that story the last time you saw her, Melinda," Melanie says, frowning.

"So?" Melinda says, displaying strong defiance. "I like hearing about how Mommy met Daddy," she adds, patting her father's left arm. "Besides, *you* wouldn't be here if they didn't!"

All the adults laugh, and Maria says, "Okay, honey, ready?"

"Ready," Melinda says, perking up.

Maria starts her story. "Your mother and I have been friends since we were young ..." Gordon looks at nothing in particular, just dreaming ...

Gordon, his hair longer and a bit of beard on his younger face, sits in a living room reading a newspaper when he hears a car with an obviously non-working muffler come down the residential street, turn around, and park in front of his apartment. Curious, he steps into the kitchen to look through the picture window to see what's going on. A young woman, featuring short, jet black hair, and wearing a T-shirt, shorts cut high and tight, and sandals, walks by his apartment on the sidewalk and cuts through his tiny front yard to the neighbors' apartment. He can hear her knock on the neighbors' door. He says, "Mm-mm." The woman is a younger Rosita ...

It's getting dark and Gordon sits at his kitchen table eating dinner when the same car with the muffler still unattended comes down the street, turns around, and parks in front of his apartment. Rosita walks in front of his apartment, but glances up to the picture window and sees Gordon watching her. Instantly, she smiles and Gordon instantly smiles back as she cuts through his tiny front yard to the neighbors' apartment and knocks on the door ...

Gordon enters his apartment from the back entrance where the garage is located and steps into the kitchen to the refrigerator to grab a Budweiser. He steps back into the living room and flops down on the sofa, pops the tab on the beer can and takes a gulp. There's a knock on his door and he gets up to answer it. Once the door is open, a portly man about Gordon's height, wearing black leather pants, a denim shirt, a black leather motorcycle cap, and an ever-present knife in its holster attached to his belt, stands outside, smiling, and asks, "Hey, man, we were wondering if you wanted to have dinner with us and drink some beer."

"Sure," Gordon says.

"Cumon, then,' the man says impatiently and starts to step to the neighbors' apartment.

"Let me grab some beer, JR. Hold on," Gordon says.

"Ah, you don't need to bring any beer," JR insists. "Cumon."

Ignoring JR's advice, Gordon turns around and races to the kitchen anyway, explaining, "I'll bring what's left of this six-pack." He returns to the door dangling four beers left of the six-pack in his left hand and the one in his right. He closes the door and follows the swaying man the two steps next door and into the neighbors' apartment.

Once inside, Gordon closes the door and follows JR the few feet to the entrance on the left into the kitchen. Seated around the table in the middle of the kitchen are a younger Jose, the couple's children, Roberto, who is eight, and Consuela, who is eleven, and the mysterious and beautiful young woman Gordon had seen twice before.

JR takes the beer cans from Gordon and sticks them in the refrigerator. Gordon notices a younger Maria stirring something in a pan at the stove. JR returns to Gordon's side and says, looking at the mysterious young woman, "This is Rosita." He looks back at Gordon and says, "This is Gordon."

Shyly, Gordon mutters, "Hi," and looks at Rosita, who is smiling confidently. He returns her smile self-consciously.

In a deep and sultry voice, not lacking in self-assurance, she loudly says, "Hi."

Jose smiles and JR motions to Gordon to an open seat at the table directly opposite Rosita. As Gordon sits down next to Jose and JR sits down next to Gordon, Maria checks the progress of the corn tortillas in the oil of a pan next to the one she was stirring on the stove and announces, "It's ready."

Maria removes and stacks the tortillas on paper towels to degrease them. When she places them on a plate, Rosita rises from the table to step to the stove, lifts the tortillas plate from the stove and places it in the center of the table next to the rest of the food. Rosita sits down and Maria pours the meat from the pan she was stirring into a bowl and places a spoon in it. Holding the bowl, Maria steps to the table, sets the bowl in the center and sits down between Jose and Rosita. She looks over at Gordon and announces, "Please, help yourself, Gordon."

Gordon sits unmoving for a few anxious moments as the others try not to stare at him. Finally, Rosita stands up and advises, "I'll fix you a plate." She scoops and lifts from the various items on the table and deposits them on her plate. When complete, she steps around the table to Gordon, lifts his empty plate and sets down the full plate before him, saying, "Here you are."

Gordon looks up at her and says, "Thank you."

Having turned away, Rosita stops, turns back and says, "You're welcome." She smiles softly as she adds, "We're all hungry, too."

Gordon laughs and, suddenly, everyone else laughs, too. Gordon comments, "I didn't do too good, did I?"

Roberto smiles as he glances at the faces around the table and observes, "You're a gringo. We forgive you." Everyone laughs again …

Consuela and Roberto have retired to the living room, and the kitchen table has been cleared of everything except the cans of Budweiser all are drinking except Maria. Rosita, Jose and Maria, at the one end of the table, speak furiously in Spanish, and JR asks Gordon, "Want to know what they're saying?"

"Not if they don't want to tell me," Gordon says, sipping his beer and turning his head to the left to look at JR.

"Not even if they're talking about you?" JR asks, raising his eyebrows. Gordon looks at him quizzically, so JR translates, "My sister says you're a good neighbor, quiet, respectful, a nice boy. Rosita says that she knows you're quiet because you've hardly said a thing, but she likes that you keep looking at her and smiling because she thinks you're hot."

Maria shouts, "JR!"

JR turns to his sister and says, "You were talking about him right in front of him and that's rude."

Gordon turns from JR to gaze at Rosita, who is watching Gordon, and asks, "She said that?"

JR turns back to Gordon and explains, "Well, she didn't say that exactly. There's not a real translation for it in English. It's kind of a slang in Spanish."

Still looking only at Rosita, Gordon raises his eyebrows as he asks, "You think I'm hot?"

Without a hint of embarrassment, Rosita replies, "I didn't say that."

Jose and JR laugh and Maria shakes her head. Jose says, "It was a little … stronger than that, my friend."

Gordon turns to JR and asks, "Well, is there a slang in Spanish like she said but for a woman instead?"

JR looks at Gordon and says, "Oh, yeah."

Gordon looks back at Rosita, who has continued to look only at Gordon, and says, "Well, then, that's what I'm thinking about her."

Everyone else turns to Rosita, who simply asks, smiling, "So, you like it?"

Gordon replies, smiling, "Oh, I could like what you have most anytime. And you?"

"I like it already," Rosita says, changing to a serious expression, "but not tonight. I have to leave in a little while."

"After all that, you're gonna bail?" Gordon asks, incredulously.

"I'll be back," Rosita promises.

"I'll be waiting," Gordon assures her …

Gordon sits on the sofa of his living room, holding a can of Budweiser and listening to rock music at a reasonable decibel level coming from the stereo in the opposite corner. A determined knock can be heard from the front door, and he rises from the sofa, steps down the open hall to his right about twenty feet to the door and opens it without asking or looking. Rosita stands on the landing outside wearing her usual T-shirt, this time solid white, with tight little pink velour shorts, but she's barefoot. She smiles as she says, "Cumon next door and drink some beer with us and talk."

Quickly deciding that they don't need any of his beer, Gordon steps out and closes the door behind him, following Rosita, who has turned to step to the apartment, but turns her head to look at him and offers her right hand and Gordon takes it into his left. They enter the apartment through the open front door and, when the two of them appear in the kitchen, Jose gets up and sits down next to his wife on her other side, so that there is space at one end of the table for Rosita and Gordon to sit together. Rosita leads Gordon to her left to the farthest chair, still holding his hand. When she stops before her chair, she lets go of his hand and motions for Gordon to sit in the chair next to hers, and, as Gordon sits down in his chair, she steps around the far side of her chair and sits down.

Jose, Maria and JR greet Gordon and he returns their greetings, smiling easily at their welcome. He quickly gulps the rest of the beer he carried and Rosita instinctively gets up, walks to the refrigerator, opens it and removes another can of beer. Deftly, she steps back to the table and sets the unopened can before Gordon. Looking up at Rosita, he thanks her as she brushes his right arm and picks up the empty can, steps to the garbage can and deposits it inside. Gordon watches her unflinchingly, noting that her movements are smooth and graceful. She steps back around her chair and sits down, knowing that he was watching her, wearing a calm and comfortable smile. Jose and Maria's children are nowhere to be seen and cannot be heard. Gordon doesn't ask.

Jose smiles and asks, "So, what did you do today, my friend?"

Gordon turns to Jose with a serious expression. "Still lookin' for work, Jose," he replies.

"I hope you find something soon," Maria says, a look of friendly concern on her face. She asks, "Isn't your unemployment running out?"

"Yeah," Gordon says, "but I think I've got a good prospect at the university."

"What do you do?" Rosita asks, and she places her right hand on his thigh under the table and out of sight of the others, rubbing it slowly.

Gordon can feel her hand rubbing his thigh and it feels good, but his expression offers no evidence of what is taking place under the table and invisible to his hosts. "Work with computers," Gordon replies, calmly, matter-of-factly, turning to face Rosita with a gentle smile, "mostly software support." He puts his left hand on top of her hand and squeezes it while he casually looks away from her. He lifts his beer can with his right hand, takes a gulp from his beer, and sets it back down on the table. When he looks at Rosita, she is smiling and he returns her smile knowingly.

"Is it hard work?" she asks.

"Nothing like what Jose does," Gordon says, "but it has its challenges."

"I'm on my feet all day as a waitress, so my legs and back hurt sometimes," Rosita says, "but I have the day off today."

"So, you're not hurting now?" Gordon asks.

"No, I'm fine," Rosita says, and her smile grows wide with anticipation. She squeezes his thigh harder and his hand rubs hers deeper.

"Good," Gordon comments. There is a moment of silence at the table and Gordon squeezes her hand and rubs it hard against his thigh, and both smile at each other. Gordon adds, "When you're hurting like that, though, you should get a back rub."

"Who would give me a back rub?" Rosita inquires with a brief quizzical expression, which immediately melts back into her anticipatory smile.

"I'd give you a back rub," Gordon offers, his eyes twinkling deviously, "but with one condition."

"What's that?" Rosita asks, smiling as she licks her lips self-consciously.

"You'd have to take your top and bra off," he says, still displaying that devious, playful expression. "I only work with bare skin." He smiles broadly and she returns his smile.

"I can do that," she replies, her smile displaying the same devious, playful expression. She suddenly slides her hand inside his leg, squeezes it, and rubs up his thigh just shy of his crotch.

Friendly small talk continues over several beers, along with the occasional gentle sexual teasing between Rosita and Gordon. Gordon lifts his left hand from hers and gently places it on Rosita's right thigh and rubs her bare skin, feeling the desire for her growing. He can feel her right hand squeezing and rubbing his thigh, inside and on top, as the result, and knows from her deep smile that she is feeling the same way.

Eventually, JR gets up and exits the kitchen. When Jose finishes his beer, he gets up and exits the kitchen. Maria looks at Rosita, whose brief and plaintive expression tells her everything she needs to know, and she rises from the table, explaining that it's late and she should go to bed so she can get up early in the morning. She leaves the kitchen to the couple sitting next to each other.

Rosita rises from the table to fetch two more beers, sits back down and places one before Gordon. She places her right hand on his left arm and strokes it, asking, her eyes wide, accepting, anticipating, "Can I go next door with you?"

Without hesitation, Gordon says, "Let's go." He grabs the beer Rosita placed before him and opens it, standing up from the table. He reaches for her with his left hand and she slips her right hand in his and they exit the kitchen through the hallway to the front door ...

Maria smiles as she looks at little Melinda and says, "And they both went back to your father's apartment, and—"

"See, Melinda," Gordon interrupts, "I didn't lock my door, so a *big* monster got inside and was waiting for us. The monster was so big, your mother peed her pants right there—"

"Gordon!" Rosita exclaims.

"And I was so scared," Gordon continues, unfazed, "I just passed out, but your mother, she's the strong one of us, she just popped that monster and chased it away, and said, 'Don't you ever come back here or you'll get more of the same.'"

Melinda looks at her mother with a smile, but Rosita says, "There wasn't a big monster in your father's apartment. Daddy's telling a story, again."

Melinda looks at her dad, smiling, and comments enthusiastically, "I like Daddy's stories."

Gordon smiles at his daughter and says, "Well, your mother did tame a monster that night, only it wasn't that big."

"You got that right," Rosita agrees. The adults laugh and Gordon winks at his wife.

Jose looks at Maria and says something in Spanish, which causes Maria and Rosita to shake their heads. Melanie turns to her father and says, "Jose said, 'We sometimes tame a woman's monster, too.' Is he talking about what I think he's talking about?"

Gordon stands up and says, "Yep, bedtime for the little one." Ignoring Melanie's disappointment, he turns to Melinda as she stands up on the chair from her booster and jumps into his arms. Gordon carries her around to the others at the table, and Melinda gets a good-night kiss from all. He carries her out of the kitchen and down the hall to her bedroom.

Meet the D. A.

The two detectives working the Rowland murder sit in the two chairs opposite the desk of the assistant District Attorney assigned to the case. An attractive, full-bodied woman, with thick blond hair falling to her shoulders, the short locks curled around her forehead, sits in a high-back, leather chair behind the desk, petite but commanding attention and respect. Her dour expression contrasting with her rather noble-looking, straight Roman nose, Sharon Pilot looks directly at Detective Lewis and demands, "So, what do we know about this suspect?"

Detective Lewis reaches into his jacket and pulls out his notebook. Flipping the tiny notebook open, he gazes down at it and states, "His name is Gordon Schell, with a C. He's in his thirties, drives a blue four-wheel-drive truck with a distinctive striping, kind of day-glow paint. Interesting thing about that: many of the neighbors on that street are very familiar with that truck."

Detective Schneider has been consulting his tiny notebook when he looks up at the D.A. and interrupts, "Several of them said they see that truck almost every day."

Sharon observes, "Then that would make him frequent the area." She looks back at Lewis. "We'll need definitive proof of that. We'll need to show that the truck these people see is his."

Looking at Sharon, Lewis nods and says, "Right." Pausing, he drops his gaze to his notebook and adds, "He works, or I should say, he used to work for a computer software company at the industrial park. He used to work, because he apparently quit or was fired the morning the victim was murdered."

Sharon wonders aloud, "Now, is that a coincidence or something else?"

"Don't know yet," Lewis replies. "In any case, our witness saw a man leave the house at ten forty-five PM, is absolutely certain of his ID, even though he says the killer had longer hair, a mustache and sideburns. Forensics puts the time of death between ten fifteen and ten forty-five."

"We've also been contacted by a woman," adds Schneider, "who claims she was jogging down the intersecting street at about that time and thinks she saw the suspect. We haven't interviewed her yet."

"What's the suspect's criminal history?" asks Sharon.

Schneider replies, "He was photographed and fingerprinted after an arrest for DUI seven years ago, but the case was dismissed for lack of witness."

"The arresting officer didn't show?" Sharon asks.

"Right," Schneider confirms.

"Great," she says, sarcastically, adding, "What other evidence do we have?"

"We're still processing fingerprints," Schneider replies. "For someone who supposedly had few visitors, there were more than a dozen separate fingerprints attributable to that many people."

"Could be she didn't clean all that well," Lewis speculates.

"We don't really want that known right now," Sharon Pilot advises. "That's not something we would want to emphasize, if you know what I mean."

"I got it," Lewis agrees. "So far, the blood is all hers. There's other trace materials that are still being processed and that could take weeks to complete."

Schneider says, "There *is* an ex-husband that we're still investigating."

"Is he tied to Schell?" Sharon asks.

"We don't know that, yet," Schneider replies, "but he did have an insurance policy for half a million on her which he's trying to collect."

"That's a pretty strong motive," Lewis states.

"If he wasn't at the scene," Sharon advises, "he's not the prime suspect. Maybe these two are tied together. If so, that should become evident as you continue to put the screws on Schell." She pauses for a moment. "Anyway, gentlemen," Sharon says, "the ID gives us probable cause for questioning Schell and that's how we should play it to begin with. If he resists the trip downtown, then I want a continuous stakeout placed on him. I want his every move watched until we eliminate him as a suspect or we get enough evidence to arrest him." She emphasizes her next sentence. "Under no circumstances, can we let him out of our grasp." She looks sternly at Lewis. "I shouldn't have to remind you how much heat we're getting to find this killer. Someone has leaked how badly this woman was tortured before she was killed and people are both worried and outraged."

"We know," Lewis says. "We're going to pay Mr. Schell a visit right now."

Sharon adds one more bit of advice. "In the meantime, we need to know about that truck and put some pressure on the fingerprint bureau. If his print's in that house, I want him arrested for murder."

Both detectives nod and stand up to leave her office.

The Snare Is Set

Gordon stands before the foggy mirror in the small bathroom of the trailer, wearing only his pants as he rubs his wet hair with a towel. He hears a knock at the front door, but he puts down the towel, lifts a comb and runs it through his hair first. Setting the comb down, he walks briskly out of the bathroom, down the bedroom hall to the front door opposite the living room. Reaching the front door, he opens it and sees two men in suits standing on his porch, Detectives Lewis and Schneider.

"Yes," Gordon says through the screen door.

Detective Schneider asks, "Are you Gordon Schell?"

"Yes."

"Mr. Schell," Lewis says, displaying his badge from his wallet while Schneider does the same, "I'm Detective Lewis and this is Detective Schneider from the Metro Police. Where were you two nights ago between ten and eleven?"

"May I ask what this is about?" Gordon asks, suddenly suspicious.

Lewis answers, "We're investigating the murder of Darcy Rowland."

"And you think I did it?" Gordon asks, incredulously, his expression one of total disbelief, while the detectives stand stone-faced. "You've *got* to be kidding!" he exclaims.

"Where were you two nights ago between ten and eleven?" Lewis repeats.

"Right here," Gordon offers. "At that time I happened to be in bed with my wife, giving her a back rub. Need more details?" Gordon asks, a little put off at the obvious insinuation of the detective's questioning.

"That's not necessary, Mr. Schell," Lewis advises, asking, "care to tell us why your truck has been seen constantly driving past Darcy Rowland's house?"

"I don't know who she was so how would I know where her house is?" Gordon insists.

"She lived at 3815 Poplar Street," Schneider advises, adding, "Does that ring a bell?"

"No," Gordon replies, glancing into the house. Turning back, he adds, "But I take a shortcut through some residential streets to get back and forth from work, just to get away from the traffic. Poplar might be one of them." He pauses. "At least, I used to, before I quit." He thinks for a moment and asks, "Didn't you say this was two nights ago?"

"Yes," Lewis replies.

"That morning I quit work," Gordon observes. "Coincidence, huh?"

"Maybe not," Schneider suggests, ignoring the brief smile from Gordon and peeved that a murder suspect would even attempt humor.

Gordon bristles as it's becoming clear to him that these detectives consider him capable of murder. Lewis asks, "Mr. Schell, why don't you accompany us downtown? We have some more questions we'd like to ask you."

"I don't know how you came to the conclusion that I may have murdered this woman," Gordon protests, his anger rising, "but you're sadly mistaken, and, unless you have a warrant for my arrest, I don't have to answer any questions from you." He looks from one detective to the other. "So, got that warrant?"

Lewis states, "No, but we thought you'd want to co-operate—"

"I'm sorry to hear what happened to that woman," Gordon interrupts, adding, "but you're wasting my time as well as yours. I haven't killed anyone. I'm not that kind of person, so if you'll excuse me, I have a very important interview for a job, and I do *not* intend to be late." Gordon steps back and closes the door.

Schneider glances to his partner and asks, "Now what?"

Lewis looks up to the sky and glances around the trailer park. "Now we camp out and wait, and we're not going to hide, either," he advises his partner and both step off the porch to walk to their car …

Two hours later, Gordon blasts out the side entrance of a hospital, pumping his right fist and scrunching his face as though he just hit the game-winning shot to decide the NBA finals. He wears a snappy three piece suit and tie, but he immediately pulls the knot open on the tie and pulls one side of it through the knot. Yanking the rest of the tie from his neck, he dangles it as he walks to his truck parked in the expansive employee parking lot.

As he nears his truck, he pulls the key and fob from his right pocket and presses the button to unlock the driver door of the truck. He flings open the door, tosses the tie on the passenger seat, flops down behind the wheel and starts the truck. Music from the CD player starts up in mid-song a moment later, but he punches the seek button on the player to the song he really wants to hear, *I Get By* from Stealer's Wheel. When the guitars open the song, he shifts the truck to reverse, backs out of the parking space, shoves the transmission to drive and exits out of the parking lot, down the alleyway and into the street running in front of the hospital.

A half-hour later, Gordon pulls into the drive of his trailer and hops out of the truck. He jogs next door and knocks on Penny's door.

Penny opens the door and Gordon steps inside, greeted immediately by Melinda screaming, "Daddy!" When she reaches him, he sweeps her off the floor, and twirls her around, pulling her to him for a hug.

Penny asks, "How did it go?"

"You are looking at the new lead support tech at the hospital," Gordon beams. "They hired me right there, gave me more money than those sad sacks I *used* to work for, and promised me a *real* opportunity to move into management, if I get my degree."

Penny shakes her head but smiles sincerely. "I am *so* glad to hear that, Gordon."

"Yeh, Daddy!" Melinda shouts.

Gordon smiles effusively as he says, "They'll cover half my tuition as long as it's related to my work. If it's computers or computer management and it's required for the degree, *no problem!*"

Penny looks at him in disbelief and exclaims, "You said you could get a job quickly, but this is *unreal!*" She holds up her hand and Gordon slaps it.

"Like that, little girl?" Gordon asks the bundle in his arms.

"You bet!" Melinda gushes, smiling. "You got it *down*, Daddy!"

Gordon glances around the room, asking, "Penny, I want to call the better half. Can I use your phone?"

Penny smiles and says, "Sure. Use the phone in the kitchen. You'll see it."

Gordon steps into the kitchen, still holding his daughter. The phone is a wall model mounted next to the refrigerator. He lifts the receiver and dials a number. After a few moments, he asks, "May I speak to Rosita, please?"

"Rosita?" a woman calls out at the restaurant above the din.

Rosita is at a table laying plates of food before customers. When she finishes, she looks over to the woman and says, "Yes."

"You've got a call," the woman shouts, and holds up the phone.

Rosita walks over to the woman and takes the phone, saying, "This is Rosita." On the other end, Gordon's voice says, "Hey, baby," in a subdued tone.

"I've got work to do, hon," Rosita protests.

"Well, that's why I called you."

"Get to the point," she admonishes. "We're really busy."

"I start my *new* job tomorrow, Rosita."

"I thought you just had an interview," Rosita says, incredulously.

"They offered me the job right there."

"Oh, baby," Rosita says, smiling profusely, "I am so happy. I love you."

"So, get your fine ass home ASAP. You've got a back rub coming, and then it's payback time, and you know what I mean."

Rosita's face breaks out like a ray of sunshine. "I know what you mean. I take care of you, don't I?"

"Yes, you do. Oh, and one other thing." There is a momentary silence on the other end of the phone and Rosita wonders what's coming. Suddenly, Gordon's voice yells, "Told ya!"

Someone calls out from the kitchen, "Rosita, your order's up!"

Rosita smiles and says, "I have to go."

"Have I told you lately that I love you like no other?"

"Not lately," Rosita insists, adding, "and you haven't been showin' it, either."

"I'll show you tonight."

"I've gotta go."

"Luv you, baby."

Rosita hangs up the phone and walks over to the counter between the kitchen and the dining room, smiling the whole trip …

That afternoon, returning from picking up the older kids from school, Gordon's truck pulls into the drive of the trailer. The kids and Gordon excitedly scramble out from the truck and run up the stairs of the wooden porch to the door, and Gordon sticks his key in the lock of the door while Melanie holds the screen door back. Unlocked, Gordon shoves the door open and they all clamber inside with shouts of glee and laughter. Across the street, a black sedan is parked between the two opposing trailers. The detectives inside the car watch the family across the street disappear happily into their trailer.

A phone rings inside the car and Lewis pulls his phone from a side pocket of his suit. "Detective Lewis," he says into the phone. He listens for a few seconds and asks, "You're absolutely sure?" After a few more seconds, he closes his phone and places it back in his pocket. He looks over at his partner sitting in the passenger seat and says, "One of the prints found in the victim's house matches our suspect."

Schneider reaches for the door handle and says, "Let's get him."

"No," Lewis advises. "We'll wait until the wife returns from work. I don't want to deal with the kids; they don't need to go through that agony." He looks to his left at the trailer. "He's not going anywhere and it would be good to have his wife watch us arrest him. Maybe that will start something to help us build the case."

Schneider looks disappointed but says, "Okay, I see your point." He looks over at the trailer, too. "Until we arrest him, though, he's still a free man, and I don't like that." He shakes his head …

The afternoon is slowly ceding its influence to the evening and, in the living room of the Schells' trailer, all of the family save Rosita are gathered. Melanie and Melinda sit in the easy chair watching PBS. Gordon has searched through his books and Mark holds the hardcopy selection his father deemed suitable for his seven-year-old son as they sit together on the sofa. Mark reads aloud and Gordon listens attentively. When Mark stumbles on a word from *David Copperfield* by Charles Dickens, Gordon patiently pronounces it and explains its meaning, often in the context of the sentence, paragraph and story, and Mark listens closely, nods his head and returns his father's ever-present smile.

Soon, a car with an obvious need for a new muffler can be heard outside. Excited, Melinda screams, "Mommy!" The car goes silent and a few seconds later the door opens and Rosita enters, smiling. Melinda hops from the easy chair and runs to her and Rosita drops on one knee to hug her daughter.

"Hi, Mom," Melanie says.

"Hey, Mom," Mark says, after handing the book to his father.

Gordon places a strip in the book before closing it and leans back on the sofa, smiling at his wife. Rosita looks at him, bites her lip before smiling broadly, and asks, "Have you kids been minding your father?"

Melanie smiles as she asks, "You mean our newly-employed father?"

"That's the one," Rosita answers, glancing to her daughter, while Gordon looks smug.

"You know Dad has no rules, Mom," Mark offers. "He just lets us run wild."

"I don't think so, little boy," Rosita scoffs.

"Nice try, kiddo," Gordon says, smiling at his son, "but your mom knows what's goin' on."

Mark snaps his fingers, shaking his head. Rosita moves to Melanie and bends down to give her a kiss. She passes her husband on the sofa and bends down to give Mark a kiss. When she stands up, she turns away from the sofa and walks into the hall to the bedrooms.

"Where's mine?" Gordon asks.

Rosita flips her head back to her husband and says, "You'll get yours." As she disappears down the hall she calls back, "Where's your patience?"

"Outside, drooling with the rest of my emasculated self, I suppose," he calls back. A moment later, he adds in a lower tone, "Story of my life, though. I gotta remember; don't get excited, because with you, it's 'hurry up ... and wait.'"

From the back bedroom of the trailer comes her answer, "Like I said, you'll get yours."

Outside, three police cars with flashing lights converge quickly before the Schells' trailer. The two detectives emerge from their black sedan and run up the stairs to pound on the trailer door.

Inside, Gordon sees and hears the commotion and wonders aloud, "What the hell is that?" The door shakes with the pounding from the outside, so Gordon gets up, walks to the door, opens it, and the detectives, along with several of the other officers, rush in. The three children retreat from the door, fearful, and Melanie yells at the officers while Melinda screams, "Daddy! Mommy!" Mark cowers, wide-eyed, on the sofa.

"Gordon Schell," Lewis advises, as he reaches for Gordon with his right hand and displaying a pack of paper in his left. "We have a warrant for your arrest for the murder of Darcy Rowland. Turn around, please."

Rosita runs from the back bedroom, pulling a T-shirt down over her brassiere, and yells, "What the hell is going on? What is this about?"

"Mrs. Schell?" Lewis turns to her and asks.

Almost hysterical, Rosita screams, "What are you doing with my husband?" She watches them put handcuffs on Gordon with his arms behind him. "What murder? My husband couldn't kill a bug, let alone a person!"

"Please stay out of this, Mrs. Schell," advises Schneider, as he moves toward her to put himself between her and Detective Lewis attempting the arrest.

She yells back at the officers, "I will *not* stay out of it! You tell me what this is about! What murder?"

Lewis calmly replies, "We're arresting your husband for the murder of Darcy Rowland two nights ago."

"Are you on crack?" she screams back, trying to move closer and being held back slightly by Detective Schneider. "Two nights ago, my husband was home all night with me and the children. You're making a big mistake!"

Lewis is now angered with the crack remark and states, "That may be, Mrs. Schell, but we have enough evidence to arrest him now and we're gonna get to the bottom of this." He swings Gordon around and pulls him to the door as Schneider motions to one of the officers to intervene with Rosita and he follows his partner outside.

As Detective Lewis begins reciting legal rights, Gordon shouts back, trying to turn to face her but restrained by the considerably bigger and stronger detective, "It's gonna be all right, babe." Pulled down clumsily so that he nearly stumbles down the porch steps, he yells even louder, "They'll see this is just a mistake."

Detective Schneider turns back to Rosita and says, "We also have a warrant to search this trailer and Gordon Schell's truck for the murder weapon or other evidence, so please stay out of our way or we'll arrest *you* for obstructing this investigation. Is that understood, Mrs. Schell?"

Rosita steps over to the sofa, kneels before it and puts her arms out for her kids. With resignation, she sighs, "I just want you out of our home ..."

Several hours later, an untidy man, of average stature and build and appearing in his forties, stumbles about the police station, adjusting his glasses while clutching a disorderly satchel full of papers. Occasionally, he scratches his head through his short brown hair or rubs his clean-shaven face in a somewhat disoriented manner as he asks anyone who looks at him for Gordon Schell. Detective Lewis spies him from the corner desk. When Schneider sees Lewis look across the room, he sees him, too, and asks Lewis, "Is that the PD?"

"Looks like it," Lewis replies, getting up from his desk. "I'll see."

Lewis steps up to the man struggling with the satchel, but the man turns away as Lewis reaches him. When Lewis touches the man's arm, the man nearly jumps. The detective suppresses a smile as he asks the startled man, "Are you the public defender assigned to Gordon Schell?"

The man just nods.

Lewis extends his hand and the two shake as he says, "Detective Lewis." Lewis looks over to Schneider rising from his chair and says, "That's my partner, Detective Schneider. We're the arresting officers and will be in charge of the questioning."

The man slowly replies, "Delbert T. Prescott from the public defender's office." He starts to dig into the open satchel, adding, "I have the papers from the Justice—"

"Let me take you to the room where we're holding Mr. Schell," Lewis interrupts, putting his arm behind Delbert, coaxing him forward, "and you get all that sorted out." The two move to a closed door with a small window at eye-level as

Schneider joins them. Detective Lewis opens the door and adds, "When you and the suspect are ready, we have some questions that we need answers to."

Lewis and Schneider close the door behind them as Delbert moves awkwardly to a seat opposite Gordon, fumbling with his satchel and almost dropping it. Paying attention to his satchel as he sets it on the table, Delbert asks before he sits down, "Mr. Schell, do you know what crime you have been charged with?"

Gordon looks up and down at the man opposite him wearing a severely wrinkled suit and realizes he is in a very bad situation now. "Murder," he calmly answers.

Delbert sits down and pokes through his case for the appropriate papers. He says, "Ah, here," as he withdraws a stapled group of papers. "This is the complaint filed with Justice Patterson, who issued the arrest warrant." Delbert looks up at Gordon as he adds, "These are very serious charges, Mr. Schell."

"Call me Gordon, please," Gordon advises. He is unnervingly calm to Delbert.

"All right, Gordon," Delbert replies, "let's go over this."

"Don't you want to introduce yourself, first?" Gordon asks.

"Oops, I thought I already had," Delbert stammers. "Let me apologize. My name is Delbert T. Prescott and I have been assigned by the public defender's office to represent you in this matter." He reaches across the table to proffer his hand and Gordon shakes it briefly.

"Now," Gordon says, "don't you want to know if I did it?"

"Not especially," Delbert replies, looking only at the papers before him.

"Well, *I* want you to know," Gordon insists.

"All right," Delbert concedes, stopping to look up at Gordon. "If it'll make you feel better, go ahead and tell me."

"I haven't killed anyone," Gordon says. "I'm not sure if I'm even capable of killing anyone in self-defense, whether my life or my family's lives are threatened." He pauses. "I was at home in bed with my wife at the time the crime was committed."

"Good," Delbert agrees. "And we'll need to establish those facts, but it won't be easy because they have a considerable amount of circumstantial evidence against you already."

"Such as?" Gordon asks in disbelief.

Delbert reads from the complaint and says, "They have a witness who saw you leave the victim's house at ten forty-five that night and the victim's time of death has been established as between ten fifteen and ten forty-five."

"It wasn't me," Gordon insists.

"The witness picked your photo after looking at more than five hundred," Delbert says, looking up at Gordon. "They will certainly bring that witness in to identify you in a lineup."

Gordon protests, "I hear people tell me all the time I look like so and so."

"We'll skip that for a defense," Delbert dismisses.

"What else?" Gordon asks.

"You drive a blue, four-wheel pickup with day-glow paint?" Delbert asks, still reading from the complaint.

"Yeah," Gordon confirms. "I had a friend do a custom paint job."

"Well, that's probably not good," Delbert says, "since they have about a dozen witnesses to choose from that will testify they see your truck drive down the victim's street almost daily."

"That's the thing," Gordon says. "I can't picture where Poplar Street is."

"You got a fairly unique license plate?" Delbert inquires.

"Maybe," Gordon says. "PEC 4 U, Peace for you."

"The prosecution has another witness from the neighborhood who says she saw your truck parked in front of the victim's house about two and a half months ago," Delbert continues, reading from the complaint, "on a Saturday, for most of the afternoon."

Gordon thinks for a moment but shakes his head. "I can't think of why I would be there, but I did install some software on a client's system about that time." He looks at Delbert. "How is this witness so sure it was my truck?"

"Well, that's the thing, Gordon," Delbert answers, slowly. "She remembers your license plate because she thought it was …" He looks at the complaint and completes his sentence, "'neat. PEC 4 U, Peace for you.' That's what she said, exactly."

"Shit!" Gordon says. "I can't remember her name. I only talked to her a couple times and never since I installed that software. I haven't seen a picture of her. Have they got a picture of the victim?"

Delbert gets up quickly and says, "I'll ask the detectives if they have one. I'll be right back." As he opens the door he advises, "Don't answer anything until I get back."

Gordon nods.

When Delbert returns, he's carrying a wallet-size picture in his left hand. He sits down opposite Gordon and hands him the picture, saying, "That's Darcy Rowland, the victim."

Gordon looks at the picture and his eyes start to mist. "I didn't know it was her."

"So, you do know her?" Delbert asks, growing disappointed.

Gordon drops his right arm slowly to the table and lets the picture fall from his grip. Somber and in a repressed tone, he states, "She's the billing manager for Emerald Medical Clinics, Inc." Slowly, he turns his head to face Delbert and adds, "was."

Delbert asks, "And you went to her house to install that software?"

"Yes."

Delbert thinks for a moment. "That would explain your fingerprint that they found in her house," he says.

"I'll bet they'll find more than one," Gordon says, shaking his head. "I was there for almost four hours."

Delbert brightens suddenly. "If this was work-related, your employer should have a record of it for corroboration. That would be good!"

Gordon drops his head when he says, "I did it on my own. The company knew nothing about it." Lifting his head he adds, "I felt bad about how we were treating this client and she had always defended my work. I liked her. She needed help getting connected from home so I said I would help her."

"That's *not* good," Delbert says. "Does anybody know about it? A colleague? Your wife?"

Gordon shakes his head. "I couldn't tell anybody at work. Performing work for a client on your own is grounds for automatic dismissal." Gordon looks away before he continues. "My wife thinks I went to visit some friends to watch a ball game and drink beer."

"So, she doesn't know the truth?" Delbert asks.

"No."

"May I ask why you told her a lie?" Delbert asks, probing into Gordon's face.

"If I told her I was going over to a single woman's house for most of the afternoon, she would have flipped out," Gordon explains. "My wife can be a very jealous woman. She's a hot-blooded Mexican with a temper you want to avoid if you've ever been subjected to it."

Delbert thinks about it a little more. He says, "Maybe, I can dig up some phone records from your former employer." He looks at Gordon with serious gravity. "I gotta tell ya, Gordon, we're in a bad situation here. They've got enough evidence, if it's not refuted properly, to convince a jury to convict." He pauses to let that sink in and asks, "Is there anything you're forgetting?"

Gordon bows his head and rubs his forehead. "That's everything. All I did was help her install that software to connect to her work system from home. Nothing else."

Delbert looks at the complaint one more time. "The detectives claim you said you didn't know who she was or where she lived. Is that right?"

Gordon straightens as he answers, "She was never the main contact for that client and I only spoke with her twice before I went to her house. Emerald Clinics is a local franchise in North Carolina. The client was Intercoastal Healthcare, a national group with more than a dozen clinical corporations like Emerald. She played a very small role in everything I did with that client." He looks at Delbert, frustrated, and says, "So, I didn't remember her name. How is that a crime?"

"It leaves the impression that you were hiding something," Delbert advises. "We'll have to convince the jury otherwise."

Gordon is worried now and says, "You're making it sound like they're definitely going to try me, Delbert, but I didn't do it."

"Unless they find the real killer before then, the DA's office is under enormous pressure from the press and public to find someone, *anyone*, to try." Delbert shakes his head. "The victim was brutally tortured before she was finally killed and everyone wants blood." He looks straight at his client. "Apparently, yours will do." He stands up. "The detectives want to interrogate you and I'll be here the whole time. Are you ready?"

Gordon looks up. "Yes," he says. Quickly, he asks, "They're not going to release me, are they?"

"No," comes Delbert's simple answer as he exits the room.

Home without Father

It is very late in the evening, the police have finally left, and the inside of the Schell trailer looks like a train wreck. Items are scattered everywhere as the police have scoured virtually the entire contents of the trailer, searching for the elusive murder weapon but have found nothing inside the trailer. The quiet is eerie, as Rosita sits on the sofa with a blank stare. The children are huddled around her, bewildered, their eyes red, tracks of tears visible on their faces. With no emotion, Rosita asks, "Is anyone hungry?"

Little Melinda replies, quietly, "I am."

"Me, too," says Mark.

Melanie gets up from the sofa slowly and says, "I'll help you fix dinner, Mom."

Rosita stands up and hugs her oldest daughter. "Thank you," she says, softly.

Mark stands up and asks, "Can I put on some music, Mom?" He bows his head briefly and adds, "One of Dad's softer CDs, please? It's too quiet for me, now."

"Okay," Rosita allows, looking to her son as she steps to the kitchen. "I'll make you turn it down if it's too loud."

"Thanks, Mom," Mark says and suddenly rushes to his mother and slaps his arms about her waist to give her a hug. She stops and puts her right hand down to his head and pushes his head against her. Mark adds, softly, muffled against her body, "I'll keep it low for you."

Rosita squats down to eye level with Mark, puts a hand on either side of his face and kisses him quickly, smiling bravely, more for influence than true feeling. Still, softly, lovingly, she says, "Thank you, little man."

Mark brightens and smiles back as his mother releases him and he steps to the CD tray and looks through the CDs for a selection to put in the CD player of the audio system. He finds one, turns on all the equipment just like his father showed him months ago, and dials the volume level off. He turns the level up slowly as he listens to the music playing and leaves it at a safe, low decibel level, satisfied …

Once the dinner is complete, a simple concoction of fish sticks and vegetables, all four sit at the kitchen table, eating quietly, the music from the living room the only sound that can be heard. The next song begins, Rare Bird's *Her Darkest Hour*, and Rosita recognizes it, setting her fork down on the table and grasping her chin with her left hand, gazing down at the table blankly. Mark looks bravely at his mother until she catches his gaze. He winks at her and she smiles.

Melinda reaches for her glass of milk, glancing at her mother, and her hand tips the glass of milk over on the table. She looks at the mess, says, "Mommy," and begins to sob. Rosita puts her arm around Melinda and consoles her with, "It's alright, baby." Mark gets up from the table, announcing, "I'll get it, Mom." He grabs the paper towels from the counter and mops up the spilled milk while Rosita watches him with new appreciation.

With dinner finished and the dishes washed, Rosita stands at the sink drying the dishes and placing them in the cupboard. She stares out the window as she grabs a glass from the strainer. As she turns it with her hands against the towel, it slips from her grasp and shatters in the sink. Melanie runs into the kitchen and the other two appear quickly behind her, but stand back between the kitchen and the living room, worry on their faces. Rosita bows her head and cries as Melanie steps up to her, puts her arm around her mother's waist and softly tells her, "Here, Mom, come and sit down at the table. I'll pick this up and I'll be real careful with the glass." She guides her mother to a chair at the table, holds her as she sits down, and turns to the sink.

The Legal Train Leaves the Platform

"What have we got?" Sharon Pilot asks the two detectives standing opposite her desk. After holding Gordon Schell over the weekend, the District Attorney's office will have to file charges or release him and Sharon Pilot wants as much ammunition as she can get. She is anxious, to say the least.

Detective Lewis doesn't bother checking his notes as he replies, "Both witnesses—the neighbor across the street and the female jogger—have positively identified the suspect in a lineup. Both still have reservations about the hair, mustache and sideburns, though."

"I can handle that at trial," Sharon advises.

Lewis continues, "The victim's house is filled with fingerprints from the suspect. He claims that he was there to install software for the victim on a Saturday when his truck was seen parked in front of the house, but his former employer neither authorized it nor could they corroborate that he was ever there for any service." He shifts his weight and adds, "He could have been there to case the house. We suspect that his wife doesn't know about it, but we haven't interviewed her yet."

"That's something we need to nail down," Sharon states sternly, drawing a deep breath, her chest expanding under her modest dress, hinting at the fullness she was carefully concealing. "Why was he there that day? That may well be the motive we're looking for."

Lewis advises, "When we first visited him, he said he didn't know her."

"Was he trying to hide it?" Sharon asks.

Lewis shakes his head but wears an expression of disbelief as he says, "I'm not sure. He said he couldn't remember her name, but if we had shown him her picture, he would have remembered her instantly." He pauses a moment before continuing. "He says he almost never watches the news, so he didn't even know about the murder."

"Maybe that's true," Sharon comments. "What else?"

"He frequently drove past her house, almost on a daily basis. We've confirmed that," Lewis continues. "Forensics concludes that the weapon may have been a scalpel, but we went through the entire trailer and found nothing. However, when we searched his truck, we found three wrinkled neckties and a small case holding a scalpel under the passenger seat. Those items are being analyzed now, but a preliminary test revealed that one of the neckties bore a blood stain. We found no other trace evidence of blood anywhere else, and there should be some, unless he disposed of his clothes and washed somewhere else. That murder scene was drenched, but we didn't find any other blood traces in the trailer, on clothes or even in his truck."

"Alright," she says. "Keep at it, there's holes that we need to fill here. However, we can establish that he was there at the house, that he was seen leaving at the time of the victim's death, and that he was in possession of a scalpel similar to the murder weapon. We have enough to arraign and bind him for trial, but I need as much as I can get."

Schneider carefully says, "We haven't been able to establish, yet, how he got there. We haven't found anyone in the trailer park that remembers seeing his truck leave or return that night."

"It's possible that he didn't use his truck at all, but keep at it," Sharon advises and looks down at her desk, pulls a file from the front of her desk, sets it before her and flips it open. "I'll need to know the results of the lab analysis on the neckties and scalpel as soon as you get them. Thank you, gentlemen."

Lewis turns to leave the D.A.'s office, but Schneider lingers, finally speaking up. "What about the ex-husband? A life insurance policy in force on an ex-wife bothers me."

Sharon looks up at Schneider and asks, "What was his explanation?"

"That's another thing that bothers me," Schneider laments. "He's hiding behind his attorney."

Sharon shows a little aggravation as she asks, "What did the attorney say?"

"The ex-wife has tax implications for the ex-husband, since they were still married part of the tax year," Schneider responds.

"That's a legitimate need, detective," Sharon advises. "Have you established a connection between the ex-husband and Schell?"

"Not yet," Schneider replies timidly, but adds, "but what if it's not Schell? What if it's somebody who looks like Schell?"

Snarling with aggravation, Sharon Pilot immediately spits, "Do you have a suspect that looks like Schell? Do you have a connection between this suspect and the ex-husband?" She glares at Schneider impatiently.

Lewis defends his partner. "We have another individual under consideration with an extensive criminal record who bears an uncanny resemblance to Schell."

Schneider adds, "But we haven't discovered a connection between the two, yet. They may have worked at the same hospital at one time but I haven't been able to substantiate it."

Sharon bristles as she advises, "Until you do, you should concentrate on the suspect with the preponderance of evidence, especially if you haven't completely ruled out that the ex-husband and Schell did not know each other. Maybe their connection is more—how shall I say it?—discreet. After all, wasn't the suspect's expertise in medical software while the ex-husband has worked at medical clinics and hospitals his entire career?"

"Yes," Schneider agrees, sheepishly.

"Perhaps, those two had *one* short, simple conversation," Sharon speculates, "but you haven't yet discovered that. All we're lacking for a reasonable explanation pointing to Gordon Schell as the murderer is a compelling motive. Find one."

Both detectives nod, stand up and turn to leave the office. Lewis opens the door and exits followed close behind by Schneider, who closes it. Schneider softly states, "I don't like it. I think the ex is the key."

Lewis frowns at his partner. "You should listen to the lady. She's taking a lot of heat. Everybody's outraged, so we need to work with her."

"I understand the outrage," Schneider comments, shaking his head as they slowly traverse the hall in the District Attorney's office complex. "Don't you want to nail the real perpetrator?"

"Yours is a hunch," Lewis replies, confidently. "The real evidence, while circumstantial, is considerable against Schell. Sharon Pilot has an enviable conviction rate. What have *you* got?"

Schneider does not respond. He drops back behind his partner, frowning ...

Late that afternoon, Delbert T. Prescott arrives at the courthouse, a gray stone monolith of classic architecture rising six floors above street level, in his dented Taurus. Shutting the engine off, he reaches into an inside pocket of his wrinkled gray suit jacket and removes a flask. He glances in both directions, opens the flask and downs a swig. He caps it and quickly replaces it to the inside pocket, reaching to a side pocket and removing a breath spray. He squirts the breath spray in his mouth and places it back in the pocket.

Drawing a deep breath, Delbert scoops his satchel of chaos from the passenger seat, opens the door and squeezes out. Flicking the lock button on the door panel, he slams the door shut and briskly walks across the parking lot to the steps leading to the building's entrance. He jogs up the many steps, past the Roman columns, through the automatic doors and to the elevator, where he punches the number 3. When the elevator doors slide open at the third floor, he hurries to his right.

In one of the courtrooms on the third floor, Gordon sits at a thick oak table at the left by himself, a county officer standing next to the table to his left. He turns around to survey his audience, a group of about fifteen, mostly reporters with notebooks and pens at the ready.

Sharon Pilot commands the table to Gordon's right, her manner prim and proper. A male assistant from the District Attorney's office sits to her immediate right, his papers neatly arranged before him, though he is engrossed in discovering a more perfect arrangement.

Sitting at a level above all others behind the bench is Judge Mildred Benjamin, a rather large, somewhat rotund, black woman in her fifties, appearing quite annoyed. To no one in particular, she asks, "Does the defendant have counsel?"

"Yes, your honor," replies Sharon in a calm, business-like tone.

"Then counsel is late," Judge Benjamin states. She turns to the stenographer and adds, "When will these attorneys learn I cannot tolerate tardiness, Beth?"

The woman to whom the Judge's question was directed just shrugs her shoulders as she sits patiently off to the left of the justice bench. Suddenly, the doors at the back of the courtroom burst open as Delbert struggles with his satchel to close the door. The officer at the back of the courtroom standing guard at the doors steps to Delbert's rescue and closes the doors for him as Delbert races to the defendant's table. Sharon betrays no expression, but her assistant tries to cover a smirk and Gordon glances to the ceiling as though appealing to the gods to intervene.

Judge Benjamin scowls, "Mr. Prescott, so nice to have you with us." She turns to the officer at the back and adds, "John, thank you for assisting our public defender." The officer smiles, knowing exactly what's coming next. Judge Benjamin turns back to Delbert, still making his way to the defendant's table. "As for you, Mr. Prescott, you are late, once again, and, once again, I don't want to hear an excuse. You will not be late for my court again. Is that understood?"

"Yes, your honor," Delbert says, contritely. He places his satchel on the table and adds, "The defense is ready."

Judge Benjamin looks to the District Attorney's table. She asks, "Ms. Pilot, are you ready to proceed with this arraignment?"

"Yes, your honor, the state is ready to proceed," Sharon says and stands up. She adjusts her immaculate royal blue business suit and instinctively pulls her matching skirt down.

Gordon looks grim when he hears the judge ask, "How does the defendant plead?" He turns to his right and listens as Delbert states, standing at attention, "Not guilty, your honor."

Sharon stares straight ahead as the judge asks, "What is the state's recommendation for bail for the defendant?"

With an expression of stern disgust, District Attorney Sharon Pilot replies, "Due to the horrid, graphic nature of the crime, your honor, the state recommends bail be set at one million dollars. Though the defendant has no criminal record, we *do* consider him a flight risk."

Judge Benjamin states, "I agree. Bail for the defendant is set at one million dollars." She slams the gavel down.

Delbert leans over to Gordon and whispers, "That means your get out of jail card will cost a hundred grand."

"Thanks," Gordon says, sarcastically, "I'm sure my truck'll cover it."

The Family That Stays Together

That evening, Rosita and the three children wait in a medium-sized, open room, with no tables, just a few chairs scattered randomly. Rosita wears a full compliment of make-up, and her eyes look full and tempting. Her appearance is stunningly beautiful, but her expression is strained, nervous. Melinda looks to her mother, sad and scared, and complains, "Mommy, that man touched my privates."

"I'm sorry about that, angel," Rosita says, concern and resignation on her face. She looks at her daughter but she speaks to no one in the room. "I wish people would listen and this would all go away."

"I don't like this place, Mom," Mark says.

There is silence for a few seconds, broken by Melinda, choking as she says the words, "When is Daddy coming home?"

Rosita steps to her youngest daughter sitting on her chair with her eyes wide and scared. She squats in front of her, pulls Melinda to her, and squeezes her tightly, clenching her teeth. A door behind them at the other side of the room opens and Gordon is led into the room in chains, wearing an orange jumpsuit. Painful expressions cross all four members of Gordon's family as they watch the two deputies unlock the chains and stand back against the wall.

Gordon smiles and moves to his family as Rosita loosens her grip on Melinda, who sprints the few feet to her father and jumps in his arms, shouting, "Daddy!" He swings her and holds her in his right arm and bends down before Mark and

Melanie and wraps his left arm around both to pull them to him. Rosita stands upright, watching her husband greet their children, and forces a smile.

Gordon looks at Melanie and puts his left hand to her cheek to wipe her tear tracks from her right eye and smiles as he says, "It's going to be alright, Princess."

Melanie looks into her father's eyes but his words of encouragement are unheeded. She moans, "I don't think it's going to be alright, Dad. I don't think you're ever coming home again." Fresh tears run from her eyes.

Gordon puts Melinda down beside him and quickly pulls Melanie to him tightly, putting his right hand against the back of her head and pushing her against his left shoulder. He whispers in her ear so only she can hear, "Don't say that. None of us know what will happen so don't be negative. Keep your head up because your mother needs you to be strong. Okay?"

Gordon releases her and Melanie leans away from him. She is still overwrought and cannot speak, so she nods her head while looking at her father through her watered eyes. She wipes her hand under her nose and forces a smile. Gordon leans to her and kisses her on the cheek and they separate.

Mark steps in and wraps his arms around his father's neck and almost pulls Gordon off his feet. Mark gives him a kiss on the cheek and asks, "Have they got real bad dudes in there, Dad?"

"Oh, no, big man," Gordon says, smiling, "we've got sewing class at eleven, cooking class at one, and group therapy every evening at six where we all talk about our feelings."

"Really?" Mark asks, looking very skeptical.

"*Not* really," Gordon says, "but don't you worry about your Pops, okay?"

"Cuz you can take care of yourself?" Mark asks.

"Pretty much, yeah," Gordon assures him.

"Okay."

Rosita steps toward him and around the children as Gordon stands up. She slides her arms around his neck, pulling him toward her and kissing him passionately. Gordon steadies himself and slips his arms around her waist, pulling their bodies together. After a few moments, she pulls her head back and says, "I can't sleep at all. I keep waking up …" Her speech drifts off, unfinished.

Gordon puts his right finger against her mouth and says, "Sshh. Let's not talk about that. We don't have much time and we need to talk about how you can take care of things for a while."

"They're not serious about going to trial, are they?" she asks. "You were home with us the whole night," she protests, loud so that even the deputies pause to look at her.

"They're not putting any stock in that," Gordon says. "They know I was in that woman's house."

Rosita appears shocked and, with some anger, demands, "What woman's house?"

"The woman who was murdered," Gordon says, glancing briefly to the ground.

"Goddamit, Gordon!" Rosita exclaims, squeezing his arm so hard he grimaces. "Why were *you* at some other woman's house?"

"I installed some software for her on a Saturday a few months back," Gordon tries to assure her.

"And that's it?"

"Yes, that's it."

"Why didn't you tell me?" Rosita demands, her anger still high.

"Tell you that I'm going to another woman's house to install software for free and watch you throw a fit, just like you're doing now?" Gordon counters.

"So you lied to me," Rosita spits, "told me you were going out with some of your friends, but now you're telling me the truth and I'm supposed to feel better?" She steps away from him, her eyes burning.

Gordon replies, sheepishly, "I can't take any of that back and I'm not trying to make you feel better. I'm trying to tell you what happened."

"Well," Rosita states, her head high but glowering at him, "now that you've had time to sit in a jail cell, have you considered that, if you had told me the truth from the beginning, you wouldn't be in this mess? *We* wouldn't be in this mess?"

Gordon turns away from her, steps to a chair nearby and slumps onto it. He looks to his wife sorrowfully, dejectedly. Softly, he finally replies, looking at the floor, "I made a mistake, yes. To avoid your jealous wrath and your incessant demand for a thorough explanation, I lied to you. I didn't trust that you would understand that I was only installing software for this woman because the company wouldn't do it, just as you can't seem to trust me around *any* women." He looks up to her hopefully. "Can we *not* beat each other up about this *now*, please? We *have* to talk about money, cuz you're gonna need it."

Rosita shakes her head and says, sarcastically, "That's a nice piece of work." Her gaze is piercing as she asks, bitterly, "Now it's *my* fault that *you* lied to me?"

Gordon springs up from his chair, lunges to his wife, slaps his hands to her shoulders and shakes her once but doesn't release her as he shouts, "Don't you get what's happening here? Let me spell it out for you. They are definitely taking me to trial, and they just might convict me, they just might sentence me to death, and they just might kill me, and there may be nothing *you or I* can do to stop it!

So you *better* get your priorities straight *right now* and take care of *our* family! Just drop this blame game and listen to me while we still have time during this visit and do what I tell you because *I can't do it from here*. Do you understand me?"

Rosita suddenly looks frightened and slumps in Gordon's grip on her shoulders. Gordon slips his right arm around her back and holds her left shoulder to guide her to a chair and sits her down softly. When she looks up at him, he says, in a measured, calm tone, "Did my paycheck come in the mail today?"

"Yes," Rosita replies, defeated.

"Did you deposit it?"

"Yes. Tonight, after work."

"Good," Gordon acknowledges. "I have one more paycheck due from them which will also have all my unused vacation and other benefits. Deposit it as soon as you get it but I need to see the stub to make sure they paid it all." He squats down before her, puts his hands on top of her thighs and squeezes them gently as he looks directly into her vacant eyes and demands, "Got it?"

She looks down at him so that her eyes stay in constant gaze with his as she replies, "Yes."

"The attorney went to interview my supervisor and I asked him to stop at the Human Resources office and get two forms for me." He pauses and reaches behind his back to retrieve some paper he had stuck in his pants. "The first was a W4 to change my withholding to nothing for my last paycheck. The attorney will take it back for me next week. It's not completely legal but it'll save us a few hundred dollars and we can claim a hardship here, okay?"

Rosita nods, "Yes."

"This," Gordon says, handing the papers to Rosita, "is a transfer form for closing my 401k account and transferring it to an IRA with no penalty. There's a little over twenty thousand in my 401k. Take this down to the bank and talk to Jack Lindblom, and *only* Jack," Gordon says, flipping the papers to the back, "here's his name, and tell him that we need to open a zero-dollar IRA with his bank to accommodate the transfer. He'll do the paperwork, you'll have to sign it, and I'll have to get it to sign it, too. Then, he'll finish this form for you, and you'll need to send it to the address listed here, certified mail. Understand?"

Rosita had been looking at the form but quickly gazes at her husband. She is beginning to sense the desperation and her eyes are misting as she simply replies, "Yes."

Gordon stands up and reaches into his right pants pocket and retrieves a folded, wrinkled piece of paper. "This," he begins, "is the web site address for the broker where I have some shares of stock from the company." He points to a section of the paper and adds, "This is my account name, my password, and this is the phone number for support help." He pauses and looks into her eyes. "Listen to me." She looks into his face. "In a few days, I'll have the chance to call them and go over everything I need to do to sell the stock and have the money sent to us. It will probably include having to close the account, but I will write down all the details." He pauses to reach down and squeeze her thighs again. "*You* will have to get on my computer and do it, though. Do you understand *that?*"

Concern overtakes Rosita's expression as she answers, "I hate using your computer because you always—"

"Don't worry, Mom," Melanie interrupts as she steps close to her mother, "I'll help you. We can do it together."

Rosita turns to Melanie and pulls her to her. Relieved, Rosita says, "Thank you, baby."

"Don't lose that paper, though," Gordon warns her. "Put it in a safe place when you get home."

"Alright," Rosita says, looking back at Gordon.

One of the deputies says, "Time's up, Schell. It's back to your cell."

Gordon quickly kisses Rosita, then each of the children as he moves toward the deputies. While they return the chains to his arms and legs, Gordon smiles and says, "I love you all."

Melinda says, "I love you, too, Daddy."

The deputies turn Gordon around and lead him out of the room. The two oldest say, "I love you, Dad." Rosita watches as they guide him a few more steps down the hall when she calls out, "I love you, dear."

Gordon twists his head to the left, smiles and winks his left eye, once.

The Trial Begins

Time is fleeting, Gordon thinks, as he is led to his seat at the defendant's table through the labyrinth of corridors and stairways that terminate in the back of the courtroom. An agonizing four months have passed at a crawl, yet Gordon perceives it accelerating. He briefly wonders if his perception is influenced only by his daily regimen of the unchanging same old thing. Entering the courtroom, his gaze immediately finds the sultry figure of the dark-haired beauty he married, sitting ramrod straight in the second row behind his table. Gordon smiles easily at her, unconcerned about any others, and Rosita forces a smile back.

The gallery of the courtroom is packed as the trial officially known as the People of the State of North Carolina vs. Schell begins. Sharon Pilot walks before the jury box at the far right of the room looking from the gallery, wrapping up her opening arguments. Her demeanor drawn and dignified, she states, "We will show, beyond any reasonable doubt, that the defendant had been in Darcy Rowland's house before, that he was familiar with the house, that he gained entry the night of the murder, that he surprised the victim, that he brutally, horribly, and sadistically tortured the victim before he slit her throat and mercifully ended her nightmare ordeal, that he was seen leaving her house immediately after he murdered her, that he had the motive and the means to commit this crime, and that he is the *only* person who *could* have committed this crime."

With the judge's instruction that he can begin, Delbert stands up and strolls slowly to the jury box, looking at each juror for a moment while he speaks, and argues, "Yes, Darcy Rowland was the victim of horrible brutality, but Gordon Schell was *not* the perpetrator of this crime. Yes, he knew the victim and her house, but he was there one Saturday to help her get connected to her employer's network so that she could work from home, something that neither Mr. Schell's employer nor the victim's employer would do for a reasonable cost. You will learn that Gordon Schell is a good and honest man and that he sits before you accused of this crime simply because he looks like the man who *really* performed this depraved act." As Delbert sits down, Gordon looks down at the table …

A young and perky woman sits in the witness box to the judge's left as Sharon Pilot asks from her table, "What do you remember most about the truck that sat parked at Darcy Rowland's house?"

"The license plate," replies the woman.

"What was special about it?" Sharon asks.

The woman smiles as she answers, "It read PEC 4 U. Peace for you. I thought that was neat."

"Let the record show that PEC 4 U is the license plate registered to the truck owned by the defendant," Sharon states, looking at the stenographer …

In the witness box sits a tall white man of average build, erect and still, wearing conservative but unspectacular business attire. As Sharon Pilot stands up, the man, who appears to be in his mid-forties, adjusts his glasses. From behind the prosecution's table, Sharon addresses the witness, "So, you found more than twenty full or partial prints matched to the defendant?"

"Yes," the man replies in a dull monotone.

"Now, this is very important," Sharon advises, continuing her questioning, as she slowly steps from behind her table toward the witness box. "Did you find any prints in the bedroom, the room where the murder was committed?"

"Absolutely," the man replies, confidently.

Rosita's calm repose gives way to anger, and her eyes narrow as she glances to the floor to hide her reaction. She listens as the man states, "There was a partial left palm print on the vanity and an index and middle fingerprint on the bedpost. There were some smudged prints on the bedpost, too." When Rosita looks up, the witness has fixed his gaze on her.

One Saturday Afternoon

In a living room with the obligatory sofa and soft, pillow-holding chairs, and in desperate need of a serious dusting, Gordon sits before a desk to the immediate left of an entertainment center with television and audio gear. He stares at a computer screen, his hands resting above a keyboard, and announces, "There it is. There's your network login." In the bottom bar on the right of the computer screen is displayed "2:30 PM." He stands up from his chair and says, "Why don't you try your login to make sure it's working."

An attractive blond in her late twenties, wearing a tight T-shirt with a low V-cut down the middle revealing the soft, white curves of her full breasts, has been standing to Gordon's left, watching him struggle to make a connection to her employer's network. As Gordon moves to his right, the woman says, "Okay." He steps back behind the chair and instinctively glances at the well-rounded butt of Darcy Rowland, admiring the fit of her waist to her hips, the ideal proportions her body posed. She sits down, taps on the keys, clicks the mouse and a few seconds later, she announces, "Yes, there's our network selections. I should be able to click on here," and she clicks the mouse, "and it should take me to the practice management login, which it did." She looks back at Gordon with a big smile. "Very good," she coos, with sincere praise. "You did good!"

Gordon smiles back and says, "I aims to please, m'am."

She gives him another big smile. Instantly, her expression changes to hopefulness as she asks, "Will you have a late lunch with me? It won't take me any time to make it and it's the least I can do for you."

"Sure," Gordon says without hesitation …

At the dining room table, located, along with the kitchen, at the opposite end of the house from the bedrooms, the plates and dishes from lunch have already been removed, and Darcy and Gordon sit across the table from each other, a glass of lemonade before each. Gordon comments, "Yeah, I remember being a little confused when I tried to reach you at work using the name the company had for you and being told by the receptionist that it was something else …"

Looking away and frowning, Darcy responds, with some lingering bitterness, "After I kicked his ass out, I had to take my maiden name back. I didn't want to have anything to do with him again."

"Oh, I can understand that for sure," Gordon agrees, wholeheartedly and nodding his head, "but going after another woman in his situation is just stupid. I mean, you're a very attractive woman, if I may say so—"

"You may," Darcy interrupts, smiling freely at Gordon.

Gordon smiles back and continues, "Anyway, you *are* an attractive woman, so I'm wondering what the hell he was thinking going after *another* woman? Were you two having any … problems?"

Darcy looks into his face as she replies, "I know what you mean by problems, so, no, there wasn't any of that, every other night, at least. But, you see, he wasn't thinking at all. He was letting his cock do his thinking for him."

Gordon looks away, partly to hide the uncomfortable identification with her assessment. "Was the divorce messy?" he asks, curious but still avoiding looking at Darcy.

"He tried to make it so," Darcy smiles, ruefully, "but I hired a very aggressive attorney and I got what I wanted from the bastard. Since then, though, he occasionally threatens me with this and that."

"Did you get the police involved?" he asks, turning to look at her with concern.

"Don't have to," Darcy assures him and stands up, walks over to the desk to her right, opens a drawer and removes a large pistol, swinging it around to Gordon.

"Shit!" Gordon exclaims, pushing his chair back. "Is that loaded?"

Darcy points it to the ceiling and smiles wickedly, responding, "Sure is, and I know how to use it, too. I go to the range every week."

"Well, let me assure you, madam," Gordon says, playfully, "that I am a *very* nice man who wouldn't harm a fly, well, almost never, and that I have a wife and three children and represent absolutely *no* threat to you whatsoever, so you can put that cannon away, thank you."

Darcy laughs and turns to the desk to return the pistol to its resting place as she says, "Oh, it's not for you, but if that fucking coward ever shows his face on my porch, I'll be ready."

Gordon observes, "Somehow, I don't think it would be wise to mess with you."

"It doesn't *pay* to, as my ex-husband discovered," Darcy replies.

After a brief pause, Gordon says, "This is a nice, old house. The woodwork is very impressive, almost antique like. How did you end up here?"

Darcy sits down as she answers, "This house belonged to my father. When he passed away two years ago, he left it to me. It's mine free and clear. I just pay the property taxes every year."

"I wish we could afford a house," Gordon laments. "That trailer is getting old."

"Would you like a tour?" Darcy offers.

"Love to," Gordon replies and they both get up from the table.

The two move down a hall to an open door on their left. Darcy leads and steps through the door, announcing, "And, this is the master bedroom, which is, of course, where I sleep."

Gordon follows her into the room, laughing, "In my book, you can call yourself master, especially with that cannon in the dining room."

She turns to smile at him and gently places her hand on his arm, letting it slide down and away. Gordon slowly steps past her, trying to ignore her obvious display of affection. On the night table next to the bed a clock displays "4:30." Gordon comments, "I love these tall bedposts. This is solid oak, isn't it?"

"Yes."

Gordon wraps his right hand around the nearest bedpost as he says, "Yeah, with bedposts like this you could have some interesting encounters with ties, or, well, other things, too." He lifts his two top fingers and slides his hand down a few inches, steps back, and turns to Darcy, smiling as he lifts his eyebrows mischievously. Darcy suddenly steps before him, placing her hands on either of his shoulders, and pushes him back to the vanity against the wall opposite the bed. When he feels the vanity against his rear and leaning back over it, Gordon extends his left arm down to its surface as a brace. Darcy quickly leans forward and kisses him aggressively, until his struggle to regain his balance succeeds and he grabs her arms at her shoulders and pushes her away at arm's length. Looking a bit surprised, he looks into her eyes, trying to sense what might happen next.

Darcy slowly regains her composure, drops her head and softly says, "I'm sorry."

Still holding her arms tight and away from him, Gordon calmly responds, "I can't do that. I'm a very happily married man and I will always be true to my wife and children. But, let me be honest," he pauses, and, when she looks up at him, he adds, "it's not that I don't want to. Trust me, I want to, but I can't."

She lowers her head again, her thick, shoulder-length blond hair tumbling across her face, and she mumbles, slowly, "I don't know. I've never …"

Gordon bends his head to her so he can look into her round, strikingly beautiful hazel eyes and says, "It's alright." She immediately relaxes and he loosens his grip and stands up straight. "When was the last time you had a hug from a man?" he asks.

The question takes her by surprise and she simply replies, "What?" She looks at him quizzically.

He repeats, "When was the last time you had a hug from a man?"

Some of her spirit returns and with mild disgust, she replies, "I can't remember."

He smiles slightly and asks, "May I give you a hug?"

She returns his slight smile and, with lowered tone, replies, "I would like that." She pauses a moment and adds, "Please."

Gordon slides his arms around her back and pulls her slowly to him until their bodies meet. She slips her arms around his waist and he squeezes her lightly. She rests her head against his left shoulder and neither move for some seconds. Finally, he pulls his arms back to her shoulders, she removes her arms from his waist and they drop to her side as they separate a bit. When their gaze meets, he says, "It's time I should be going. Will you walk me to the door?"

As his arms drop to his side, wordlessly she turns to the bedroom door and steps toward it. Her left hand grasps briefly his right hand and lifts it slightly, but she lets it fall as she walks past him. He turns and follows …

Rosita wears a half-blouse minus the brassiere, cut low to reveal her beautiful breasts and barely reaching her torso. Her gym shorts are so high and loose almost any movement would expose her fully-rounded butt. Holding the phone in the kitchen to her ear, she listens to it ring. After the third ring, on the other end, a man's voice, a bit sing-songy, says "Hello?"

"Barry?" she asks.

"Yes."

"It's Rosita."

"Hi, Rosita. What's up?"

"Can I talk to my husband?" Rosita asks. "I want to know when he expects to come home."

"I can't tell you when he expects to come home, Rosita, because he's not here."

"Where is he?" Rosita demands, disbelieving.

"I don't know," Barry replies. "I haven't seen him all day."

Rosita thinks for a moment before speaking. "Okay, I was just trying to reach him," she says, stumbling slightly through the words, "and I thought he said he would be with you, but I must have misheard him."

"No problem," Barry says. "Are you alright?"

"I'm fine," Rosita replies as cheerfully as possible. "He must be with one of his other friends. Thanks."

"Are you sure?"

"Oh, yes," she says. "I just wanted to know when to have dinner ready. I'll find him."

"Okay," Barry says, adding, "If there's—"

"Thank you," she interrupts. Replacing the handset back on the receiver without looking, worry combines with anger to overtake her expression, and she stares for minutes at the blank wall.

The Witness Parade

Trying to establish the fact that Gordon Schell frequented the neighborhood where Darcy Rowland lived, Sharon Pilot stands behind the prosecution's table and asks the very same question to five different witnesses, "How often would you see the defendant's truck drive through your neighborhood?"

The first witness, an elderly man, short and skinny wearing small, wire-rimmed glasses, sits stiffly erect in the witness box. He simply replies, "Daily."

The second witness, a shorter woman in her mid-forties of average build, sits confidently in her smartly matching woman's business attire. Her jet black, curly hair is brushed back and reveals an attractive face belying her age. She pauses to think about her answer before she responds, "Almost every day that I can recall."

The third witness, an elderly, overweight and frumpy woman with graying hair over-sprayed, sits in the witness chair fidgeting and nervous. She can barely be heard as she replies, "Every time I would be watching the traffic."

The fourth witness sits proud and defiant. Her demeanor fits perfectly with her appearance, an attractive, full-bodied black woman with short, stylish hair, mid-thirties and full of confidence. She quickly states, "Just about every business day."

The fifth witness looks like the president of a successful corporation. In his early forties, the man is snappily dressed in an immaculately tailored suit and projects confidence and authority. His short black hair is brushed back and looks wet and he is ruggedly handsome as he smiles easily. In a matter-of-fact tone with just enough emphasis to make his point, he replies, "Every morning when I would walk down the driveway to my car to go to work, that truck would drive by."

Sharon quickly follows up with the fifth witness. "How could you tell it was the defendant's truck?"

The man smiles confidently before he replies, "Oh, that truck was pretty easy to spot, with that day-glow blue stripe thinning to a point at the back. That was a custom paint job I haven't seen before …"

A young and slight woman sits in the witness stand as Sharon moves out from behind the prosecution table, asking, "Were you jogging that night?"

The woman, her plain appearance almost calculated to avoid attention, shyly answers, "Yes,"

"Do you always jog that late at night?" Sharon asks.

"Only when it's been hot during the day," the jogger slowly replies, "or when I don't get an opportunity to do so during the day. I don't mind being out at night in the neighborhood. It's usually a very quiet, sedate place to live."

"Now, do you remember what happened as you approached Poplar Street?" Sharon inquires.

"Can't forget it," the jogger replies firmly. "A man turned down the sidewalk from Poplar on the street where I was jogging and I immediately did not like the way he looked. I jogged into the street and kept my eye on him the whole time, even looked around behind me when I passed him."

Sharon steps right up to the stand, puts her hand on the rail and asks, "Did you get a good look at him?"

"I passed him right under the streetlight, yes," she insists.

Sharon turns to the jury as she asks, "Is that man here in this courtroom today?"

"There's no doubt in my mind," the jogger insists further.

Still looking at the jury, Sharon asks, "Can you point to him?"

"He's sitting over at that table," the jogger replies, pointing at Gordon. "His hair's shorter and he's clean-shaven, but that's him."

Still scanning the jury, Sharon states, "Let the record show that the witness is pointing to the defendant, Gordon Schell …"

Bill, the victim's neighbor from across the street, squirms a bit on the stand, obviously uncomfortable. Despite the incessant cooling in the courtroom, he feels the sweat accumulating under his arms and tries to avoid moving them. He speaks cautiously. "I watched the man leave the victim's house and walk to the end of the block and turn left on the sidewalk, disappearing behind the houses on that street. Only a moment later I saw a female jogger come up to the intersection in the street, and I noticed that she was looking behind her almost until she ran into the street."

Sharon stands behind the prosecution table and says, "You have identified the defendant as the man you saw that night leaving the murder victim's house, but you've also stated that his hair was different from the original photo that you identified. Is that correct?"

"Yes," Bill says, adding, "his hair was longer, he had a mustache and long sideburns and they were missing in the photo."

Sharon steps out from behind the table to the middle of the courtroom and nods to the man still sitting at the prosecution table before a computer. He begins typing and moving the mouse of the computer as Sharon says, "Mr. Atkins, if I may direct your attention to the large screen near the wall over here," and she points to the screen at her left, which displays the police photograph of Gordon. Sharon asks, "Can you see the original police photo of the defendant?"

"Oh, yes," the witness confirms, "quite clearly, yes."

"We're going to add some features now," Sharon states, and nods again to the man at the table. He clicks the mouse and the photo of Gordon Schell on the screen suddenly has longer, stringier hair, a mustache and long sideburns. When the additions are complete, Sharon turns to the witness and asks, "Is that the man you saw the night of the murder?"

The witness blinks once and his eyes grow wide as he blurts, "My God, that's him. That's the man I saw that night, just as he appeared."

"Objection, your honor!" Delbert shouts, standing up. "The prosecution is manipulating evidence. That is *not* a photo of my client. They have doctored it and it is therefore inadmissible."

Nonplussed, Sharon turns to the judge and states, "Your honor, we are simply demonstrating how easily the defendant could have altered his appearance in an attempt to hide his identity." She has stepped back to the prosecution table, bends down to lift a bag from the floor and set it on the table. She pulls out its contents, one by one, lifting each to display it for all to see before she sets each one on the table. "We found these items at a local costume shop. Here's a wig, just like the one on that screen. Here's a paste-on mustache, just like on the screen. Here is a pair of long paste-on sideburns, just like on the screen. *All* of these items are easily obtainable and just as easily disposable." Returning to the center of the room and facing the judge, she adds, "Your honor, we could make the defendant don these items for the witness, as is our right."

Justice Benjamin looks to Delbert as she ponders for a moment. She calmly says, "The prosecution has a valid point, counselor. Do you wish your client don the costume items instead?"

Delbert, defeated, drops his head and simply replies, "No." He slumps back down in his chair as Gordon looks at him sympathetically.

"I'll allow the manipulated photo, then, counselor," the judge states. "Objection overruled …"

Sharon Pilot stands behind the prosecution's table and announces, "The state calls Edward Keller to the stand."

A tall, thin man, a bit scruffy with his shirt hanging below his waist and short whiskers, rises from his seat in the gallery, scoots to the aisle, walks up to the witness stand and places his right hand on the book held level before him by the bailiff. The bailiff asks, "Do you swear to tell the truth, the whole truth, and nothing but the truth, so help you, God?"

The man replies, "I do."

The bailiff advises, "You may sit down."

The man sits down in the witness chair, shuffling his brown locks to his right with his left hand, as Sharon moves out from behind her table. Delbert is looking over some papers, a bit perplexed.

Sharon commands, "Please state your name and occupation for the record, please."

The man says, "My name is Edward Keller and I tend bar at the Cogent Coxswain Restaurant and Bar."

Delbert stands up and says, "Objection, your honor, under the rules of discovery. This witness is not on my list of witnesses provided by the prosecution."

Sharon, undeterred, moves back to her table to retrieve a document, saying, "Your honor, the prosecution is prepared to demonstrate that the defense was provided with this witness and the relevance to this proceeding at the time of discovery."

Judge Benjamin glances to both attorneys and advises, "Counselors, approach the bench."

The two attorneys step to the bench before the judge as she covers the microphone and asks, in a lowered tone, "Ms. Pilot, what do you have?"

Sharon answers, "Your honor, the evidence that Mr. Keller will provide came to light eight days ago. At that time, we sent, by certified mail to the Public Defender's office, this witness' name, along with the next witness who we intend to call, along with the relevance." She pauses for a moment as she hands a document to the judge, who looks it over, as Sharon continues. "This is a copy of the certified return from the Public Defender's office. Note, your honor, that the date of signature is seven days ago, well within the guidelines for rules of discovery."

Delbert pleads, "I haven't seen that from the prosecution, your honor, therefore, I have had no time to prepare for this witness."

"Then, you had better talk to Ms. Adams—is that her name?—in your office," Judge Benjamin responds, handing the document to Delbert, "because the prosecution has met its obligations."

Delbert looks at the document. Dejected, he hands it to Sharon, and the judge states, after removing her hand from the microphone, "Objection overruled. Please continue, Ms. Pilot …"

Chance Meeting

A tall, thin, and scruffy man wearing a bright Hawaiian style shirt and brown corduroys, wipes drinking glasses from behind a bar, his back turned away from the patrons as he looks up at the television to his left. Gordon steps through the door of the bar entrance, separate from the restaurant section, and saddles up to a stool to sit down, pulling his dress shirt out from its position tucked into his dress pants.

The man behind the bar turns around, recognizes Gordon and sets the dishcloth and glass down on the sink under the bar. "The usual?" he asks.

"Nothin' but, Eddie," Gordon replies to Edward Keller, the bartender.

Edward turns around, slides a cooler open, pulls out a bottle of Corona, grabs a bottle opener, pops off the cap, and places the bottle before Gordon. Gordon leans to his right to slip his hand into his left pants pocket but Edward stops him, saying, "I'll run a tab." He picks up his cloth and another glass and continues drying, adding, "You're in pretty early. How's your day going?"

"Sucks," Gordon replies with disgust. "Let me put it that way. Just don't ask anymore."

Edward smiles as he replies, "If it's that bad, I don't want to know."

The clock above Edward shows four minutes past four, as Gordon draws the bottle to his lips and tips it to take a drink. When the contents of that bottle eventually disappear between his lips and down his throat, Gordon orders another and proceeds to handle it in the same fashion. With the bottle almost empty, he glances above Edward to the clock, which now shows five minutes to five.

Seconds later, Darcy Rowland steps through the door of the bar entrance. She slinks to a booth in the back corner while the handful of men in the bar stare at her as she passes. The waitress working the tables and booths in the bar steps over to her booth. Gordon spins on the stool before the bar and watches the two women exchange words he can't hear until the waitress approaches the bar. Darcy glances toward the bar and sees Gordon looking at her and both exchange brief smiles. As Edward turns to satisfy the order, the waitress, a short, attractive woman in her early twenties, steps over to Gordon, smiles, and says, "The woman at the booth wants to buy your next round if you'll sit with her."

Gordon had turned to the waitress as she neared him, but he swivels to glance past her at Darcy. Still watching Gordon, she beckons to him with her right hand to join her at her booth. He turns back to the waitress, her attention riveted on Edward, and he glances briefly at the small mounds on her chest covered by her dark blue T-shirt. Smoothly, his eyes move up to her face and he says, "Thanks."

She twists her head to him and smiles. "Corona?" she asks.

"Yeah," Gordon answers, "but I'm not ready for another yet."

The waitress smiles again as she replies, "When you're ready, just give me a signal."

Gordon slides off the stool, strolls to the back corner to Darcy's booth, and sits down across from her. Wearing an easy smile, he asks, "So what's a blue ridge cowgirl doing in a bar at five in the afternoon? Don't you have horses to break, cows to feed, chores to do around the barn?"

Returning his smile Darcy replies, "I don't get much time to ride horses anymore." The waitress places a drink before Darcy and steps away. Darcy, looking a little hurt, asks, "Won't you let me buy you a drink?"

"She'll bring me another when I'm ready and she'll put it on your tab so you'll be paying for it, sooner or later," Gordon assures her, still smiling.

"Good," Darcy replies, her smile returning.

Gordon's eyes widen in a devious manner as he notes, "Besides, I wouldn't refuse a free drink from an attractive woman. I may be slow, but I'm not stupid." He glances away, lifts his beer and downs a mouthful.

Darcy lets out a little laugh and Gordon turns back to look in her eyes and smile widely. Back and forth, they trade small talk and semi-horror stories, both smiling frequently. Gordon orders the beer Darcy offered and the waitress sets it before him. On they go, talking easily, both occasionally glancing down to the table or around the bar but paying no heed, only listening raptly to the other.

They reach a break in their continuous conversation and both look about the room. Darcy turns back to Gordon and in a low tone says something to him that causes his expression to immediately change to serious concern. His gaze focuses solely on her eyes as he leans forward and softly states, "I couldn't do that."

"Yes, you could," Darcy argues, her eyelids narrowing. "You could do it easily and your wife would never know."

"*I* would know," Gordon argues, his expression now severe.

Darcy leans forward so their faces are inches apart, replying, "You don't like me?"

Gordon shakes his head and replies, "I like you, but—"

"Then, it can't be that you don't find me attractive," Darcy interrupts. "You've said so yourself. You *don't* want me?"

"That's not the point," Gordon argues back. "I love my wife and I'll always be true to her."

"What she doesn't know won't hurt her, and she'll never know."

Gordon leans farther forward and says, "I wonder if this was the same argument the other woman used on your *ex*-husband."

Darcy's face flashes anger as she stares at Gordon but she doesn't respond immediately. After a few moments, she states, "Maybe you just don't like white women. Maybe you prefer Mexicans. After all, they're ready to roll in the hay at the merest suggestion, and they're easier to control, probably because this isn't their country and they're just naturally afraid of being discovered being here illegally and being sent back."

Gordon leans back and sits up straight. Disgusted, he shakes his head and says calmly, "That's asinine."

As she leans back away from Gordon, Darcy shakes her head with an aggravated frown and replies, "It would be asinine if it wasn't true so damn often. You men are all alike."

Gordon shakes his head and looks around the bar, preferring to ignore her last remark and wondering how their friendly, casual, flirting conversation turned to this.

"Where were you today?" she asks.

Gordon turns back to look at her, frowning. He says, "I had a meeting with my supervisor this morning to determine if the setup we've been testing with your company was going to be formally adopted or rejected."

Darcy looks back with as big a frown, saying, "I'm not going to want to hear this, am I?"

Gordon glances away as he says, "I think he knew I recommended and installed software to connect remotely from your house, though he didn't say anything."

With complete disdain, Darcy shakes her head and comments, "Yep. I don't want to hear this."

Gordon continues, "He refused to accept my documentation to begin the formal development process and told me I had to roll back my setup, so I quit right there."

Darcy still shakes her head and says, "Well, that explains why everyone was in a panic today and all the higher-ups were in meetings." Seething, she leans forward and adds, "Now, because you couldn't keep it together, billing is going to go back to a disaster." She shakes her head. "You're not a partial fuck-up, you're the complete, real deal."

Gordon starts to get up from the booth seat, saying, "I didn't have any choice."

Darcy watches him get up and states, in a louder voice that all can hear, "I want to thank you for making my life more miserable than it already was. Now, I'll have to call your office and convince them that you were incompetent to begin with and that your little trip to my house was all *your* idea, that you assured me that it was *no problem*."

Gordon stops and turns around to answer, "They won't believe you."

Darcy smiles wickedly. "Oh, they'll believe me, because you don't have any credibility with them or us. I'll make sure you *never* get a good reference from us." Gordon turns back around and starts to walk away but stops when Darcy adds, "And, for good measure, I should call your wife and let her know about your trip to my house, but, of course, you've already told her because you tell her everything, don't you?" Gordon stands still but makes no acknowledgement. After a few moments, he takes one step further, but stops when he hears Darcy shout, "Oh, so you *didn't* tell her, did you? Well, what she doesn't know won't hurt her, right, Gordon?"

He walks over to the bar and pulls out some bills and flips two twenties on the bar toward Edward, asking, "Will that cover it?"

"And then some," Edward replies.

"Keep it," Gordon advises and walks out through the door to the sidewalk, turns right and disappears …

The Defense Confers and Counters

With the bar waitress' testimony concluded, Judge Mildred Benjamin calls a recess and the courtroom slowly empties. As the two deputies approach Gordon sitting at the defense table, he stands up and glances back into the gallery for Rosita. Unmoving, she sits two rows back, watching her husband stand and look back to her. Her gaze moves up his frame to his eyes, her face saddened, dejected. He looks for just a small sign of belief, but she offers none. Instead, she slowly turns her head to the right and drops it, staring at the floor as if it held an answer. One of the deputies motions for Gordon to step from behind the table, and he turns away to heed the request. Escorted by the deputies, each with a firm grasp of one of his arms, the three exit the courtroom to the left of the judge's stand.

After a few minutes, Rosita stands and scoots along the bench to the aisle. Dignified and ignoring everything around her, she walks to the courtroom door, pushes it open and is immediately surrounded by several local reporters. She avoids looking at any of them and silently walks down the long hall to the elevators, enters the first one that opens going down and exits that elevator at the first floor.

Down the hall and out of the building, she walks slowly past the columns at the front of the building and down each step toward the sidewalk. Sitting cross-legged on the wall buttressing the grounds of the building, a skinny, middle-aged man with sunglasses, T-shirt and shorts, bobs his head to the music playing from the portable box next to him, loud enough for all to hear gathered at the front of the building, David Gilmour's *There's No Way Out of Here* ...

Gordon sits behind a table in a small room and the door bursts open as Delbert quickly steps to the table opposite Gordon. Though he struggles with his satchel, he still slams it down on the table and Gordon jumps in his chair.

"They're gonna hang you, Gordon," Delbert states, his voice loud.

"They don't hang people in North Carolina," Gordon responds, calmly, smiling.

"You can drop the false bravado," Delbert advises, still loudly. "The weakness in their case was motive, and those last two witnesses just gave them the motive, but, because you never told me anything about meeting the victim in the bar on the day of her death, I have no defense to counter it."

Gordon looks down and says, softly, "I forgot all about it."

Incredulous, Delbert practically shouts, "How could you forget *that*?" He quickly pulls a chair out from under the table and plops down. "Did I *not* tell you to never hold anything back from me, no matter how irrelevant? That I would be the judge of that?"

"Yes."

"So, tell me, Gordon, *how* could you forget to tell me that?" Delbert asks, lowering his voice a bit.

Gordon lays his forearms on the table and interlocks the fingers of his hands. He looks to his left and away from Delbert. Delbert waits patiently, though his expression is one of extreme concern. Finally, Gordon meekly offers, "I forgot about it."

Delbert peers at Gordon, who refuses to look back at him. He says, "You're still hiding something from me. What is it?"

After some time, Gordon turns his head to look directly at Delbert, and angrily says, "I blocked it out okay? Is that what you want to hear? I blocked it out like I block out a lot of things. If I think you don't need to know, you won't." He lowers his head and his tone is calmer as he adds, "If Rosita doesn't need to know, she won't."

Delbert nods his head, like he understands now. He says, "Please don't tell me you did this to protect Rosita."

Gordon replies slowly, deliberately, "You don't know what it's like to be married to her. You don't know her like I do. You don't know how insecure she is, how racked with self-doubt she is." He pauses and draws a long breath. "And how much that contributes to her jealousy ..."

Delbert looks confused as he asks, "So, this is all about her jealousy?"

"No, that's just the tip," Gordon continues, slowly, deliberately. "That's just her reaction if I look at another woman, if another woman shows me the slightest interest." He is silent for a moment, until he adds, "It comes from a place much deeper than that."

"I'm still listening."

"When she first came here from Mexico, she had to trust people she didn't know." Gordon takes a sip of water from a cup before him. "She met another Mexican boy here, liked him, trusted him. She considered him her boyfriend, he was showing her how to make it in the Anglo world, until …" He is silent for a moment, and looks directly into Delbert's eyes. "… he sexually abused her, he raped her. Do you know how many people in this world know Rosita was sexually abused?" he asks, choking some as he poses the question.

"No. Tell me."

"Four people. Rosita, the boyfriend, and me," Gordon replies, "and you're the fourth." He pauses before adding, "Do you know what it's like to live with a woman who was sexually abused?"

"No. Enlighten me."

"When you live with a woman who was sexually abused, it's almost like you're victimized, too."

"That's a little drastic, don't you think?" Delbert asks, skeptically.

Gordon narrows his eyes and bitterly spits, "When you live every waking moment in pure dread that something you'll say, something you'll do that day, will trigger a memory of that event, that incident, that man?"

"That's still not as drastic as what she went through," Delbert counters.

Gordon shakes his head and looks at Delbert in disdain as he says, "So it shouldn't matter that you'll always be considered the enemy simply because you're a man, just like he was?"

"I still don't see it," Delbert says, softer, trying to understand.

"When she was so ashamed of it, like it was *her fault*, that she couldn't even tell me about it until we were married for a year and a half and she was pregnant with our first child?" Gordon takes another sip from the cup. "That we can never afford counseling so she can get past the shame that she still feels to this day?"

"I think I know—"

"You don't know jack-shit about it," Gordon interrupts. "You don't know that her only instinct when she realizes she was jealous for no reason is to give me her body, to make me have sex with her, because that's what every man wants, isn't it? That why she was sexually abused, wasn't it?"

"Sexual abuse is about power," Delbert advises.

Gordon quickly adds, "And it's a crime of violence, just like beating the crap out of somebody, or shooting them. It's violent. It's not about a man wanting sex, so convince Rosita."

Silence ensues, broken by Delbert saying, "Let me see if I understand." He pauses, collecting his thoughts. "You have established a pattern with your wife, then, where you don't share things that happen in your life because you anticipate it will 'set her off', so to speak. So you're not completely honest with her—you block out those events—because it has proven useful in the past, since what she doesn't know won't hurt her, right? Is that a fair assessment of your life with her?"

"Unfortunately, that's pretty much how it's evolved, yes," Gordon agrees. "That's a fair assessment, except for one thing."

"What am I missing?" Delbert asks, leaning forward.

"I was going to split from Rosita—it wasn't working out—until all that happened."

"You mean when she told you she was pregnant and had been raped?" Delbert asks for clarification.

"Yes," Gordon simply replies, his head bowed.

"So, you've been trapped in a less-than-ideal marriage with a wildly jealous wife," Delbert observes. He thinks for a moment and adds, "Would it surprise you, then, if I told you that Rosita knew you weren't with your friends that Saturday afternoon *before* you came home and less than a week later knew you were at another woman's house instead?" Incredulous, Gordon stares at Delbert, who just stares back, frowning. He adds, "She knew all along, Gordon, even while you were playing that game."

Gordon drops his head and speaks in a very low tone. "I'm not perfect, never was. None of us are. I'm trying to protect my family, my wife and kids, the only way I know how." He looks away as he adds, "If they were to leave me that would kill me."

"That's how your life has changed, Gordon, but you can only see part of it because you're still somewhere else. At one time, you wanted to leave. Now, it would kill you if your family left *you*." Delbert stands up from his chair and reaches for his satchel. "And, it's funny you should say that, Gordon, because, after all this, you may end up losing your wife and kids anyway, and the state just may kill you."

Without moving, Gordon responds, "I didn't kill her."

Delbert picks up his satchel and shifts it under his right arm as he replies, "I know that, Gordon. Now, I have to go back in there and reverse the damage as much as possible." He steps to the door but turns back to add, "And hope that the *jury* is convinced that you didn't …"

Rosita sits in the witness stand, straight and proud, a figure of radiance in her attractive blue dress, the make-up on her face highlighting a sexual attraction impossible to ignore. Delbert stands behind the defense table and says, "Tell us what happened on that Saturday afternoon."

Rosita calmly replies, "My husband, Gordon, told me that he was going to visit some friends to drink a few beers and watch a game and would be back in time for dinner."

Delbert asks, "What happened next?"

Rosita thinks for a moment and replies, "Well, it was getting late in the afternoon, so I called his friend, Barry. He told me that he hadn't seen Gordon all day."

"How did that make you feel?" Delbert asks.

Rosita looks at Gordon as she replies, "At first, I was angry, because my husband had not been truthful with me."

"Were you still angry with him when he returned about a half-hour later?"

"No."

Delbert looks shocked for the jury as he asks, "Why not?"

Rosita smiles as she replies, "I've been married to my husband for almost thirteen years. What I've learned about him over the years is that, despite his outward appearance of strength and his carefree attitude—here's what all the wives will understand—in a lot of ways, he's still just a little boy." The courtroom erupts in laughter and the judge bangs her gavel for order, while Gordon lowers his eyelids in mock anger and Rosita steals a glance at him and flashes a smile.

When the laughter subsides, Delbert asks, "Well, what does that mean?"

A woman in the audience bursts out, "We all know what that means." The courtroom erupts in laughter, again, and the judge bangs the gavel for order. Gordon looks away, shaking his head, but he can't help smiling and Rosita sits up straight, smiling comfortably.

Judge Benjamin looks down at Rosita and asks, "Can you answer the question without causing yet another disturbance, Mrs. Schell?"

Rosita looks proudly at the judge and replies, "Yes, I can, your honor."

Judge Benjamin advises, "Please do."

Rosita continues, "Just like a little boy, when my husband does something embarrassing or something he shouldn't be doing and he doesn't get caught immediately, he'll pretend like it never happened, like he wasn't there at all."

Delbert looks a little suspicious as he asks, "Well, Rosita, how often does this take place?"

Rosita laughs for a moment and replies, "I love Gordon, but he's a little boy every day."

A woman shouts, "Amen," and the courtroom erupts in laughter. Sternly, the judge bangs her gavel, looking at Rosita, and shouts, "I'll empty this courtroom at the next outburst. Do you understand me?" The courtroom grows quiet and the judge says to Rosita, "Now, Mrs. Schell, you promised me."

Rosita flashes a look of innocence as she replies, "I'm sorry, your honor, but I promised to tell the truth, the whole truth, and nothing but the truth, so help me, God."

The judge says, under her breath, "I could use His help now." Looking to Delbert, she advises, "Counselor, you better get to a point very soon or you'll try my patience."

Delbert answers, "Yes, your honor, we're getting there, I assure you." He turns back to Rosita and asks, "Why wouldn't you still be mad at him after he came home and you knew he wasn't truthful with you?"

Rosita thinks for a moment and replies slowly, "As much as I hate it when he's not truthful with me, I discovered long ago that he's not a devious man. He doesn't play around. Instead, in his little boy way, he's just over-protective."

Delbert asks, "What do you mean by 'over-protective?'"

"He's trying to protect me from being hurt," she replies. "He's been that way ever since I told him."

"Told him what?" Delbert probes.

Rosita looks down as she speaks in a lower tone, "When I was pregnant with our first child, I told him that I was sexually abused," and she pauses, looking up and around the room defiantly, "that I was raped when I was fifteen." A hush fills the courtroom and many of the women in the gallery focus squarely on Rosita's face, concern and empathy replacing much of the skepticism.

Delbert asks, "How did Gordon take that?"

Rosita looks to her husband, painfully, as she answers, "He was very quiet, not saying anything. Then, he got up and came over to me, put his arms around me, and held me for hours." She looks at Delbert and continues, "Ever since, he's been very protective of me. He tries very hard to keep me from being hurt."

Delbert looks up, thinking, and asks, "Do you ever get jealous?" He pauses and looks at Rosita, adding, "For instance, when you catch him looking at other women."

Somewhat offended, Rosita answers, "I'm not *jealous* about that. I'm mad."

Delbert interrupts, "So, you *do* get mad at him?"

"Yes," Rosita confirms. "When I'm out with my husband, he needs to pay attention to me. I'm the love of his life, not those other women."

Delbert asks, "How did you find out that he was at another woman's house?"

"Quite often, when I call his work, he's on the phone, so I'll talk to one of his work friends, Barry," Rosita explains. "That week, Barry told me that he knew where Gordon had been that Saturday. I had called Barry at his home that Saturday trying to find Gordon, so he thought I should know."

Delbert asks, "Did you get mad then?"

"No," Rosita replies. "Barry told me that he was there to install software and that's just like him."

"How so?"

Rosita pauses to look at the ceiling and think of her answer. After a moment, she replies, "Gordon's the person who will help people when no one else will, even if it means putting off our plans."

"Can you remember a time when he did that?" Delbert inquires further.

"Yes. Last winter—"

"Objection, your honor!" Sharon Pilot interrupts, standing up quickly from her seat at the prosecutor's table, peeved and annoyed. "I fail to see the relevance of any of this testimony."

Delbert spins to the judge and argues, "Your honor, the defendant is on trial for his life, and it is our contention that he is here on a case of mistaken identity. We are trying to establish his true identity—a caring and compassionate man, your honor, and *not* a cold-blooded killer."

Judge Benjamin looks at Delbert and says, "I'll allow it, for now. Objection overruled." Without comment, but shaking her head vigorously, Sharon Pilot sits back down, glancing briefly to the jury with a look of concern. The judge ignores Sharon's display, turns to Rosita and advises, "You may continue, Mrs. Schell."

"Last winter," Rosita says, "when we had that big snow, our son wanted to see a movie for his birthday, so, even though the snow was coming down heavy, we got in Gordon's truck and started driving to the theater. Gordon saw a car had slid off the road into a ditch, so he pulled over to check on it, even though we all asked him not to—that we would be late for the movie—but he got out, anyway."

Pleased, Delbert looks at Rosita with encouragement and asks, "What did he do, then?"

"Gordon checked on the driver first," Rosita continues, "and tried to push the car out of the ditch for the next half-hour, while cars just kept driving by. I kept rolling down the window to remind him that we were missing the movie, but he just kept at it. Finally, two men stopped and the three managed to push the car out of the ditch—and Gordon even fell into the wet snow—but the car drove off."

"Were you late for the movie?"

"Yes."

"How did you take it?"

Rosita pauses to look at her husband, her expression soft and warm, before answering. "I knew why he did it. When he got back in the truck, our son said, 'Good job, Dad.' Gordon said, 'Thank you, Mark. I'm sorry we're gonna miss the start of the movie,' and our son said, 'That's okay.' We stayed to the next showing and caught the start of the movie." She pauses and her eyes mist when she adds, "That's how Gordon is. He'll stop to help total strangers, people he doesn't even know."

Rebuttals

Sharon Pilot stands to announce, "The state calls Kelly Cook for rebuttal."

The courtroom doors open. An average-looking, young woman, her brown hair falling freely past her shoulders, enters through the opened doors, exhibiting a bit of bewilderment and anxiety mixed with an odd sense of sincerity. Rosita watches her move to the witness stand, uncertain what might take place in the next few minutes and concerned because of it.

Once the witness reaches the stand and is sworn in, Sharon, standing behind the prosecution's table, begins, "Now, Ms. Cook, how do you know the defendant's wife?"

Kelly Cook smiles as she answers with a thick, Southern drawl, "Oh, Rosita and me both work as waitresses at the same restaurant."

Sharon asks, "Very good, Ms. Cook. Do you recall a conversation you had with the defendant's wife, Rosita Schell, on the afternoon of the twelfth last month?"

Kelly beams, "I sure do."

"Can you tell us where this conversation took place first?" Sharon leads her.

"In the back room of the restaurant," Kelly confidently replies.

Sharon smiles and comments, "Excellent." She steps out from behind the table and advises Kelly, "Please tell the court, in your own words, about this conversation."

Kelly thinks for a moment. "Well, I was sympathizing with Rosita about her husband and all of this," she begins, speaking slowly, carefully. "I knew it must have been very hard for her, and I just wanted her to know that I was there for her. I asked her what she was going to do, and that's when she said, 'I don't know, but I'll do anything to save my husband. Anything.'"

Sharon tries to look skeptical as she asks, "You're sure she said that?"

"Yes, m'am."

"How can you be so certain?"

Kelly's expression is deadly serious as she answers, "Because she emphasized 'anything', even said it twice. When she left, Jimmy even said, 'Did she say 'anything'?'"

"Who's Jimmy?"

"Jimmy's one of the cooks …"

A slight black man in his late twenties, with short cropped hair and a neatly trimmed beard, sits at the witness stand glancing slowly around the courtroom, careful to avoid eye contact, as Sharon approaches him. She asks, "Please state your name."

The man turns to face Sharon and smiles at her as he replies confidently, "James Edward Brandon."

"Where do you work, Mr. Brandon?" Sharon asks.

"I work at the Beverly Restaurant as one uh the cooks," he replies.

Sharon turns away from the witness toward the jury box without focusing on anyone, asking, "Mr. Brandon, do you recall overhearing a conversation between the defendant's wife, Rosita Schell, and Kelly Cook on the afternoon of the twelfth last month?"

Jimmy smiles while he hesitates with his answer, but states slowly, confidently and emphatically, "I couldn't *help* but hear it since I was standing but *five feet away!*"

Sharon spins slowly back to Jimmy to ask, "Do you remember Ms. Cook asking Mrs. Schell what Mrs. Schell was going to do?"

"I shore do."

"Do you recall what Mrs. Schell said in reply?"

"She said, and I'll never forget it," Jimmy replies, and suddenly looks at the juror in the first seat closest to him, "'I don't know, but I'll do *anything* to save my husband. *Anything!*'"

A few minutes later, Delbert slowly walks before the jury, scanning their faces, as he asks, "Mrs. Schell, did you say to your friend, Kelly Cook, and I quote, 'I'll do anything to save my husband. Anything'?"

Rosita sits at the witness stand, wearing the same attractive blue dress as before. She fidgets a moment, a sad expression on her face, and replies as she gazes at Delbert, "Yes, I said that."

Still facing the jury, Delbert asks, "Did you use the word 'anything' as a figure of speech?"

Rosita sits up straight, strong and defiant, as she answers, "I did not mean that I would do 'anything.'"

"Would you lie for your husband?"

Insulted, Rosita snaps, "Never!"

Turning to face Rosita, Delbert argues, "But, Mrs. Schell, your husband's on trial for murder and his life may be at stake. You're telling the court that you would *not* lie to save his life?"

Rosita turns to glance at several of the jurors as she answers, "I don't have to."

"And why not?"

Rosita scans over the jurors, her head high, as she answers, "Because on the night that woman was murdered, my husband was home with me, in our bed, giving me a wonderful back rub, and then he made love to me."

Delbert turns in the direction of the jury box and glances at some of the jurors, continuing to turn completely around to walk back to his table. As he strides confidently, he calmly says, "Thank you, Mrs. Schell."

Deliberation

After two weeks of testimony and courtroom wrangling by both sides, the trial concludes and the judge instructs the jury as to their responsibilities under the law. With the fate of the defendant now in the hands of twelve of his peers, the press speculates about the probable outcome. Coverage of the trial is particularly nasty in the state where the crime was committed, since public outrage over the senseless brutality of the murder has barely subsided in five months.

Much of the sporadic national commentary is skeptical of Gordon's extremely brief testimony that the real suspect must have planted the evidence discovered in his truck. Most find Gordon's demeanor in the witness box arrogant and his explanations unconvincing and self-serving, as do most of the jurors. What Gordon cannot refute is that the blood found on the neckties belongs to Darcy Rowland, a positive DNA match to the murder victim. On top of that, the murder weapon is a scalpel, just like the one discovered in Gordon's truck. While the technicians discover blood on the scalpel, too, it is too small of a sample to subject to DNA testing. Still, they can and do determine that this blood is the same blood type as the murder victim.

Who is the mystery suspect that the defense claims committed the murder of Darcy Rowland? No one offers a single name from the defense or the prosecution, so the vast majority of those who follow the trial conclude that there is no mystery suspect. It's merely a defense ruse, as Sharon Pilot ably argues in her jury summation ...

In a secluded room behind the courtroom, a short, slight man in his early thirties, sits in the middle of one side of a table with eleven others scattered around it.

He opens a piece of paper, looks it over and sets it down next to a pile of small papers before him, and says, "That's ten for conviction and two for acquittal."

An older white man of average height and build sits across and to the left of the jury foreman, glances down the table and comments disgustedly, "Who's holding out here? This man had the motive—the victim threatened his ability to gain employment—he knew his way around her house, he may have had something going on with the victim, he was seen at the scene of the crime when it happened, and I don't believe his wife, period." The jury foreman nervously pushes the short locks of his black hair to his right but says nothing.

An attractive woman with a shining dark complexion and stylishly short, straight hair, smartly dressed, leans forward from the opposite end of the table from the older white man, staring straight at him, and defiantly demands, "What have you got against his wife? You've been ripping on her since we started."

The older man focuses on the woman and snaps back, "Is she from here?"

The woman lifts her eyes to the ceiling in disbelief as she responds, "What does that have to do with anything?"

The older man, a little calmer, replies, "I'll ask it, again, and I'll answer for you. Is she from here? No, she's from Mexico and came into this country illegally. Do you *really* think, if anyone asked her if she was here legally, she replied, 'No, I'm an illegal immigrant?' Of course, not. But, when she married her husband, she became legal, didn't she? And, the prosecutor pointed out, correctly, that she worked at various jobs before she married and she always stated that she was in this country legally. She's lied before, my fellow jurors, and you're not going to convince me that she wouldn't lie to save the man who put her in this country legally, *and* permanently."

The faces of the jurors appear resolute. Most nod, though the black woman rubs her face with a look of worry. One young man, of Latino appearance, sitting directly across from the smartly dressed woman, looks down the table, turns his head back and away from the others and frowns.

CONVICTION AND SENTENCE

Following two days of deliberation, the jurors file into the courtroom to take their seats. When the courtroom is finally quiet, Judge Benjamin asks, "Mr. Foreman, has the jury reached a verdict?"

The jury foreman responds, "Yes, your honor."

Judge Benjamin orders, "Please stand and read the jury's verdict, Mr. Foreman."

The jury foreman stands and opens a paper he was carrying in his right hand. He reads matter-of-factly, "On the count of first-degree murder, the jury finds the defendant, Gordon Schell, guilty." He closes the paper and looks over to the judge.

Under his breath, Delbert says, "Shit!" He shakes his head.

Rosita screams, "No!" Gordon spins around to look at his wife, gritting his teeth, his face emotionless. Her face ashen and eyes misting, she stares unblinking at Gordon. They gaze only at each other until two deputies appear next to Gordon to remove him from the courtroom …

Delbert paces back and forth in a small room while Gordon sits at a table calmly, his hands folded and resting on the table. Delbert says, "Gordon, your only hope to avoid execution at this point is to throw yourself at the mercy of the court." He stops before the table to look at Gordon. "Son, you're going to have to swallow your pride and just do it, if you want to live to see your children grow up. You can get life in prison."

"That'll never happen," Gordon replies, eyes narrowing. "I'll never confess to a crime I didn't commit."

"Dammit, Gordon," Delbert says, trying to remain calm, "you've only two choices: life in prison or execution. You can save your own life, and your wife still has a husband, your children still have a father." Gordon remains silent but looks away from Delbert, who adds, "Don't forget that twelve disinterested people think you did it."

Gordon is unimpressed as he replies, his tone rising, "I don't care if there were seven billion people in that jury box and they all agreed that I did it. They'd all be wrong, all seven billion of 'em."

"And you'd be right, Gordon," Delbert concedes, "and dead, anyway." He steps away and looks at the wall as he adds, "In good conscience, I cannot advise you to do what you insist on doing."

Gordon leans back in his chair and states, "I can't show remorse for something I didn't do. That's just absurd, but there's a bigger dilemma than that, Delbert." He pauses for a moment, looking at his attorney as Delbert turns around to look back. "With life in prison, I get to see my kids grow up through the occasional prison visit for, what, an hour or two every month, two, three months? I can't hold them in my arms and comfort them. I can't play with them, can't read to them, can't help with their studies, can't advise them through their lives, can't be there when they need me. How about my wife? Can I hold her for hours, dance real slow with her tight against me, kiss her passionately, rub her back, have her rub mine, plan our lives together, take vacations, make love with her? Is that going to be my life? No, I get limited prison visits for the rest of my natural life. How *natural* is that?" He pauses to glance down at the table. "All my life, I've done what others have told me I should do, and paid the price when it wasn't right. This is just another example, Delbert, where everybody knows what's right for me. They all think I'm a brutal murderer and I should pay, but you're asking me to make a choice for a life that I cannot possibly live." He stops for a few seconds to place his hands back on the table. His hands slowly form into fists. "I only feel an intense anger for this foolish judgment against *me*, so, fuck 'em," and he slams his right first on the table and leans farther forward staring intensely at Delbert, "let 'em kill me ..."

Judge Benjamin looks down from her bench severely at Gordon sitting at the defendant's table. She asks, "Gordon Schell, do you have anything you wish to say on your behalf?"

"Yes, your honor," Gordon replies, calmly.

"Please stand," the judge advises and Gordon stands up behind the table.

"Your honor," Gordon begins, "I understand what you, the victim's relatives, the community, perhaps the entire civilized world expects from me. To display remorse for an action that I never performed, however, is impossible and, on a personal level, repugnant. I will *never* do that, not in *this* life, not *ever!*"

Perhaps shocked by the defiance, Judge Benjamin gathers herself and returns a gaze of intense sternness at Gordon. Finally, she speaks. "In light of that remark, Gordon Schell, I am now ready to pass sentencing upon you. For the most horrific torture and murder of Darcy Rowland, I sentence you to be executed by lethal injection at the earliest possible date that the state of North Carolina can arrange. May God have mercy on your soul." She bangs the gavel down on the peg of her table, stands and quickly exits the courtroom without looking at anyone.

The Big Bucks Cometh

A Latino man, about six feet tall and well-built with short, slicked back black hair, clean shaven and extremely handsome, wears an impeccably dazzling dark gray Armani suit as he strolls confidently from the elevator to a glass enclosed office suite. Holding a polished black leather briefcase in his left hand, he reaches for the handle of the glass door once he reaches the suite and flings it open like he belongs there. The door reads "Lambert, Sheehan and Goldsmith, LLP, Attorneys at Law" and he strides into the office with the poise and confidence of a celebrity movie star. He walks by the reception desk and the attractive young woman behind the desk looks up at him and unconsciously sweeps back her brown hair from her face and smiles easily. When the man catches her gaze and smiles back just as easily, she says, "Good morning, Mr. Rodriguez."

The man replies, with a new day enthusiasm, "Good morning, Amy."

Amy's expression changes to seriousness and she advises him as he walks past her, "Mr. Sheehan asked that I tell you to come to his office as soon as you get in."

The man immediately stops and turns to face her. Smiling as he looks over her as she sits in her chair, he says, "Thank you, Amy. Incidentally, I love that outfit. It's very smart and professional."

She flips her head up and her hair falls freely below her shoulders as she flashes her radiant smile. "Thank you," she coyly replies. "You're looking dapper as usual."

The man returns a smile and teases, "This thing? I found it at the Salvation Army." He raises his eyebrows for emphasis.

Amy reveals a mock frown and comments sarcastically, "Sure." The man turns away and walks down the hall.

A few moments later, the man approaches a desk situated just left of a closed office door with the name "Adam Sheehan" written on it. A tall and attractive middle-aged woman with blond hair to her shoulders and wearing a red dress to her knees is bent over slightly before a filing cabinet behind the desk, pulling files from a list she holds in her left hand. When she hears the man approach the desk, she turns around, steps to her desk and lays down the file in her right hand. As she reaches for the phone with her now free right hand, the man asks, "Is Adam busy, Joyce?"

She smiles at him and punches a button as she says, "Not for you, Manny."

She looks at the phone as a voice from the speaker says, "Yes, Joyce."

Joyce replies, "Mr. Rodriguez is here, Mr. Sheehan."

The voice from the speaker says, "Send him in."

Manny smiles as he says, "Thank you, Joyce." Immediately, he steps to the door and reaches for the handle.

Joyce watches Manny approach the door and says, "You're welcome."

Manny opens the door and enters the office. He looks at the older man sitting behind a mahogany desk in an oversized leather chair and asks, "What's up, Adam?"

Adam Sheehan, his average height and build and sincere impression belying his status as the senior partner of the law firm, gestures to one of the chairs surrounding his desk and says, "Have a seat, Manny." He waits for Manny to sit down and get comfortable before he continues. "We just got a new habeas corpus, *People of the State of North Carolina vs. Gordon Schell*. The mandatory appeal is scheduled in ninety days and I'm assigning you to the case." He lifts from his desk a blue folder and hands it to Manny, who reaches forward to take the blue folder. "That's the brief filed by the prosecution, along with a summary of the trial proceedings, and the judgment. The full transcript and evidentiary documents are in several boxes in the records room. Evan will help you get all that together."

Without looking inside the folder, Manny asks, "What's the prognosis, Adam? Are there grounds for reversal for improper jury instruction, prejudicial misconduct, improper discovery, rights violations, improper search and seizure, witness tampering, anything?"

Adam shakes his head as he answers, "The intern who prepared the summary didn't see anything obvious, but that's why you'll go over everything, of course."

"Well, of course, "Manny replies, jovially, smiling somewhat deviously, "don't I always?"

"No complaints, here," Adam agrees. "How was the art exhibition last night?"

"It went well," Manny says, slouching comfortably. "There were quite a few people who dropped by, and Sharona sold two pieces, which is not bad."

"So when are you going to make an honest woman out of that beauty, Manny?" Adam teases.

"You keep asking me that same question, Adam," Manny protests, smiling, "and I keep telling you the same answer. We're just good friends from our college days."

"That's what I always thought about Beatrice," Adam muses, smiling back, "until I woke up one day and realized I couldn't live without her."

"I still haven't decided which one of you to believe," Manny jokes. "Every time I hear Beatrice tell it, *she* woke up one day and realized *she* couldn't live without *you*."

"Funny how that happens, isn't it?" Adam asks, still smiling, but looking away while thinking about something else. "I'm sure it was just a coincidence that it was the same day for both of us." He turns back to look at Manny and winks when he adds, "Maybe, some day both of you will wake up."

Manny stands up smiling, shifting the folder to his left hand to hold it and the briefcase, and says, "I get so much more accomplished when I sleepwalk, who needs to be awake?" After a moment he looks at Adam seriously. "I'll assemble this in my office and start going over it this morning. Do you want to meet in a few days for an assessment?"

"When you're ready, yes," Adam replies, satisfied.

"Alright, I'll check with you then," Manny replies and steps to the door.

CRIBBAGE ANYONE?

A very tall, muscular, black man, in his mid-forties, wearing a corrections officer's uniform, appears at the bars of Gordon's cell holding an opened box. "You got mail, Gordon," he announces with officiousness. "Looks like a cribbage board and a pack of cards." Looking a little sheepish, he adds, "We had to open it, you know."

"Excellent," Gordon says, turning to look at the officer and bouncing up from his bed. When he reaches the bars and takes the box offered through the bars, he smiles at the guard and says, "That's alright, big man. It's the right size for a file, ain't it?"

The guard smiles back, saying, "Yeah, it is. Don't you need two people to play cribbage?"

Gordon removes the board and cards from the box and steps to a shelf to place them on it. With his back turned to the guard, he replies, "To make a game of it, yes." Turning around and holding the box in his left hand, he steps back to the bars, and offers the empty box to the guard, adding, "You can play by yourself for practice, though, but you're playing both hands."

The guard takes the empty box through the bars and asks, when he looks back at Gordon, "How long's it take for a game?"

Gordon thinks for a moment and says, "Oh, anywhere from a half-hour to an hour. Depends on the hands, I guess."

The guard shakes his head and says, "You won't have much time to play a game with anyone."

Gordon puts both hands on the bars, leaning against them, and replies, "True. One hour in the exercise yard isn't much time."

"Think any of the other Death Row boys play cribbage?"

"Don't know," Gordon replies. "You ever play cribbage, Big Man?"

"Nah," the guard drawls, "where I come from, nobody's ever heard of it."

"I could teach you how to play, if you want," Gordon offers. "It's a simple game to learn but it takes a little strategy to be good."

The guard smiles, saying, "You'd probably whip me good every time."

Gordon smiles, but hunches his shoulders, saying, "Sometimes, ya get lucky."

Trailer Trash Meets Armani

Gordon Schell waddles in full leg and arm chains through the maze of corridors in the maximum security prison apprehensive about his coming confrontation. Over the last month he has listened to fellow Death Row inmates, guards, studied law proceedings in the prison library and now knows the process which is just beginning. His apprehension stems from years of little appreciation, underestimation, ignoring and overlooking, enduring a complete lack of faith in him until he demonstrates conclusively the failed merit of this initial judgment. All of this comes from the suits, those who are more formally educated than Gordon but have earned a thorough disdain and disregard, since he invariably leaves once it's clear that the expectations placed upon him have been blown away. After all, those who cannot believe in him do not deserve his presence.

Apprehension dogs him as he makes his slow progress through the prison because he knows that he will soon sit across from yet another suit and be subjected to yet another round of no appreciation, underestimation, ignoring and overlooking. *How quaint,* Gordon thinks. *I just can't wait.* He feels a growing sense of disdain and disrespect, an uncooperative attitude attaching itself to his conscious perception like a leech sucking the life blood from him.

Patiently, Manuel Rodriguez sits at a table in a small room with cinder block walls, painted gray, a folder and papers spread out before him, a blank pad of yellow paper directly in front with a pen sitting atop it. He glances around the room, lifts his left arm and notes the time on his watch. He returns his left arm to his lap, interlaces the fingers of both hands, and waits.

A few moments later, the door opens, and Gordon Schell is led into the room with his full leg and arm chains by a single guard. The guard pulls the chair across from Manny out from under the table and Gordon waddles in front of it and plops down. No one says a word until the guard leaves the room, closing the door behind him.

With a now seething conflict raging inside him, Gordon views the Armani suit sitting across from him as the enemy and demands, with open sarcasm, "So, you're the heavy hitter?"

"Not really," Manny explains. "In capital murder cases like this, appeals are automatic. When a public defender serves as counsel at the trial, law firms like ours are assigned the appeal to ensure that all the rights of the accused have been met."

"For big bucks, I presume," Gordon remarks, glancing to his right.

"We have an important duty to perform, Mr. Schell," Manny replies, a little perturbed.

"That's a lawyerly answer," Gordon replies. "Did they teach you that at law college? Always avoid talking about fees."

"We need to discuss—"

"I guess I shouldn't complain," Gordon interrupts. "Why, I got the best defense money could buy, considering I didn't have any money." He looks at Manny, his eyes narrowing, and adds, "You know what I ask when you get something for free?"

"No."

"How much is it worth?" Gordon replies. "So, how much is something for free worth?"

"I don't know," Manny thinks, playing along. "It would depend on what that something for free is."

"Nothing," Gordon spits out. "Something for free is not worth anything. *Anything* is worth nothing when it's *free*." He looks away from Manny.

"I still think it would depend," Manny argues, but Gordon ignores him. "Listen, let's go back to the beginning." He stands up and offers his right hand all the way across the table to a few inches from Gordon's right hand. "My name is Manuel Rodriguez."

Gordon looks at Manny and lifts his right hand the few inches and grasps weakly Manny's hand. He says, "You'll excuse me if I don't rise and reach across the table. I'm tied up at the moment."

"You've got a sense of humor," Manny says, smiling, as he sits down. "That's good."

Gordon turns to look at the wall and says, "Ain't it amazin'! They can force you out of your home, remove you permanently from family and friends, throw you in jail, whip up a mistaken eyewitness, concoct some circumstantial evidence, convict you, sentence you to death, eventually kill you, but they *just can't* fuck with your mind," and Gordon pauses to look Manny straight in the eyes, spitting, "unless, of course, you let 'em."

Manny looks back at Gordon for a moment, but an uncomfortable feeling overtakes him. He drops his gaze to a pile of papers, searching for a particular paper, and says, "I can sympathize with your plight, Gordon. May I call you Gordon?"

"You can call me shithead, if you want," Gordon deadpans. "Just don't expect to get my attention on a crowded street, as if that'll happen."

"Gordon, I can sympathize," Manny continues, "but, here, I found it, your courtroom comments were ill-advised. You challenged the judge and, really, gave her no choice but to pass a sentence of execution."

"Sympathy from a lawyer," Gordon laughs. "That would make a great Neil Young tune. I'll have to write him a letter."

"Didn't your counsel advise against that sort of outburst?"

"Of course the lawyer advised against it," Gordon shoots back, offended. "So did my wife and everybody else." He adds in a mocking voice, "Throw yourself at the mercy of the court! Say anything, so long as you save your life!" He pauses to look at Manny, and continues, suddenly calmer, "There are two sides to this conflict, the entire state of North Carolina versus me, and each side has obligations. Twelve impartial jurors didn't believe in me and rendered their verdict, the judge issued the sentence, and I could have done a lot of things."

"But your outburst forced the state to sentence you to death, Gordon," Manny advises.

"Like I said, I could have done a lot of things," Gordon replies. Contritely, he adds, "I'm sorry, I forgot your name. I'm not good with names."

"Manny Rodriguez. You can call me Manny."

"Is your given name Manuel?"

"Yes."

"I'll call you Manuel. I always call my wife Rosita, never Rosie, or Rose, always Rosita." He pauses and looks at Manny. "I could have begged for my life, yes, Manuel. But if I want to retain any dignity as a human being, I must insist on my innocence and never, *never*, express remorse for an act I did not commit. Let me ask *you* a question."

"Okay," Manny agrees, smiling.

"Did your mother ever accuse you of something one of your brothers did?"

"Yes," Manny confesses, "more times than I can count, probably."

"Did you ever plead for her mercy and confess, because you knew she was absolutely convinced and there was no hope of her changing her mind, so, at least, the punishment might be lessened?"

"No," Manny says, thinking, "and I would take my brother's punishment anyway, but I would always maintain my innocence." Manny looks straight in Gordon's eyes until Gordon looks away briefly. When Gordon returns his gaze, his eyelids are narrow and his expression is severe and Manny is suddenly impressed. Softly, Manny adds, "I see your point."

"Good," Gordon replies, with a thin smile. "That makes two of us."

Manny glances at some notes on the table. "What about the evidence they found in your car? How do you think that got there if you didn't commit the crime?"

"I would imagine that the real murderer or an accomplice put it there."

Manny leans forward. "That would imply that you were set up," he states. "Haven't you thought about who would hate you enough to set you up for murder?"

Gordon leans back in his chair and calmly replies, "Everyone has enemies, real or perceived. That's life." He smiles warmly as he pauses a moment. "Everyone builds defenses for that very reason, creating a safety and security zone. We even do it collectively and alter the world in the process, even though it's just an illusion."

Manny appears confused but smiles and says, "You lost me. What does that have to do with being set up for murder?"

Gordon smiles widely. "Have you ever seen a picture of the continent we call North America from a satellite photo?" he asks.

Manny stares at Gordon with visible skepticism but decides to play along. "Of course I've seen that. Most everyone has."

Gordon raises his eyebrows as he demands, "Ever notice what's missing?"

Manny shakes his head in disagreement as he replies, "Nothing's missing, Gordon. It's all fairly straightforward."

"You weren't paying attention," Gordon counters. "That nearly straight line which runs from the Great Lakes to the Pacific and separates what we call Canada and the United States on maps doesn't appear in satellite photos, because it *doesn't exist*. It's a fiction, an illusion some men dreamed up years ago and we accept as reality today, but it's not real. It's nothing more than an imaginary boundary, a limitation, meant to keep us safe and secure and ordered, but it only serves to keep us separated, divided and apart."

Impatiently, Manny drops his pen on his notepad, having lost desire to take any further notes, leans back in his chair and crosses his arms defiantly. "What does that have to do with you being set up for murder?" he demands.

"Nothing, Manuel," Gordon calmly replies, "but you were taking notes and I thought I should remind you that not all appears as it should be."

Manny shakes his head slowly. "Those lines denote nations, countries."

"Those lines denote tribal boundaries," Gordon argues, "and with more detail, more lines and more tribal boundaries. Sure, the tribes have grown bigger, more complex, more sophisticated, but they're still tribes. We still use 'chief' to designate the leader, like Chief Executive Officer, Commander in Chief, but they're all tribes and nothing more. Tens of thousands of years have passed and we still behave like tribes. We beat our chests, scream a war cry, yell, 'My tribe is better than your tribe,' and the lines on the map change to denote the change in separation, division, apartness."

Manny rubs his face but lifts his pen. "What are you getting at, Gordon?" he asks, softly.

"Those satellite photos are proof that this is nothing but a big, blue spaceship hurtling through the void at sixty thousand miles an hour. Its fate is our fate. We are all locked in its grip, held here tightly to ensure that we are all in this together. Yet, we cling to our tribes and fight amongst our divisions as though we truly believe that one tribe will win, our tribe. All along, there has only been one tribe, the tribe of human beings, but we were all separated long ago, and, even with the truth staring right at us, we hold on to the fantasy of superiority and create more tribes daily, rejecting the one true tribe for new impostors."

Manny finishes writing on his notepad and bows his head. He rubs his eyes while Gordon sits back in his chair, calm, a wisp of a smile on his face. Manny states slowly, softly, "I think that, deep down, we all know that we're in this together." He lifts his head to look at Gordon.

"Have you heard the Santayana quote," Gordon interjects. "'Those who cannot remember the past are condemned to repeat it?'"

"Yes," Manny replies.

Gordon smiles but his eyes are vacant. "Here's a peek at our future with a twist on Santayana. Those who cannot live together will surely die together. Failure to reject the past, to reject the impostor tribes, will seal our collective fate. We will remain the tiniest speck of insignificance in the universe and our extinction won't even cause a blink. There will be no survivors as none deserve to survive. Do you feel superior now? Our own host, the big blue spaceship, finds us revolting, reminding us frequently how pathetic our rank truly is. Let's see you badasses plug a volcano and snuff the next eruption, or dampen the next earthquake, or build an impenetrable wall to repel the next tsunami." Gordon smiles and lets out a short laugh as he leans forward. "They say elephants can't fly but I can do the impossible, Manuel. With the help of our host, I can put an elephant in the path of an F5 tornado and I guarantee you that fucker's gonna fly!"

Manny smiles weakly. This is not the conversation he had expected and his usual confidence and cockiness wanes. Growing tired, Manny sighs, "When can we discuss your case, Gordon?"

Gordon smiles and leans back in satisfaction. "We've pretty much discussed it all, counselor," he replies confidently. "The appeals court will uphold the trial court's proceedings, the death sentence will be upheld, it will be carried out and I'll be dead."

Manny looks at Gordon somewhat incredulously and asks, "Is that what you want, Gordon? Do you want to die?"

Gordon smiles infectiously and says, "Death is not permanent."

"You don't know that," Manny scoffs.

"You don't know that it *is* permanent."

Manny argues, "I know I can get the sentence reduced to life in prison. The prosecution did not have a clear preponderance of evidence."

"And when the proposal reaches me, I'll never agree to it," Gordon counters. "It will contain some admission of culpability or statement of remorse and I will *never* agree to that." Gordon pauses and stares unblinking at Manny, his eyes narrowing. "Besides, most of this state's citizens, the police, the prosecution, twelve jurors and the judge didn't think there was a clear preponderance of evidence lacking. Attack with that argument and you force the appeals court to put the entire legal system on trial and they're not going to do that."

"You can't be sure of that, Gordon," Manny tries to assure him. "It's not as rigid as you think and even I am surprised at times which argument worked and which didn't."

"Yet, your options at the appeals level are limited, Manuel," Gordon asserts. "You certainly cannot argue my innocence. That belongs at the trial court level and I had my one shot at that and lost. A judgment for reduction of sentence requires my agreement and you can't get that, either. In practical terms, your only hope is finding enough evidence to identify the real murderer and convince the appeals court that my sentence should be suspended until that person can be thoroughly investigated." Gordon pauses to roll his eyes. "Good luck on that one."

Now, Manny leans forward with his eyes narrowed. "Then, let's get right to it," he demands. "Did you commit this crime?"

"No," Gordon calmly answers.

"How can I believe you?" Manny further demands.

"Only you can answer that for yourself, Manuel," Gordon offers. "You can't know if I committed Darcy's murder or not and I can't make you believe that I didn't do it. You can only come to believe it or reject it over time, but you have to do it on your own." Gordon hesitates a moment and looks away. "You see, we all have beliefs. We need them, since belief is that reasonable understanding we create to fill in the gaps in our knowledge, those gaps where we don't know or cannot know." Gordon slowly turns his head back to look at Manny. "And that's the problem with belief."

"What problem?" Manny asks, intrigued.

"Be careful what you believe in," Gordon advises, "because belief is not knowing. It's not based on indisputable evidence, so, if you're not extremely careful, you might just act on your beliefs and hurt or kill innocent people. Then your reasonable understanding isn't so reasonable, is it?"

"Then what should I believe, Gordon?"

"I said I can't make you believe anything," Gordon states, calmly, softly, patiently. "For all you know, I could have killed her. That's possible, from your clouded point of view." Gordon draws a breath and sighs as he looks down at the table. "I've had the strangest feeling all my life, that I'm merely a visitor, that I'm not from here. Long ago, I did something despicable and so I was placed here for penance, in a virtual prison where the inmates run the asylum. The many tribal leaders try to convince you that, despite sharing far more similarities, those other tribes are not like us. It's us versus them and you should fear them. The argument is quite effective because fear runs rampant and unchecked in this virtual prison, but I've had enough. My penance is nearly over now and here you come today to create yet one more conflict for me."

"I'm not fighting you, Gordon," Manny protests. "I'm here to try to help you."

"And that's the source of my conflict," Gordon replies, looking up. He smiles freely as he adds, "I like you, Manuel. You're a decent human being, and, for that, I want you to do well, to grow, get better and improve as a human being. However, you could solve this case and convince the appeals court and they would release me from this prison of visible walls, but I would still be locked in the prison of virtual walls, and I'm tired. I'm so near the end that I'm looking forward to it. I'm ready to leave and leave it to you, all of you, to discover the one undeniable truth of a virtual prison: those who cannot live together will surely die together. It's your choice." Suddenly, Gordon struggles with his chains and stands up to waddle to the door. Looking through the door, he makes eye contact with the guard outside and nods. The key can be heard inserted into the door as the guard unlocks and opens it.

Manny stands up quickly and pleads, "I have more questions, Gordon."

"You come back anytime you want, Manuel," Gordon replies, turning back to face Manny, a smile of genuine sincerity on his face. "I'll tell you some more, and I'll try to help you, though I'm sure it won't be much. May you know peace in all you do."

Slowly, Gordon turns away and the guard guides him out of the room. The two make their way down the corridor and disappear at the first turn to the right. Manny bows his head, still standing, and rubs his right hand over his eyes, now suddenly tired …

The day after his meeting with Gordon Schell, Manuel Rodriguez sits uncomfortably in one of the chairs in Adam Sheehan's well-appointed office. Adam sits in the oversized leather chair behind his desk, leaning back, the fingers of his hands pressed together forming a triangle as he stares benevolently at his protégé, sensing his discomfort. Adam asks, "How was your consultation with our new client?"

Shaking his head lightly, Manny replies, "Not very good, Adam."

Adam leans forward and places his hands on the desk, looks at Manny quizzically and says, "Tell me what happened."

Manny drops his head and replies, "How do I start?" He pauses to look up at Adam. "Gordon Schell is a smart man, intelligent. He knows some about the law, he knows how the system works, and he knows the difference between right and wrong." Manny looks up at the ceiling to form his next statement. "He claims to be an innocent man and he'll never even imply guilt to reduce his sentence." Again, he pauses for a moment and adds, "He spent most of the time rambling about his philosophy and belief." Manny pauses to glance over the legal pad in his left hand.

"Belief?" Adam asks, curious. "What belief?"

"I've got it here," Manny replies, finding his place in the notes. "Belief is 'the reasonable understanding we create to fill in the gaps in our knowledge, what we don't know or cannot know.'"

"Interesting," Adam says, leaning back in his chair and rubbing his chin. "He said that?"

"Yes," Manny replies, his face displaying the confusion he feels.

"So, Manny, tell me what you're struggling with," Adam coaxes. "Something else he said has you unsettled and I can tell."

Having it squarely in his mind, Manny leans forward and sets the pad on Adam's desk, interlaces his fingers and leans on his elbows across his legs. He wants Adam to understand his frustration, so he states, "You know, Adam, I began by telling his that his comments before sentencing were ill-advised, so he tells me that if he is to retain his dignity as an innocent man he's not going to show any remorse for an act he didn't commit."

"I'd heard about that comment from people I trust and I know Judge Benjamin. She's an intelligent, fair-minded woman, but you don't challenge her in her courtroom." Adam looks at Manny and lifts his right hand. "Yesterday, I looked up the transcript so I could read it myself and, *now*, I understand Judge Benjamin's sentence. He challenged her, but I've thought about the words he used. In over thirty years of practicing law and listening to colleagues, I have *never* heard a defendant justly convicted in a fair trial state that to express remorse for his conviction is 'personally repugnant.' I have come to the conclusion that he's either the embodiment of diabolically clever evil or pure, unrestrained innocence. So, which one is he, Manny?"

"That's what I was trying to get at, Adam," Manny complains in exasperation. "I asked him how I can believe he's innocent and he replied that he can't make me believe anything." Slowly, staring straight at Adam for emphasis, he adds, "Then, he looked me straight in the eyes and said, 'For all you know, I could've killed her.'"

"And, so, we're back to belief," Adam observes.

"Exactly," Manny agrees.

"But you haven't decided yet, have you?"

Manny leans back in resignation. "Adam, he went on about tribal boundaries and philosophical meanderings—"

"As defense counsel," Adam interrupts, "we're not interested in our clients' beliefs unless it's pertinent to the case. Is it?"

"No," Manny replies, a measure of calm returning. "I don't think it is."

"Didn't they discover some murder evidence in his vehicle?"

Manny nods his head. "He said that the real murderer or an accomplice must have put it there."

Adam smiles reassuringly. "You don't decide his innocence, Manny. That's not your job, but we always assume he's innocent, even during the appeals process. That's the only way we can represent our clients' interests properly." Adam pauses to let his advice register. Manny nods his head and Adam smiles. "So, if he's an innocent man, we need to find something we can use to reverse this. There's nothing in the trial proceedings?"

Manny frowns as he responds. "Nothing. The judge was not prejudicial, the prosecution conducted itself properly, the instructions to the jury were correct. His defense could have been better—a lot better—but it wasn't deficient or incompetent. The appeals court will see that." He leans forward and adds, "I've gone through it several times, Adam, and, while most of the evidence is circumstantial, the trial was conducted fairly. Perhaps, the jury should have concluded there was reasonable doubt, but all twelve found him guilty."

Adam rubs his chin before he answers. "What about the police investigation? Didn't I hear something about an ex-husband?"

Manny replies, shaking his head, "They couldn't find anything definitive to tie him to the murder." He leans back in the chair and rubs his hands absent-mindedly as he adds, "Adam, I've done some checking on him, too. This guy had the motive. His wife took him to the cleaners at their divorce six months before her murder, but," he pauses to lean forward and lift his right index finger as a point, adding, "he argued with the life insurance company to keep his policy on her in force for a year."

Adam leans forward on his arms and asks, "What are the details behind that?"

Manny replies, "He had a policy on her life for a half-million, but once the divorce was final the insurance company cancelled the policy because he had no vested interest in her life, as the law requires." Manny looks at Adam and smiles as he says, "So, here's the interesting part. He argues that because the divorce became final during the year, he carries a tax liability for the portion of the year when they were still married and cancellation of the policy puts him at severe risk if she should die." He pauses and looks knowingly at Adam. "And the insurance company bought it, reinstating the policy."

"Very clever," Adam remarks.

"Now, while the police had given up on him, the insurance company had not," Manny continues, "but they couldn't dig up anything on him either." Manny shifts forward and rests his left elbow on the edge of Adam's desk and adds, "A few weeks ago, he had his attorney draft a very polite letter threatening them with legal action and they cut him a check two weeks later."

"Where is he now?" Adam asks.

"He quit his job as the hospital's HR director that day with no notice," Manny says, shaking his head, "and left for a long vacation in Bermuda. He's still there as far as I know."

Adam leans back in his chair, frowning, as he glances around his office. After a moment, he says, "As soon as he gets the money, he quits a job with considerable prestige and responsibility with no notice." He pauses to look at Manny and adds, "Those are *not* the actions of a man of honor, Manny." Thinking for a moment, he asks, "The witness who saw a man leave the victim's house said the man had longer hair, a mustache and sideburns, so the prosecution at trial showed a picture of Mr. Schell and added the missing pieces and the witness said that was the man, correct?"

"Right," Manny confirms. "They claimed that those could easily be purchased and discarded as a means of disguising one's identity."

"And the ex-husband could not possibly be that man?"

"No," Manny replies, "the ex-husband is six inches taller and considerably heavier than Mr. Schell."

Adam looks at Manny with a serious expression as he asks, "Do you believe Gordon Schell is innocent?"

Manny drops his gaze and shakes his head slowly as he replies, "I don't know what to believe about him, Adam, other than he's probably delusional." Manny stops shaking his head and looks seriously at Adam, who appears somewhat mystified. "He told me he was just a visitor, that he's not from here, and what he meant by 'here' is the planet Earth, Adam. What do you think?"

"You really want to know what I think, Manny?" Adam challenges his protégé.

"Yes."

Adam thinks for a moment and calmly says, "The killer is not the ex-husband, so, if Gordon Schell is innocent," and Adam pauses to gauge Manny's reaction, which is a simple shrug of the shoulders, and adds, "then, there's a man in this community who looks so much like Mr. Schell they could easily be mistaken for one another. This man is going to have a connection with the ex-husband, too, somewhere from their past."

"How can you be so sure, Adam?" Manny asks.

"The likelihood of a human resources director with connections to organized crime is very low, in my opinion, Manny," Adam explains, "but the likelihood that the ex-husband met a man who is pathological enough to commit this murder is much higher."

Manny listens but remains unconvinced. "Of course, that is all based on the assumption of Gordon Schell's innocence," he counters.

Adam nods his head and looks straight at Manny unflinchingly. "You've had direct contact with him, Manny, and I respect that and any opinion you have derived. However," Adam begins and stands up to move to the front of his desk and lean against it, looking down at Manny, "when a convicted killer can stand before a court and claim that to show remorse for an act that he did not commit is 'personally repugnant,' I'm going to pay attention. Would you like to know what one of the definitions for 'repugnant' is?"

"Sure," Manny replies, a bit intrigued at Adam's growing passion.

Adam smiles and states, "Characterized by contradiction and irreconcilability. This from a man who knew *exactly* what he was doing." Adam shakes his head demonstrably as he adds, "You can't convince me that a man of that intelligence is only smart enough to dispose of his disguise but leave the damning evidence from the crime scene under the front passenger seat of his truck, so I *do* believe he's innocent, Manny. And you believe he's delusional."

"I would at least prefer that he undergo a psychiatric evaluation."

"Then, do it."

Manny smiles at Adam, who hasn't budged from leaning against the desk and looking down at him. "You have more, don't you?" he asks, good-naturedly.

"Absolutely," Adam replies, equally good-naturedly as he crosses his arms.

"What else would you suggest I do?"

"We need to research every workplace, club, group and organization with which the ex-husband had affiliations within the last ten or twelve years or so," Adam advises. "What we need to find is a list of all the men who were also affiliated at the same time. A roster with pictures would be best, because we're looking for a picture of a man who looks like Gordon Schell, enough that you can see the resemblance right from the photo."

"That's going to be a lot of work, Adam," Manny says.

"Would you feel better if the state executed an innocent man and you didn't do anything to prevent it?" Adam argues.

Manny drops his head and says, softly, "No, but I'm not as convinced as you."

"Then, wait until the psychiatric evaluation comes back to clear him, if that will help convince you," Adam counters. "At that point, Manny, you'll have your work cut out for you and you'll have lost time that you can't get back. You can recruit some of the staff to help," Adam offers, "but you'll have to get on it."

Manny smiles as he asks, "What if the psychiatrist finds him delusional and unfit?"

Adam returns the smile as he counters, "Then, you'll be right and you finish the appeals process and move on." Adam stands upright, leans forward over Manny and pats his left shoulder as he observes aloud, "We'll see, won't we?" As he stands upright, Adam turns to gaze out the window …

"Your boy is no more delusional than you or me," proclaims the pretty blonde sitting stiffly in the chair near the edge of Manny's desk one week later. Smiling, her expression displays a mild regret, knowing that Manny was hoping to hear a different conclusion, and she braces her right hand on her right knee crossed tightly over her left leg set solidly on the floor in a perfect ninety-degree angle.

Manny frowns as he leans forward in the chair to rest his forearms on his desk. He glances briefly at the open folder on the desk and complains, "That's not what I wanted to hear, Angela." Looking up at her smiling face, his frown fades to a smile, though feeling defeated. "He didn't go into any of those things we talked about?"

Still smiling, Angela says, "Of course he did, Manny. All of that and more, over three hours, but none of that makes him delusional from a psychiatric perspective." She pauses as Manny's frown re-appears and her smile is replaced by a more professional demeanor. "Everyone has a set of beliefs to explain the unknowable and Gordon Schell has a very solid idea of how those beliefs are created, meaning his 'reasonable understanding' statement. In fact, he knows quite a bit about psychology, much to my surprise. Did he tell you about his amygdala paradox? It's fascinating, actually."

"Perhaps he just said what he needed to convince you," Manny suggests, as he turns away.

Curt with a bit of resentment, Angela replies, "As I said, we all have a set of beliefs. Yes, Gordon Schell's set of beliefs are way off the beaten path, so to speak, but he's *not* delusional, Mister Rodriguez. He knows what he was convicted for, he knows he's in Death Row awaiting execution in a maximum security prison, he knows what is going on around him at any moment. What I was most impressed with was his sense of humor, which he uses quite effectively to create a common bond between himself and all others. He made me laugh at times."

Manny looks up and states, "As I said before—"

"His attempts at humor were very revealing. For example, he told me his joke about the one true God, which he read from this paper." Angela puts her right leg down tightly next to her left and leans forward to open the folder on the edge of Manny's desk. Lifting the top paper, she offers it to Manny, who turns it around it in his hands and looks it over as Angela continues. "It's not so funny as it's telling about the position some hold concerning religion, that religions started not so much as a set of beliefs but as a conscious effort to keep a group of people together against external elements trying to destroy them."

Manny looks up from the paper in his hands and says, "It's also irreverent and possibly heretical and would create a good deal of animosity, so I think we'll just keep this to ourselves." He sets it upside-down on his desk and glances at Angela to gauge her acceptance.

"Suit yourself," Angela says, shrugging her shoulders. Immediately, she regains her professional demeanor and adds, "Here's my last finding. Your client is a smart man, smarter than you or me. I gave him a standard intelligence test at the end of my visit and when I totaled it, he scored on the genius scale." She smiles warmly as she asks, "Do you qualify for Mensa?"

"No," Manny blurts, suddenly laughing.

"Your client does," Angela states calmly, definitively. "Any questions?"

Manny shakes his head and replies, "Not at this time but I may have some later as I review your report."

"Well, you know how to reach me," Angela invites him as she stands up from her chair and straightens her skirt. Before she takes a step, she looks at Manny severely and admonishes, "You owe me a dinner in a *very* fancy restaurant, Manny, for changing my schedule so I could see your client quickly, and I expect you to honor that soon. Don't you make me wait!"

Manny smiles broadly and assures her, "Soon, it is."

Angela smiles broadly, too, and in a soft, sensual tone, says, "I'm actually looking forward to it. Aren't you?"

Manny nods as his eyes flicker down her body and he agrees, "Oh, I'm sure I'll enjoy it, too."

Behind the Plexiglass Window

The door of Gordon's cell opens and the Big Man strolls down the hall to the opened cell. He calls out before he reaches the cell, "You got visitors, Gordon. I think it's your wife and kids."

Gordon steps out from his cell into the hall and smiles at the Big Man. "Well, alright, then," he replies. "We shouldn't keep them waiting." He starts to walk toward the guard, who stops and waits for Gordon to reach him, and turns around to follow Gordon down the hall to the guard's observation room.

Once they're both inside the small room with a desk and chair, the cell door and observation room door close as they wait patiently. In the next room, a guard presses a button on a console before him and the door to the control room opens and both step inside with the other guard. To the left of the control room guard sits a small box and a song plays at a low level. Gordon stops to listen, hearing something familiar in the song. The others hesitate for a moment, watching Gordon stand with his head tilted slightly to his left. Suddenly, Gordon says, "Huh, that's a Buddy Holly song, but that's not Buddy Holly."

The Big Man and the control room guard glance at each other until the Big Man says, "Oh, that's one of those satellite radio players." He steps over to the small box on the table and adds, "I think we've got one of the country rock channels on." He turns back to Gordon and offers, "Take a look at it, if you want."

Gordon steps to the table and looks at the box. The digital display on the box reads "TALBOT BROS EASY TO SLIP." "Yep, that's the song, but I never heard that version before," he observes. "Good tune, though."

Standing up straight, Gordon turns around and steps to the opposite door while the Big Man steps up behind him. The open door to the control room closes, the opposite door opens and both men step into the next prison wing, making their long way to the visitor room. Both are silent the entire time it takes to reach the visitor room, but Gordon imagines whether the family waiting for him is real. *Is it just my imagination? Is any of this real or just a clever delusion? What if none of this is real, none of us are real?*

Huddled in a small cinder block cubicle, Rosita sits in a chair while the children stand next to her, wide-eyed and frightened. Immediately before her is a plexiglass window and to the side hangs a phone receiver. On the other side of the window is an identical cubicle and phone receiver. Gordon steps up to the chair on the other side of the window, pulls the chair out, sits down and scoots it toward the table. Smiling, he lifts the phone receiver from the hook and puts it to his ear. With an expression of grave concern, and remembering what Gordon had told her about their recording visitor conversations, Rosita lifts her phone receiver, puts it to her ear, and with a shaking voice, says, "I got your package the other day."

Noting the concern on her face, and her tone of voice, Gordon calmly asks, "Which package was that?"

Rosita pulls her purse close to her, setting it in front of her. She barely reaches inside and lifts the top of a bill of United States currency so that Gordon can see it. Still nervous and straining to keep her voice from cracking, she says, "The one where you wrote all those notes," and she pauses to lift the currency and push it down into her purse, adding, "about your love for me. I just loved the—"

"Sentiment?" Gordon interrupts. "Was it too much?"

With her eyes widened, she looks down at her right hand, her fingers and thumb spread wide, as she tries to regain her calm. Slowly, she says, "Not at all. I appreciate when you tell me you think of me a *thousand* times a day."

Grasping her meaning, Gordon says, "I wish I could send you money, instead. I know you could use that more, but they don't pay diddly here."

Alarmed at his reaction, Rosita carefully says, "I know you would, but the sentiment comes in handy. It's been a difficult time."

In a deliberate tone, Gordon says, "Listen." He stares in Rosita's eyes and she stares back, afraid.

She lowers the headset and mouths, "OK."

Gordon speaks very slowly as he says, "I've heard what people say about you and the kids. It's not right. Maybe, though, there are some people out there that we don't know who are beginning to speak that same sentiment. No matter. You hold on to that sentiment, keep it close at hand, use it sparingly, carefully, since it's for you and the children. Don't let anyone know about it since it's none of their business."

Rosita shakes her head, still unconvinced. "Do you think that could happen?" she asks.

"Yes," Gordon assures her. "It could be anyone at any time, but you can count on one thing. People hate me, so *sentiment* will never come to you by my instigation." Gordon looks hopefully at Rosita and she slowly nods her head and lifts her eyes to his. Satisfied, he asks, "Have you had any more problems getting the money for the stock?"

"No," Rosita says softly. "We got the check two weeks ago. It was close to twenty thousand, Gordon."

"Don't spend it all in one place," Gordon says, smiling.

Rosita's expression does not change from concern and fear. She blurts, "I'm so scared, Gordon. This is tearing me apart."

Gordon says, calmly, "Imagine what I'm thinking every night."

Rosita moans, "I miss your body next to me so much."

Gordon looks away briefly as he says, "That's what I'm thinking every night. Good guess."

"Stop," Rosita says. "This isn't funny." She looks at him sternly. "You have been sentenced to death, Gordon, and you're still trying to be funny. It's *not* funny."

"Look at your children, Rosita," Gordon says, motioning with his head to the children. "They're scared to death to be here, you're scared to death, I'm the one *sentenced* to death, but this is *not* killing me. I'll be damned if they take away the one thing they can't have, *me*."

Gordon looks at his wife in condemnation, but immediately softens, as he glances at Melinda, who has been watching both intently, expectantly. Gordon smiles and Melinda bravely returns his smile. Rosita drops her head. She can't look at her husband. Gordon calmly advises, "The children need someone, anyone, to lift them up. That's what I did before. That's why they came here, and that's what I'm going to do today. But, you need to look at me, now." Gordon pauses until Rosita lifts her head to stare into his eyes. "It doesn't matter whether I die in a few months or fifty years from now. This is the most you can expect. You will never hold me, touch me, kiss me, *ever again*!"

Defiantly, Rosita says, "I don't think that." She waits until her husband is paying attention, looking for that specific click in his eyes, in his face. When she sees it, she continues, "That new lawyer has called me twice, Manny …"

"Manuel," Gordon interrupts.

"He said you would say that," Rosita confides. "He also said that you could only call me Rosita."

"Your name is Rosita, not Rosie, or Rose," Gordon explains. "I love Rosita."

She flashes a smile briefly, but gets serious again as she says, "He's trying to find the man who did this." She tries to express hope in her voice and face. "He thinks there's a tie between this man and the ex-husband."

Gordon seems unimpressed as he replies, "He sent a shrink to evaluate me. He thinks I'm delusional."

"He was concerned, Gordon!" Rosita exclaims, raising her voice. "It's like you don't even care any more!"

"There isn't anything I can do, Rosita," Gordon replies, calmly, "but I told him I would help him any way I can, *except* to imply my guilt and show *any* remorse. *That*, I will *never* do."

Rosita is quiet, her expression disappointed. She looks over at the children and Melanie asks, "Can I talk to Daddy now?" Rosita responds, "In a moment, Melanie." She turns back to Gordon, frowning, and asks, "Why are you like this? Don't you want to get out of here?"

Gordon frowns back and says, "Of course, but I'm not getting my hopes up. Nobody's found this guy yet, and, even if they do, then what? Will he confess? Uh, don't think so. What will the courts do? Give me a new trial? Release me? Apologize? Uh, not likely."

Despairing, Rosita looks down at the table, moving her head from side to side as she says, "So, that's it, you just want to leave. You want to leave us forever?" She looks up at his face.

Sadly, Gordon slowly says, "It's not my choice. I've never had any choice in this."

Her expression changing to one of convincing hope, Rosita argues, "You can save yourself. It would give us more time to expose the real killer, Gordon." She looks into his eyes to gauge his feelings. "Time is all we need, you and me. We can make it through this if you would only give us more time."

Gordon shakes his head, resolutely, as he explains, "I have to show remorse for an act I never performed, a crime I did not commit." He pauses to let it sink in. "I cannot do that."

Rosita looks away in the direction of her children, looking at none of them. She lets her arm holding the headset fall to the table. Melanie taps her arm and Rosita looks at her and hands her the headset. Rosita scoots the chair back and softly says, "Talk to your Father." She doesn't look at Gordon.

Melanie moves to the spot her Mother just vacated and leans forward on the table, saying, "Hi, Daddy."

"How's my big girl?" Gordon asks, brightening.

"Scared," Melanie replies. "Why are you even here, Daddy? You didn't do this. You were at home with us and Mommy. Why can't they see that? What's wrong with these people?"

Concerned, Gordon looks at his daughter and says, "Twelve people believed I did it." Melanie had been looking down at the table in anger, but looks up at her Father, and he adds, "In this life, Melanie, sometimes the truth doesn't matter to people. They just ignore it and believe what's easiest for them to believe." He stops to look at her expression, determining whether she understood. He adds, "The truth is hard to find and sometimes harder to accept, but if you've already made up your mind, you'll never find the truth."

"It's not fair," Melanie laments, and sniffles as her head drops.

"Look at me, Melanie," Gordon commands and her daughter dutifully lifts her head to look in her Father's face. "I know you're not going to accept this, but I want you to remember what I'm going to tell you, now. Promise?" Melanie nods her head. Slowly, Gordon says, "Things happen for a reason. We may never know what that reason is. You're going to be hurt by this, but it's going to make you stronger and a better person. It may take a long time, but you'll be all right in the end. You'll be better for it, *unless* you let it keep you angry and mad. You can't be angry and mad at ignorant people. *You* have to show them the better way. Show them that the search for truth is harder but it's far more rewarding."

"Daddy," Melanie chokes, her eyes misting, "I won't remember that."

"You'll be all right," Gordon says, softly. "I'll be all right. Please don't be angry at people who don't know what they're doing."

"That's too much for me, Daddy," Melanie complains. "I'm not a grown-up."

"It's not for now, Melanie," Gordon explains, "you won't be eleven forever, but there will be a day when you'll get it. I'm speaking to you for that day."

Melanie frowns briefly, not really convinced, and sadness returns to her expression as her eyes mist and she mumbles, "I miss you so much, Daddy. I want you to come home."

Gordon's eyes water as he looks into his oldest daughter's eyes. "I do nothing but think here, think about all of you. I miss everything about you, big girl, and it hurts."

Both are silent for a few moments, examining the other's face. Mark leans forward and says, "I want to talk to Daddy." Melanie says in the headset, "Mark wants to talk to you." She pauses and adds, "I love you, Daddy."

Gordon replies softly, "I will always love you, Melanie."

Melanie holds the headset out to Mark and steps around him so that he can lean on the table where she had been. Mark says, "Hi, Dad."

"Greetings from the big house, big boy," Gordon says, smiling.

"Is it bad in there?" Mark asks.

"I get room service three times a day," Gordon replies, still smiling. "Beat that."

Mark drops his head as he says, slowly, "I got into a fight at school."

Gordon asks calmly, "What were you fighting about?"

Mark looks up at his Father and his face displays anger as he says, "This boy, Carl, said you were nothing but a rotten killer, and I told him he didn't know anything about you, but he wouldn't stop, so I hit him, and we both started punchin' and wrestlin'."

"You got in trouble, didn't you?" Gordon asks.

Mark hangs his head again as he replies, "Yes, detention for a week."

Gordon says, "If I told you I could control you, would you know what I mean?"

Mark looks up and replies, "I think so, like, making me do something I don't want to do?"

"Exactly," Gordon says, nodding approvingly. "Do you know what the word 'reaction' means?"

Mark squints and says, hopefully, "Maybe."

Gordon smiles briefly and says, "I'll give you an example. Think of me as Carl, okay?"

"Okay," Mark says.

"I keep telling you that your dad is a rotten killer," Gordon says, adding, "and I won't stop until you hit me. Follow me so far?"

Mark looks more understanding as he says, "I think so."

"When you hit me," Gordon explains, "that was your reaction to my telling you that your dad is a rotten killer. Your reaction was to hit Carl. Do you see that?"

"Yes," Mark replies, simply.

"Before Carl even talked to you, did you want to hit him?"

"No."

"Carl has figured out how to control you, Mark," Gordon says. "He knows how to get the reaction from you that he wants. He wants you to try to fight him."

Mark frowns as he explains, "But, Dad, he wouldn't stop."

"The easy thing to do is react, son," Gordon says, softly, "but you let other people control you when you do that. It's hard to ignore them and walk away quietly with your head up, but that's what you have to do, what you need to do." Gordon looks at his son for a sign of acknowledgement. Mark finally lifts his head and, seeing his Father looking at him anxiously, nods his head twice. Gordon adds, "You can't let other people control you, Mark. It's hard to walk away, but after a while something good comes from it."

"What's that?" Mark asks, skeptically.

"They stop trying to get that reaction because they've learned that they *can't* control you," Gordon says. "You will have earned their respect because you showed them you're a strong person that they cannot control."

"Are you sure?" Mark asks, a little less skeptically.

"Been there and done that, big boy," Gordon affirms.

"How can you be so sure that will work, Dad?" Mark asks. "Carl shouldn't have said that."

"You wanted to control Carl," Gordon says. "You wanted him to shut up, didn't you?"

"Yes, he shouldn't have said that," Mark argues.

"That's the other side, Mark," Gordon confides. "You can't control other people, so don't even try. Let them learn their own lessons. Just control your actions but protect yourself."

"Okay," Mark says softly, hanging his head some.

"Hey, you, don't be droppin' your head to me," Gordon teases, and Mark looks up. "I'm not disappointed in you, Mark. You'll never disappoint me. You'll always be my big boy and I love you, son. I always will."

Mark's expression brightens and he smiles for a moment. "Thanks, Dad," he says.

Melinda taps several times on Mark's arm. When Mark looks at Melinda, she asks, "Is it my turn, yet?" Mark says in the headset, turning to look at his Father, "I love you, Dad." He gives the headset to Melinda and steps out of the way.

Melinda climbs onto the table and leans with her free hand against the glass. Shyly, she says, "Hi, Daddy."

"Hi, baby doll," Gordon says, smiling.

"Have you been okay?" Melinda asks.

"Yeah, I'm okay. You?" Gordon asks.

"I've been okay, but I miss you," Melinda says. "Are you coming home soon?"

"I wish I could come home, but I don't think it will be soon."

Melinda frowns as she says, "Do we have to come here to see you? It's kinda scary, Daddy."

"I'm sorry about that, baby doll," Gordon says, frowning. "I wish it could be different."

Melinda brightens and smiles as she says, "That's okay, Daddy. I love you."

"I love you, too, Melinda," Gordon says, smiling back warmly.

"Can you do the thing with me?" Melinda asks hopefully.

Gordon motions against the glass and says, "You have to get up against the glass. You'll probably have to put this," and he looks at his headset, "down, too."

Melinda drops the headset and pushes her torso and head against the plexiglass. Gordon taps his heart, his nose, the glass before Melinda's nose, and the glass before her heart. He says, "The nose knows all," but the others behind the plexiglass window can't hear him.

The Appellate Court Rules

Less than three months later, the Big Man sits comfortably in a chair before the observation room desk at one end of Death Row. He rocks slowly in the chair, calmly and silently watching a small television planted on the desk a few feet away. On the screen of the television is an attractive woman of medium build with short, black hair parted down the middle and brushed back, holding a microphone and talking.

The woman on the television is a reporter, and, as she looks down periodically at a sheet of paper she holds in her left hand, she states, "While many anticipated that the defense for Gordon Schell would mount several challenges to the trial court's ruling, that was not the case today. Accepting the trial court's verdict in full, the defense requested that an execution date be set as soon as practically possible.

"The most interesting exchange during the proceedings was when one of the justices asked the defense, 'Hasn't your client maintained his innocence all along?' Manuel Rodriguez, counsel for the defense responded, 'Yes.' The justice then asked, 'Assuming for a moment that your client *is* innocent, why would an innocent man accept the trial court's verdict and push for his own execution?' Rodriguez replied, 'Your honor, would there be grounds for a new trial if I stood before you and maintained that my client is innocent of this crime and that the jury's verdict was incorrect?' The justice replied, 'No, there would still be no grounds for a new trial.' Rodriguez replied, 'Continuing with the assumption your honor introduced, should I, as counsel, advise my client to display remorse for a crime he did not commit in the hopes of having his sentence reduced to life in prison?' One of the other justices asked, 'Counsel, we should not be executing innocent people, don't you agree?' Rodriguez then argued, 'Your honor, we are only following an assumption here. The innocence or guilt in this matter has already been decided by the courts, and, unless you determine that a new trial is warranted, the innocence or guilt of my client is not a matter for this court to decide.'

"The chief justice affirmed that there were no grounds for a new trial, so the appellate court has ruled to deny the defense's automatic appeal of the death sentence for Gordon Schell and has ordered the Corrections department to set a date of execution. That date is expected to be no later than six months."

The Big Man leans over the desk from his chair and flips the television off. He looks through the window of the solid door to his left and makes eye contact with the guard, a tall, muscular hulk with very short, blond hair sitting on the other side of the door. The Big Man signals to him to open the main door to the Death Row wing as he gets up from his chair and moves toward the door.

Hearing the door unlock and watching it slide open, he slowly steps inside the wing. He listens disinterestedly as the door behind him closes and locks as he strolls halfway down the hall, his head straight, never turning to look inside any of the cells he passes. Once he reaches the sixth cell on his right, he stops before it and peers inside. He waits for a moment and says, softly with his deep voice, "They denied your appeal, Gordon."

Gordon sits up in his bed and looks at the Big Man, emotionless, expressionless. Nothing is said for a few seconds until Gordon asks, "Did they set a date?"

"Corrections sets the date," the Big Man advises. "The reporter said it would probably be within six months."

Gordon looks to his left and scratches his head with his left hand. "In six months," he says, "I could make you a pretty good cribbage player."

"Ah, I ain't never gonna beat you in that game," the big man complains.

"Everybody wins in cribbage, Big Man," Gordon assures him, "eventually."

"How long is eventually?" the Big Man asks.

"Less than eternity," Gordon says with a big smile.

The big man smiles back, but his tone is disheartened as he says, "That's not reassuring."

"Cumon," Gordon enthuses, "let's play a game."

"Awright," the Big Man moans.

Gordon hops out of bed and grabs the board and deck of cards off the shelf while the Big Man disappears down the wing to get his chair. Gordon pulls up a chair to the bars and places the board on the chair. He removes the cards from the deck and places them on the chair. Lifting the board from the chair, he turns it over and slides the back cover open to remove four pins. He sets the board back on the chair upright and places the pins in the starting position. He sits down on the floor and crosses his legs, grabs the cards and shuffles.

When he sees the Big Man's chair enter his peripheral vision, Gordon places the deck of cards on the chair and says, "Shuffled and ready to deal, you deal first. You can shuffle 'em some more, if ya don't trust me."

"Won't make a bitta difference," the Big Man complains.

"Now that's a losing attitude, ya know," Gordon cajoles. He lowers his eyelids as he adds, "Maybe, that's your problem."

"You're too good is my problem," the Big Man jokes, cracking a smile. "Six cards, right?"

"Right."

Cards are dealt, hands are played, points are assessed, and, close to an hour later, the Big Man stares at the four cards he holds in his right hand. He lifts one of the cards out and places the five of spades on the chair after putting his arm through the bars. Gordon looks at the cards he holds in his right hand, lifts one and drops the five of hearts on top of the five of spades, declaring, "Pair of fives. Two points. Game." He moves the back peg past the line at the end of the board.

"Yer making me hate this game," the Big Man complains, but he smiles anyway.

"Don't lead with a five, Big Man," Gordon instructs. "Any card that's a ten, including all the face cards, will put me at fifteen and that's two points to start."

"It didn't matter," the Big Man observes. "You just popped me with that pair."

"I had three tens," Gordon says, laying his cards face up to show a jack, queen and king. On top of the big pile of cards sits another queen. Gordon remarks, "That was a nice cut you made. Fifteen eight and a double run of three for eight gave me sixteen in my hand. I can live with that."

"You've got this game down, Gordon," the Big Man says, admiringly. "That's for sure."

"Years of practice," Gordon advises, standing up from the floor, adding, "instead of mowing the lawn." The Big Man laughs. While he puts the game away, Gordon says, "You know how our moms would warn us about the big, bad world, and say things like, 'It's a jungle out there?'"

"Sure do," the Big Man agrees.

"Well, when *my* mom would say, 'It's a jungle out there,' she *meant*," Gordon says, stopping to turn and face the big man, "the grass is six feet tall, I better cut it real soon."

The Big Man laughs and says, "Ha! I'll bet that happened a lot with you."

"True," Gordon says, smiling, "the things you can get away with when the grass is taller than you are."

Strolling with a smile back to the observation room, the Big Man suddenly stops and turns to Gordon. With his head down, he recalls, in a low, barely audible tone, "It was just me and my mom and my two sisters growing up." He stops to raise his head and look squarely in Gordon's face. "Was it just you and your mom?"

"Yeah," Gordon answers, but glances around the wing of Death Row. "I never knew my father, never even knew his name."

"Well, I knew my father's name," the Big Man scoffs, "because that was all he left us."

Gordon turns his head back to the Big Man and says, "I have my mother's maiden name. She used to tell me that she didn't know who my father was, but, one day, she told me that she had to leave him because he raped her, and she hid from him and put 'Unknown' on my birth certificate. She said she was telling me now because he was dead." He bows his head. "She was crying when she told me that."

Feeling a common empathy, the Big Man struggles a bit as he asks, "Did she tell you his name?"

Gordon shakes his head and replies, "No, and I don't really see her much anymore. She and my wife just never got along." He turns his back, crosses his arms and stares at the wall of his cell …

Two days later, Manny sits across the table from Gordon, shackles around Gordon's arms and legs, in the same room as before. This time, the papers of briefs and documents remain in Manny's briefcase on the floor. All that rests on the table is a legal-size yellow note pad and Manny's right hand cradling a pen above the pad.

"You got what you wanted," Manny states flatly.

"Good," Gordon replies, nodding his head to Manny. "Thank you."

"No evidence arguments, no mention of a more likely suspect, nothing like I usually argue," Manny advises, frowning slightly. "My boss was not very happy. He thinks you're innocent and I should have been more aggressive. I should have argued something to at least buy us more time, but I didn't."

"But you don't believe I'm innocent, do you, Manuel?"

"I haven't decided, yet," Manny replies, staring intently at Gordon. "My job doesn't require that I believe in my clients' innocence, either."

"Nope, you just need to maintain an argumentative posture," Gordon remarks, smiling smugly.

Manny shakes his head. "You still find all this amusing, don't you?" he asks.

"What's the alternative?" Gordon counters, unaffected. "I could find it maddening and they could put me in the nuthouse, although that wouldn't be so bad if that Angela would come and visit me every month. She's a looker, isn't she?"

"That she is."

"That she is, indeed," Gordon responds quickly, "but I like amusing instead. It's like I have a *big* secret and if I share it with everyone I can stop something that will surely cause embarrassment, perhaps even shock. Yet, no one will give me *any* credence, so I have to laugh at everyone's decision to remain blissfully ignorant. I can get mad or I can get humorous. I choose humor."

"Maybe that won't be the outcome after all," Manny says. "We have quite a few of the staff searching for the link between the ex-husband and a man who looks like you. My boss says there's a man connected to the ex-husband who looks so muck like you, one can tell just from a photograph."

"A lotta guys look like me," Gordon jokes. "I hear all the time that I look like so and so. I think I'm a pretty popular model."

"There you go again," Manny complains. "I'm trying to tell you that we haven't given up, we're trying to help set you free, and you're throwing out the one-liners."

"But, you, personally, are doing it reluctantly," Gordon laments, "and that bothers me some. Like I said before, though, I can't make you believe anything. You have to do it on your own."

Manny feels a twinge of guilt for a brief moment. It's a strange feeling to him, and he can feel it expressed on his face as confusion and doubt. He looks down and away from Gordon and races to find something to change the subject. Trying to regain his composure, he glances at Gordon and says, "Tell me about this amygdala paradox."

"Can't," Gordon states, smiling with would-be triumph. "You're not a shrink."

"Tell me about some of the other things."

"You should talk to Barry, my colleague from my old work. He gives me credence."

DATES

In his small, cramped and crowded office, Manny Rodriguez stands before a table crammed with pamphlets and papers. Brushing up next to him is a tall and slender young woman, her ample endowments emphasized through her tight skirt and blouse each time she bends over the table to look closer at a paper or pamphlet, often sweeping her long, straight blond hair away from her face. Manny, however, pays it no heed, scanning his office and gauging the extent of his work still to perform, noting that virtually every surface, including the floor, is saturated with papers and pamphlets.

The attractive assistant, a paralegal not assigned to any particular attorney, stops searching through the papers on the table. Instantly, she stands upright and turns to face Manny, who is growing disheartened at the enormous task still left before him. Holding a stapled document in her right hand, she announces, "I've got the entire employee roster for Good Samaritan Hospital for the time that Simon Edwards was HR director there, Mister Rodriguez." She patiently waits for him to snap out of it, and Manny finally turns to her with his full attention after a few seconds. "I've matched most of the male roster to their pictures from the hospital, but some do not have pictures available."

Manny scans the table and asks, "How many, Cathy?"

The young woman glances over the pile before her on the table and replies, "I don't have an exact count, but roughly two dozen."

Manny rubs his forehead and closes his eyes for a moment. Softly, he laments, "It keeps adding up, Cathy. That's a good amount of research left." He opens his eyes and turns to look in Cathy's face and she tries to display an expression of hope and encouragement. He smiles briefly but asks, "Have you checked the pictures we have against Gordon?"

"Yes," Cathy replies, shaking her head, and placing the document in her hand back on the table. "None are even close."

"Okay," Manny says, and takes two steps to his desk to retrieve a clipboard. He spins around and hands it to Cathy and she takes it in her right hand and lifts it so she can read the paper attached to it. Manny advises, "Cross off Good Samaritan from the list. I'll need those employee names as soon as possible, because we're going to run out of time." He pauses to look at the calendar on his desk as she bends forward to lift a pen from the table and scratch it across the paper on the clipboard. Without focusing on anything in particular, Manny observes, "I just wish I knew how *much* time we have left. It's been three weeks since the appeal and still no date."

Cathy glances at Manny and asks, "What do you think is taking them so long, Manny?"

Manny focuses his gaze on her, shaking his head, and replies, "I don't know, but I don't like it."

Holding the clipboard against her body with her left arm, she gathers up the papers she was working on from the table, and announces, "I'll put together the names with pictures missing and get it to you right away." She steps to the door and struggles trying to open it without dropping the papers she's holding in both arms. Manny swiftly steps to the door to open it, twisting around her to avoid striking her, and she takes one step through the door until both hear a shout.

A young man steps quickly to them from the hall and states, "I was coming to your office, Manny. Corrections just announced the execution date." Both Manny and Cathy freeze and glance at each other.

Concern crosses his face as Manny anxiously asks the young man, "How long?"

Reaching both and looking up at Manny, the man replies, "We've got nine weeks."

Without further hesitation, Cathy simply assures Manny, "Give me fifteen minutes," and she turns and walks away quickly, struggling to avoid dropping the papers she carries.

Manny gazes at the face of the young man suspiciously and asks, softly, "They really want to get rid of him, don't they?"

The young man, his average height and build dwarfed next to Manny, nevertheless draws himself up and comments, "A lot of people want to get rid of him,

Manny. I heard the news on a TV at the coffee shop and a couple of people said, 'Ain't soon enough.'"

Manny simply shakes his head and glances down as he twists his left arm to note the time on his watch. Immediately, he turns and steps back behind his desk as the young man steps down the hall and disappears in another office.

Lifting his briefcase from the floor, Manny places it on his desk, opens it, bends down to open a drawer, pulls some files from it and places them in the briefcase. He slams the briefcase shut, steps out of his office and closes the door, making his way down the hall to exit the law office.

Pausing at the reception desk, he announces, "I'll be in court until lunch, probably about 11:30. After lunch, I have an appointment until 2, so I should be back at the office about 2:30, but I'll call first."

As he steps to the door leading out of the office, Cathy runs to him, shouting, "Manny, here are the names."

Manny waits for her to reach him and takes the paper offered, slipping it into a side pocket of his briefcase. He asks, "Will you put a copy on my desk, please, Cathy? I'll take this over to David while I'm out."

Cathy nods, smiling, and states, "Consider it done."

"Thank you," Manny says, returning her smile, and turns to the glass door, pushes it open and steps into the hall. In seconds, he's out of sight …

Rosita sits at the end of the kitchen table nearest the living room in her trailer while Jose and Maria sit next to each other at the opposite end. Since the language to which all three were introduced from birth is Spanish, when all three are together and no one else is in the room, they feel more comfortable speaking Spanish, not English. When Rosita's children are present or are the subject of address, they speak English, which was always Gordon's wish and Rosita usually honored it. In the kitchen by themselves, they speak Spanish, and Maria asks Rosita, "How are things? Can I help you with anything?"

Rosita looks at her friend, strong and resolute, and replies, "We're doing all right." She shakes her head, though. "Someone slashed a tire on my car yesterday, so I had to have it towed and the tire replaced."

Jose asks, "Do you think it was someone who knew about you and Gordon?"

Rosita grits her teeth as she replies, "It's been getting worse at the restaurant. When someone recognizes me as his wife, they say some nasty things. It's happening more often, so I'm going to finish the week and quit."

Maria looks a bit shocked as she asks, "Don't you need the money?"

Rosita's expression softens as she answers. "Not right now. Gordon saved a lot in his retirement account and received stock that we sold for a lot of money." She looks up and lets her eyes wander about the kitchen as she adds, "We've got enough money to last awhile."

"That's good," Maria comments. "You know that Jose and I will do anything we can for you."

"I know," Rosita says, sincerely. "I appreciate it. I appreciate both of you."

Jose hesitates a moment, bowing his head as he says, "I heard they set the date. That's not much time to save him."

Rosita's face tightens as she sighs, "I can't think about that now."

Concerned, Maria declares, "There must be something we can do to help."

From the living room, Melinda screams, "Ahhh! Mark." All at the kitchen table stop and look toward the living room. Melinda screams, "I hate you!"

Rosita rises from the table, enters the living room and spies Melanie and Mark struggling on the sofa with the remote control for the television. Melinda sees Rosita enter the living room and gets out of the chair to run to her, her face flushed with anger. As Rosita squats down to accept Melinda, she looks over at the older children wrestling on the sofa and calmly says, "Please stop." As Melinda wraps her arms around Rosita's waist, Rosita slowly stands upright, so Melinda's arms settle around her hips. Rosita looks down at her youngest daughter and slips her left arm around Melinda's neck, resting her left hand on the opposite shoulder.

The older ones continue to wrestle, so Rosita, a little louder but still calm, says, "Melanie."

Melanie, angry, stops to look at Rosita and protest, "Mom!"

Rosita immediately counters, "Please stop."

Mark beams triumphant until Rosita says, "Mark, bring me the remote." His triumph is soon replaced by sheepishness on his face as he scoots off the sofa and walks slowly to his mother holding the remote. When he reaches her, he hands it to her, and Rosita takes it in her right hand. She looks sternly at Mark but still quite calm says, "Mark, you seem to be in the middle of this, so tell me what happened." She glances to both daughters briefly and announces, "Everyone else needs to be quiet. You'll get your chance to speak."

Mark grows animated, fidgeting as he looks around at both siblings, and loudly proclaims, "Mom, Melinda's been hogging the TV—"

"Everyone's going to talk to me in a calm tone," Rosita interrupts, "or you're not going to talk at all."

Mark flashes a look of pain, ready to protest, but stops himself. After a few moments, his face relaxes and in a lower volume, he says, "We've been watching the shows Melinda wanted to watch and I wanted my turn, Mom."

"So you did what?" Rosita asks.

Mark looks down as he says, "I changed the channel until I found something I wanted to watch."

"And did you ask either of your sisters first?"

"It was my turn, Mom."

"That's not what I asked, Mark," Rosita counters. "Did you ask them if there was something they wanted to watch and, if not, could you watch what you wanted?"

Mark hesitates for a moment, but simply replies, "No."

Rosita looks at Melinda and asks, "Young lady, have you watched your shows all day?"

Melinda protests, "Mom." She stops as her mother cocks her head to the right and narrows her eyes. Melinda looks down and adds, "Yes."

"Is it your TV?" Rosita asks.

"No."

"You need to share," Rosita advises Melinda. "You shouldn't wait for someone to ask. *You* should ask the others if there's something they want to watch when you've had plenty of turns. Okay?"

Melinda looks up to her mother and displays a half smile as she says, "Okay."

Rosita looks over to Melanie and asks, "Melanie, what was your role in all this?"

Melanie frowns as she answers. "Mark chose some show that I didn't like, so I tried to get the remote from him, but he wouldn't let go, so I tried to yank it from him, and we started wrestling for it, and ..." Her voice trails off for a moment, when she adds, "I was wrong, Mom. I'm sorry."

Rosita brightens as she replies, "That's all right, Melanie. I don't have to tell you, because you know you were wrong and you're harder on yourself than I am." She pauses for a second. "We all have to share, we have to talk and ask each other, and I look to you to set an example for the younger ones."

Melanie looks up at her mother with a determined expression but contritely says, "I will. I'm sorry, Mom."

"That's okay," Rosita assures her. To all three, she announces, "TV time is over for the night. You can listen to music." She glances at Mark and adds, "You can read until bedtime." She glances at Melanie and adds, "You can work on your homework and get ahead on it or play a game, but I want you to get along and please be quiet and behave."

Both Mark and Melanie say, "Okay, Mom." Melanie gets up and turns on the radio but dials the volume low.

Rosita looks down to Melinda and asks, "Will you come with me to the kitchen and visit with Maria and Jose?"

Melinda smiles and says, "Yes, if you carry me."

"You can't walk?" Rosita asks.

"You won't carry me?" Melinda counters.

Rosita squats down, wraps her arms around Melinda's knees, lifts her up as Melinda grins, and carries her to the kitchen. Rosita returns to her seat with Melinda in her lap.

Speaking English, Jose observes, "You handled that well."

Maria looks at Rosita and asks, "You know who you reminded me of?" Rosita shakes her head. Both Jose and Maria glance at each other and speak at the same time, Maria saying, "Your husband," while Jose says, "Gordon."

Rosita frowns slightly as she replies, "Maybe you haven't noticed, but I don't get upset with the kids as much as I used to. You seem to always see me after I've had an argument with Gordon, which was getting to be almost every morning, and my anger would last all day. Sure, we would make up that night, but it takes *so much* out of me." She turns away and gazes out through the kitchen window above the sink into the blackness outside. She sighs, "At least, I haven't been mad all day in a long time."

Jose and Maria drop their heads but instinctively lift each to search into the eyes of the other ...

Manny slumps back in the chair of his office desk, beat. Lifting his left arm, he pushes the sleeve of his jacket away from his left wrist with his right hand and notes the time on his watch shows it's after nine in the evening. When he rests his right hand on his right leg, he feels a rustle of paper in the pocket. He shoves his hand into the pocket to retrieve the paper and unfolds it with both hands to read it. It's the scrap he wrote from his visit with Gordon at the prison when he wrote Barry's home phone number and tore it from the pad.

With renewed vigor, he sits up and leans forward against his desk and lifts the receiver from its set. Placing the scrap on the desk, he glances at the number and punches it on the set and listens to the phone ring.

A slightly effeminate voice at the other end of the phone says, "Hello?"

Smiling with curiosity, Manny asks, "Is this Barry?"

"It is," confirms the voice. "And who might you be?"

"Oh, I'm sorry," Manny replies, contritely. "My name is Manuel Rodriguez. I'm Gordon Schell's attorney. I apologize for calling so late, but do you have a few minutes to talk about Gordon?"

"Of course," Barry replies. "Will it help spring him?"

"What?" Manny replies, surprised. After a brief moment, he adds, "Oh, I don't know about that. I wanted to know more about Gordon and he said I should talk to you."

"Well, I've known him for more than six years, since I met him at the university." Barry pauses for a moment. "He's told me quite a few interesting ideas over that time, some I agree with and others I don't."

"Good," Manny says, smiling with satisfaction. "What about this amygdala paradox thing?"

"Did he tell you that one?"

"No."

"Because you're not a shrink?" Barry anticipates.

"Yes," Manny replies. "How did you—"

"That just means he doesn't think you would appreciate it," Barry interrupts.

"Well, what is it?" Manny asks, again.

"Did he tell you about the circle of influence?"

"No."

"Or my world?"

Manny sounds confused as he says, "Your world?"

"Everyone's world, in the context of whose world is strongest, and the advantage of its mobility," Barry explains. "How about fear and trust?"

"Do you mean," Manny asks, remembering what Gordon had told him earlier, "how fear keeps us divided, separated and apart?"

"That's some of it," Barry assures Manny. "He must have gone into the tribes."

Manny shakes his head when he hears that. "Something about tribal boundaries."

"Have you ever seen a satellite photo of what we call North America?" Barry asks, in an impersonating manner. "What's missing?" Barry waits for a moment. "Did you know what's missing?"

Manny thinks back to that conversation. "Well, I think I told him that there wasn't anything missing."

"Oh," Barry exclaims, laughing. "He chided you for not paying attention, didn't he?"

Manny smiles with the memory. "As a matter of fact, he did," he confirms.

"Yeah, he loves springing that one on college graduates, and, if you don't know, he calls you 'degree sheep', from sheepskin, because you're being led around by professors—shepherds—without really learning anything." Barry laughs. "He got me with that one, and when he was done, he said, 'So, now that you've learned something about paying attention from a college dropout, which is more than any of your professors taught you, do you feel better about your education? You should demand a tuition refund, after you ask the dean about the satellite photo and they validate that they have no clue, either.'"

Manny pauses as he leans back in his chair. He says, "I think Gordon suffers from an inferiority complex."

Shocked, Barry exclaims, "You must be joking with me, right?" Manny frowns as Barry adds, "If he *suffers from anything*, it's a lack of tolerance for fools masquerading as superior intellectuals."

Quickly leaning forward to rest his elbows on the desk, Manny asks, "Then, what is his angle, Barry?"

Ignoring the question, Barry asks, "Did he tell you how love is a delusion?"

Surprised, Manny simply exclaims, "What?"

"That's part of his fear and trust monologue," Barry advises, "where he tells you about the three attachments, those being, physical, mental and emotional. Everyone bears evidence of their physical attachment, you know."

"No, I don't know," Manny says, a bit lost.

"Don't you look at your body in the mirror and notice that scar over your belly?"

"What? My bellybutton?" Manny asks, letting out a short laugh.

"Your bellybutton is evidence of your one and only physical attachment," Barry explains, confident from the knowledge of having heard it many times. "As soon as you're born, they cut that cord, hand you to Mom, as though they're saying, 'Here ya go, kid. You're on your own.' From that moment forward, you are a single, independent entity, which, by definition, *is* alone, and you will spend your lifetime creating the other two attachments to combat your loneliness. Since they are creations of your own mind, *that*, by definition, makes them delusions, because they are not real. You made them up."

Manny is unimpressed. "That all sounds far-fetched, Barry," he complains. Suddenly, he smiles as he asks, "What about sexual intercourse? That's a physical attachment."

Barry laughs before he replies, "That's exactly what I said, but it's not a physical attachment in the sense of…" He pauses before adding, "conjoined twins. Physical attachments end after birth, which is good, because if they persist after birth, they're usually fatal. Witness the fact that when one conjoined twin dies, the other normally expires within hours. Does that normally happen after sexual intercourse?"

"No," Manny agrees, smiling. "Why didn't Gordon tell me this?"

"Probably because he doesn't think you'd appreciate it, yet," Barry reassures Manny. "But he has more. Did he talk about kindred spirits?"

"What?" Manny blurts. "No."

"Did he explain love and desire?"

"No."

"Or life is pain?"

"No."

"Or the only true tribe is the tribe of human beings?"

Manny hesitates a moment. "Well, he might have," he stammers.

"You would have remembered it," Barry insists. "How about patches of dirt?"

"No, not at all."

"Did he explain the difference between identity and identification?"

Manny perks up. "No," he replies, "would that make a difference in freeing him?"

"I doubt it," Barry says. "Gordon didn't kill that woman, but that fact didn't make any difference at his trial."

"How do you know that?"

"Did he tell you that there is no such thing as a coincidence?"

Manny persists as he asks, again, "How do you know that, Barry?"

"He really didn't tell you much at all, did he, Mr. Rodriguez?" Barry fires back.

Manny puts his left elbow on the table to rub his forehead with his left hand. He mumbles, "No, he wasn't much help. So, please, tell me what *you* know, Barry."

The line is silent for several seconds as Barry considers his next response. Finally, he calmly explains, "A few months after I met Gordon, he was telling me his opinion about sexual preference. It made me nervous, because I didn't know what he was getting at, and I thought he was going to criticize homosexuality, and me, by inference. Instead, he told me how ironic it was to live in a country full of sexual prudes who consider any sex bad but are absolutely obsessed with knowing everybody's sexual preference, like it's their business. He says that he never tells anyone his sexual preference *unless* they want to have sex with him. Then, he surprises me by saying, 'So, Barry, do you want to have sex with me?'"

Spellbound, Manny asks, "How did you reply to that?"

Barry's speech slows perceptibly as he carefully chooses the words. "I lied to him. I said, 'No, of course not, Gordon.' I told him that I knew his sexual preference and he just said, 'Sure you do, Barry.' And that conversation stayed with me for months as I grew to trust him more and more and remembering that I had lied to him." Barry pauses for a few seconds and Manny leans forward against the desk. "Finally, I reminded him about that question and told him that I had lied to him, that I had wanted to have sex with him from the first moment I saw him. He said, 'That bothered you all this time that you lied to me, didn't it?' I said, 'Yes.' He said, 'And you feel better now that you told me, don't you?' I just said, 'Yes.' So, he lowered his voice like he does for a punch line of a joke and said, 'You still can't have sex with me, though. I'm already spoken for. Sorry.' He smiled and that made me laugh and he added, 'Barry, have you ever heard about a woman scorned?' I said, 'Yes.' And, he delivered the punch line, 'Wait until you've seen a *Mexican* woman scorned.'"

Manny sits up and says, "Meaning his wife, Rosita." He thinks for a moment and says, "Rosita told me she considers you a friend of both of them. Is that true?"

"I imagine she thinks that when she seeks my help or advice, but she hates homosexuals and occasionally reminds me about that."

"How so?" Manny inquires.

Barry pauses a moment before he replies, "Oh, she'll be going off about fags, and faggots, and homos, and queers, and then she'll stop, look at me, and say something like, 'No offense to you, Barry,' or 'I don't mean you, Barry,' or 'Except for you, Barry', but her meaning is pretty clear. When Gordon hears her say that, though, he really comes down hard on her about generalizations and such, and they usually get into an argument. Maybe 'friend' is bit of a stretch, but do you want to know what's *really* ironic about her?"

"What's that?"

"I had no idea until the trial that she had been raped. Neither Gordon nor Rosita had ever talked about it before. So here's Rosita, raped by a heterosexual and she hates homosexuals, none of whom *ever* hurt her. *That's* irony."

"Perhaps," Manny comments with some disinterest. Suddenly, he remembers something Gordon had talked about, so he says, "Barry, there was one thing Gordon said. He was talking about being a visitor, not from here, serving some kind of penance—"

"And he probably told you," Barry interrupts, "that those who cannot live together are doomed to die together."

"Something close to that, yes," Manny confirms.

"That's a bad precursor," Barry warns. "When he starts talking like that it usually means he's falling into a depression, and you don't want to be around him when he's in a full-blown depression."

"Have you seen him like that?" Manny asks, deciding that he needs to take notes and begins to jot on the pad on the desk.

"Twice, which was once too often," Barry bemoans.

"What's he like when he's in a depression?"

"It's not what he does or what he says, though he's quite short and curt," Barry explains. "It's the expression on his face. I can only explain that it looks like you're bothering him and if you don't leave him alone *real soon*, he's going to rip your beating heart out with his bare hands, stuff it in your mouth and make you swallow it."

Manny forces a chuckle, unexpectedly, but comments, "That's a little severe, don't you think?"

"When you've seen it, you don't ever want to see it, again, and I'm not the only one. I've seen the entire office in dread of having to confront him, even bosses and the biggest guys in the building. When we have to deal with him, we all do it delicately, like we're walking on eggshells and the sound of one of those shells cracking is going to set him off." Barry pauses a moment while Manny waits with anticipation, fascinated. "Don't get me wrong, when he's over it, he's a sweetheart with everyone, joking, apologizing, and it's forgotten. Still …"

"What sends him there?"

"I don't know, Mr. Rodriguez" Barry replies. "The only thing he's ever told me about it is that he doesn't want to see anyone, talk to anyone or be talked to, unless he absolutely has to. He wants to be left alone, period. But it *is* bad. It's almost like he hates everyone, that we're all hopeless and deserving of the despair that he feels." A moment of silence ensues as Barry considers what started this part of the conversation. He adds, "I heard that visitor talk the day before one of those episodes. That's why I think it's a precursor."

"I appreciate your being so open and honest with me, Barry," Manny says. "I'm starting to get an understanding about Gordon Schell that I didn't have before."

"I hope it helps you get him out of there," Barry remarks. "I need to take care of some things now before I go to bed. I have an early day scheduled."

"Thank you for taking my call," Manny acknowledges.

"I want you to know one more thing, Mr. Rodriguez," Barry insists. "I love Gordon, with a love that's free and pure. You should make him explain love and desire and then you'll know how free and pure love truly is, that it's caring, consideration, appreciation, concern, compassion, empathy, all these intangible qualities one can give to another without *any expectation of return*, which is what makes it free and pure. It's the hardest thing a human being can do, to continue to give love without receiving *any* in return. And I was just as confused about love as everyone else, but I learned that from him. In all the years that have passed, I am a better person having met him. There aren't many other people about whom I can say that."

"Love and desire?" Manny asks as a reminder.

"Love and desire," Barry reaffirms. "You'll learn something very valuable."

"I'll be certain to do that next time I visit him," Manny assures him.

"Good night, then, Mr. Rodriguez," Barry says.

"Good night," Manny replies and he immediately hears a click on the line. He leans forward to place the phone receiver on the handset and leans back in his chair in contemplation …

Two days later, Gordon sleeps on his right side on the bed facing the wall as the Big Man steps up to his cell and asks, "How are things today, Gordon?"

Unmoving, Gordon replies softly, "I'm not feeling well today."

The Big Man looks concerned as he says, "They said you didn't go out to the exercise yard. You need a doctor?"

"No," is Gordon's short reply.

"Are you sure?" the Big Man asks. "You don't sound too good."

"I'll be all right."

The Big Man stands straight but tilts his head, looking at Gordon's unmoving body. "We haven't played cribbage in a while," he says. "I'll play a game with you if you want."

Still unmoving and speaking softly, Gordon says, "Not today, Big Man. Not in the mood."

"Are you sure you don't need a doctor?" the Big Man inquires again, visibly worried. "You don't sound like you usually do."

There's no response from Gordon for several seconds. Finally, he says, "I just need rest." He pauses but makes no movement as he adds, "I just want to be left alone."

Disappointed, the Big Man flippantly states, "Suit yourself," and turns to walk away.

Gordon quickly says, "Sorry, Big Man. Maybe tomorrow."

The Big Man says, unconvincingly, as he disappears from view, "Maybe."

THE PRIVATE EYES

The following day, Manny sits in a chair in a comfortably-sized office kept reasonably tidy by the man sitting across the desk from him. A short and stocky chap, balding with short brown hair on the sides and back, he appears considerably older than Manny. At the front of the desk is a nameplate which reads "David Samuels, Private Investigator." Manny asks, "What progress have you made so far?"

The man behind the desk replies, "I could ask you the same question. Have you completed all of the rosters?"

"Yes," Manny replies, and glances at David's desk to a folder as he adds, "In there is the last of the names that we could not match with a picture."

"How many?" David asks.

"About fifty more," Manny replies.

"That's close to three hundred, fifty," David moans, shaking his head. "I'm only halfway through that list, Manny. Here," and he pauses to retrieve a large brown envelope from a drawer in his desk, hands it to Manny, adding, "these are the pictures with the names that I matched from the last time." He shakes his head as he says, "I gotta be honest with you, Manny. I didn't see any resemblance with this set to your man."

Manny takes the envelope and slips it under his right arm as he says, "We've got less than seven weeks, David. Can you finish this before then?"

"Depends," David says, looking away with a frown. "Some are well-hidden and others aren't so. If I have to find a picture of them buried in some bureaucracy file because there are none more available, that takes a *lot* of time, Manny."

"I understand, David," Manny assures him. "That's why we hired you, but we're running out of time."

"I'll do the best I can," David says, "but I can't guarantee I'll get through the whole list."

"I know," Manny says, reluctantly, "there are no guarantees in life."

Absentmindedly, talking more to himself than Manny, David mutters, "Maybe in the next one." He reaches for the newest folder on his desk, sets it before him and glances through the contents …

Manuel Rodriguez sits behind the desk in his office a week later, leaning back in his chair reading a legal brief. From the speaker phone comes the announcement, "David Samuels is on line one for you, Manny."

Manny looks up from the papers he holds, stares at the phone, annoyed, and barks, "I asked not to be disturbed, Jackie."

The woman's voice from the phone is apologetic as she responds, "I told him that, Manny, but he insisted that you need to hear this."

Perturbed, Manny capitulates, "All right, send him through."

The woman's voice softly states, "Just press line one, Manny."

Manny leans forward until he reaches the phone, presses a button and says, "David, I'm preparing for trial, so make it quick, please."

From the phone, David says, "I'm looking at a picture of your man right now, Manny." There's a momentary pause until he adds, "I need you to look at this as soon as possible and tell me if you agree."

Manny brightens for a moment but frowns as he answers, "Can't meet with you until the end of the day. I'm in court until probably five."

David's voice is assertive as he says, "Okay. While you're in court, though, I'm going to start some background research on this guy."

"You're sure it's him?" Manny asks, adding, "You still have some on the list with no pictures to match, don't you?"

"Wait 'til you see this picture, Manny," David's voice says reassuringly.

"All right, then," Manny says, "I'll call you as soon as I get out." He presses the same button as before and the phone goes silent …

Having rushed directly from the courthouse to meet in David's office, both men stand before a table scattered with pictures and papers in a smaller room of David's office space. David calls the room his work area, which he usually keeps locked unless he's using it. David lifts a four inch by six inch picture from the table, holds it so that both men can see it, and says, "This is the original picture that one of the former employees at Good Samaritan Hospital let me have." The picture is one of many people taken at an outing. With his right index finger,

David points to a man in the picture standing at the far left side. "That's him right there, posing with a number of employees at a picnic."

He hands the picture to Manny, who holds it to his face for a closer examination. David reaches for another picture, which is a cropped blow-up of the man in the original picture. Holding it up so Manny can see it, he says, "So I had it blown up around him." He reaches for a picture of Gordon Schell with his right hand, holds the two side by side, and says, "Then, I compared it with Gordon's picture. Check this out." Manny sets the first picture down on the table and grabs a picture with either hand, pulling both close to his face. He glances from one to the other several times and lowers them.

"If I didn't know any better, David," Manny comments, "I'd say these pictures were of the same man."

"Exactly," David agrees, excitedly. "That's what I thought, too."

Manny looks at David, frowning, and says, "Only one problem, though. We don't have the long, stringy hair, the sideburns and the mustache."

David smiles broadly and reaches for a folder and says, "Oh, yes we do." He opens it and removes another picture, a mug shot from the police. He holds it before Manny and says, "This is where connections with the city's finest come in handy."

The mug shot shows Gunther Rankin with long, stringy hair, long sideburns and a mustache. Manny looks at the picture without taking it from David and appears shocked. After a few moments he says, "That looks just like the picture of Gordon the prosecution doctored to add the hair, sideburns and mustache."

"Except that it's not," David says. "*This* is Gunther Rankin."

"When was this taken?" Manny asks.

"A couple months before the murder," David says, adding, "and this guy is definitely a bad dude. This was taken after his arrest for armed robbery, but he made bail and was out at the time of the murder. Then, he missed a trial date, was arrested and he's still in jail awaiting trial."

Both David and Manny set their respective pictures down on the table. Manny asks, "What do you know about him?"

David replies, "He's thirty-three with an enormous rap sheet, with arrests for everything all over the board, robbery, assault and battery, attempted murder, murder, you name it. He's been convicted twice and served time. His juvenile record is sealed but I've talked to several juvenile officers and they remember him. He was, shall we say, troubled way back then, from age twelve, when he cracked an adult male with whom he was having an argument with a baseball bat."

"You said he was arrested for murder?"

"Sure was," David confirms. "He was released for lack of evidence and the case is still open. He's still the leading suspect."

Manny takes a deep breath and turns toward the table to compare the pictures of Gordon and Gunther again. He shakes his head as he says, "The resemblance is amazing. They're like twin brothers." He turns his head to David and asks, "What happened here? Why did they go after Gordon and not this creep?"

David leans to Manny and in a conspiratorial tone says, "Between you and me and no further, I had a conversation that never took place with the junior detective that worked this case. They knew about Gunther Rankin but they never seriously pursued that investigation, because the DA's office was convinced about Gordon when he initially denied knowing the murder victim. Once they got the fingerprints, and, *then*, they found the murder evidence in his truck, they just conveniently forgot about Rankin." David shrugs his shoulders, adding, "To be honest, Manny, the evidence against Gordon, *so far*, is more compelling."

"So far," Manny agrees, "but the more I get into this, the less I believe in Gordon's guilt." He shakes his head. "Rankin's the prime candidate, so if you ask me," and he points to the mug shot of Gunther Rankin, adding, "that's the killer right there."

"No argument from me," David agrees.

Manny turns to David, anxiously, and says, "Now, we need to establish the link between Rankin and the ex-husband, and we need to find it fast. My client has one month to live."

David smiles and pats Manny on the arm. "Already working on it," he says.

The Big Man Loses Again

After dinner, Gordon and the Big Man are playing cribbage again. The peg positions on the board show that this game is much closer than the last. Still, the look on the Big Man's face shows resignation as he says, "Looks like you got me again."

"Perhaps," says Gordon, "but you took all the points on the showdown just now. You did good."

"It's not going to be enough, though," the Big Man observes.

"Let's see what you got," Gordon advises.

The Big Man lays his cards on the chair inside Gordon's cell next to the board and announces, "Double run of four for ten and fifteen four for fourteen."

"Good hand," Gordon encourages him. "Nice draw on that six there. That was six extra points just from the luck of the draw."

The Big Man reaches through the bars to move his back peg fourteen holes beyond his front pin, past Gordon's front peg and only five points from the end. He says, "Yeah, that was lucky, wasn't it?" He looks up at Gordon and shakes his head as he adds, "I'm still short, though, and you're counting."

Gordon lays his cards down, revealing two fours, an ace and a jack. He says, "A pair for two and fifteen six for eight." Gordon moves his back peg eight holes beond the front pin, only two points from victory. He reaches for the discard pile and turns over an ace, a four, a seven and the top card is a six. He says, "A pair of sixes for two." He moves the back peg past the end line to the starting peg position. He looks up at the Big Man from his cross legged position on the floor, smiles, and says, "That's game."

The Big Man smiles and says, "That six didn't hurt you at all, did it?"

As he starts to put everything away, Gordon responds in a mock mystical voice, "It's the cribbage way."

"Yeah, sure," the Big Man responds skeptically with a chuckle. "I think you're right about one thing, though."

"What's that?" Gordon asks.

"I'm gonna beat you one of these days," the Big Man promises.

Gordon stands up from the floor, grabs the board and deck of cards and steps to the shelf to set them down, saying, "There's hope for you yet, Big Man."

The Way and the Will

"Tell me about love and desire," Manny demands, as he sits opposite Gordon in the attorney room at the prison. It's two days after his meeting with David and Manny has brought along a picture of Gunther Rankin to show Gordon and ask about him, but he's more curious about the things that Barry talked about earlier.

Gordon smiles as he shifts his weight with some effort and the chains rattle softly. "They're synonyms," he replies. "Why, I hear people all the time say they love someone when they mean they desire someone, or they desire someone when they mean they love someone. They're interchangeable." He nods several times and his smile grows a bit more devious.

Manny shakes his head. "Not the way Barry tells it," he says, unconvinced.

"You talked to Barry?" Gordon blurts, his face in shock.

"As a matter of fact, I called him late one night, and he spent some time talking with me about you," Manny confides. His face grows more serious when he adds, "So, are you going to tell me about love and desire or are you just gonna joke around?"

"Barry loves me, you know," Gordon admits.

"That's what he said," Manny advises.

"Did he tell you he's wanted to have sex with me for years?" Gordon asks.

Manny nods and replies, "Not so much in those words but he said you told him you were spoken for."

"Yeah," Gordon agrees, "and in Spanish, no less."

Manny frowns slightly and in a polite business tone again demands, "Love and desire, Gordon. Let's hear it. I want to know."

"All right, Manuel," Gordon says, with apparent surrender. "Gosh, you're so demanding," he adds, shaking his head but smiling anyway. "Love and desire. Did Barry tell you about the three attachments?"

"Yes," Manny confirms. "The three attachments are physical, mental and emotional. I don't get the significance of the physical attachment, though."

"Did he mention the conjoined twins?" Gordon asks.

"Yes."

"Good," Gordon says, nodding his head. "That's what I like about Barry. He pays attention." He pauses for a moment and looks away from Manny. "The conjoined twins argument is important in explaining how all the attachments work, but mostly for the physical, because a physical attachment between human beings links their very lives together. Your one and only physical attachment ends at birth when they cut the umbilical cord." Gordon turns back to look at Manny and leans slightly forward. "If you get high some time and stare at your belly button, you can start thinking about how you're linked to your mother and she's linked to her mother and to her mother and on and on, all the way back to the beginning, where we're all linked through our belly buttons, or navels. Although, they don't really have any similarity with navel oranges, so what's up with that? Anyway, to properly appreciate all that linkage way back, I think you have to be *really* stoned."

"I get the linkage, Gordon," Manny says, peeved. "Get on with it."

"Physical attachment links two human beings together. As the one goes, so goes the other. They live or die together. There is no separation, unless that cord is cut. Once it is, you are on your own from that moment forward, where we use the other two attachments to combat our loneliness." Gordon halts to look at Manny and gauge how he's following. Suddenly, he asks, "Ever been married, Manuel?"

"No," Manny replies. "Haven't met the woman yet."

"Doesn't *have* to be a woman," Gordon insists as Manny frown disapprovingly, adding, "not in Massachusetts." Manny continues frowning and starts shaking his head. "Okay, well, you'll have to use your imagination to consider what it's like. You get up in the morning and your wife makes some vague comment about how disappointed your life has turned out up to this point. The kids wake up and start round one thousand, seven hundred and forty-nine of their incessant boxing match, except for the little one, who is still in a constant state of shock and awe, not to be confused with a certain military incursion into a certain Middle Eastern country. And all is good in your marriage. Looking forward to it?"

Manny frowns as he responds, "That's not very romantic."

"Ah, romance," Gordon comments. "Yes, there's still that, during those few moments when the kids are in bed or away visiting friends or relatives and your wife's in the mood and not on her period, which is, on average, once every six or seven fortnights, and usually starts something like, 'Is that thing hard, again?' Reality bites, man."

Manny calmly states, "You're getting off the subject, Gordon."

"Older couples face this on a daily basis," Gordon explains. "What am I going to do if my spouse dies before me? If your loved one dies suddenly, *you're* not gonna die, unless you're both in the same accident, for example. You may *want* to die, but that would be by your own hand, which is not the same thing. And, when they *do* die, you're alone, on your own. But you were *always* on your own, since, once that umbilical cord is cut, you are a single, independent entity. By common and accepted definition, that *is* alone, and you will create mental and emotional attachments to counter that loneliness until you die."

"I'm not alone now," Manny counters. "I'm with you."

Gordon smiles as he answers, "That's what some psych student said about twenty minutes after he met me. You're not alone because you have already created mental and emotional attachments directed at me, and your loneliness is thus abated." For a moment, Gordon stops to shake his head slowly. "And, really, they're both mental, since emotions are still just mental processes, but I include them both to avoid meaningless arguments, because I want you to understand how it works."

"But I can't be alone if I'm in some room with another human being," Manny argues.

Immediately, Gordon counters, "Which overlooks the feeling that I know you've had in the past when you walk into some room, like an airport terminal, or a bus stop, or some huge hall to register for something, and there is not a single human being with whom you are familiar and you feel, *alone*." Gordon pauses for effect. "You can all be packed in that room like sardines, bodies pressing on you from all sides, and you will *still* feel alone, because you have no mental and emotional attachment to *anyone*. Then, suddenly, someone looks at you and smiles, and you smile back and say, 'Hi,' and that person says, 'Hi.' You share a funny observation and that person laughs, and, *bam!* You don't feel alone any more, because you have just created a mental and emotional attachment directed at that person, and it is exactly what that person has created, which is directed at you. *That's* how fast it works."

"That is a mental and emotional attachment?" Manny questions skeptically.

"Would you feel mentally and emotionally attached to anyone *other* than that person at that moment?" Gordon counters.

"No," Manny says, nodding his head. "I see your point."

"And, this was for the psych student," Gordon says, "since it is only a creation of your mind, that makes it a delusion, because it is no different than a schizophrenic who *hears voices*. Oooh! So, what does this mental and emotional attachment consist of? Love, Manuel, one which is free and pure. It is caring, consideration, appreciation, empathy, compassion, concern, all the intangible qualities we can give to another without any expectation of return, which makes it free and pure."

"In your example, though," Manny says, "I return that person's love. Wouldn't that person have expected a return?"

Gordon smiles and hesitates a moment before he replies, "That's a good point. What would have happened if you had just turned away from that smile?"

"I would think that person would also turn away and, possibly, be disappointed," Manny replies.

"Perfect! With this development we now establish three rules about love and desire," Gordon declares. "First, it is unilateral, meaning it only goes one way, so that there is no such thing as mutual love. Second, there is always some level of desire involved, even if it's only a *desire* to find out what this human being thinks about me. Third, it is unfulfilled *desire* which affects the hurt and pain we feel or, in this case, the disappointment. The *level* of desire is affected by sensory feedback one receives from the human being to which an attachment is directed. In this case, the level of desire falls because that person *sees* you turn away, in essence, reject the attempt to attach, which will certainly result in some amount of pain from unfulfilled desire."

Manny smiles with newfound appreciation. He remarks, "You've thought a lot about this, haven't you, Gordon?"

"With all the shit that passes for wisdom about love and desire, all of which is complete and utter stupidity, do you blame me for trying to figure it out?"

"No, not at all," Manny replies, smiling.

"For example," Gordon states, "I'm with some woman who says, 'Let's make love.' We tear our clothes off, hop in the sack, and get to it, but, despite my best efforts, I can't get her to climax, to have an orgasm, to cum for me. As I roll off her, do you think the first words that pop out of her mouth are going to be, 'I love you so very much?'"

Manny laughs and struggles to say, "Probably not."

"Does that mean we failed to make love?"

"Well, do you think you succeeded?" Manny asks, still chuckling.

"Yeah, it must be my fault," Gordon remarks, sarcastically. "It's always the guy's fault. No, seriously, we didn't fail in making love, we failed in having a fulfilling sexual experience, which is *not love*. It's sex. Love and desire might lead to sex, but sex is sex, love is love and desire is desire. Yet, the vast majority of human beings wander around the big blue spaceship confused about why it didn't work out with so-and-so and so-and-so, and I think that, maybe, it might be you're all *clueless* about love, and desire, and sex. Every one is so confused about why it doesn't work out because they don't have a *clue*."

Again, Manny laughs. He looks at Gordon, smiling, and says, "I've got no argument with any of that. Making love does seem an inappropriate term."

Gordon laughs briefly, smiles, and states, "It's completely ridiculous. Fucking is fucking. Making love sounds like two magicians about to perform a magic act. Hey, watch me pull a rabbit out of my pants. Ooh, watch me make a rabbit disappear in my pants. But, really, it's not a rabbit. We made love, right out of thin air. How's *that* for magic?"

Manny laughs and smiles as Gordon smiles back. He notices a sort of twinkle in Gordon's eyes as he glances over his face from that easy smile. A thought quickly flashes in Manny's consciousness. *If this guy's a killer, he's the smoothest at setting a comfort level I have ever witnessed.* Still smiling, Manny asks, "Watch me pull a rabbit out of my pants, huh?"

Gordon's smiles grows wider as he replies, "Like that one, do you? Gotta be magic!"

"I like it," Manny says, sincerely, "but how does love and desire work with couples? What happens when couples break up, split, or divorce? What role do they play?"

Gordon lifts his chained hands awkwardly to rest on the table and leans forward, never breaking his fix on Manny's eyes. He calmly states, "First, those attachments are created, with love and desire, and they're always in your mind. We periodically clean out the unused attachments, kind of like spring cleaning, but I suspect that they always remain. We just render them inactive."

"What brings two people together?" Manny inquires.

"That's a mutual decision," Gordon explains, "affected by a number of forces, many of which are external to either. None of that really matters much, because both eventually decide to make some kind of life together, and that is a desire in and of itself." Gordon pauses a moment and looks away when he continues. "See, desire is anything one can desire from and for another. It can be anything you want, anything. It can be as innocent as a desire to help another improve their situation, their lives, to something as hard-core as the kinkiest, freakiest sexual escapade. It's all desire, wanting, so when two people desire to be together, that starts a dance of levels, since the level of desire of one is independent of the level of desire of the other." He looks back at Manny and glances down at Manny's arms resting on the table. "Leave your elbows on the table, lift your arms and set your hands flat with your palms up," Gordon commands Manny.

Manny looks down at his arms and lifts them, keeping his elbows on the table. He flattens his hands with his palms turned up and sets them at the same height. "Like this?" he asks.

"That's good, yes," Gordon commends. "Assume that your hands represent the levels of desire of a couple, one for each human being. Now, raise your right hand about six inches but keep it flat." Manny raises his right hand about six inches above the height of his left hand. Gordon says, "Good. The love remains the same, but the *level of desire* of each changes, constantly changes. What affects the level of one is sensory feedback from the other, meaning what one sees, hears, smells, feels, and—my favorite because it means you're really close to that person—how the other tastes. Trust me. When someone shoves their tongue in your mouth, they're tasting you. Disagree?"

Manny smiles as he says, "No, I would agree with that."

"These levels are independent of each other, being unilateral," Gordon says, "and they are constantly going up and down, based on sensory feedback."

Manny moves either hand up and down, below and above the other. He asks, "Like this?"

"Exactly," Gordon affirms. "They can never be exactly the same. That's perfection and impossible in this life, but the goal is to keep each in relative equilibrium, where each level is close to the other, even though one can be higher than the other, and vice versa, at any time."

Manny sets the height of each hand close to the other and lifts and drops each, keeping them within an inch or so as to height, but allowing one to be higher, followed by the other several times. "Like this?" he asks.

"Absolutely."

"I think I'm seeing how this all works," Manny observes.

"What you're showing with your hands the way they are now," Gordon says, "is how couples who have remained together for a long time have learned how to do it. Their levels of desire rarely get far apart, and when they do they take steps to bring them back to equilibrium. How do they do that? Put your right hand back up six inches higher than the left and move your right hand over your left."

Manny quickly does as Gordon commands, smiling as he notices the gap between the two. "See that gap, Manuel?"

"Yes," Manny confirms, adding, "this isn't good, is it?"

"Not if that couple wants to stay together," Gordon advises. "If that gap continues, that couple will be pushed apart by their own incompatible levels of desire. One will feel strangled, and the other will feel a growing sense of detachment. However, the successful long-term couples learn to recognize these gaps and act to bring their levels to equilibrium." Gordon glances at Manny's hands. "Bring your right hand down while you bring your left up until one is above the other." Manny complies until his right hand rests flat above his left. "One will lower the level while the other will raise the level. In fact, many long-term couples get so good at it, that they do it without a conscious effort. It also has nothing to do with the irrelevant human attributes, or the ones I call accidents of birth: gender, race, place of birth, or the primary language learned. They are irrelevant."

Manny sets his hands down on the table, gazing intently at Gordon. "So, it's just the amount of desire that forces couples apart, nothing more? It's not something like betrayal or abuse or a change in behavior and interests?"

Gordon shakes his head and replies, "All of that will affect the outcome and more, but, remember, sensory feedback affects the level of desire. Do you not think that all of those will affect one's level of desire?"

"Good point," Manny admits.

"Put your hands out like you just did, Manuel," Gordon commands, "and put your right hand way above your head but keep your left hand way down." He waits, watching while Manny performs the requested action. When Manny has his right hand up above his head, Gordon says, "That is an example of 'being in love' or 'madly in love.' As you can see, it's nothing more than an abnormally high level of desire, but how long do you think that couple will stay together with a gap that huge?"

"Not long, I would imagine," Manny offers.

"Correct," Gordon agrees. "And when it comes crashing down—drop your right hand to the table," Gordon commands, and Manny lets his hand fall freely to the table with a thud. Gordon continues, "That's the end of those two. I hear people frequently say, 'Oh, I'm in love with so-and-so,' and a few weeks or months say, 'Oh, I'm out of love with so-and-so,' and I just have to walk away shaking my head, because I know they have *no clue* what love is. Love is not something you fall in and out of, like it's some hole in the ground. It's just a level of desire so intense that your every waking moment is consumed by thoughts of the other to the point that you can barely function, until you finally burn out completely or the other person runs away because they are being suffocated."

"You don't really think that people can get burned out from desire, do you?"

"Human beings are fragile creatures," Gordon counters. "Trying to maintain a level of desire that's too intense will eventually fry your brain."

"Come on, Gordon," Manny argues. "That can't really happen."

Gordon shakes his head slowly and says, "Everyone thinks they're somehow superhuman, even you, I'll bet, but I'm telling you, human beings are fragile creatures. You give me five days and I could turn you into a bumbling lunatic ready to be locked up in an insane asylum, *and* I can do it without physically or mentally abusing you."

With obvious disgust on his face, Manny simply says, "I don't think so, Gordon."

Gordon smiles. "Sure I could," he says,"with the help of a couple friends. We just shake you when you start to go to sleep and keep you up for five days straight, and we'll turn you into a mumbling incoherent and a stumbling incompetent. Display you to some shrinks and the boys in white coats will come to take you away, for sure. If you haven't stayed up for more than two days straight, you haven't even been in that territory and you're gonna argue that I can't make you a complete crazy?"

"Well, Gordon," Manny says, rubbing his chin, "that *is* intriguing."

"Let's get back to 'out of love,'" Gordon suggests. "What do you think happens when that level comes crashing down and the two separate?"

"One of them's going to be hurt, don't you think?" Manny proposes.

"Both are going to be hurt, Manuel." Gordon struggles to pull his hands from the table and rest them in his lap while leaning back. He looks at Manny and adds, "The hurt, the pain that everyone feels, even from an early age, is just unfulfilled desire. Both will have unfulfilled desire and both will feel pain, and it will always be there, diminishing over time until something happens to bring it back fresh, but it will never go away." He smiles and waits for a few seconds before he says, "So, my friend, life is pain, all from unfulfilled desire and always there. If you don't feel pain, then you're dead. You're certifiably dead because you're not breathing and your heart's not beating. You're clinically dead because there is no discernible brain wave activity, or you're emotionally dead and cannot feel *anything*, pain or otherwise. And there *are* some of those walking among us, but in any case, you're *dead* if you can't feel pain." Gordon turns away, satisfied and remains unmoving.

Manny stares at Gordon until he recognizes that the lecture is over. Softly, he asks, "What about you and Rosita?"

Gordon turns back to look at Manny as he asks, "What about us?"

"Didn't you think about leaving her at one time?" Manny asks, delicately.

"Yes," Gordon replies, still looking at Manny but closing his eyelids some.

"Why didn't you?"

Gordon smiles briefly as he calmly answers, "Melanie greeted us."

Manny nods his head, his expression sympathetic. He observes, "And you couldn't leave her then, could you?"

"Not like that," Gordon says, "no."

Manny looks down at the table briefly. Looking up, he says, "She told me that there were problems early in your marriage, but you both worked through them, to the point where she said you loved each other very much." Manny slows his speech as he asks, "So, is Rosita the love of your life?"

"No," is the only sound Gordon utters.

Shocked, Manny blurts, "What?"

"Oh, she might be and I just don't know it," Gordon responds calmly, a thin smile appearing through an otherwise lack of expression. "Or, maybe she will be eventually, but that's not why we're together, why we've stayed together."

"Is it the kids?" Manny asks, softly.

"We won't ignore our responsibilities and obligations, but that's not what drew us together in the first place." Gordon pauses and twists his head from side to side. "She's with me to teach me patience, selflessness, to respect differences in cultures and traditions. I'm with her to teach her peace, calm, forgiveness, to help her forget and to trust a man, again. I think I'm with her to restore her faith and belief, but I also think that I failed. I think that she believed in me once but not any more."

"I disagree with that assessment, Gordon," Manny tries to assure him, looking into his eyes for acknowledgement. Gordon just looks at the table. Manny adds, "I don't think she ever stopped believing in you, not from the way she talks about you. Sometimes, it sounds almost like reverence, and when she talks about how you act with the children, I can see the tears watering in her eyes." Gordon looks up at Manny and quickly turns away. "I think you're wrong, Gordon," Manny concludes.

"Perhaps," Gordon says, trying hard not to choke on the words while he continues looking away. "I don't want to talk about her right now, though, Manuel, so may we change the subject?"

Manny drops his head and says, softly, "I understand." He looks down to his briefcase on the floor next to him, reaches inside and retrieves some photos. As he brings them above the table, Gordon turns to look at them and Manny sets them before him. He lifts the top photo and twists it to set it before Gordon right side up. He states, "Take a look at this photo. Notice the resemblance?"

Gordon looks at the photo and says, "To me? Well, the eyes are farther apart, the nose is slightly longer. Um, the cheeks are more angular, the chin is a little lumpier—"

"Okay, then, compare it with this," interrupts Manny, as he lifts the next photo and twists it to set it next to the first. He points to the new photo and says, "This is the photo the prosecution gave the jury of you with the longer hair, sideburns and mustache added."

Gordon glances from one to the other and back. "We do look quite a bit alike," he observes.

Manny points to the first photo. "That is a man named Gunther Rankin," he states. "We think he's the real killer."

Gordon looks up at Manny and says, "I've never seen him before, Manny." He looks again at the first photo. "I have no idea who he is. Why do you think he did it?"

Manny smiles as he answers, "We thought he would have some relationship to the ex-husband, so we looked for a photo of a man who looked like you with that in mind and we found it. They both worked at the same hospital at the same time."

"Why would he set me up?" Gordon asks.

Manny shakes his head. "We don't know that, yet, but he must have known about you," he says.

"Well, I certainly don't know him," Gordon reiterates. Suddenly, he narrows his eyes as he stares at Manny and states, "Say, I thought you didn't believe in my innocence."

Sheepishly, Manny looks away and says, "I don't know what to believe right now, Gordon, to be honest." He turns to look directly at Gordon. "But, I don't think you should die, so I'm going to try to do everything I can to prevent it."

"I don't mind dying, Manuel," Gordon says, softly, his gaze locked on the counselor. "I welcome death."

"You shouldn't say that," Manny advises, holding his gaze.

"Maybe it's my time and there's nothing anyone can do about it," Gordon says. "In any event, our time's about up. You're gonna be busy, I'm sure, so there's no need to come back here, especially since I can't really help you."

"Maybe there's something I can do for you, if I do come back," Manny offers.

"Then, I'll tell you what I dream about," Gordon says.

Manny smiles at the response. "What's that?" he asks.

Gordon returns the smile and says, "I want to touch Rosita, to hold her, to kiss her."

Manny's smile grows even wider as he jokes, "I thought she wasn't the love of your life."

"I can't deny what I desire, Manuel," Gordon responds, grinning now.

"I'll see what I can do, Gordon," Manny says, winking. He grabs the photos on the table and returns them to his briefcase. Leaving the briefcase in its place on the floor, he rises from the table to open the door and summon the guards …

Rosita sits alone in the living room of the trailer a few hours later, a pervasive silence occasionally broken by some activity taking place outside. The phone rings in the kitchen, awakening her from her self-imposed daze. Rising from the sofa, she unhurriedly walks into the kitchen to lift the receiver from its wall mount. Flat and emotionless, she says into the receiver, "Hello?"

Through the other end, Manny's voice asks, "Rosita? It's Manny."

"Yes," Rosita says, guardedly, "Hi."

Manny's voice says, "We need to meet. I have some papers for Gordon and you."

"What papers?" Rosita asks.

The phone is silent for a moment until Manny's voice answers reluctantly, "I think Gordon should have a will made and I want to talk to you about it." There is a pause to let it register and his voice adds, "When can I come over?"

"Here?" Rosita asks.

"Yes," Manny's voice replies.

Angrily, Rosita insists, "You can't come here to my house. My husband's not home."

Sitting comfortably in the chair in his office, Manny suddenly looks down to his desk, realizing the mistake he has just made. He attempts to rescue the phone conversation by saying, "I'm sorry, I wasn't thinking about that. Let's meet in my office as soon as you can make it, please."

To Manny, Rosita's voice sounds resigned when she asks, "Are you giving up?"

"What?" Manny blurts, surprised, quickly adding, emphatically, "No."

Rosita's voice sounds confused and saddened as she asks, "Then why are you asking about a will for Gordon?"

Manny softly replies, "It's just a precaution, Rosita. Everyone should have a will. If the worst happens, at least we can keep it out of probate, keep the state out of it. Otherwise," he says, pausing for effect, "they could demand half of everything. I can't let that happen."

Rosita's voice sounds more reassured as she says, "All right. You're the one who's busy all the time so tell me when."

Manny's face displays relief as he says, "I'm in the office all afternoon. Please come by at your convenience."

"I pick up the kids from school at three fifteen," Rosita's voice says. "I can come to your office from there with the kids. Would that be a problem?"

"No," Manny assures her. "Bring those kids. We've got room."

"It'll be about four," Rosita's voice advises him.

"Good," Manny says. "It won't take long, I promise you."

"Goodbye," Rosita's voice says.

"Goodbye, Rosita," Manny says. He places the receiver back on the phone set on his desk.

Immediately, the speaker on the phone relays a female voice saying, "Manny, David Samuels called while you were on the phone and said he needs to talk to you."

Manny glances at the phone and asks, "Did he leave a number?"

The voice from the speaker says, "He said you could reach him on his cell phone. Do you have that number?"

Manny replies, "I have it programmed in the phone. Thank you, Jackie."

The voice from the speaker says, "You're welcome."

Manny lifts the receiver from the set and holds it to his right ear while he pushes three buttons on the set. The phone rings and when it's answered, a voice says from the other end, "Yes."

Manny says, "David? It's Manny."

David's voice is excited. "Manny, hold on a second and I'll pull over. I was on my way to your office and I've got some very interesting stuff to show you."

Manny shakes his head as he says, "Don't stop. Hang up and I'll wait for you."

David's voice says, "Okay." The phone goes silent.

Twenty minutes later David bursts open the door to Manny's office and announces confidently, "Manny, I've got just the connection we needed."

Displaying a look of seasoned skepticism, Manny stands up and walks around his desk as David steps to the front of it and places his case on the chair next to the desk. Manny demands, "Let's see it."

David pulls out several folders from his case and places them on the desk. He looks for the appropriate folder and opens it, saying, "First, Simon Edwards has known Gunther Rankin more than *half* of Rankin's life." He looks at Manny who looks back at him, puzzled. "I found this," David adds. He hands him a photocopy of a newspaper article titled "Big Brothers hosts annual baseball tournament" and a picture accompanying the story. Manny looks at it still puzzled. Gauging Manny's reaction, David says, "That's what I thought when I saw it, because the caption doesn't identify anyone in the picture, but I knew Edwards volunteered with Big Brothers Big Sisters for several years. You can't really make anyone out, so …" David's voice trails off and he lifts another picture, continuing, "I found the photographer, who still had the original negative. When I looked at his photos, I thought I saw something very interesting, so I bought his negative, had it developed and blown up. Here." He hands the next picture to Manny, showing an older man and a boy who looks about fourteen. David continues, "The older man is Simon Edwards with his arm around guess who?"

Manny looks up from the photo to David and guesses, "Gunther Rankin."

David replies convincingly, "Bingo." He looks down at the photo and adds, "Rankin has always looked younger than his real age, but he was sixteen in this photo and barely a month removed from juvenile detention."

Manny says, excitedly, "Great. That establishes their connection, and it's a long one."

David smiles as he says, "Oh, it gets better."

"I'm listening," Manny assures him.

David removes some hand-written papers clipped together and hands them to Manny as he explains, "Those are my notes from conversations with people who were at Good Samaritan Hospital when Edwards and Rankin were both there." He pauses to collect his thoughts. "First, Edwards personally recommended Rankin for the maintenance position that he eventually worked for three years. Second, Edwards' department, Human Resources, instituted the internal identification system requiring pictures of all employees. When picture day came around to the maintenance department, Rankin was absent. The maintenance supervisor at the time told me that Edwards, more than once, promised to take care of Rankin's missing picture but he obviously never did. Third, drugs, some quite expensive, were constantly missing while Rankin worked there. Several people suspected him but nothing could be proven. He was finally fired for 'conduct dangerous to fellow employees.' He got into a fight with one of his co-workers and beat the guy unconscious."

Manny shakes his head and asks, "How does a little guy like Rankin beat someone into unconsciousness?"

David smiles as he answers, "With a steel broom handle. It was bad enough that he was arrested and charged with assault and battery." David pauses for effect and adds, "Who do you think put up his bail?"

Manny asks in disbelief, "Edwards?"

David replies, "He explained it to some of the people there that Rankin was a victim of circumstances. To his credit, the charges were dismissed when the evidence suggested that Rankin was provoked and acted in self-defense. Still, everyone I talked with said Rankin was a person they avoided. One of them said that he always worried Rankin would go off any time."

Manny asks, "What about the murder charge?"

"The interesting thing about that," David says, "was the attorney who represented Rankin. He wasn't from the public defender's office, as you would expect. Instead, he was the personal attorney for Edwards."

"Did you find out how that came about?" Manny asks.

"Not definitively, no," David replies. "He invoked attorney-client privilege when I talked to him over the phone, but when I asked him how he could expect me to think that Gunther Rankin could afford his retainer when it was certainly more plausible that Edwards had paid it, he hung up."

"To be expected," Manny observes.

"He's the same attorney who drafted and sent the threatening letter to the insurance company, too," David adds.

"I know him," Manny comments. "You won't get anything from him. His reputation precedes him, whether deserved or not." Manny steps away from the table and around his desk to sit in his chair before he asks, "So, what have you found to tie these two together for the murder of Darcy Rowland?"

"Unfortunately, Manny, not much," David says with resignation. "There's no paper trail that I have found. I can't see phone records without a court-ordered subpoena. They were careful never to be seen together since the murder charge, and, when Rankin was recently arrested, the public defender's office served as counsel, not Edwards' attorney." David brightens as he adds, "I did discover some things that are suspicious. First, Edwards withdrew five thousand and then seven thousand a week later about a month before Rowland's murder. According to Edwards' accountant, this was an investment in a local company run by a friend that went sour shortly thereafter and Edwards lost the entire amount."

David pauses as he reaches for a set of papers and hands them to Manny. "Here's what doesn't add up: that money was never deposited into the investment's bank account. The friend says he immediately used it to pay off pending debts. One of the investment partners, less than satisfied at the outcome, claims that the friend pocketed two thousand of it but has no idea where the rest went. In the bankruptcy proceedings, Edwards is not listed as a creditor. Then, I found two people familiar with Rankin who claim that he came into a lot of money at the same time, and, best of all …" David pauses for effect.

Manny looks up from the papers he was glancing over and says, "You have my attention, David."

"A week before Rowland was murdered," David continues, "Rankin went to Atlantic City and dropped over five grand. You've got the photos and casino records right there to prove it."

"Thank you, David," Manny gushes, gratefully. "This will give us some ammunition with the state Supreme Court." David gathers the rest of the papers scattered on the table and places them on Manny's desk on the only open spot. Manny adds, "With just four weeks to Schell's execution date, I've got to get to work on this brief and file it as soon as possible …"

Manny writes on a yellow legal pad diligently and feverishly, stopping briefly to rub his forehead and think. A beep sounds from his phone and he presses a button on the phone and says, "Yes, Jackie."

A female voice from the phone set states, "Rosita Schell is here to see you, Manny."

Immediately, Manny advises, "Please, send her in." He rises from the chair and steps out from behind the desk. The door opens and Melanie steps in cautiously holding Melinda's hand. Mark follows her inside and Rosita steps into the office last, closing the door behind her as Manny steps around the children and approaches Rosita. Extending his right hand he says, "Ah, Mrs. Schell. Thank you for coming on such short notice." As he reaches her, Rosita limply extends her right hand and Manny grasps it and squeezes gently, releasing her hand immediately. He adds, "Please, take a seat." He scans the children and asks, "How are you three? Behaving?" All the children nod their heads but retain a look of displacement. Manny asks, "Would you like something to drink? We have water."

Rosita sits erect in her chair as she interrupts, "If you would bring them one bottle of water, that would be fine, Mr. Rodriguez."

Manny looks at Rosita and asks, "Nothing for you?"

"No, thank you," Rosita replies, dropping her gaze to the floor after she speaks.

Manny shuffles to the door and opens it, saying, "I'll be right back. Make yourselves comfortable, children, please." Quickly, he steps out the door, closing it behind him.

As Melinda saddles up to her mother and Rosita picks her up and deposits her on her lap, Melanie looks over to her mother and asks, "Why are we here, Mom?"

Softly, Rosita returns her daughter's gaze and says, "Mr. Rodriguez wants to ask me some questions about your father's property so he can create a will for him."

"What's a will?" Mark asks innocently.

Rosita grits her teeth before she answers. "A will is a set of instructions for how someone's property should be distributed to someone else."

"You mean Dad's things?" Mark asks.

"Yes," Rosita replies.

"But if it's Dad's, don't you own it, too, Mom?" Mark asks.

The door opens swiftly to interrupt the questioning and Manny steps back in, closes the door, twists the cap off the bottle of water and holds it out to Mark and Melanie. Melanie grasps the bottle and takes a sip as she looks at Manny, who hands her the cap. Melanie holds it with her left hand and shifts her gaze to the cap in her hand. Manny steps behind his desk, opens a drawer and retrieves a file folder, opening it and placing it flat on his desk. Melanie offers the water to Mark but he shakes his head so she replaces the cap on the bottle. Melinda sits quietly on her mother's lap and Rosita stares at Manny, stone faced.

Manny turns to face Rosita and asks, "Shall we get to the matter at hand?"

"Please," Rosita replies.

Placing a blank pad of paper before him and lifting a pen from his desk, Manny asks, "Does Gordon have any living close relatives? Brothers, sisters, parents, grandparents?"

"Just his mother," Rosita replies. "He never knew his father. His mother never told Gordon who his father was. His birth certificate says 'unknown' for father."

"All right," Manny says, scribbling on the pad. Without looking up, he asks, "Do you have any family heirlooms that she would want? Furniture, jewelry, or the like?"

"No," Rosita replies resolutely, "none of that."

Manny looks up and says, "I'll need her address. I'll have to send her a copy."

Rosita remains stone faced as she says, "I'll have to get it from home. I don't remember it." She pauses and her face displays a frown as she adds, "We were never close to her. Gordon wanted to find his father, but she wouldn't tell him his name. Then, he found me." She glances away from Manny and adds, "His mother never liked me and I never liked her."

Melinda looks up at her mother and asks, "Are you talking about Gramma?"

"Yes," Rosita replies softly, looking down at her daughter.

"Are we going to see her soon?" Melinda asks.

"Maybe," Rosita replies, painfully, and strokes her daughter's face.

"Does he or you have any items that someone else would want or lay claim to?" Manny asks, adding, "Something that he may be holding for this person?"

"No," Rosita replies simply, shaking her head slightly with a frown.

"All right, then," Manny declares, looking up from his pad, smiling, "that makes it simple. He leaves everything to you and the children."

A look of concern and disappointment crosses Rosita's face as she says, "I thought you were close to finding the killer, and you would stop this whole nightmare. Are you?"

Manny's face turns serious as he replies, "I'll be filing a brief with the state Supreme Court for a stay of execution next week, but I can't guarantee the result. I have to be prepared for anything."

Quietly, as she closes her eyes and her face saddens, Rosita asks, "What did we do to deserve this?" Melinda looks up, turns around and puts her arms around her mother's neck and squeezes. Rosita opens her eyes, wraps her arms around her daughter and hugs her tightly.

Manny's face tightens and he looks down at his pad. Without shifting his gaze, he asks, "I need to ask of you one more favor."

Rosita is peeved as she replies, "What?"

Drawing a breath, Manny looks up at Rosita and says, "Your husband asked me not to come back to see him, *unless* I bring the one person he really wants to see." Manny pauses to look at Rosita, narrows his eyes and nods once. "You," he says.

Angry and hurt, Rosita replies, "I can't go there anymore. I can't look at him through a glass wall, speak to him through a filthy phone."

Looking assured, Manny counters, "That's why I've been thinking about how we can do all of this, why I should draft a will and take it to him and get it signed by him and witnesses, and how I need … help." Manny looks hopefully at Rosita, and sees the cue he was searching for, as she suddenly sits up straight, the anger and hurt dissipating. Calmly, he states, "You won't be seeing him in the visitor's area. We can see him in the attorney's rooms, if you'll come with me."

Brightening, Rosita asks, "No glass wall?"

Manny smiles as he replies, "The rooms are open with a desk and chairs. You can touch him and he can touch you, if you want." He pauses for effect. "The problem is that he probably won't want to see me, so we have to convince him to see me."

"How?" Rosita asks, intrigued and suddenly cooperative.

"When we get to the prison, I'll tell them that I'm there to see Gordon," Manny says, "and they need to deliver this note to him when they tell him I'm there to see him." Manny looks at Rosita confidently, adding, "You're going to write the note, so that he sees it in your handwriting, for one ..."

"One?" Rosita asks, somewhat confused. "What else?"

"The note will read, 'Manuel Rodriguez to see Gordon Schell to take one final deposition along with his secretary, Rosita ...'" Manny says, adding, "but we can't use your married name."

A slight smile appears on Rosita's face as she recognizes Manny's ploy. She says, "Suarez. That's my maiden name. Gordon will know what's going on when he reads that."

"Good," Manny says, smiling. "You'll help me, then?"

Rosita turns serious, saying, "If you can get me in there so I can touch him, hold him, then I'll go."

"That's a given," Manny promises.

Destiny

The date is less than two weeks until Gordon Schell's scheduled execution, and Manuel Rodriguez stands before a long mirror with four sinks, a public restroom in a large motel in Raleigh, the capitol of North Carolina. His face appears tired as he stares at his reflection for several seconds and turns the water on, cups his hands under the stream and splashes the captured water on his face. Pulling out several paper towels from the dispenser above his sink, he dabs them over his face and stares at his reflection again, blankly, emotionless, drained.

Quickly pulling a comb from inside his suit jacket, he runs it through his hair from front to back and from right to left. When he returns the comb to its pocket, he twists his left hand to glance at his watch, turns the water off, gathers the paper towels, spins around to his left, steps forward and tosses the towels in a receptacle at the end of the sink to his right. He marches to the exit, but, reaching for the door, it suddenly opens toward him and a short, heavy man immediately stops, having startled both.

Manny jumps back and smiles briefly at the businessman, saying, "Excuse me."

The shorter man, a bit older in appearance than Manny, treads into the restroom slowly and flings the door open for Manny, joking, "Sorry. Didn't mean to scare you." The businessman smiles and moves to Manny's right, past the divider between the urinals and the sinks.

Manny flicks his right arm to push the door back and laughs, "You had me frozen with terror." Manny hears the businessman laugh out of sight as he turns to his left out of the restroom and marches past the elevator station on his left.

Clearing the elevators, he reaches a corridor where he turns right and marches fifty feet. The motel's restaurant is straight ahead, to his right is a sports bar, closed until dinnertime, but he turns left where double glass doors provide an exit to a parking lot. A moment later he passes a second set of double glass doors and is outside the motel, moving quickly to his car quite a distance away, certain that he will not be late for his next meeting.

In the motel's restaurant, a television mounted on a tray bolted to the wall displays the same slight female reporter who had covered the first meeting between Manny and the state Supreme Court justices. A slightly overweight white man, dressed in a smart, dark blue business suit, his short brown hair thinning on top, momentarily puts his right hand down on his table, still holding the fork, and stares at the television intently. The reporter can be heard saying, "Again, the latest attempt by Gordon Schell's defense team to win a stay or new trial has been dismissed this morning by the state's Supreme Court, which clears the way for Schell's execution late next week." The man shakes his head, lifting his fork to his plate. Glancing to his right, he spies the short businessman who nearly ran into Manny at the restroom. A colleague of the white man, the shorter one approaches his table and sits down across from him.

Settling into his chair, the shorter man turns to look at the television over his right shoulder and asks his colleague across the table, "I missed that. What did they say?"

The white man replies, "Schell's attorneys tried to have the Supreme Court issue a stay or order a new trial based on some new evidence that they supposedly uncovered. They say they have evidence that another man committed the murder."

An older black woman, sitting at the next table to the white man's right and dressed in casual tourist attire, has her neck craned to see the television. She turns her head even further to the white man and asks, "Isn't he the one who cut and tortured that poor young woman before he finally killed her?"

"That's the one," he confirms.

The woman proclaims loudly, "He's sick. They should fry him."

The shorter businessman glances to the woman and calmly states, "They don't fry people in North Carolina. They use lethal injection." He turns to his companion and asks, "Haven't they always contended that someone else committed the murder?"

"Yep," replies the white man, taking a sip from his coffee and setting it down. "At the sentencing, Schell refused to show remorse for a crime he says he didn't commit. Pretty arrogant about it, too."

A bit confused, the shorter businessman asks, "So, what was new?"

The white man thinks for a moment before replying. "Well, the defense showed that their suspect and the murder victim's ex-husband have a long history together." He pauses, glancing to the ceiling, adding, "Their suspect came into a lot of money just two weeks before the murder and blew about five grand in Atlantic City."

"Five grand?!" exclaims the shorter one. "If that was murder money, that wasn't too bright."

"Their suspect said it was cash he had saved over the years and felt like partying in Atlantic City," replies the other man. "They showed a picture of their suspect and Gordon Schell side by side, though, and, man, if those two aren't dead ringers."

The black woman at the next table has turned back to continue with her meal but lifts her head when she hears the white man's comments. With complete disdain for her subject, she announces, "Frying or injecting, it don't matter. Sick bastards like that don't deserve to live."

The two men glance at each other and each raises their eyebrows in reaction. The white man looks down at his plate and stabs a piece of sausage with his fork …

Having already delivered the news to Gordon earlier that day, the Big Man gazes through the window down the corridor of Death Row. Turning to his fellow guard behind the glass encasement between the observation room and the rest of the prison, the Big Man says, "Open the door, Jeff. I'm going to play a card game with Schell."

The muscular Anglo guard smiles wickedly as he shakes his head and asks, "What is that game you play with him? Cribbage is it?"

"Yeah," the Big Man says.

"You ain't won yet, have you?" Jeff asks as the door buzzes open.

"Nope," is the Big Man's simple reply, stepping into the corridor. After walking about fifty feet, the Big Man stops before Gordon's cell as Gordon sits propped up in his bed against his upright pillow, legs crossed yoga fashion, reading a book. The Big Man smiles as he says, "I'm here for my punishment."

Gordon looks up from the book, smiles and asks, "Your cribbage whippin'?"

"You could call it that," the Big Man says, adding, "but this could be the time I take you."

Gordon sets a piece of paper in the book for a placeholder, rises from the bed and steps to the shelf, placing the book on the shelf. He removes the cribbage board and the deck of cards, turns to the Big Man, and says, "True." He swings the chair under the shelf to the middle of the cell before the cell bars and places the board and cards on the chair. As he sits down cross legged on the floor next to the chair and the Big Man steps away to retrieve his chair, Gordon says loudly, "Then again, I could whip you worse than ever in this game."

The Big Man returns and sits down in his chair before the cribbage board, the cell bars separating the two players. "Nope," the Big Man dismisses Gordon's claim. "That was when I didn't know what I was doing." He smiles as he looks at Gordon confidently, adding, "I do now."

"You are improving, no doubt about it," Gordon says. "You deal."

The Big Man reaches through the bars for the cards, pulls them through and shuffles them on his leg. He puts them through the bars and alternately places six cards each in two piles, sets the cards face down on the board and reaches for the pile closest to him.

After each plays the hand dealt, the board now shows two pegs only a few holes from the start of the board, a third closer to the start but its pair near the first corner. The Big Man places the four cards he's holding face up and announces, "A run of three and fifteen two for five." He moves the peg closest to the start past the first corner, smiles broadly and teases, "How do you like that, Skinny?"

Gordon smiles back as he says, "That was a very good hand. Puts you more than a quarter of the way to victory." His smile thins and his eyes narrow as he adds, "Hope you don't fizzle out altogether."

After several more turns, the Big Man's right hand moves his rear peg beyond his forward peg only three holes from the end. The forward peg of the other pair is four sections of five each from the end. The Big Man observes, "Well, I almost got there. I can get you in the next hand."

"First, let's see if a 'next hand' is in the cards," Gordon says, placing the cards in his hand face up on the chair. "Two pair for four and fifteen twelve for sixteen." The Big Man's face sours as Gordon moves his rear peg sixteen holes ahead. Gordon turns over the discard hand, looks it over as the Big Man realizes the result and shakes his head. Gordon announces, "That's a run of three and a pair for five. Gotcha." He moves his rear peg past the end line and sets it in the hole beyond it. He looks at the Big Man comfortingly and adds, "You're gonna get me pretty soon, I just know it."

The Big Man still shakes his head as he replies, "Maybe, but I sure wanted it to be this game." Still shaking his head, the Big Man rises from his chair to push it slowly back to his room and back to his normal job, watching over Death Row …

The following week, Manny and Rosita walk down a corridor in the prison, escorted by a guard in front and behind. Manny is wearing his usual sharp business attire, but Rosita wears an attractive print dress that falls to her knees and a matching buttoned shawl over her chest. She carries a large satchel while Manny carries his usual briefcase. As they walk toward the attorneys' meeting room, Manny turns to Rosita and says, "We have a meeting scheduled with the governor's office in two days and we think we can still get a stay."

Rosita frowns and disappointingly remarks, "His execution is at midnight after that day. Aren't you cutting it too close, Mr. Rodriguez?"

"Why won't you call me Manny?" Manny asks, ignoring her question.

Rosita shoots him a scathing look as she reiterates, "Aren't you?"

Manny appears contrite as he drops his head and replies, "The governor won't see us until that day."

Rosita glances away as she softly says, "That's his last chance." She looks back at Manny as she adds, "Please tell me you have something that will convince them to stop this."

Manny tries to reassure her as he says, "We have some additional evidence concerning Rankin that we didn't have when we went to the Supreme Court. The court, also, deferred the stay to the governor. They wanted us to go there for a stay." Manny pauses to gaze seriously at Rosita, adding, "I think the governor will listen. We have compelling evidence that the real killer is not Gordon and the mood all over the country is to be absolutely certain that a guilty man is executed." He shakes his head as he adds, "The governor will not want to let an innocent man be executed if he can stop it."

For months Gordon has let his hair grow unrestrained, to the point where it now appears strikingly similar to the suspect's hair. Even in the shared lavatory with the other inmates, the resemblance never occurs to Gordon whenever he stares into the mirror and sees the head of the fellow staring back at him. It seems quite natural to him so the irony never registers. Now, he sits propped against his pillow on the bed reading as two guards appear at his cell and one announces, "Schell. Your attorney is here to see you. Let's go." The other guard, a tall, well-built black man with a shaved head and face, carries the chains.

Gordon looks up but makes no movement as he calmly replies, "I don't have any business with my attorney."

The first guard, a stocky white man of average height and short brown hair parted to his left, replies, "He said to give you this note." He dangles the note through the bars.

Gordon rises from the bed, still holding the book in his left hand, with a finger stuck between the pages marking his place. He steps to the bars and takes the note with his right hand and flips it open. The handwritten note reads, "Manuel Rodriguez to see Gordon Schell to take one final deposition along with his secretairy, Rosita Suarez." Gordon gives the note back to the guard, grabs the placeholder and sticks it in the book. He turns and sets the book on the shelf, saying, "Okay. Let's go."

The first guard looks back down the corridor and spins his outstretched index finger. Immediately, the door of Gordon's cell opens and the guards motion for Gordon to step into the corridor so they can put on the chains.

Manny and Rosita sit at a table in a small room opposite the one door leading into the room. Two empty chairs are placed on the opposite side. Manny has papers spread before him and Rosita looks officious with a pen in one hand poised over a pad of paper as the door opens and the two guards lead Gordon into the room. They sit him down in one of the chairs across from them. Manny addresses the guards, "Gentlemen. I have a will for Mr. Schell to sign but I need three witnesses. Could you, perhaps, find another of your fellow guards and sign as witnesses, please? I would be most grateful."

The stocky, smaller guard turns to his taller colleague and suggests, "Go down the hall and see if Bernie can spare a few minutes to come down to the meeting room."

The taller black guard replies, "Sure." He turns to Manny and Rosita and assures them, "It'll be just a few minutes."

Manny replies, "Excellent. Thank you very much."

Five minutes later, the taller guard returns with Bernie, a tall, pockmarked man, with short black hair and rippling muscles, trailing behind. Middle-aged and officious, Bernie asks, "You need a witness signature for a will for one of the prisoners?" Gordon turns around and Bernie and Gordon nod to each other as Bernie adds, "I thought it would be you, Schell."

"Yeah," Gordon replies, sitting quietly in his chair seemingly oblivious to the chains still hooked to his arms and legs, "I got a big day comin' up."

Manny displays a document stapled together and says, "I've prepared Mr. Schell's will. I need his signature and then I need each of you to sign on one of the lines reading 'Witness.'" Manny flips the document to the last page and hands it to Rosita. Rosita stands up from the table, placing the document on the pad and steps around the table. Once she's before Gordon, she squats down to hold the document steady and puts her pen in Gordon's chained right hand.

Gordon moves the pen over the page. Smiling at Rosita, he hands the pen back to her, and says, "So good to meet you, Ms. Suarez." Rosita smiles innocently as she stands up and he adds, "Would that ring on your left hand mean that you're married?"

As she places the pad and document on the table, Rosita replies, "Very happily married." She motions to the shorter guard and he steps to the table and takes the pen that she offers. As she points to the document for the guard to sign and he bends down, she adds, "I love my husband very much."

Manny says to the guard as he stands, "Please write your name under your signature, too. Thank you."

The shorter guard bends down and writes on the document as Gordon says, "Your husband must be a lucky man, Ms. Suarez." He turns to Bernie and adds, "What do you think, Bernie?"

The taller guard moves to the table and Bernie replies, "I don't think about those things. I've got enough dealing with you guys every day."

Gordon responds, "You haven't had to deal with me much, have you?"

The taller guard stands erect, sets the pen down on the document, and moves out of the way as Bernie steps to the table. As he writes on the document, Bernie says, "No, Schell, I haven't. In fact, if there was such a thing as a model prisoner, and there isn't, you could be one."

Gordon smiles as he says, "I should get an extra helping of dessert for that, shouldn't I?"

Bernie sets the pen down and stands erect, turning to face Gordon, smiling. He says, "Speaking for all of us, you just don't belong here, Schell. You're not the type." Bernie moves toward the door, but places his right hand on Gordon's shoulder briefly. As he steps to the door and opens it, he turns back to Gordon and says, "I don't know what happened, but what they're going to do to you in two days just don't seem right." He shakes his head once and exits through the door, followed by the other two guards who close the door behind them. Manny scoops up the signed document and places it in his open briefcase.

Gordon and Rosita turn to gaze at each other smiling and Rosita says, "Mr. Rodriguez, please watch the door for us."

"I always liked that dress," Gordon says.

"Of course," Manny replies as he walks around the table toward the door. As he moves past them, Rosita pulls up her dress to the top of her thighs, slips her hands up to her panties and pulls them down. When Manny sees that, he turns his head away quickly and warns, "I don't think that's a good idea."

"You and I may have had ideas about this meeting, Manuel," Gordon says as he watches Rosita lift first her right leg and slide her panties past her leg and shoe and then the left, "but I see my wife has made other plans." Wearing a half-smile, his eyes wide, he slowly lifts his gaze over her body, stops to watch her unbutton and remove the shawl to expose a considerable extent of her sizable breasts, the rest barely hidden under her low-cut top, and smiles widely when his eyes meet hers.

Rosita steps to Gordon's right and slides her right hand over his crotch, rubbing it hard to induce his erection. Manny stands at the door, taking quick glances through the window and hiding his head out of sight. He says softly, "We could get in a lot of trouble."

Rosita lifts her gaze from Gordon's crotch to his face, smiles, and says, "Feels like you're ready."

"Oh, yeah," Gordon says, smiling, "we've reached maximum hardness." Rosita feels for his zipper, pulls it down, reaches into his jumpsuit as he shifts his weight on the chair and pulls out his erection. Gordon folds his chained hands open as Rosita lifts her dress slightly, swings her right leg over his legs, and settles on his folded hands and legs. Gordon's smile disappears briefly as he says, "You spelled 'secretary' wrong."

Rosita smiles as she places her right index finger over his mouth and softly says, "Shh." With her left hand under her dress, she moves and lifts her hips, stopping for a moment. Slowly, she raises and lowers her hips rhythmically, closing her eyes, her face tightening.

Gordon feels his wife's vagina envelope his erect penis, closes his eyes briefly, opens them, smiles deviously, and says, "You got me in chains and there's an unwitting voyeur in the room." Looking at her closed eyes, he pauses for effect, and adds, "Is this a new fantasy for you?"

Rosita opens her eyes, frowns, and admonishes, "Be quiet. We don't have much time." Constantly raising and lowering her hips over him, she leans forward to whisper in his ear, "You always tell it to me. Now it's my turn." She pulls her head back from his and, as they gaze in each others' eyes, she whispers, "Cum for me." Gordon closes his eyes and begins to actively push his hips up and down in perfect synchonization to her movements. He leans forward as she leans back and buries his face between her breasts and kisses each breast separately, lifting his head to look in her eyes. Both moan in growing anticipation.

Manny listens to their efforts helplessly and raises his gaze to the ceiling, shakes his head, quickly peeks through the window, and retreats behind the door. He mumbles to himself, "What's the worst that can happen to you, Manuel?"

Consciously avoiding looking behind him, he gazes to the ceiling, and continues, "Let's see. You could be forbidden never to enter this prison again, which isn't so bad. You could be called before the ethics board for conduct unbecoming of an attorney and sanctioned for a year." He pauses for a moment as the moans grow louder and he rubs his face. "You could be dismissed from your lucrative and prestigious position with the firm, with no hope of any reference, escorted to the door in abject humiliation." He sneaks a peek out the window, and ducks his head behind the door to stare into the corner next to the door. "Nope. Disbarment from practicing law in the state of North Carolina. That would be the worst." He peaks through the window again and retreats. The groans from Gordon, the moans from Rosita, become noticeably louder and Manny continues, "Disbarment from the state of North Carolina for aiding the sexual intercourse between a prisoner and his wife. That'll look good on my resume."

Gordon lets out a loud, "Ahhh!" His hips push up hard and drop. Rosita responds with an encouraging, "Yes." Seconds later, Gordon repeats, and Rosita says, "Yes, my love. Give it to me, all of it." After a few more thrusts and "ahhs", Gordon slumps in his chair, tilts his head back, and he exhales loudly, spent. Rosita pulls his head forward and kisses him passionately.

Manny peeks through the window, retreats, and asks, "Are you kids about done?"

Rosita rises from Gordon's lap and swings her right leg over his legs to stand up. She walks behind the table, says, "Almost," and removes a washcloth from her satchel. She turns away from both men to wipe herself, turns around and walks back to Gordon and hands him the cloth. While Gordon wipes his member, she returns to her satchel, removes a tampon, turns away from the men and sets it in place.

Resting the cloth on his leg, Gordon pushes up his zipper, and Rosita retrieves her panties from the floor, slipping them over her right foot, her left, and pulling them quickly over her hips under her dress. She takes the cloth from Gordon's leg, returns to her satchel and sets it inside. Gordon turns to Manny and asks, "In law school, did you think you'd make a good lookout?"

Manny turns around slowly, not amused, and asks, "Are you about through?"

"Yes," Gordon says.

"Good," Manny says, walking back to the table, glancing at Gordon but avoiding a look in Rosita's direction. "As for law school, they could never design a course for something like this."

"Well, they could," Gordon replies, "but it would never be accredited."

"Very funny," Manny says sarcastically, sitting down in the chair behind the table, rubbing his forehead. Rosita walks to the side of the table where Gordon sits, picks up her shawl from the table, throws it over her shoulders and begins buttoning it from the bottom up. Manny turns to look at Gordon and says, "Tell me, Gordon. How can you be so nonchalant about your situation? Pardon me for being blunt, but you *are* facing death."

Gordon and Rosita catch each other's gaze, and Gordon motions for her to sit on his lap, which she does, sitting from his right side. Gordon replies, "That's out of my control, Manuel. What's still within my control is who I am. This is who I am, what I am. Nobody can take that away from me, unless I let them."

Rosita lifts her right hand to stroke Gordon's face, and he momentarily closes his eyes. She asks softly, "Don't you want to live?"

Gordon opens his eyes to look into her eyes as he replies, "With you and our children, yes. And that's what hurts me the most, that I have *no* life with you and our children."

Softly and slowly, she says, "It's possible that you could stop it."

"Life in prison is not an option," Gordon insists, "and we've had this discussion before. That would be worse than death for me, since I still could not live with you and our children." Animated now, he shakes his head demonstratively, his eyes slits of anger, as he continues, "Feeling constant pain and anguish with the occasional visit behind a glass partition? No! Fuck that!"

Manny says, "There's still hope. We meet with the governor and his staff the day after tomorrow." Gordon looks over at Manny and Rosita turns her head to face him, too. Manny continues, "He could grant a stay or even commute your sentence, so it's not over, yet."

Gordon looks away from Manny and his countenance becomes contemplative and emotionless. He says softly, "That's all fine, Manuel, but maybe there's a reason why this is all happening the way it is." Gordon pauses and looks directly at Manny, adding, "Maybe, I know something you don't, or maybe I'm just delusional and I don't really know anything." Gordon looks away again and drops his head as he says, "Except, I do know this. No one is guaranteed tomorrow. No one."

Rosita rests her left hand gently on Gordon's right cheek, pushing and lifting his head so that he looks directly at her as she says, "Gordon, please, no more." She waits while he drops his gaze down away from her eyes, adding, "Melinda misses you so. She misses 'Daddy's thing', so I have to do it with her, but I've always wondered why you did that with the kids."

"You want to know what 'the nose knows all' means, don't you?" asks Gordon, looking up at Rosita, smiling.

"Yes," Rosita replies.

"Smell used to be the most important sense for humans," Gordon explains. "Now, it's sight and hearing, but smell is still very powerful. Tell me you haven't been so overpowered by the smell of the kids' vomit that you didn't have to run to the toilet and throw up yourself."

Rosita produces a weak smile as she stares at the wall, remembering exactly what her husband is saying. "You cleaned up some, too, but you never threw up yourself."

"Cleaned up after you, too," he says, "and felt it stirring in my stomach a few times, but I just concentrated on getting the job done." He pauses and looks at his wife. "So, smell is still powerful, would you agree?"

"Yes," she agrees.

"We smell things all the time, some that register and some that don't," Gordon continues, "and we still smell fear, because fear has a distinctive, uncontrollable smell. Usually, it doesn't register, but we smell it anyway. We know it's there and fear does serve a useful purpose." He looks over at Manny as he asks, "Do you know what useful purpose fear would serve, Manuel?"

Manny has been listening with his head down, but lifts it to look at Gordon and reply, "I suppose it would serve to keep us out of harm's way, to help protect us."

"Unless it's irrational and unjustified," Gordon replies, "as in fear of all strangers."

"Children should fear strangers," Rosita insists.

"Children should be protected by adults," Gordon continues, "and not be left unsupervised for long periods, but many of us have to make a living now, don't we? And, we bear the fruits of that today, don't we, with so many having to make a living, leaving their children unsupervised?"

"What's your point?" Manny asks, having heard this before from others and a little peeved.

"My point's not with the children, Manuel, it's with adults," Gordon explains. "The mutual fear of strangers from adults that's irrational, unjustified, and serves to keep us apart, divided, separated. It's fear that keeps us from trusting, because when you fear someone, you cannot trust them. When you trust someone, you have no fear of them. Fear is the inverse of trust."

"Most people are not trustworthy," Manny counters.

"You can believe that, Manuel, but in my experience, that's a crock of shit," Gordon explains, a bit angry. "Most people try to be good, try to do the right thing, as a matter of course. When they're confronted by someone lacking fear, they manage to overcome their own fear, mutual trust is achieved, and then, unbelievable, incomprehensible things occur." Gordon pauses and looks severely at Manny and adds, "Because I've seen it happen."

Manny shakes his head, unconvinced, and Rosita looks straight ahead with a somewhat glazed look in her eyes. Manny says, "I don't understand why you're telling us all this, Gordon."

Gordon turns back to look at Rosita's face and says, "What I'm trying to do, clumsily at best, is apologize to my wife." Rosita snaps from her daze and turns to stare at her husband, her eyes searching his entire face. "I have never trusted her completely, I've been afraid to confide in her, and I've lied to her, and all of it's the reason I'm here today." He pauses a moment to lock his eyes on hers. "And, I know it's going to be the end of me soon."

"No! No, it's not," Rosita pleads, shaking her head. "Don't say that."

Still looking in her eyes, Gordon laments, "It's true, Rosita. While you grew, you learned, you got better, I didn't. I never changed from the day we first met, always thinking I was protecting you, while you had already grown past that." He drops his head and Rosita slips her arms around his waist and leans her head against his chest. "I denied meeting that woman to the company, to you, and even to the police, and I'm going to pay for it."

She squeezes him and softly says, "Stop."

"Once, you believed in me, and I know I don't deserve it, now" Gordon says, slowly, trying to keep from choking on the words. Tears form in his eyes and slowly run down his face. "I'll have another chance and I'll do everything I can to come back to you, to be back for you, but only if you believe in me, again."

Without lifting her head she says, "You're not making sense. You're not going anywhere. You're not leaving me."

Gordon pleads, "*I* believe in you. *I* believe that you can take care of you and the children, that you can and will do everything necessary to do that, without me to help. *I* will look after you and be back for you as soon as I can, but only if you believe in me." He cranes his neck to look at her head still buried against his chest. "If you won't believe in me, I'll do *nothing* for you."

Lifting her head from his chest and seeing the tears running down his face, Rosita admonishes, "Stop this talk now! Don't you know I love you, that I will always love you?"

"This may be the last time, Rosita," Gordon insists. "You need to tell me you believe in me. I have to hear it from your lips. I have to *know*."

Manny sees a movement through the window in the door. A guard is looking through the window and immediately reaches for the handle as Manny says, "Busted."

Two guards immediately enter the room and Rosita stands up from Gordon's lap and cries out, "No! Stop!" Bernie is the second in the room and he shouts to all of them, "That's the end of this deposition. I'm sure the warden will want to have a word with you, Counselor." The two guards each grab one of Gordon's arms and yank him out and over the chair, which tumbles to the floor.

As they swing him around to carry him out of the room, Gordon shouts, "You need to tell me."

Bernie places his hand over Gordon's mouth and shouts, "That's enough, Schell. Keep it up and you'll be hurting."

Hysterical, Rosita continues shouting, "No!" As the guards drag Gordon into the corridor a few feet, she suddenly shouts, "Gordon, I believe in you! Do you hear me? I believe in you!" Gordon tries to twist around, but the grips of the guards carry him down the hall straight and away. Rosita bends down to set the chair upright, tears running down her face. She slumps into the chair and sighs, "I believe in you …"

Gordon sits unmoving on the edge of his bed in his cell. It is late that evening, nearing time when the guards will turn off all the lights on Death Row. He hears a voice across the corridor ask, "Did you whip the Big Man again, Gordon?"

"Yep," Gordon replies, "but he keeps making a game of it more and more."

"Think you'll go undefeated?" asks the same voice.

"Don't know, Johnny," replies Gordon. "I'll just have to wait and see."

"I'm pullin' for ya," says the voice.

It's quiet for a few moments, and there is no other sound to be heard on Death Row. Suddenly, Gordon begins singing the second verse and chorus of *Don't Do It*, more like The Band's version but with a single change of one word, omitting *girl*. When he finishes, it's eerily quiet, again.

From across the corridor, the voice says, "I didn't know you could sing, Gordon. That was good." Gordon looks down at the floor and makes no acknowledgement. A moment later, the voice says, "They're gonna be letting you go pretty soon. Do you know where you'll go from here?"

"I think so," Gordon replies. "I've thought about it a lot."

"When it's my turn, I'm going to hell. I know that."

Gordon looks up and out to the corridor. "I'll see you there, then," he says, calmly.

The voice laughs in disbelief. "I don't think so, amigo. You haven't done anything, not like the things I've done."

"This is hell, Johnny," Gordon insists, "A proving ground, so to speak."

"Nah," the voice disagrees. "It's just this one time around, my friend, so you better get it right. I didn't and I'm gonna pay for it."

Gordon shakes his head and says, "See, I don't believe that, Johnny. I don't believe that anyone can get it right the first time. We keep coming back, fixing our previous errors, until we finally get it right."

"You don't seriously believe that, do you?" the voice asks, incredulously. "There's just this one life, Gordon. That's it."

"And that's your belief, Johnny," Gordon answers. "That's what it comes down to. What do you believe? Because no one knows. No one!"

A guard shouts down the corridor, "Quiet for lights out." A few seconds later the lights on Death Row go dark and all is quiet again.

A Reversal of Fortune

The following day, the cribbage board sits on the chair in Gordon's cell with competing lead pegs just eight holes from the end of the game. The Big Man, sitting in his chair outside the cell, looks worried. Gordon's face appears blank, expressionless. He lays down the cards he holds onto the chair, sitting on the floor cross legged as always, and says, "A run of four and fifteen two for six." He moves one of the back pegs six holes beyond one of the lead pegs, two short of victory. "You're up, Big Man," he says.

The Big Man looks at the cards on the table first, confirming that an ace, two, three, four and the seven sitting atop the deck equate to six points. He lays the cards in his hand onto the chair through the cell bars, showing a ten, queen, king and five, and says, "Fifteen six for six." He moves his back peg six holes beyond his lead peg to a tie with Gordon. Reaching for the discard pile, he turns them over to show an ace, ten and a pair of sixes. The Big Man smiles as he says, "A pair of two for two." Triumphantly, he moves the back peg beyond the finish line and declares, "I finally got you. That's game!"

Gordon extends his right hand through the bars, smiling warmly, and the Big Man engulfs it with his own as Gordon says, "You did good. I told you you'd beat me one of these days." Gordon smiles even more widely as the Big Man beams back at him.

"You were right," the Big Man observes, "but it sure took long enough."

Gordon stands up from the floor and begins to put everything away. He says, "Nothing worthwhile comes easy or quickly. It takes time and practice."

The Big Man sits back in his chair watching Gordon clean up and agrees, "True." After a moment, he asks, "Do you want to play again tomorrow, same time?"

Gordon stops and turns to the Big Man and says, "No. I'm not going to be in a game-playing mood tomorrow."

The Big Man suddenly stops gloating on his first victory as the significance sets in. A look of concern crosses his face as he protests, "You should at least beat me one more time." He pauses for a moment and adds, "That would make me feel better."

Gordon places the board on the shelf, turns and places the chair back against the wall, and replies, "Somehow, Big Man, it's fitting that it should end this way." He looks up at the ceiling and nods his head as he adds, "I like it."

The Big Man stands up from his chair. He waits for Gordon to look at him and when he does, the Big Man's face is sorrowful as he softly says, "Tomorrow, they're gonna do something that hasn't happened here in a long, long time." He drops his head as he continues, "All of us that work on this floor were thinking about what we should do, so we decided we should grant you a privilege for the afternoon."

"Such as?" asks Gordon, a bit mischievously.

The Big Man looks up at Gordon and replies, "We could bring a TV in and you could watch whatever you want, even pornos."

"None uh that, thanks," Gordon declares, shaking his head.

"Or let you stay out in the yard longer," continues the Big Man, adding, "or let you play music, or something we can provide that you would want."

Gordon brightens as he says, "Music. One song in particular."

"What's that?" asks the Big Man.

"I wanna hear *Midnight Blue*," Gordon says.

"Never heard of it," the Big Man comments.

"*Midnight Blue* by Lou Gramm," Gordon says. "He used to be in Foreigner, but that's from his solo album. That's what I want to hear. If you could get that, I would appreciate it."

The Big Man nods his head as he says, "I've got the boom box, so I'll see what I can do."

"Thanks," Gordon says as he watches the Big Man scoot his chair down the corridor and out of sight …

In the evening, just before the lights out call, Death Row is quiet. The single window at the end of the corridor is black, without even the hint of moonlight, but, like the night before, Gordon breaks the silence to emote a song from his past in a low, haunting tone. The third verse and chorus of *Blue Ridge Mountain Skies* carries throughout the Death Row corridor and no other sound can be heard. Even the guards at the other end of the corridor listen intently.

When he finishes and silence permeates the big room, the voice of Johnny Morales cracks the peace. "Damn, Gordon, why the singing now?"

"Just feel like it, Johnny," says Gordon. "I just feel like it."

"Well, you carry a tune pretty good," the voice responds. "Sure would have liked to hear more."

There's a hush for a moment until Gordon says, "I've got a deck of cards that I won't have any use for soon. Want 'em?"

"Yeah, I'll take 'em," Johnny replies, "but don't be so sure that you won't need 'em. The guv's granted stays before. Happens a lot, my friend."

"Let's just say, I know it's in the cards," Gordon says. Immediately, a deck of cards shoots out from between the cell bars six down from the guard station on the right, slide across the floor and between the bars into the cell opposite.

"Thanks," the voice says.

"See you in the morning," Gordon promises.

The guard watching the activity or lack of it on Death Row doesn't even bother to shout the words required as stated in the book for "lights out." He can't recognize the need for it on this night. He flips the switch in the station and the big room goes dark.

Passing

The following morning, the Big Man sits at his kitchen table, holding a cordless phone in his left hand and punching the buttons to dial a number with his right. He holds the phone against the right side of his head and listens to the phone ring twice. He hears the phone on the other end go off hook and a man's voice say, "Yeah."

"Jeff, this is Clarence," the Big Man says into the phone. "I need your help."

"Shoot," comes the answer through the phone.

The Big Man explains, "I need to find a recording of a song—CD or tape—for a friend."

"What's the name?"

"*Midnight Blue*," the Big Man replies.

"Hmmm," the Big Man hears through the phone. "Is that a rock tune?"

"I think so," the Big Man answers. "I heard Foreigner."

"I'm not much on rock, but I know who is," comes the reply. "I'll try Charlie."

"Thanks, Jeff," the Big Man says, appreciatively.

"No problem."

Jeff, the tall, muscular guard who works at the prison with the Big Man, paces in a modest living room wearing gym shorts and white T-shirt. He presses the "talk" button on his phone, waits a moment, and punches some numbers. Still pacing, he holds the handset to his head with his left hand to hear the phone ring once and a voice answer, "Hello?"

"It's Jeff, Charlie," Jeff says. "Got a rock question for you."

The voice on the other end mockingly says, "You're not listening to rock 'n' roll now, are you? You know that'll subvert you, your family and your friends and send you all spiraling downwards, doncha?"

"Funny," Jeff replies, not amused. He pauses a moment and adds, "Ever hear of a song *Midnight Blue* by Foreigner?"

"It's not by Foreigner," corrects the voice. "I know that, for sure. I remember that song, though. That was quite a while ago. It could have been from one of the guys from Foreigner in a solo release."

"Have you got the recording?" Jeff asks. "A friend needs it."

"I don't," says the voice, and Jeff's face displays disappointment. "That was when I wasn't buying much music—didn't have the money—sometime in the late eighties, early nineties."

"Do you know anybody who might have it?" Jeff asks, desperation in his tone. "It's kind of an emergency."

"More than one," replies the voice, "but I'll try Tommy, first. Gimme a few, ok?"

"Sure," Jeff says and the phone goes dead.

Charlie, a tall, skinny man with medium length brown hair, punches some numbers on his cordless phone as he sits in a lazy chair in his den. He listens to it ring several times against his right ear. Finally, the phone connects with another phone and a voice on the other end answers, "It's me. Who are you?"

"Scorpion?" Charlie says, "It's Lunatic."

A chuckle comes from the phone and the voice says, "Say Loonie-bin, 'sup?"

Charlie, the mid-thirties rocker, smiles as he says, "Got a favor to ask. Need to take you down memory highway."

The voice good-naturedly says, "As long as we ain't stoppin' to re-visit my accidents."

Charlie laughs and says, "Nah, I think this one's just a passenger evacuation."

"One of the many," the voice interjects.

"One of your exes, if I remember correctly," Charlie continues, "used to love that song *Midnight Blue*. Remember that? Who was that?"

"Hell, I used to like that song, too," says the voice, "but I always liked the cherry red part."

"Cherry Red, that's right," says Charlie, excitedly. "That was Cindy."

"You got it!" says the voice. "Cherry Red."

"Boy, her face used to turn beet red when you called her that," Charlie comments.

"Had to," confirms the voice. "That was one of her favorite songs. I couldn't resist." There's a pause in the conversation and the voice adds, "It's amazing we're still on speaking terms, as long as I don't call her Cherry Red."

"Think she's got that recording still?" Charlie asks.

"No doubt, Loon," the voice says. "After I stepped on it one night and shattered her copy, I had to get her another one, and then she lost that one and bought still another one."

"Can you call her and see if we can borrow it?" Charlie asks. "A friend needs it just for a short time."

"If I can get ahold of her, yeah," says the voice, "if she's in town. The guy she's hangin' with now likes to travel around, so they could be gone for days."

"Whatever you could do would help, Scorp," says Charlie, "but don't put yourself out. I've got some other possibilities, too. Just let me know if you can as soon as possible."

"I'll call her right now, dude," says the voice and hangs up …

An hour later the phone rings on the Big Man's kitchen table. He anxiously steps into the kitchen, lifts the phone, presses the "talk" button and says, "Hello?"

"I'll have the CD with that song *Midnight Blue* at work," says the voice of Jeff. "I'll see you then."

"Great, Jeff," replies the Big Man, relieved. "I really appreciate it."

"My pleasure, Clarence," Jeff's voice acknowledges. "This wouldn't be for the condemned one, would it?"

"Yes, it is."

"That's what he wanted, huh?" Jeff's voice asks with some disbelief, "of all the things?"

"He just wanted to hear *Midnight Blue*," the Big Man says. "That was all he wanted."

"I'm glad I could help," Jeff's voice assures the Big Man. "I wouldn't want to ruin his last request." A momentary pause ensues until the Big Man hears the other end go dead …

That afternoon the Big Man appears outside Gordon's cell, holding a boom box and a CD jewel case. He says, "I got somethin' for ya, Gordon." He nods down the corridor and the cell door is unlocked and opens. Once the door has opened fully, he steps inside as Gordon sets his book down and rises from the bed.

"You actually found it?" Gordon asks, a mild surprise on his face. The Big Man smiles broadly as he hands Gordon the CD case.

"It took a little passing from one friend to the next," the Big Man explains, "but one friend managed to borrow this one from his ex-girlfriend."

"And so it goes," Gordon says and smiles as he looks up at the Big Man towering over him. He glances at the front of the CD case, flips it over and sees a name written on the back paper, "Cindy Benson." He comments, "Huh, I worked with a girl named Cindy Benson quite a while ago. She used to love this song."

"Really?" the Big Man asks. "How long ago was that?"

"That was more than five years ago, out at the university," Gordon says, reflecting. "When she would get rattled and I'd run into her, I'd say, 'Life is simple. It's either cherry red or midnight blue.' And that would always make her smile." Gordon steps to the bed and tosses the CD case on it. The Big Man steps behind him and sets the boom box on the bed, too. Gordon spins quickly and looks at the Big Man as a thought occurs to him and he says, "I just remembered that her boyfriend, when he'd tease her, would call her 'Cherry Red' and she'd blush pretty heavily." He laughs at the thought and the Big Man smiles. Gordon asks, "When do you want this back?"

"You can play it until ten," the Big Man replies.

"That's too long," Gordon says, shaking his head. "Everyone will go crazy if I play one song until ten. I'll just start it at nine and play it for an hour. I think that's about the limit of everyone's endurance."

"Suit yourself," says the Big Man as he steps out of the cell. "I'll be back for it at ten." He twirls his right index finger as he glances down the corridor, and the cell door closes as he begins to stroll back to his station.

"Thanks, Big Man," Gordon says and the Big Man stops and turns around. "I appreciate it."

The Big Man drops his head to look down at the floor as he says, "I wish I could do more." He looks up at Gordon and the two stare quietly at each other and Gordon nods his head knowingly …

In the evening, Gordon sits cross-legged on his bed, his back pressed against the pillow propped against the wall. The Big Man's boom box sets on the chair across the cell, blaring music from the CD that spins on top. A thick magazine rests in his lap, while atop that are several sheets of blank paper, as Gordon holds a pen in his right hand and moves across the top sheet. Occasionally, he closes his eyes, rests his hand on the sheet, and bobs his head in a distinct rhythm.

He finishes with one sheet, looks it over, and sets it to one side. He begins writing on the next sheet, pausing to think, or close his eyes to listen to the music for a few minutes. He writes a little more on the second sheet, lifts it to look it over, and sets it down. Toward the bottom of the sheet, he moves the pen across the paper quickly, and sets the sheet on top of the first.

Rising from his bed, he sets the magazine and remaining sheets of paper on the shelf. He lifts a small envelope from the middle shelf of the three shelves, and sets it on the open area of the bottom shelf. With the pen still in his right hand, he writes on the front of the envelope the name "Rosita." Reaching for a letter-size envelope on the middle shelf, he sets it next to the small envelope on the bottom shelf. Again, he writes on the front of the envelope, but this time it reads, "Manuel Rodriguez, Attorney at Law."

Stepping around the bed, he leans over and lifts the top sheet, glances briefly over it, and folds it in half three times. Returning to the shelves, he lifts the small envelope and slips the folded sheet inside. He flips the envelope over, brings it to his lips and runs the glue edge of the flap over his tongue and presses the flap tightly against the rest of the envelope. Calmly, he sets the sealed envelope on the bottom shelf. He steps to the bed, leans over and lifts the remaining sheet of paper, spins suddenly and steps back to the shelf, in a half-dance, bobbing his head. He folds the sheet twice length-wise, lifts the letter-size envelope from the shelf and slides the sheet inside. Holding the bigger envelope in his left hand, he grabs the small envelope and places it inside the bigger one. Flipping the big envelope over, he runs the glue edge from the flap over his tongue, flips it over and seals it. Nonchalantly, he places the envelope on the bottom shelf conspicuously visible, and steps to the side of the bed and hops onto it. He spreads his body over the bed on his back, and slips his hands with his fingers interlaced under his head, his feet lifting and dropping with a regular beat.

His fellow inmates are annoyed at the same song playing over and over again, but none say a word. All of the inmates, and even the guards, sit quietly where they are, detached, solemn, reflecting. Gordon glances to the clock on the shelf, and it reads "9:57," as *Midnight Blue* fades again. He rises from the bed, takes two steps to the boom box and turns the power off.

Providence

The Big Man sits in his chair in the outer guard station. The clock on the wall shows "11:40." When the door to the inner station buzzes a few moments later, three guards, the warden and a priest all enter the outer station while the Big Man stands, awaiting the closing of the first door and the buzz to signal the outer door to the corridor has been released. Hearing the buzz, he pushes the door open and steps out of the way to let the three guards and the warden pass by and march quickly down the corridor to Gordon's cell. The Big Man follows slowly behind.

Gordon lies quietly on his bed until he sees the guards clear his cell block and come into view. As his cell door unlocks and slides open, he sits up, swings his legs over the bed and rises from it. The warden, a tall black man with short hair, fit, dressed in modest business attire and carrying a serious demeanor, calmly announces, "Gordon Schell, it's time. Step out, please." One guard steps into Gordon's cell and reaches for him, but Gordon calmly steps out to the corridor, and the guard pulls his arm back and simply follows Gordon. Another guard, holding the chains, drops the leggings to prepare them while Gordon holds his hands together before him and stands with his feet about a foot apart, still and calm.

"Big Man," Gordon says, eyeing the Big Man a few feet away, "I'd like you to have the cribbage board, if you want it. I gave the cards to Johnny Morales."

With as little emotion as possible, the Big Man replies, "Sure, I'll take it. Thanks." He steps past all the commotion into Gordon's cell, up to the shelf and removes the board, resting it in his cupped left hand as he steps back into the corridor. Walking past the warden, he stops to glance at Gordon, and, as both men look into each other's face, the Big Man confides softly, "My name is Clarence."

Gordon smiles as he answers, "I've known that ever since I got here, Big Man." The Big Man frowns as he turns and steps away from the flurry of the guards preparing the chains, and Gordon asks, "Did you ever play the saxophone, Clarence?"

The Big Man stops and turns around before he answers, "When I was a kid, yes."

"But it was your mother's idea for you to play, wasn't it?" Gordon asks, as the chains are just about in place.

"She wanted me to learn a musical instrument," replies the Big Man.

"And you quit because you weren't playing for you, you were playing for your mother, and that wasn't enough, was it?" Gordon asks.

The big man looks puzzled as he asks, "How could you know that?"

"Don't matter," Gordon says, shrugging his shoulders, adding, "if you ever see an old sax for sale, you should buy it, take it home and play it for yourself."

Still puzzled, the Big Man mutters, "Maybe." He turns and walks down the corridor about ten steps.

Gordon suddenly shouts, "Clarence!" The Big Man stops but doesn't turn around as Gordon continues, "I'm glad I met you." The Big Man grits his teeth, trying to suppress an emotion he does not want to display, while there's silence for a few moments. Finally, Gordon offers, "As Jimi says, I'll see you in the next world," and, after a moment, adds, "and don't be late." The Big Man drops his head and quickly wipes the back of his right hand across his face and over his eyes. He strolls as calmly as he can muster back to his station and sits down, looking away from the corridor.

The priest, a man of average height and build with prematurely graying short hair belying his mid-thirties age, emerges from the station to walk down the corridor to his charge. As soon as he spots him, Gordon shouts, "Save it, padre! I don't need it nor want it."

The priest continues until he reaches Gordon and calmly says, "Now, son, I can read from any faith, so don't let that stop you."

Gordon leans to the priest and says, "I practice voodoo. Got anything for that?"

The priest looks shocked and protests, "Voodoo is not a faith."

"Stop," interrupts Gordon, "I don't want to hear it and I'm thanking you in advance for honoring my last wishes."

Disappointed, the priest says, "You could change your mind. I'll come with you."

Gordon shakes his head but smiles as he says, "Not where I'm going. You know where that is, padre, doncha?"

"Now, son," says the priest.

"Where I'm going," Gordon quickly assures him, "there's no hurt, no pain. It's calm, peaceful, exquisite warmth." Gordon smiles at the priest again as the warden nods to the guards and two of them grab an arm each and escort Gordon down the corridor. He adds, "Oh, you were probably thinking I meant Hell, weren't you, padre?"

The priest follows behind and says, "I didn't say anything."

"But you were thinking it," Gordon says, "and you'd be wrong. It's called 'home,' padre. I'm going back home." Gordon turns to the warden leading the procession. "Warden," he says, and the warden stops and turns around and the guards halt. Gordon continues, "I just want you to know that when you see me smile when they swab disinfectant on my arm before they stick that needle in, it's because we *all* sure don't want me to die of a bacterial infection, now, do we?"

The warden never changes his serious expression as he says, "Let's go, Schell." He turns and walks toward the guard station and the procession begins anew. Once they reach the station, the warden adds, "And put a lid on it." Gordon can't repress a smile. As soon as the warden said "lid," Gordon thought about marijuana. *Maybe they'll have a bong waiting for me in the execution room,* he thinks …

As midnight approaches, the scheduled time for Gordon Schell's execution, the governor is seated in the chair behind a delicious mahogany desk in his office at the governor's mansion. The office is spacious and richly appointed in mostly dark colors but befitting for one with such an officious position. A nameplate on the desk reads "Governor Jobe." Tall and lean with gray hair immaculately styled and wearing attractive casual attire, he flips a pencil in his right hand, sliding his hand to the bottom of the pencil, flipping it over and repeating the process. He focuses on nothing as he laments, "This is the time in this job that I hate the most. Why do I, alone, have to decide the fate of someone else?"

The only other person in the office, a short, stocky man in his late thirties wearing a business suit, steps to the desk to the right of the governor, leans against it, and consoles, "That's the beauty of polls, Thomas. You don't have to make the most difficult decisions on your own."

"What concerns me, Oliver," the governor says to his aide, "is that this man may be innocent. So I do nothing and we execute an innocent man. *That* is an outcome I will have a difficult time living with."

The governor's aide sweeps his thinning brown hair across the top with his left hand. "The evidence presented by Schell's defense that another man committed the murder is compelling," he confides, "but it's not definitive, Thomas. They can't show that the money came from the ex-husband, that he wanted his ex-wife killed and hired this Rankin to do it. There's no unbroken trail and no one has confessed to it. That's just not enough to overturn an impartial jury's verdict, nor the judge's sentence. This was a fair trial, Thomas. Never forget that."

The governor shakes his head, suddenly looking older than his mid-fifties, as he replies, "The two eyewitnesses bother me. The jogger picked Rankin when shown both photos on a recent news show!" The governor looks sternly at his aide and friend and adds, "Jesus, Ollie, if she can make a mistake like that, we can't undo an execution when we make the same mistake."

"She was ambushed and obviously rattled," his aide calmly counters. "I saw the same program, Thomas. She was pressured to make a decision without proper consideration."

Wearing a pained expression, the governor says, "I also have never appreciated the prosecution's characterization of his wife." He narrows his eyes as he stares at his friend. "That was appalling and completely uncalled for."

"*She* was the one who said she would do anything, *anything*, for her husband," the aide argues. "The prosecution didn't make that up."

Governor Jobe shakes his head, unconvinced. He argues, "That stuff about illegal aliens and her marriage making it impossible for her to be deported, *that's* what I mean by uncalled for. Hell, Oliver," he complains, looking severely at his aide, "one of the jurors interviewed after the trial called her a 'wetback!'"

"Nevertheless, Thomas," the aide counters, "the means of the victim's murder were found in Gordon Schell's truck, *right under the seat where his own children sat*. So, his defense is that the murderer found the man who looked just like him, Gordon Schell, and set him up. What murderer does that?" The aide pauses to look at the governor, who merely shrugs his shoulders in dismay. "But, there's one more thing, Thomas," the aide adds, "something only a few people know."

"What's that?" the governor asks.

The aide turns away and takes a few steps away from the desk while he says, "This afternoon, I took a call from the prosecutor's office, because you wouldn't speak to them."

"They just wanted to remind me that justice was served," the governor protests.

"No, Thomas," the aide informs his friend, spinning around, "they wanted to tell you about the evidence they suppressed with a judge's order. Evidence they expected would definitively reveal the real killer, by confession, if nothing else. You see, the killer left a calling card at the scene."

"A calling card?"

"The killer left a message written in the victim's own blood on the floor," Oliver explains. "The letters were printed, but they were distinctive enough that they could possibly be matched. When they searched Schell's trailer, they found notes he had written. The interesting thing is that he always *printed* what he wrote, and he used the same distinctive style with the letters, such as an 'E' printed similar to an ampersand. The prosecution had a handwriting expert examine the Schell samples with the message from the murder scene, and that expert concluded with ninety-nine percent certainty that they were from the same person. There's no such thing as one hundred percent certainty in these things."

The governor leans forward over his desk, bows his head and rubs his right hand hard against his forehead. When he looks up, he asks, "Why didn't they present this at trial?"

"They fully expected Schell to confess, revealing that one detail," the aide explains, "but they now realize that Schell is truly the killer, one with a complete absence of conscience."

"That's just speculation, Oliver, pure speculation," Governor Jobe argues.

"And how many people do you know, Thomas, that *never* write in longhand? They *always* print and their 'E' *always* resembles an ampersand." The aide stares down the governor, and asks, "Just how many people do you know that do that?"

The governor frowns deeply and mumbles, "No one." Suddenly, his expression changes to hope and he states, "Still, if we grant a stay, that gives everyone more time to get to the bottom of all this. It's much better to be right than timely, don't you think?"

"In a perfect world," Oliver concedes, "that would be judicious. But you exist in the political world, Thomas," and Oliver leans forward to make his point more persuasive. "You have constituents to represent. If you ignore their wishes, your re-election bid will fail." He stands up straight and moves slowly to the front of the desk, not facing the governor, as he continues, "The poll from two days ago shows more than two-thirds think Gordon Schell is guilty and deserves execution." He stops and faces the governor as he adds, "Don't forget another constituency: the prosecuting attorneys and investigative detectives in this state. They support your policies, Thomas, more than any other group. If you grant a stay, how do you think they will react?"

"Not well, I'm sure," Governor Thomas Jobe reflects, frowning. He looks up at his friend, and flips the pencil in his right hand again. Slowly, he asks, "So, you suggest that we do nothing?"

"We do nothing," the governor's aide pronounces ...

Gordon is led down a long, bare corridor, waddling almost like a duck in the constraints of the chains. With the warden leading the way, Gordon is flanked by two guards, followed by a third guard and the priest bringing up the rear.

They reach a door and the warden pushes it open. Inside is a table with straps for the forearms and hands, the head, and the ankles. Off to the side is a contraption holding two bottles. From the bottles stream transparent plastic cables wrapped around an arm sticking from the middle of the contraption. The cables converge to one and at the other end is a plastic connector.

The room has glass on three sides, all closed with drapes. Gordon is led to the side of the table and his chains are removed. One of the guards motions to Gordon to sit on the table from his right and he complies. The two guards help lift his legs onto the table and he is pushed flat. Each guard pulls an arm to the arm strap, the one tending to his right arm first unbuttoning and rolling up his shirt sleeve before wrapping the strap around Gordon's arm and buckling it. Moving to his legs, each guard pulls a leg to the strap, wraps it around the corresponding ankle and buckles it.

While the two guards are engaged with the arms and legs, the third guard positions Gordon's head in its spot, lifts the head strap, wraps it around his head and buckles it. The guard on Gordon's left lifts the chains from the floor, while the other two each pull a forearm straight, push it against the table, wrapping the wrist strap around the corresponding wrist and buckling it. Their mission complete, the guards move back from the table, as the warden walks around Gordon, testing each strap for tightness. Once he has completely circled Gordon and tested each strap, he nods to the two guards who escorted Gordon, and they step outside the room, single file. The priest, waiting for some sign from Gordon which never appears, reluctantly follows the guards out of the room.

The warden glances at his digital watch. It displays "11:59." He nods to the lone guard and moves to the other end of the room and pulls open one side of the drapes. The guard opens the other end, moves to the middle drapes and opens them, too. Through the middle glass are more than a dozen people, all sitting somberly in their seats, some appearing startled as the drapes open and they see Gordon lying on the table, ready for his moment.

A man of medium height and build in a white medical coat with a stethoscope wrapped around his neck enters the room and steps straight to the contraption, sliding it next to the table on Gordon's right. He stands straight, looking like a medical doctor ready to begin a procedure, but stares only at the warden. The clock on the wall outside the room where the people are gathered shows a second hand ticking four, three, two, one, twelve o'clock, as the minute hand moves from the 59 minute position to straight-up midnight.

The warden glances at the man in the white coat and nods once. The man in the white coat pours a mixture from a small bottle onto a cotton swab, and rubs it on Gordon's exposed right arm. Gordon smiles. The man ties a rubber cord around the top of Gordon's arm tightly. Staring at Gordon emotionless, the warden moves his lips, forming the words, "Any last words?" Gordon simply closes his eyes.

As the man in the white coat inserts the needle into a vein and connects the single end of the plastic cables to the needle in his arm, Gordon accesses his mental jukebox and selects for play, Marshall Tucker's *Blue Ridge Mountain Skies*. With the music playing only in his head, oblivious to his surroundings and the dripping of the chemicals into his body, he remembers a trip into the mountains ...

The old man sitting in the rocking chair with a beagle dog laying next to him on the porch of the remote grocery store as the whole Schell family scramble inside ...

Mark tries to pound one of the stakes for the tent into the ground, turning it the wrong way and Melanie shakes her head, trying to pry the stake out, calling for help, and Gordon steps around from the other side, laughs, pries the stake out, holds it steady for Mark, who misses with the hammer and strikes his Father's hand, Gordon looks at his son wearing a painful expression without moving his hand, points to the stake, and Mark strikes the stake into the ground, Gordon lifts his wounded hand for a high-five, pulls it back to high-five his son with the other hand while he shakes the wounded one in mock pain ...

Everyone holds a long-handled fork with a hot dog at the end over a fire, Gordon coming around to check if they're done, pulling the hot dog off the end of the fork with a bun and handing it to the tender, pulling off one and setting it on a plate, giving the plate to Melinda, who bites into the hot dog without a bun ...

At the stream, Gordon assembles three fishing rods. Gordon pulls a worm out of the bait cup and tears it apart as Melanie watches in horror and disgust, he wraps it around her hook, a second piece he wraps around Mark's hook and the last he wraps on his hook …

Melanie's rod bends dramatically and she struggles with the reel, finally pulling the fish to the shallows, Gordon grabs the line and holds up the fish as Melanie jumps up and down, Melinda claps on the shore in front of her smiling mother …

Mark's rod bends but as he reels it goes limp and he stomps his foot and grimaces …

Mark's rod bends and he reels hard, he and Gordon can see the fish in the water getting closer until the line goes limp as the fish spits the hook out and Mark and Gordon look at each other in wide-eyed amazement and laugh and shake their heads …

Mark's rod bends again and he reels and reels, Gordon wades into the deep water keeping hold of the line while holding a net, scooping the fish with line still attached into the net, lifting for Mark to see and slipping and falling back into the water but keeping the net and fish together, while everyone laughs …

Rosita wears overalls with a knit tube blouse under it as Gordon holds one of the fish, pulls open the front of her overalls, threatening to drop the fish down it while she pushes him away, swinging at him until he stops, he puts his free arm around her waist, pulls her closer to kiss her until she sniffs, and pushes him vigorously away, so he takes the fish and attacks her from the rear, never touching her with the fish but chasing her around their camp area as the kids laugh mightily …

Framed by the sunset, Gordon and Rosita stand facing each other, his arms at her waist and hers around his neck, each speaks, and when Gordon speaks, five times Rosita taps his head with her finger, they gaze at each other and Gordon speaks, glances away, looks back at her and speaks again, Rosita slowly turns her head to rest it on his shoulder and softly answers him and they squeeze each other tightly …

The memory slowly disappears and the music playing in Gordon's mental jukebox fades completely into nothing. The man in the white coat, the one end of the stethoscope in his ears, holds the other end against Gordon's chest, bent over. Standing up, he lifts the end from Gordon's chest, and pulls the other end away from his ears to drape his shoulders. As he glances at the warden, his lips form the words, "No heartbeat. He's dead." The warden nods once, solemnly.

The clock on the wall in the visitor room shows the minute hand pointing just past the mark for "1." A dull blue glow, imperceptible to human eyes because it is composed of a substance well outside the visible human spectrum in the ultraviolet range, slips outside the room at the bottom of the window and veers slowly to the left. A moment later it veers back and moves slowly to the right and slightly up. A few moments later it veers back again to the left and crosses to the middle of the window, getting smaller for a few seconds while remaining steady. Suddenly, it veers straight up and the power of its glow dissipates until there is no longer any to detect.

Schell Shock

The phone on the kitchen wall at the Schell home rings. Rosita appears quickly and reaches to the phone, hesitates, closes her eyes, takes a deep breath, and lifts the receiver. Pressing the receiver against her face, she says, "Hello."

She stands unmoving, silently listening to the phone. Occasionally she blinks, but otherwise she stands still, betraying no emotion at all. After nearly half a minute, she pulls the receiver from her face, glances briefly at it, and replaces it back on the hook. She turns around and pulls the chair closest to her away from the table and steps around it to drop down. She places her arms on the table, hands clasped tightly together. Slowly, her head falls to the table between her arms, and she lifts her clasped hands above her head, setting them on top. She sits quietly in this manner until she begins to sob softly …

The two guards step back into the execution room and undo all the straps holding Gordon's body. Another white-coated man pushes a gurney into the room and positions it flush with the table. The two guards, one at Gordon's head, the other at his feet, lift his body off the table, scoot toward the gurney and lay his body on the gurney. The white-coated man pulls a strap from either side of the gurney and slips them together, tightening around Gordon's chest. He follows the same procedure around Gordon's knees. Moving to the rear of the gurney, he pushes from Gordon's feet and wheels it through the door and quickly down the corridor …

In a dimly lit loading area in the underground bowels of the prison, the white-coated man pushes the gurney next to another gurney, a few feet from the back of a vehicle looking similar to a hearse, except that it's pained white with the word "Coroner" on the side. On the bare gurney sits a translucent bag zipped fully open. Two men waiting lift Gordon's body, one from the head and the other from the feet, position the body into the bag, and zip it closed. One pushes the gurney to the vehicle and the legs of the gurney collapse as he pushes it completely inside, sets a lock on the wheels at the end, and closes the left door, followed by the right. He jogs to the passenger side of the vehicle and climbs in to join the other man waiting behind the wheel. The vehicle zooms from the loading area up a ramp and away from the building at considerable speed in the dead of night …

Later in the morning a man wearing a long lab coat escorts Rosita, Jose and Maria to a door labeled "County Morgue." He stops and motions with his right hand to Jose and Maria, both of whom immediately stop, while the man enters through the door with Rosita close behind. He steps to the side of the room covered with doors about three feet equidistant apart. Pulling up the handle of one at chest height, he opens the door and grabs the front of the tray and pulls out a body zipped in a translucent bag. He unzips about a foot of the bag at the front and Gordon's face appears. Rosita stares blankly at the face, looks at the man in the lab coat, and nods. The man zips the bag closed, while Rosita turns and exits the morgue. Pushing the tray back inside, the man closes the door and drops the handle …

That afternoon the same door is open as another gurney is positioned flush with the tray by a man wearing a lab coat over a suit and tie, his back to the wall. He grabs the end of the bag nearest him while the man wearing the long lab coat grabs the other end. They lift the bag and place it on the gurney. The suited man straps the bag to the gurney and wheels it away, out of the morgue, into the hall, down the hall to a set of double doors, through the doors and into a large open area. He pushes the gurney to the opposite end of the large area to a garage door raised open, the tail end of a black hearse parked under the door. The back door of the hearse is swung open to the left side and the suited man pushes the gurney into the back of the hearse, locks the wheels, swings the back door closed and walks to the driver's side of the hearse …

The next afternoon Gordon's body rests in an open, unadorned casket in a waiting room. He is dressed in a white T-shirt with a pink open shell printed on the front and blue jeans. Rosita cautiously steps up to the casket and Gordon's face, gazing at his face for a few moments. She instinctively and delicately pushes the long bangs parted in the middle farther to either side of his head with her right fingers. Stoically, she looks away from Gordon and everyone else in the room and steps away from the casket.

Melanie and Mark pass by, glancing briefly at Gordon's face, misty-eyed and baffled. Jose steps to Gordon's face, holding Melinda in his arms. Melinda looks unconcerned and glances at Jose. She says something and Jose nods. Her face turns into a smile as she touches her heart, her nose, then tries to touch her Father's face. Jose has to lean her closer to the body, but she manages to touch Gordon's nose and his chest above his heart. Snapping her eyes shut, Rosita quickly turns away ...

The black hearse cruises down a street with a tiny flag on the antenna with "Funeral" in red written on it. Several other vehicles with the same flag attached to the antennas follow.

Inside the vehicle immediately following the hearse, Jose drives, Mark sits in the middle, and Maria sits in the front passenger seat. Melanie sits in the back directly behind Maria, Melinda sits in a child seat in the middle, and Rosita sits behind Jose. Jose turns briefly to Rosita and says something but Rosita stares unblinking out the window, watching the scenery pass in a blur. Jose reaches for a CD jewel case set in the opening of the dash level with the shift lever. Handing the case to Maria, she opens it and removes the first CD labeled in handwritten marker "Rokn33" and slides it into the opening of the audio portion of the dash. Jose presses a reverse seek button three times, the display changes to "T 20" and the opening notes of UFO's *Getting Ready* fill the vehicle, drowning all noise from outside ...

Headstones are everywhere as the hearse is parked in a cemetery and the funeral attendant pulls the casket out from the back partway. On the left side of the casket, Jose is at the front, Alan, Penny's husband and a large man, is behind him and the funeral attendant waits for the last position. Barry is on the right side at the front, with Manny behind and Manny's boss, Adam, at the rear. Jose and Barry grasp their handles and pull the casket out and each succeeding pallbearer does the same. When the group has secured the casket, they carry it to a hole in the ground surrounded by green carpet and draped with two green lines across the hole. The group sets the casket over the hole, slowly dropping it against the lines.

Rosita pulls a piece of paper from her purse, unfolds it and reads from the paper. Struggling to keep from breaking down completely, she occasionally wipes tears from her face, finishes speaking, folds the paper and places it in her purse on the ground. She turns and glances briefly at the casket, turns away and steps to a chair at the end of the first row with the others and sits down.

After a few moments, all stand and step single file to the casket and past it. As a group, they all step away from the hole, some gathering together, some moving to cars parked haphazardly in the cemetery. Maria hugs Rosita tightly, the funeral attendant flips a switch hidden from view and the casket descends into the hole.

Revelation

The previous day, a television mounted on a tray attached to a wall shows the warden as he says, "At twelve oh six this morning, inmate Gordon Schell was pronounced dead of heart failure upon completion of the sentence of execution, which we began precisely at midnight ..." The screen on the TV switches to a female reporter, who states, "That was from the press conference immediately after the execution of Gordon Schell, which took place earlier this morning ..."

The television is located in the commons area of another prison. Prisoners sit around tables, some watching the television, others talking, or quiet and disengaged. Among them sits Gunther Rankin unmoving in his chair, a satisfied smile on his face as he watches the television, his hair cut short and bearing a remarkable resemblance to Gordon just a few months earlier, especially now that his face is clean shaven. Eventually, his gaze appears to be unfocused, as though he is reminiscing ...

Later that day, when inmates are allowed to make outside phone calls, Gunther stands before a phone connected to the wall, holding the receiver up to the right side of his face. Into the receiver, he calmly states, "You need to come out here to the prison right away. I have something to tell you."

He listens for a few moments and shakes his head. "If I were you, I'd find some excuse to pass on it and come out here instead. I can't tell you about it on this phone," he confides, turning to face the room with a confident smile, "but consider it a bombshell."

He listens to the receiver a few more moments and turns to place it on the hook. He spins back to face the room, a half-smile on his face, his eyes narrowed …

The following day, Gunther's attorney, an attractive woman of average height and build in her late twenties, sits behind a table in a small, enclosed room, wearing a frown signifying a desire to be elsewhere. The door to the small, enclosed room opens and Gunther is escorted inside, wearing jeans and a blue prison shirt with a number stenciled above the heart. He takes a seat opposite the attorney, her long, full blond hair seeming to fill the room, and the guard exits, closing the door behind him.

With obvious displeasure, the woman spits, "Rescheduling that deposition is going to set me back a week on that case, Gunther, so this had better be good."

Gunther smiles, enjoying the moment, as he replies, "Depends on your definition of good."

"Cut the crap, Gunther," she responds, angrily, "and get to the point."

"Fine," he relishes. "Point One. You're going to schedule a press conference," and he scans the small room, "where you will announce that your client—me—has undeniable proof that he knows who killed Darcy Rowland and that it wasn't Gordon Schell."

"What?" the woman exclaims, shock flashing across her face. "They just executed him!"

"Isn't it beautiful?" Gunther gushes, relishing the thought. He adds, "Point Two. I will only tell the two detectives that investigated the murder and you'll state that in your press conference."

Shaking her head, she insists, "You need to tell me what you know."

"I don't need to tell you shit!" Gunther barks, peeved. "You'll find out when everybody else does."

"Why?" she asks, hurt. "I'm your attorney. You can trust me."

Gunther smiles as he says, "You're not my partner in crime! It's more fun this way."

"There's something I don't like about this," the woman says. "What are you up to, Gunther?"

"Spite," Gunther confides, smugly, "and here's the last point."

She pauses a moment before asking, "What is it?"

Gunther's face turns a solemn seriousness as he warns, "Point three. If those two detectives do not meet with me in one week, I will call every news outlet and tell them the whole story of that murder. And I *know* what I'm talking about."

"That sounds like a threat," the attorney remarks. "What do you have on them?"

"The whole story," he replies, nonchalantly, "all of it." He glances randomly about the room ...

The next day Gunther's attorney stands before a podium with a half-dozen microphones in front of her face. She sets a single page of paper on the podium and calmly states, "I've called this press conference to announce that my client, Gunther Rankin, possesses intimate knowledge of how the murder of Darcy Rowland was committed and, more importantly, who killed her, and that it was *not* Gordon Schell. Further, he will only tell the detectives who investigated the murder, but they have one week to meet with him. After that time, if they have not met with him, he will tell his story to every news outlet willing to listen, which, I imagine, will be every reporter in this state." She lifts the page from the podium and folds it in half and adds, "Thank you for coming. I have nothing further to add and I will not take questions." She turns to her left and exits the room.

Amid the confusion, different reporters can be heard simultaneously saying, "What does your client know?" "Why did your client wait until now to talk?" "Jesus! They executed Schell just three days ago!" Gunther's attorney heeds none of it and disappears through a door that closes abruptly ...

Just a scant three days later, Gunther sits in a chair behind a table in the same room where he met with his attorney, smugly smiling at his company. Detective Lewis sits in a chair directly across from Gunther, menacing and threatening. Detective Schneider stands next to Lewis, a chair turned around before him, his right leg resting on the seat, leaning forward on his bent knee toward Gunther, sizing him up. In the middle of the table stands a small tape recorder.

Detective Lewis speaks first. "Alright, Rankin, you got us here, so, spill it."

"First, though," Detective Schneider adds, "tell us how you know who really killed the woman."

Gunther narrows his eyes, lips drawn into a half-smile, more like a smirk. "That's easy," he says, calmly. "Since I killed her, I should know all the details, doncha think?"

The two detectives glance briefly at each other but hardly display any other reaction. Lewis turns toward Gunther and asks, "What happened that night, then?"

Gunther briefly closes his eyes and says, "First, I slit open the screen on the right window in the dining room, because the lock was broken and had never been repaired or replaced, so that window would always be open."

Schneider stops him to ask, "How did you know that?"

Gunther opens his eyes and glares at Schneider. "I knew it."

Lewis seethes as he remarks, "You're not cooperating, Rankin!"

"You're interrupting," Gunther calmly counters.

There is a momentary silence. Lewis drops his head and resignedly says, "Get on with it."

Gunther begins speaking again, punctuated by interjections from the two detectives. Lewis writes in his notebook occasionally and Schneider drops his leg to walk around the room, only to re-position himself in the same manner.

"And that's it?" Schneider asks incredulously. "You walked out the door and the neighbor and the jogger saw you, not Schell, and you made it to your car parked two blocks away and drove off undetected?"

Lewis adds, "There's nothing except the window that you couldn't already know from the trial and news reports, Rankin." He grabs his notebook and stands up quickly, disgusted that the trip seems a total waste of time. He shakes his head as he turns to Schneider and spews, "Let's go."

Schneider reaches for the recorder and clicks the stop button. He lifts it and deposits it in a side pocket of his jacket and turns to follow Lewis, who has reached the door and is pulling the handle to open it.

"I left a message for you and you haven't even asked me about it," Gunther states matter-of-factly. Lewis immediately releases his grip on the handle and both detectives freeze. As Gunther stares at the backs of both men, he adds, "I could have written 'rest,' but 'eternal respite' added a touch of class, wouldn't you agree? Besides, it was fitting, too." Gunther smiles broadly at their backs.

Schneider appears distraught as he complains, "Dammit, Ed, my gut *told me* that sleezeball did it!" Lewis stares forward blankly, unmoving, unable to speak.

"Ever play chess, gentlemen?" Gunther asks facetiously, continuing without waiting for a response, "because it's at this point I get to say, 'checkmate.'"

Detective Lewis leans against the door as though unable to stay upright. Detective Schneider suddenly takes charge, steps back to the table as he removes the tape recorder and places it on the table. He depresses the record button, sits down in the chair in which Lewis was sitting, and demands, "All right, Gunther Rankin, tell me again what you just said."

Gunther smiles broadly as he calmly says, "I wrote the words 'eternal respite' on the floor of the murder scene with the victim's own blood. That fact was conveniently omitted in the press coverage and never revealed at trial. I know all about it, because I killed Darcy Rowland." He pauses for a moment to stare at Schneider and grin widely. "I wouldn't feel too badly about it, though. You can console yourselves with this: at least, the state exacted its revenge and executed *somebody* for that murder. It just wasn't the *right* somebody." He opens his eyes wide, looking like a little boy caught with his hand in the cookie jar, and places his right hand over his mouth as he blurts, "Oops!"

Lewis turns around and leans against the wall, his arms separated a bit from his body but pressed hard against the wall. Softly, he asks, "Why, Rankin? Why?"

"When I'm hired to do a job, I do it," he replies.

"Who hired you?" Schneider demands.

Gunther glowers at the question. "Are you guys *really* that slow?" he mocks them. "I mean, *really*, who scooted out of the country with half a million clams to sail contentedly in Bermuda?"

"Simon Edwards," Lewis states in a low, dejected tone.

Gunther smiles insidiously as he says, "You won't be able to extradite him right away, though, considering that his safe, little bungalow caught fire a few nights ago. It's a shame. I hear he got burned pretty badly and he's lucky he managed to wake up and crawl out."

Schneider shakes his head and looks incredulous as he asks, "How do you know that?"

Gunther glances from Schneider to Lewis and back to Schneider. He warns, "As far as I'm concerned, a deal's a deal with me. You *better* keep your end of the bargain." He pauses to stroke his chin. "He'll still be in the hospital when this breaks, and he'll run, even if he has to sneak out of the hospital, because he knows *now* that, if you catch him and put him in prison, he won't survive. It pays to have friends on the inside. I've got a few, scattered here and there."

Schneider comments, "That's how you knew about the window, isn't it?"

"Of course," Gunther confirms, pausing to lift a cup of water and gulp it down. "You're catchin' on," he says, staring at Schneider with a smile.

Detective Lewis pushes away from the wall and slowly steps forward to the table, saying, "Tell us about Gordon Schell. What did he have to do with this?" When Lewis reaches the other chair he slowly pulls it away from the table, turns it around and sits down. He crosses his arms and wearily stares at Gunther.

"Gordon Schell didn't have anything to do with it," Gunther states blankly. "He really was an innocent man who got caught up in the circumstances."

Schneider shakes his head and asks, "Why did you set him up? You did, didn't you?"

Gunther turns his head to look squarely in Detective Schneider's eyes. He calmly replies, "Well, I didn't want to get caught, if that's what you mean." As he sits back in his chair and looks up, he continues. "When Simon talked to me about killing his wife, I knew where she lived because I had been there before when Simon was still married. Then, I remembered that Gordon had been there once, too, because I had followed him that day." Schneider looks puzzled and Gunther smiles. "Sometimes, when I would get bored, I'd go over near Gordon's trailer and follow him around. Did it for years and he never knew."

"Why would you do that?" Schneider demands.

With a serious expression, Gunther explains, "I was always curious about him. I've known about him for a long time, and you're probably wondering how I knew about him, aren't you?"

"I want to know, yes," Lewis says.

"Gordon Schell is my brother, half-brother," Gunther replies calmly. He looks from one to the other as both detectives lean back in their chairs and glance at each other stunned.

When Schneider regains his composure, he states, "Gordon Schell had no siblings, Rankin. His mother was raped by some man she didn't know and Gordon was the result."

Gunther smiles as he answers. "Well, she *may* have been raped. That would make perfect sense, knowing Gordon's father, since he was mine, too. Dear old dad was a mean bastard when he wanted to be, which was most of the time, but she knew he was the father. She ran away from him and hid while she was carrying Gordon, so she couldn't exactly advertise that fact." He looks from Schneider to Lewis and asks, "Know what I mean?"

"How did you know about him?" Lewis softly asks.

"Dear old dad would talk about her, in between slugfests with my mother, almost like bragging," Gunther explains. "He would brag about his women, threatening to leave my mom. She just wasn't a strong person."

"So, how did you meet Gordon," Schneider asks.

Gunther shakes his head and corrects, "We never met. I was just always curious about him, because I knew he was my brother. Finally, I met this guy years ago who thought I was Gordon. I told this guy I was his cousin and wondered how Gordon was doing, so he told me where he worked and I just went over there one day to see him. I was just curious, so I followed him around the rest of the day, wondering if he would spot me, but he never did."

Schneider is unconvinced as he asks, "If he was your brother, didn't you *want* to meet him?"

Gunther frowns. "I thought about it a few times," he says, but grows agitated as he adds, "but when he started dating that spic whore and, then, married her, I really didn't want to have anything to do with him." He shakes his head demonstratively. "She *was* a whore, too. She went out with several guys while she was dating Gordon and I don't think he knew about that. She's good-lookin', no doubt about that, but a whore's a whore, you know."

Lewis leans forward and asks, "So you knew all about him but he didn't know anything about you, is that what you're saying?"

"That's what I'm saying," Gunther replies, smiling. "The more I found out about him, the more it was like we were from two different worlds and I didn't want to be a part of his world."

"Did you hate him?" asks Schneider.

"Nah," Gunther says, calmly, "I didn't hate him. I didn't *know* him. We may have been blood related but that doesn't mean I have to be in his life. It was just kinda fun to follow him around once in a while, keep tabs on him sorta." He laughs as he adds, "Hell, a lot of times people would think I was him. That was always funny to me."

"You put the evidence in his truck, right?" Schneider asks.

"Yep," Gunther confirms, "the day after." He grabs the cup of water and gulps down a swallow. "I don't think anybody saw me, either. I was pretty careful about that."

"What about the writing, the printing?" asks Lewis. "How did you know about that?"

"Didn't" Gunther insists. "That's just how I write, or print, to be exact. I had no idea how Gordon wrote. Coincidence, huh?" He smiles deviously. "I covered my tracks by getting rid of anything I wrote down, just to be on the safe side, but that's what convinced you guys, wasn't it?" Gunther notes that the two detectives avoid looking at him, frowning, before he continues. "Look, let's save us all a lot of time and aggravation. I fully expected you guys to come after me. Gordon was my trump card. I would plant that evidence, you would arrest me, a mysterious call would be placed, you would search his truck and find the evidence and I had my 'reasonable doubt.' *I* expected to be on trial and I was going to beat it, *until your witness* identified Gordon instead of me. Even *I* couldn't believe how lucky I was. The writing, the fact that she just happened to run into Gordon that very afternoon he quit work, that she was so poor at cleaning house that his fingerprints from *two months before* were still easily retrievable, that he actually interviewed for a job at Good Samaritan Hospital, was hired and actually met with Simon, that he constantly took a shortcut through that very neighborhood, that he didn't even know about the murder, didn't even remember her name and lied to you guys about being at the house. I mean, *seriously, how lucky can a killer with no conscience be?* Fuck!"

Schneider looks at Lewis and Lewis hangs his head. When Schneider turns to Gunther, he says, with complete disdain, "Fuck you, Rankin. I knew it was you the whole time, but I couldn't find the thread that tied you to Edwards. When he got his life insurance money and flew off to Bermuda with no notice, that was just my confirmation that I was right. By then, though, you had covered every alibi and everyone wanted Gordon Schell's blood. No one had the guts to stop the legal proceedings already started. It was a fucking nightmare, and nothing was going to stop it from reaching its bloody, disgusting end. Still, I knew it was you the whole fucking time."

Lewis, appearing to finally wake up from his daze, asks, "Why did you have to cut her up and torture her like that?"

Gunther smiles and nods his head as he replies, "Who would've thought? I just knew I had to change my MO, because I've killed a few people before but not like this. That scalpel, though, sure cuts fine and true. Shit! I could've skinned her alive, completely, taken her skin with me! I wasn't thinking that it would set everybody off. That was what I asked Simon for, a weapon that couldn't be traced back to me and that's what he gave me." He smiles triumphantly as he grabs the cup of water and downs the last of its contents. Flicking the cup to his right with his right hand on the floor, he looks at Schneider with an expression of contempt and says, "You couldn't tie me to any evidence because I didn't leave any. I drove to a motel six hours away in Virginia for a job interview, even had the interview. But I took a friend and he drove Simon's car and stayed behind to make the call from the motel room to my girlfriend, all pre-arranged. I had a sheet over the driver's side of Simon's car and I burned that sheet, my clothes and the latex gloves I wore. You weren't going to find anything on me, not even from my alibi accomplices. I would kill them before I would allow them to testify against me and they knew it."

Schneider glares at Gunther with total disgust. He speculates, "And, you're still doing the same thing with Edwards, too. Keeping him quiet."

Gunther shakes his head and smiles at the officer's incomprehension. He calmly states, "A deal's a deal. Simon owes me quite a bit of cash for my services. I knew he stood to walk away with half a million, so I wasn't going to do this for some fucking ten thousand. Hell, I'm killing two birds with one stone here, making you guys look like idiots *and* putting the heat on Simon, too. It's beautiful, actually."

Lewis shakes his head slowly, deliberately, and says, with a deep sadness, "You could've stopped this at any time, Rankin. Edwards had screwed you, the state was going to execute your own half-brother, you could've stopped it, but you let it happen the way it did, anyway. Why?"

"I had to see if you were really going to go through with it," Gunther replies, smiling insidiously, almost infectiously. "Would you, all of you, haul a completely innocent man out of his home, arrest him, try him, convict him, sentence him to death and execute him?" He pauses and glances at one detective and the other, his eyes glimmering with inner glee, as he adds, "Well, ya did, didn't ya?"

Principal Reaction

The District Attorney, three staff members, Sharon Pilot, and Detectives Lewis and Schneider are congregated in a slightly darkened room around a conference table, later that week. Sharon argues, "We need to go after this Gunther Rankin."

"Sharon," the District Attorney, a slightly overweight man, calmly interrupts, "we have a growing crisis to address and it has nothing to do with prosecuting another offender."

The lone female staff member remarks, "The governor has scheduled a conference today. He intends to issue an apology and offer the family reparations." She shakes her head as she adds, "Oliver spoke with me just before the meeting. He wanted to convey the governor's, quote, 'extreme disappointment with the District Attorney's office', end quote."

"So, Sharon," the District Attorney observes, "with the governor's disappointment added to the outrage people have expressed in the last few days and the beating we're taking from the media, mounting a prosecution against Rankin is self-serving now, at best." Concerned, he looks at Sharon Pilot and continues. "I know you did your best and this should not be construed as a loss of confidence in your, or any of the other prosecuting attorneys', abilities. However, we need to develop some policy changes, beginning today, to ensure that the outcome of a prosecution like Gordon Schell's never happens again." He scans the table for reaction. No one is compelled to speak, so he continues. "The first change I wish to suggest is a further separation between the DA office and the investigative units of the various police agencies." He looks at the two detectives. "As examples of the investigators in this district, you two are charged with discovering as much of the truth behind a crime as possible. If nothing else, I am realistic and pragmatic and completely understand that you have limited resources. Don't we all? The DA's office, though, must provide you with no more than guidance concerning the burden of proof required to mount a successful prosecution and nothing more. You investigators, on the other hand, must control all aspects of your investigations and never close the investigation of any suspect unless and until you are completely convinced that the suspect can be eliminated from any consideration." With a little more emphasis, he adds as he looks around the table, "Your offices will investigate and this office will prosecute. Should you feel that overstepping is being suggested, your responsibilities as investigators require you to remind all representatives of this office of the boundary between both, and that includes me as well. Is that understood by everyone?"

No one speaks but all nod their heads in agreement. Detective Schneider glances at Sharon Pilot briefly, his face blank and unrevealing, while he successfully conceals a certain smugness …

In a different conference room appointed with rich and elegant furnishings, as expected from a leading, highly profitable and experienced enterprise, a television mounted in the wall is tuned to a news channel. Seated around the large, oval table constructed of solid, luscious maple are staff and attorneys from the law office of Lambert, Sheehan and Goldsmith, including Manny and Adam. On the television screen, an attractive black female reporter in her mid-thirties with swept hair flowing up from her forehead down to her shoulders is seated at a desk on a studio set. Her voice is excited as she says, "For a live reaction from the Schell family to the governor's statements just concluded, let's go to George Sanderson on the scene. George?"

Immediately, the television screen changes to the side porch of the Schell trailer in the background. Many reporters with microphones and cameras and onlookers are gathered before the porch, and one reporter's voice can be heard saying, "Thank you, Kelly. I'm at the home of the late Gordon Schell, waiting for his wife, Rosita Schell, who has promised to take questions after the governor's statements."

The reporter's voice pauses but before the voice can begin again, the door of the trailer leading to the porch suddenly opens and Rosita steps onto the porch, solemn, angry, but poised and strong. Several of her trailer park neighbors and friends, including Penny and her large husband, Alan, and Jose, have stood vigil on her porch and instinctively close around her, allowing her a space to address and be seen by those in front of the porch. With no instinct to move closer to the uplifted microphones scattered around the front of the porch, she moves to the side rail, built by her now-dead husband, and leans on it with her right arm for much-needed support.

The reporter's voice quickly comments, "Here she is now."

In the background, a bit muted, another reporter's voice can be heard asking, "Mrs. Schell, can you tell us what you feel about the governor's statements?"

Scathingly, Rosita looks down at the reporter as she barks, "What do I feel? What should I feel?" She pauses for a moment, looking around the grounds where she had lived for so long, the only home any of her children had ever known. Curiously, no one dares speak and the silence is eerie, unpredictable, disconcerting.

She turns her head back to the crowd but looks over their heads as she confides, "I read something the other day that I need to share with you." Waiting a moment to gather her thoughts, she glares at face after face in the crowd with indictment as she states, "Take a foolish thing and even if a million people believe it true, it is still a foolish thing. That is what I have felt throughout this whole nightmare. This was all a foolish thing, and not one of you can undo this."

Rosita glares at several in attendance and turns around to take one step back to the door. Several reporters begin to yell more questions, which she pays no heed. Instead, she stops in mid-stride, spins around and quickly steps to the rail and slaps it once to loudly proclaim, with seething, visible anger shaking her countenance, "Fools killed my husband, Gordon!" Scanning the faces with no change in her expression, she slaps the rail yet again. "Fools made my children fatherless." Holding the rail to keep from falling, feeling suddenly spent, her voice is much softer as she blurts what she has always known for the entire ordeal, "You are all fools."

Expending considerable effort, she turns around and steps back toward the trailer. Penny grabs her waist and holds her upright as the two enter the trailer amidst a growing chaos of comments, questions, and rumor coming from the crowd before the porch.

Alan suddenly steps to the edge of the porch, with Jose right behind him, and in a loud, booming, bass voice, his arms crossed defiantly, he commands, "Mrs. Schell thanks you all for coming and now asks that you respect her request to vacate her property now." Two more men, neighbors from the trailer park, step out to create a phalanx on the porch as Alan adds, "I should remind you that this trailer park and each lot in it is private property. Unless you have the permission of the property owner, we can request the police have you removed. We would appreciate not having to resort to that, so please leave."

Jose smilingly moves around Alan down the porch one slow step at a time, waving his arms to persuade the reporters and onlookers to disperse. Reluctantly, all retreat from the porch.

In the conference room, Adam lifts a remote control from the table and pushes a button to turn off the television. No one offers any verbal comment at all.

After a few moments, everyone departs the conference room save Manny, still sitting in the same spot at the table, and Adam, who has stood up to return the control to its spot next to the television and watch everyone file out from the room. Manny asks softly, looking down at the table, "May I have a moment with you, Adam, before you return to your office, please?"

"Of course, Manny," Adam replies and, sensing that Manny is about to propose something of which will pack a considerable impact, sits down at the head of the table to be at eye level.

"Adam," Manny begins, "you heard the governor. He's acknowledged the irreparable harm that the state has incurred upon the family. He wants to negotiate with them for a just reparation."

"I think I know where you're going with this," Adam interjects while Manny pauses.

"That woman and her family have been through a torment none of us can imagine," Manny continues, shaking his head, still looking down at the table. "She has been a rock of stability and restraint through the very worst that can happen to rip a family apart, all for her children. They have looked to her for guidance and understanding and have received it in abundance." Manny lifts his head, rubs his hands over his eyes, and looks at Adam. "That woman will never receive her due if she negotiates with the governor's office on her own."

Adam lifts his right hand like a stop sign and advises, "Stop before you go any further. I know what you propose to do and have to advise you that you will have to resign from the firm to do so."

"She needs proper, adequate, aggressive representation, Adam," Manny counters.

"I agree," Adam says, nodding his head, "and you are going to provide that representation." Adam leans casually back in his chair and presses the tips of his fingers on each hand together. "Let me explain what I have learned about you since you first came here. While I have worked hard to make you a partner, maybe in the hopes that one day you would be the managing partner, I have always sensed that you feel constrained. We have a singular focus at this firm and I like to think we're good at what we do. You, however, have broader objectives."

Adam pauses to sit up and lean forward with his hands on the table, looking directly in Manny's face. "My advice to you, Manny, is to seek those objectives, set out on your own, and this opportunity can be the launching of your own successful practice."

Manny shakes his head but smiles at Adam as he says, "I really expected you to be disappointed in me, Adam, and feel that I was abandoning you."

"This whole thing has been a disgusting mess," Adam confides, "and, to date, only Gordon and Rosita Schell have held up to it with any dignity. Everyone else has fallen away but I think that is going to change." Adam pauses to reflect and looks away to the door of the conference room. "People are going to change because I refuse to lose hope in every human being's basic decency." He turns to Manny and smiles encouragingly. "You now have your place in this, Manny. Fulfill it." Adam rises from his chair and steps around the table to Manny, still seated. He stops behind Manny, places a hand on either shoulder, squeezes Manny's shoulders and pats Manny's right shoulder with his right hand. Manny hangs his head as Adam steps around the other side of the table and exits the conference room without looking back …

"I don't understand what you want, Mr. Rodriguez," Rosita complains to Manny as they stand on the courthouse steps where Gordon's trial was conducted one week after the governor's statements.

Manny drops his head, standing below Rosita, as she looks down at him sternly. After a moment, he lifts his head to look at Rosita as he explains, "I don't want anything from you, Mrs. Schell, except the opportunity to represent you when you talk with the governor's office about the settlement."

Unfazed, Rosita responds rapidly, "And how much is this representation going to cost me?"

Manny smiles to ease the tension but returns to a serious expression as Rosita's display of stern distrust remains unbroken. He comments, "You have your husband's contempt for attorneys, I see."

"Tell me, Mr. Rodriguez, what exactly did lawyers do for us?" Rosita asks bitterly.

Suddenly, Manny drops his act of attorney bravado, relaxes, and his face saddens as he replies, "Nothing, Mrs. Schell. No attorney did you any good at all, not even me." He pauses and looks slightly away from her as he continues. "I tried, and I'm sure I made mistakes." His gaze returns to her as he adds, "In the end I accomplished nothing."

Rosita softens her expression a bit and her tone is less combative as she says, "Then, tell me why this is different."

Softly, Manny replies, "They'll simply give you as little as they can to make you go away, to keep you silent."

Rosita defiantly says, "I won't take their first offer. I know that much."

Manny begins to fall back into his attorney bravado as he insists, "And they'll expect that and make another, bigger offer, and it still won't be enough." He pauses and puts his right hand in his pants pocket. "You see, they let the system break down by rushing every step to show they were making progress, letting public pressure drive the process. The public, however, has no place in the system or justice will never be served, yet they invited the public into the system and, for that, they need to pay."

Rosita is intrigued now and asks, "What should they pay?"

"They should pay a lot," Manny says, "to serve as a deterrent. Just as we sentence the convicted to harsh punishments, harsher than usual, to hopefully send a message, to set an example, we must do the same here. This rush to judgment must never happen again."

Rosita's eyes water a bit and she looks away as she says, "It won't bring Gordon back but I think he would be pleased if we could do that for him." Both look down until Rosita lifts her head to look at Manny and asks, "What do we do?"

Manny suggests, "Let me go with you from the beginning. Call me your friend and advisor. We'll listen to their explanations and offer and respond in kind."

Skeptically, Rosita asks, "How much is this going to cost me?"

"A percentage of the settlement and nothing until then," Manny replies.

"Minus their first offer," Rosita says, sternly.

"Alright," Manny says and smiles.

"And their second offer since I won't take their first," Rosita insists, unsmilingly.

"Agreed," Manny says, letting out a short chuckle. "You drive a hard bargain. Are you planning on starting your own business? You should, you know."

"Maybe I already have," Rosita suggests, still unsmiling. "What's your percentage?"

"Normally, I would take a third," Manny replies, and smiling, he adds, "but I'll save you the trouble and take a quarter. Agreed?"

"Deal," Rosita replies, extending her right hand. Manny reaches for hers with his right hand and delicately wraps his fingers around hers and gently squeezes …

A few weeks later, Rosita and Manny stand before a hotel elevator door, silently waiting for the car. A moment later, the bell rings and a few seconds later the door opens and they enter the empty car. Manny presses the button for the bottom floor and the door closes. He turns to Rosita and commends, "You did well for your first meeting with big-time lawyers. I was very impressed."

Rosita scowls thinking about what took place and remarks, "After two weeks of excuses, they really pissed me off when they wanted to chit chat like we were old friends. They really had some nerve."

"That's a feeling out process," Manny advises, "trying to see if they can build trust in you." He turns to her and rests his right hand on her left arm below her shoulder as he adds, "You did exactly what you needed to do. You kept your composure and made them stick to the task at hand."

Rosita looks down at his hand on her shoulder and glances at him severely. Manny quickly removes his hand and flashes an expression like a boy caught with dirty magazines by his mother. Rosita comments, dryly, "It won't do any good to be angry. I know that."

The elevator slows and, seconds later, the door opens to the hotel lobby. Manny points his left hand while holding his brief case out to the lobby. As Rosita steps out first, he puts his right arm behind her but avoids touching her. As they walk through the lobby side by side, Manny says, "Now that they have made their first play, we need to talk about our strategy and what I can do to make it as painful for them as possible."

"I'm listening," Rosita says, looking forward as they approach the hotel front entrance.

"Not here," Manny says, "and I don't have an office, yet." Rosita steps through the automatic door and stops a few paces out of the way of people coming and going and Manny steps up to face her. They look at each other a moment until Manny says, "May I suggest we gather at your kitchen table and discuss what we need to do, please?"

"As long as my neighbor is home and can sit with us," Rosita counters.

Manny shakes his head and says, "No, we can't have anyone knowing what we plan to do. It has to be just you and me." He hangs his head as he adds, "I know what it looks like to have a strange man in your home and I wish I didn't have to suggest it but we need to discuss this and be ready for our next meeting with them." He lifts up his head and, appearing contrite, quickly and resolutely adds, "Let me apologize right now for putting my hand on your arm. That was uncalled for and wrong of me to do and it will *never* happen again."

Unblinking, Rosita stares at his face up and down for a few moments. "All right," she says, seriously, "and you *should* apologize. I am your *client*, not your *date*."

"You are absolutely correct," Manny agrees, still contrite. "I am your attorney and should act like one at all times." He hangs his head as he adds, "You should have slapped me. I deserve it still."

"That won't be necessary," Rosita insists. "I think you get the point." She turns around and begins to walk to the parking lot, briefly smiling to herself …

"When you said, 'My mother taught me never to accept a first offer. Try again,'" Manny says, sitting across the Schell's kitchen table from Rosita, three hours later the same day, "that was perfect." He nods approvingly, showing genuine admiration. "Then, you threatened to end the meeting and leave when they hesitated to give you a better offer, and I thought you were going to blow it. Did you see my reaction?"

"Not really," Rosita says calmly. "I wasn't paying attention to you, but I learned that trick from Gordon." She looks away from Manny, and adds, "He always said if the other party thinks you won't walk away from a deal, they'll never budge. You have to always be prepared to walk."

"Well, it's good that you didn't have to," Manny remarks, unimpressed, "because that was not our strategy."

"No, you're right," Rosita agrees, straight-faced, "it was *my* strategy."

"Are we in this together, or not?" Manny asks, concerned.

Rosita, holding her own, narrows her eyes as she responds. "Now we know how serious they are, but even their million dollar offer doesn't make up for killing my husband." She leans back in her chair and crosses her arms. "Now they know how serious I am," she says, calmly.

Manny's concern softens and he nods in agreement as he says, "Okay, you won round one." Rosita smiles until Manny adds, "They are not going to cave, though. They are not going to just give you what we want, especially when they have the 'government is harmless' precedent working for them."

Now Rosita appears concerned as she asks, "What do you mean?"

"Long ago," Manny explains, "the courts set to limit, even eliminate, private citizens' ability to sue or seek redress against the government for alleged wrongdoing by governments and their agents, or government employees."

Rosita's expression displays her lack of understanding. "Why would they even offer me anything if they can't be held harmless?" she asks, concerned.

Manny smiles as he enters his element. "The courts could never eliminate it. Other courts, legislatures and even people wouldn't allow it. There are precedents for it and precedents against it and that's where I come in."

"Is that why you asked them for thirty days to give our answer?" Rosita asks.

"Partly," Manny replies. "It gives me more time to research the law, yes, but it makes them consider what we're up to, and," Manny emphasizes with a pause, "it allows me to use public pressure against them, too."

"What's our next move?" Rosita asks, curious and excited, too.

Manny looks a bit worried as he gazes at Rosita. "We'll meet with them again, but from now on I do the talking," he replies cautiously.

"I don't think I like that idea," Rosita disagrees, frowning severely.

"No, you won't like it at all," Manny says, dropping his gaze to the table, "but if you want to set an example with them, as I do, you have to acknowledge that it is now a matter of my legal expertise against theirs." He pauses and lifts his gaze back to Rosita's eyes and her unconvinced expression. "And, you must remain **silent** until the end. You can't talk to anyone, not the governor, friends, family **and** especially not the media." Rosita frowns but Manny adds before she can **speak**, "From now on, you must trust me and do everything I tell you to do, without exception."

Rosita continues to frown as she thinks over Manny's recommendation. Finally, she warns him with an unmistakable strength of conviction, "You better not blow it, Mr. Rodriguez."

Manny straightens as he replies, "I'll hold up my end, Mrs. Schell, because you and your family are my only concern now." Flashing a display of great confidence he adds, "Do only what I ask of you and we will prevail." He looks at her unconvinced expression and smiles with conceit, narrowing his eyes, imagining the battle to come …

The phone in the Schell kitchen rings and Rosita gets up from the sofa and walks into the kitchen to answer it. Picking up the receiver from the hook, she says, "Hello."

Penny's voice on the other end excitedly shouts, "Turn on channel seven."

"What?" Rosita asks, confused. "Why?"

"Just do it, Rosita," Penny replies. "Hurry."

Rosita drags the long cord from the phone pressed to her ear into the living room and to the table. She lifts the remote from the table and punches the channel selector to seven.

A female reporter is speaking into a microphone on the screen, and is heard in mid-sentence, saying, "… may have reached an end. While the governor's address has been scheduled under extremely short notice, news outlets were advised, as you know, Jordan, as early as last night that there may be an announcement concerning the negotiations between the governor's office and the Rosita Schell family. And, I have learned from a source close to the negotiations, that both sides have reached an agreement and that the governor will deliver the outline of the settlement in his address, which should begin in about ten minutes."

The screen changes to a male reporter behind a desk, his average build contrasting with his silvery, polished hairstyle cut reasonably short and placing him somewhere in his fifties. Looking directly into the camera, he says, "Thank you, Kelly. We will return to the capitol once the governor reaches the conference podium. Earlier this morning, in Charlotte …"

Rosita presses the mute button and says to Penny, "I've got to hang up, Penny. Manny may be trying to call me. Thank you."

"God, I hope it's what you want, Rosita," Penny says. "Is it okay if I come over?"

"Yes," Rosita says, stepping into the kitchen to hang up the receiver. She steps slowly around the kitchen table, nervously darting her gaze all over the room but looking at nothing. A few seconds later, a pounding on the front door can be heard and she walks to it and opens the door, stepping out of the way of an excited Penny bursting into the room.

"Have you heard from the attorney, yet?" Penny blurts out.

"No," Rosita replies, calmly, "not yet." She looks at Penny chidingly and adds, "It's only been a moment, you know."

Penny gazes at Rosita apologetically and mumbles, "I know." Suddenly, she extends her arms out to Rosita and steps forward and Rosita stands still and straight as Penny puts her arms around her and hugs her, saying, heavy with emotion, "Oh, Rosita, you have been through so much …" Penny begins to choke and has to stop thinking about the recent past to regain her composure.

The phone in the kitchen rings and both look toward it and Penny drops her arms as Rosita steps into the kitchen and lifts the receiver. "Hello," she says.

In a car flying down the interstate, Manny says into his cell phone, "I know I didn't think it would take six months and I apologize for that, but the governor is expected to announce the settlement any moment and if he says what I expect him to say I'll be at your home in two hours with a bottle of champagne."

Rosita hesitates for a moment but finally says, "I won't be in the mood to celebrate."

"I understand, Rosita," Manny says, "but I think you'll be pleased at what you accomplished." He passes a truck and looks in the rear view mirror and moves into the right lane. "Anyway, don't talk to any reporters until I arrive. I should be there in two hours or less. Okay?"

"Yes," Rosita says, feeling a little tired, "Thank you. Goodbye."

"Bye," Manny says, and flips his phone shut ...

The governor steps to a podium holding some loose papers in his right hand, setting them on the stand in front of the many microphones. He begins, "Thank you all for coming. I will be brief and I will not take any questions at the conclusion.

"As you know, my office has been negotiating with the family of Gordon Schell—who was convicted and executed for a crime he did not commit—and their representative for reparations. This morning, both sides have reached a tentative settlement, subject to acceptance by the family and budget authorization from the state legislature. The agreement reached includes a payment to the family of ten million dollars. In addition, at the insistence of Mister Schell's widow, Rosita Schell, we have also agreed to clear every Death Row wing and judiciously, systematically and thoroughly review every current case which has resulted in a death sentence, and, further, to suspend all death sentences in the state indefinitely or until every current case has been reviewed completely. My office will create a board of inquiry to conduct these reviews and details will be forthcoming. As of this moment, all Corrections facilities have been notified to empty their Death Row wings and move the affected inmates back to the general prison population immediately. Thank you."

The governor quickly steps away from the podium to his right and his aide, Oliver, steps to the podium from the other side. Oliver announces, "I will take your questions, now, but, please, keep in mind that there are some questions that I cannot answer at this time ..."

Not two hours later, Manny drives his car into the trailer park and is confronted with the sight of several television trucks, and a huge number of other vehicles, including police squad cars. He spots an opening at the side and parks his car somewhat haphazardly into it, resigned to gathering his briefcase and grocery sack in the back seat and walking to the Schell trailer several hundred feet away.

When he reaches the trailer he is deluged with reporters and onlookers spilling into the road and neighboring yards. A few reporters sit casually on the porch as Manny pushes through the crowd and up the steps of the porch, ignoring the questions and pleas for comments until he stands atop the porch. He glances from person to person residing on the porch and says, calmly, "I'll make a brief statement but only after you clear this porch. I shouldn't have to remind you that this is private property."

Manny sets down his briefcase and sack next to the door and waits a few more moments as the reporters step down from the porch. Finally, he addresses the audience, saying, "As the governor has already stated, we have both reached a tentative agreement. I'd like to further clarify that it was my client, Rosita Schell, who resolutely insisted that the settlement include the provision for death sentence reviews and a temporary moratorium on executions in this state. In memory of her husband, she has vowed to do everything possible to ensure that the tragedy which befell her family should never be endured by any other family ever again. Last, let me tell you in no uncertain terms about this woman. There is absolutely no amount of money or action taken by the state that can give her what she wants most of all: to have her husband, completely innocent of any crime, returned to her. She can *never* have what she wants most of all and nothing will make up for that."

Manny bends down and lifts his briefcase and sack from the porch, turns back to the crowd and adds, "Now, if you'll excuse me, I have to consult with my client. I will take questions later and my client will deliver a statement soon." He turns to the door, shifts the sack to his left with the briefcase, opens the screen door, steps inside it as it rests against him, opens the front door, steps inside the trailer and closes the door behind him quickly.

Inside the trailer, Rosita and Penny sit together on the sofa, holding each other's hand. The phone rings and Penny exclaims, "That damn thing's done nothing but ring all morning."

As she gets up to answer it, Manny asks, "You haven't let Rosita talk, have you?"

From the kitchen, Penny reaches for the receiver and replies, "Just listen, Manny." She puts the receiver to her ear, waits a moment, and says into the receiver, "No, Mr. Morris, she is not available to answer any questions or speak with anyone, and do not call her, again, please. Thank you." She removes the receiver from her ear and drops it onto the hook. She glances at Manny and asks, "Satisfied?"

"Perfect," Manny replies as he steps into the kitchen and deposits his briefcase and the sack on the table. He calls out to the living room, "Rosita, I need you to review the settlement and, if you're comfortable with it, we'll need your signature, please." He reaches for his briefcase and opens it as Rosita steps into the kitchen, dazed and emotionless.

Watching Manny lay out the documents from his briefcase on the table, Rosita says flatly, "If money means opportunity and security, do you know that we probably never would have achieved that while Gordon was alive?"

Manny stops and turns to Rosita and Penny remarks, "No amount of money could ever replace Gordon, and you know that, Rosita."

Defensively, Rosita responds, "That's not what I meant."

Manny looks away from Rosita to stare at the draped window, which would have shown the front yard overrun by strangers. "I only spoke with your husband three times, Rosita," he says, his gaze fixed on the drapes, "and I've thought more about who he reminded me of. I know, now, that he didn't remind me of anyone. He reminded me of who I *wanted* to be."

Rosita sniffs and confidently states, "You're hardly the only one. He wasn't ambitious or driven or hardworking or much of a provider, but he sure reminded everyone of who they wanted to be. It always would have been a struggle living with him, but who replaces that?"

"Nobody," Penny says. "We all know he left a hole that probably can't be filled."

"Then we should pick up the slack," Rosita comments. "I'm giving half of the money to the university for a permanent endowment for students who otherwise would not be able to attend." Rosita pauses and glances at Manny and Penny. She adds, "And, I'm going to school, too." She looks at Manny and asks, "What do you think I want to be?"

Manny moves from the table to stand before Rosita and replies, "Tell me."

Innocently, she reaches with her right hand to lightly grasp his left forearm as she says, "I'm going to study law so that I can represent those who can't afford an excellent attorney."

Manny quickly responds, trying to appear unaffected by her grasp of his arm, "I have no doubt you'll make an excellent attorney and I hope I *never* face you in court, and," he pauses to glance at Penny and adds, as his gaze returns to Rosita, "I'll do you better. My cut is two and a quarter million. I'll add a million and a quarter to your university endowment."

Manny smiles and Rosita slowly smiles back, slipping her right hand off his arm and slowly reaching around his back with both arms. She turns her head to her left and rests it against his right shoulder and hugs him gently while he stands unmoving, closing his eyes.

Requiem for a Lightweight

Several months later, an older model Chevy pulls into an empty parking space in a large lot and comes to rest. Jose sits behind the wheel and Maria sits in the passenger seat. Jose, in Spanish, turns to his wife and asks, "Are you ready to do this?" Maria, who was looking to the side at the surroundings, turns to her husband, smiles nervously and nods her head. The doors open and both slide out of the car.

As they walk along a sidewalk to the walk leading to a large building, several people casually dressed sit around a small music box chatting and laughing. Jose can hear strains from the music box playing a song that sounds familiar, but he can't remember the song's name, *Anyday* by Derek and the Dominos. Quietly walking to the door of the large building, he listens to the first verse and recognizes that he heard the song in Gordon's trailer.

Reaching the door, he holds it open for Maria and she steps through, but he hesitates as he hears the last line of the first verse. Suddenly overtaken, he glances to Maria with growing emotion barely controlled and, as unaffected as possible, says, in Spanish, "That's what Gordon said, that he was going back home."

Instinctively, Maria steps back to him, puts her right arm around him and gently pats his shoulder with her left, smiling openly. Jose moves with her out of the doorway and softly reaches around her to squeeze her once as they stare into each other's eyes. Instantly, they break apart and grasp each other's hand and walk down the hall looking for the right room. When the door closes, the lettering on the door contains three lines, with the first reading "Blue Ridge Community College," the second "Administrative Offices," and the last "Admissions and Records." The two disappear through a door halfway down the long hallway on the left …

Three half-full glasses of champagne sit together on a solid wood table in a nook off a kitchen, a big bay window looking out to a sizable yard, now the new home for Rosita and the children. Rosita sits in a chair, her back to the room, staring out the window, while Manny, to her left, retrieves a legal-size document from his briefcase and sets it before her on the table.

Penny leans against the wall to Rosita's right, watching Rosita with concern. Penny's husband, Alan, stands on the other side of the kitchen leaning against the counter, occasionally glancing to the others but content to remain where he is, away from the others.

Manny explains, "Okay, Rosita, this is the document that spells out the terms for the endowment between the university and us." He pauses and leans forward, resting on his left arm, as she flips each page and glances briefly. "All of the conditions that we stipulated are here, including that the student must not be eligible for any other grant, will not be able to attend without obtaining an educational loan, has a letter of recommendation from one or more of the student's teachers, and has submitted an essay about the student's plans and hopes for the future, and that two students will be awarded full rides each year, one male and one female." Manny stands erect and crosses his arms as he continues, his voice more friendly, less official. "I've met with the chancellor personally, Rosita, most of his staff and everyone who administers grant programs. They're all sympathetic to your ordeal and are excited and looking forward to doing anything they can to help you make this endowment a success." Rosita looks up at Manny and he stares back. "Of course, it will be known as the Gordon Schell Endowment. Are you ready?"

Almost in a daze, Rosita snaps out of it and says, "Absolutely. Let's get started."

Manny hands her a pen from his suit coat and says, "Sign your name on the last page on the line above your typed name. That's it."

She takes the pen he offers and signs the page and hands the document back to Manny, who places it in one of the dividers in his briefcase before retrieving a second legal-size document and setting it before Rosita. He says, "This is the document that establishes the trust with the bank for the endowment. The investment choices, initially, are reasonably safe and secure, but we can review and make changes every six months."

He reaches for the document as Rosita leans back in her chair and he turns it to the last page. "You need to sign here," he says, "above your name." Still holding the pen, she leans forward and signs on the line where Manny has pointed and leans back. "I'll need a check for a hefty four million dollars made out to the bank before I leave," he adds, gathering the document and dropping it into his briefcase.

"Those bloodsuckers," Penny says, in mock anger, stepping to Rosita to place her left hand on Rosita's left shoulder and rubbing it. Rosita rests her right hand on top of Penny's hand, and smiles at Penny, who smiles back warmly.

Manny bends forward over the table to reach two of the champagne glasses. He hands one of them to Penny from behind Rosita and says, "I'd like to propose a toast to Gordon, if I may." He looks down at Rosita as she looks up and quickly pushes the chair back from the table to stand up. Manny reaches for the third glass and hands it to Rosita and she holds it up steady. Manny adds, as he lifts his glass, "To your husband, Gordon Schell. May his death not be in vain nor his life forgotten."

Both Manny and Penny wait for Rosita's reaction. After a moment, still holding her glass at arm's length and steady, she softly says, "I only think of Gordon as alive, even though I know he'll never return to me." She pauses and looks up to the ceiling and, finally, lifts her glass high, adding, "Wherever you are, silly boy, I hope you approve and will always smile down on me."

"Amen," Penny says. Rosita turns to Penny and they clank their glasses together. Rosita turns to Manny and their glasses clank together and Manny leans to do the same with Penny. All take a small sip from each of their glasses.

Rosita sets her glass down, steps up to Penny and puts her arms around Penny and rests her head on Penny's right shoulder, saying, "Thank you for being such a good friend."

Holding her glass away with her right hand, Penny reaches around Rosita with her left and squeezes her, saying, "Anything I can do to help you, girlfriend, I will do it."

Manny turns away to look out the window and sips from his glass, partly from a desire to respect the women's privacy and partly as a matter of self-contemplation. When Rosita and Penny release each other, Rosita turns to see Manny has turned his back to them, so she taps him on his right shoulder. When Manny turns to her, Rosita asks innocently, "Can I get a hug from you, too?"

Without waiting for his response she steps up to him and puts her arms around his back as he opens his arms slightly, moving his right arm, holding the champagne glass, out of the way. Rosita gently rests her head against his chest and squeezes him. Slowly, Manny sets his glass on the table and puts both arms around her back and squeezes her tightly, closing his eyes. They remain in their embrace for a few moments until Rosita leans away from him and he relaxes his grip and drops his arms and she slides her arms around him and drops them at her side.

Moving back one step, Rosita says, "I have some place I need to go soon. I appreciate all you have done for me, both of you." She turns to acknowledge Penny as she says this. Both Manny and Penny take their glasses and down the last of the champagne and set the glasses on the table but Rosita leaves hers untouched. Instead, she asks, "When will the trust and endowment be established, Manny?"

Manny replies, "It will be ready and serviceable by the start of the next semester." He bends down to lift his briefcase from the floor and adds, "People from the university's grant administration will want to talk to you about its requirements and practice as you envision it, but I will help coordinate that contact with you."

"Thank you," Rosita says appreciatively.

"I should be going now, too," Manny says, moving toward the exit from the kitchen. "I'll stay in touch but don't hesitate to call me, Rosita, for anything." As Rosita moves to follow him, he adds, "I can find my way out, thank you." Rosita immediately stops following him.

Still standing away from the others in contemplation, Alan suddenly blurts, "I've never said this before, but I loved Gordon like he was my own brother." Everyone looks at Alan, even Manny, who has stopped in the doorway of the kitchen. "I can remember when you first moved in," he says, looking directly at Rosita, "and I invited him to meet my racing buddies. I thought they'd just tear him up, but he acted like a good ole boy and they all liked him right away. He was that way. He never judged anyone and he was fearless and he was always there when I needed him." Alan pauses and gazes in Penny's eyes as he adds, "I can't count the times he saved my marriage just by listening to me and helping me understand my own wife."

Penny steps from the other side of the kitchen to her husband and wraps her arms around him. She turns to Rosita and says, "Well, we should probably be going, too."

Manny quietly turns around and leaves the room. A moment later they hear the front door open and close.

"I won't be gone for long," Rosita says, turning to her friend. "Unless you have something planned, I'd like you both to be here when I return, please."

With an arm around each other, Alan and Penny lean against the counter. Each glances at the other and to Rosita. "Nope, we don't have anything planned," Penny says, and nods once. "You go and do what you need to do and we'll be right here when you get back."

From Rosita's new home Manny drives to a gas station and pulls up to one of the fuel stands. Exiting his car he steps up to the stand while lifting a small wallet from his jacket and removing a credit card. He slides the card in and out of the slot, lifts the fuel dispenser, and punches his fuel selector. Spinning around, he twists the gas cap open and deposits the dispenser inside and locks the dispenser open. He stands up and surveys his surroundings, his arms crossed as he waits.

When the fuel dispenser in the tank opening of his car clicks shut, he lifts it from the opening and places it back on its holder of the fuel stand. As he looks at the panel to press the button for a receipt, he glances to the street and notices a car driven by a woman.

Behind the wheel of the car sits Rosita, as she stops the car at the intersection for the stop sign, the signal light on the right side of her car blinking. Seeing no cars coming from her left, she makes a right turn onto the intersecting street and drives on.

Manny rips the receipt from its opening on the fuel stand panel, places it in a side pocket of his suit coat as he steps to his car, opens the driver's door and sits down behind the wheel. He turns the key still in the ignition switch and starts his car. The radio blares on with a song playing somewhere in the middle. Paying little attention to the music, he drives his car out the exit from the gas station onto the street where Rosita has just driven and stops at the intersection. Looking left, he quickly accelerates, turning the car right onto the intersecting street and zooms away, while the song on the radio, *Anyday* by Derek and the Dominos, moves into its second verse.

The car Rosita is driving comes to a stop at the side of the road in a cemetery. The driver's door opens and she emerges from the car holding a single white rose in her right hand. Slowly, resolutely, she meanders over the grounds between the headstones and markers, avoiding a trespass over the remains of some buried loved one laid out from its marker under six feet of dirt. Eventually, she stops some forty yards from her car to stand before a small marker on the ground, a dying white rose laying on it, which reads, "Gordon R. Schell."

Bending her knees to squat, she places her free left hand on the ground and settles to her knees. She lifts the dying rose from the marker with her left hand, places it on the ground to the side, and she sets the fresh white rose on the marker with her right while she softly whispers, "My love, sometimes I wonder why I talk to you, since I imagine you knowing what I think, but you always knew that I needed to talk anyway, so maybe I just do it for me and you let me." She looks down to the ground and continues. "So much has happened and I have tried to help others. That was your way so I hope I've made you happy."

While Rosita brushes some dirt from the marker, Manny's car slowly comes to a stop behing her car, but Rosita does not seem to hear it at all, her back facing both cars. She whispers, "Melanie got her grades this week. She's the top student of her class but you always knew she would be, didn't you?" She glances up from the marker to look across the cemetery for a few seconds. "Mark is reading *David Copperfield* now. His teacher thinks it's too much for him, but you would never agree with that, would you, Gordon? I try to help with your dictionary when he has trouble with the words." She shakes her head briefly, looks down at the marker, and adds, "Mark is so patient with me. Does that surprise you?" She pauses a moment. "No, I didn't think it would."

Manny pulls the door handle and the driver's door of his car swings open a little as he observes Rosita. He hesitates and remains seated in the car, watching quietly, respectfully.

Rosita whispers, "Melinda stopped asking to do the 'thing'. She doesn't remember you much anymore, Gordon, but I remind her all the time and she loves to hear me talk about you. She always says at the end, 'I love my Daddy.'" She pauses a moment, her eyes misting, and she instinctively wipes her eyes with her right hand. "She starts school in the fall," she whispers.

Manny opens the door further and begins to slide out of the car, but stops when Rosita, still on her knees, bends down further to almost touch the ground with her head. Frozen for a few moments while he studies her unmoving body, he slowly closes the door, holding the handle to dampen the sound. He turns the ignition switch and starts the car, pulls around Rosita's car and drives away.

With her head bowed deep before the marker, Rosita whispers haltingly, emotionally, "I miss you every moment of every day and I will love you always, silly boy. Share with me your strength so I can make it through each day until I see you again." She remains prone and silent for several minutes, until she gathers the strength to stand up on her own …

In another city not far from Clayville, Clarence sits relaxed on a couch in a modest living room watching television, his large body dwarfing his immediate surroundings, his legs extended so that his feet rest on the carpeted floor beyond the table placed before the couch. The only item on the table is the cribbage board that Gordon left him.

Suddenly, a plump black woman of average height, her smooth complexion straining with the huge luggage piece she is pulling, struggles through the living room to reach the front door just a few feet from Clarence. She frequently stops to sweep her straightened jet black hair back from her face to fall to her broad shoulders. Clarence ignores her and the enormous effort she is expending, and sits unmoving on the couch, his attention riveted to the displays beaming through the television. When the woman finally reaches the door, she leans the luggage upright and carefully removes her hand to test its steadiness. Satisfied, she glowers at Clarence and complains, "Ever since you brought that thing home," and she pauses to point to the table, "you've changed to someone I don't know, someone I don't like. You'd better get your act together, Clarence, or it won't just be *me* leaving you." Turning away from him to open the door, she struggles outside to the porch with the luggage, and closes the door behind her.

A man sitting behind the wheel of a car parked on the street a few houses away flings open the car door, lunges out of the car and runs to the porch of the house, He struggles with the luggage to grasp it by the side handle and lug it back to the car. He sets it on the street by the door and reaches inside the window to push a button and the trunk lid pops open. As the man lifts the luggage and carries it to the rear of the car and deposits it inside the trunk, the woman steps between cars and opens the passenger door of the man's car and sits down comfortably, smiling as he returns to the driver's door, opens it and sits down behind the wheel. They glance at each other briefly and lean toward each other and press their lips together. He starts the car, shifts it in reverse and backs away from the car before him, turning the wheel to point his car toward the center of the street.

Clarence lumbers forward and stands up from the couch. He turns around to look out the window between the blind shades and watches the man's car move forward around the car parked against the curb before it, and slowly pass before his house. He turns his head with the car passing until it's out of his sight …

A few days later Clarence sits behind a long, portable conference table playing cribbage with a young boy at the local Boys and Girls Club. Before him on the table taped to a small stand is a handwritten paper that reads, "Sign up for Cribbage Club" and next to the stand is a clipboard with lined papers clipped to it. A taller black girl, about thirteen, and a black boy, about twelve, both slender, step up to the table and the girl asks, "What is cribbage?"

Clarence sets his cards down and answers, "Cribbage is a card game played for points that you tally on a board like this." He points to Gordon's old cribbage board. He adds, "It builds math, probability and strategy skills. The more you build of those, the better you play."

The boy is unimpressed and replies nonchalantly, "So does poker."

Clarence looks down at the boy severely and says, "Poker is a card game of probabilities. It's only good for gambling and that requires money, so that the best poker players are people readers." Clarence pauses to look the boy up and down before adding, "Do you play poker for money?"

The boy stands erect and with bravado replies, "That's the only way to play, man."

"Does your mama know you play poker for money?" Clarence asks.

The girl turns to the boy and crosses her arms, daring him to answer truthfully. The boy's bravado immediately sinks as he sheepishly replies, "No."

"Should I tell your mama that you play poker for money or should I wait for *you* to tell her?" Clarence asks.

"Oh, man,' the boy protests, "don't make me have to do that."

The girl brightens and her eyes sparkle as she looks directly at Clarence. "I want to learn cribbage," she blurts.

Clarence turns to her and, pointing to the clipboard with the lined papers on the table, says, "Just print your name on that sheet there. We meet here every other Wednesday at 4 PM after school. Everyone gets their own cribbage board and a deck of cards so there's nothing you have to buy or bring."

She lifts the pencil next to the clipboard and writes on the sheet. When she's done, she says, "Thanks, mister."

"Brown," Clarence says, holding out his hand. The girl shakes his hand and he adds, "Clarence Brown."

The girl smiles as she says, "Thanks, Mister Brown." She turns to the boy and asks, "You gonna tell Mama?"

The boy reluctantly lifts the pencil and writes on the sheet, saying, "I like poker. I don't know nuthin' 'bout cribbage."

He drops the pencil to the table and as both scoot away, Clarence calls out after them, "First meeting is next Wednesday." Clarence looks down at the clipboard and lifts it to see the names "Jasmine" and "Jade" that the two children have written on the sheet …

The following Wednesday, two conference tables are set up parallel to each other with a dozen children, boys and girls, scattered around both. Each child is paired with the other across the table, a cribbage board between them. Clarence walks around the tables, watching the play, stopping occasionally to gauge the action, bending down to look at the cards proffered by one of the children, offering advice.

One of the children grabs a pin on the board and counts past the end line, setting the pin behind it and raising his arms triumphantly. Clarence moves to the other child and rests his large hand on the boy's shoulder, providing words of encouragement and advice …

A few months later, three girls and two boys, including Jasmine and Jade, enter a hotel lobby with Clarence in tow. They walk through the lobby to an intersecting hall and stop, looking confused, until Clarence points to the left, and they all turn left and move down the hall.

The group reaches a conference room where a portable sign stands outside, the letters on the sign reading, "State Cribbage Tournament, Junior Division." All enter the conference room slowly, awed by the sight of hundreds of children scattered around tables chatting and bragging and waiting for tournament play to get started …

The following month, Clarence shepherds Jasmine and Jade through the airplane ramp into an airport. As they move through the airport they pass a sign that reads, "Welcome to New York City."

In the darkness, a taxi arrives at a hotel entrance and all three emerge from the taxi and retrieve their bags as the driver hands each to them from the trunk. Clarence hands the driver some bills and walks away to catch up with the children while the driver nods his appreciation several times and retreats to the driver's side of the taxi …

In the daylight of the next morning, the three walk down a sidewalk and pass a window full of musical instruments. Prominent in the display is a golden tenor saxophone, held upright next to its case and a sign that reads simply, "Sale." Clarence stops to admire the instrument. Jade says something and Clarence responds. Jasmine pleads, and Jade pleads, but Clarence shakes his head unconvincingly. The girl takes his arm and starts to pull him to the door, while the boy quickly grabs his other arm and more rigorously pulls him to the door and inside all three disappear. After a few minutes all three emerge from the door, Clarence holding a case by its handle as he smiles from one of the children to the other and each returns his smile …

Later that day, the three step into a large ball room with a sign just outside the door that reads, "National Cribbage Tournament, Junior Division." During her first game, Jasmine lays down her hand, says something to her opponent and moves her back peg beyond the front one a few pins.

Jade lays down a five on top of a jack and moves his back peg two pins. His opponent lays down a five and moves the back peg two pins. Jade lays down another five and moves his back peg six pins beyond the front peg …

With the tournament concluded, a middle-aged man stands at a podium and makes an announcement and Jade steps from the side to the front of the podium. The man lifts a trophy from a table to the side and hands it to the boy, who is all smiles and lifts it for all to see.

The man makes another announcement and Jasmine steps from the side to accept a larger trophy from the man. Holding it in her right hand, she raises her right arm and stretches her left arm up like a victorious combatant. Clarence looks on from the audience, smiling proudly …

Back home, Clarence places a CD in a tray in one of the shiny gear boxes on his entertainment stand, presses a button and the tray retreats into its box. He walks past the couch in his living room but stops to gaze at the saxophone case laying on it as the music from the CD fills the house. He looks away from the couch, as he suddenly remembers something …

"Did you know you have a '14' on your cheek?" Clarence asks Gordon from his chair outside Gordon's cell.

Gordon glances up from his gaze on the cribbage board, surprised. Seated cross legged on the floor, he says, "You're only the second person who ever mentioned that. The first person who told me made me realize what it was, because I could only see it in the mirror, reversed."

"How did you get that?" Clarence asks.

Gordon smiles as he replies, "The result of an intersection with my face and a broken tonic water bottle."

"What?" Clarence exclaims, dumbfounded.

"Long story," Gordon assures him, as he returns his gaze to the cribbage board. "Anyway, it's served as my protection ever since it happened."

Clarence shakes his head in disagreement. "It didn't protect you from this," he comments.

Gordon nods. "True," he says, "and for one of two reasons. Either everyone involved has not recognized it for what it is or this is my fate, my destiny." He pauses and looks away. "I've thought about it a lot. This *is* my fate, my destiny."

Clarence shakes his head in disgust, looking down at the floor, and remarks, "I don't believe in fate, destiny …"

Back in the present, listening to the strains of a guitar and slide guitar competing during the instrumental break of the song currently lilting from the sound center, Clarence bends down to open the saxophone case. He removes the saxophone, licks his lips, puts the mouthpiece to his mouth, licks it, and puts the mouthpiece between his lips. The instrumental break concludes and he pauses as the first lyrics can be heard from the final verse of Derek and the Dominos' *Any-*

day. He opens his mouth and drops the saxophone in surprise, recognizing the familiarity of his own personal life with the words sung. Suddenly, he lifts the sax to his mouth and begins to wail as he walks out of the living room.

The Wake

Five years after Gordon Schell's execution, Manuel Rodriguez publishes a book chronicling his experiences working the case that propelled a national re-examination of the legal system and capital punishment, in particular. The last chapter of his book contains Manny's observations of most of the people who were involved in this story, much like a "where are they now" section. Following are quotes from *The Wake* by Manuel Rodriguez.

"In the five years since Gordon Schell's execution, almost everyone involved has undergone considerable change, some better than others. Governor Jobe's bid for re-election failed and, during his press conference to concede defeat, he surprised most people by also announcing his retirement. He has since moved to California, trying to enjoy a simpler life. Oliver, the governor's trusted aide, was immediately left without a job and disappeared from public life with little fanfare. No one in the state seems to have missed him and many wonder if he still lives in North Carolina at all.

"Edward Lewis, the lead investigator, was so shaken from Gunther Rankin's confession that he resigned from the police force less than a month later and did not work for an entire year. He has since started his own business, Computer Forensics and Disposal, specializing in data discovery of impounded or discarded storage devices and the secure and environmentally safe disposal of computer equipment. In his spare time he puts his investigation skills to work for the public defender's office, refusing any and all compensation for it. When anyone asks about the Gordon Schell case, he often replies 'I can't bring that man back, but I'll do whatever I can to ensure that it never happens again.'

"Cory Schneider, the junior member of the homicide investigation team, is now the senior homicide investigator for the Metro Police. Successfully cracking several high-profile cases since the Schell debacle, he has never commented publicly about his role in it, but when anyone stands before his desk, he frequently points to the plaque sitting prominently on it. The plaque reads, 'We'll find *all* the evidence. You do the rest.'

"The attorney who defended Gordon Schell at trial, Delbert T. Prescott, continues to work in the public defender's office. Having always maintained that hiding the fact that another suspect was under serious investigation for the murder of Darcy Rowland hampered his defense, and, compounded by the judge's decision to withhold the message left by the murderer at the scene, Delbert mounted a successful campaign to strengthen the rules of discovery and the penalties if circumvented. Unfortunately, he still battles the demons that only frequent alcoholic drinking can assuage.

"Sharon Pilot remained with the district attorney's office as a successful prosecutor for two more years, effectively shaking off the stigma left from the Schell prosecution through persistence, consistency and an unflagging determination to rid the streets of dangerous criminals. Courted by a large national cable network, she is seen regularly by millions of people on her own television show, which features stories of criminal investigations, mostly of the sensational or particularly heinous type. Most viewers, including critics, have ignored her progressively conservative attire, which rarely, if ever, offers any revealing look, which was much more of a staple during her prosecutorial days.

"Judge Mildred Benjamin remains on the bench today, still ruling over her courtroom with vigor and an overly serious, humorless demeanor. Deflecting criticism of her role in the Schell case by correctly revealing the defects in the system outside her control, she still commands the respect of most in the legal profession. Still, Judge Benjamin has produced one anomaly in her rulings for which she has refused to address or explain in any manner: until Gordon Schell's execution, she had sentenced several convicted murderers to a sentence of death; since Gordon Schell's execution, she has not issued a single death sentence.

"Barry Avila, Gordon Schell's most trusted confidant, left the area for places unknown less than two years later. Calling me at my office with some prescient mystique, since I had not considered writing this book yet, he said, 'Mister Rodriguez, this is just to let you know that if you, or anyone else, decides to tell this story, you have my complete permission to use my actions and quotations in any manner you or anyone else choose. That will save you a lot of time in trying to find me to get that permission later, since you won't be successful.' When I tried to ask what he meant, the phone immediately went dead. The very next day, Barry disappeared without telling a single person, even members of his own family, where he was going. All subsequent attempts to reach him proved fruitless. To this day, not one person who knew him has any knowledge as to his current location.

"Jose and Maria Montanez, the oldest friends of the Schell family, and Rosita Schell most of all, both received their college diplomas on the same day just last year. Jose was awarded a bachelor of sciences degree in biology. He is currently pursuing a Master's degree with an eye toward a doctorate, his ultimate goal being work toward discovering new methods of sustainable agriculture and reversing environmental degradation in developing areas around the world. Maria was awarded a bachelor of arts in education and is already teaching bilingual students in a third grade classroom in a severely impoverished educational district in the state. She has also started a non-profit organization to establish a better balance for funding education other than through property taxes. Arguably, her position that property taxes fuels a cycle of diminishing returns for districts which are less economically fortunate is difficult to overcome. As she correctly states, 'You, as a member of this society, are going to pay for these deficiencies sooner or later. Your choice is pay now and provide these children with the means to fuel their hopes and dreams, or pay later when they're dashed and you put them in prison or cover the necessities of their children born to young girls out of wedlock. You choose, but you're going to pay this bill sooner or later.'

"After his conviction for armed robbery, Gunther Rankin was transferred to the same facility which housed Gordon until his execution. The Death Row wing had been emptied and Johnny Morales had entered the general prison population, a move which proved crucial three years later. At that time, Rankin, Morales, and two other inmates performed one of the most daring escapes from a maximum security prison ever undertaken. The resulting manhunt, lasting over three months, succeeded in capturing all the prisoners except Rankin. Morales was quoted as saying, 'I always thought that Gunther Rankin was a sleezeball, until he came up with this escape idea. You have to admit, it was pure genius.' Thus, Gunther Rankin, the mastermind of the prison escape, still remains at large, a focus of continuing investigation, but leads seem to get fewer and less reliable as time goes by. Even when he was the subject of a segment on a television show featuring stories of criminals on the run, the leads from that exposure were useless. Perhaps, the host of the television show was right when he observed at the segment's conclusion, 'It's as though Gunther Rankin has fallen off the face of the earth.'

"A scant three years after embarking on her educational pursuits, Rosita Schell had achieved her G. E. D., a law degree and had passed the law exam on her first attempt, allowing her to practice law in the state of North Carolina. If the above hasn't convinced one of the extraordinary level of conviction and determination that this woman possesses, try facing off with her in a courtroom. Fortunately, I haven't experienced the displeasure of that event, but I have witnessed her thoroughly dispatch her lesser competition with arguments, logic and preparation unequaled. That she refuses to represent affluent clients, concentrating instead on those clients with no means at their disposal and usually of Spanish-speaking origin, is admirable. She has also overseen the successful graduation of the first four students who received a university education through her endowment exclusively. Currently working a case seeking compensation for taxes withheld from several illegal immigrants deported back to Mexico, I predict that she will prevail in the end. It will certainly send chills through those among us attempting to stem illegal immigration by deporting those immigrants who work jobs none of the rest of us will undertake but who still pay more than their fair share for services that benefit all of us.

"Why do I think Rosita Schell will prevail? Rosita has an uncanny ability to separate the right from the wrong and argue in a way that easily distinguishes both so that only an unreasonable zealot would hold onto their tenuous position. I would simply advise avoiding her wrath. As a personal note, every weekend, she visits the grave where the body of Gordon Schell lays under six feet of dirt, without fail.

"As for me, I own and run a humble law practice which does reasonably well. If I have developed a specialization, it would be defending those caught in the over-reaching snare of changes to due process through seemingly well-meaning efforts of 'Homeland Security.' The idea that we should allow government to peer into every aspect of our lives because only criminals have anything to hide is misplaced ignorance at best. I'll defer to Benjamin Franklin, however, who may have phrased it more aptly. 'Those who relinquish liberty in the name of security deserve neither liberty nor security.' I couldn't say it any better than that, but I will offer one warning. Continue down this slippery slope on which we are now sliding and one will soon have neither."

Turn! Turn! Turn!

A dozen years later a labor delivery room inside a hospital conceals the darkness of midnight sprinkled with stars at the top. Outside the range of human eyesight waits a dull blue glow as it hovers above the hospital as though poised to enter the single window of the room.

A nurse says, "Are you ready, Melinda? Give us one more push and then you can relax for a few minutes 'til the next contraction."

A woman grunts, growls, and finally lets out a distinct, "Ahhhhh!!"

Another woman, the obstetrician, says, "That's beautiful, Melinda. The head is crowning so it's not going to be much longer."

Melinda blurts, "Oh, god, it hurts."

A man's voice calmly says, "You're doing great, hon. You're almost there so don't quit just yet. We're almost through." A pause follows and he adds, "I can see the head."

The doctor says, "Maybe two or three more pushes, Melinda. Are you feeling the contraction coming, yet?"

With a deep grunt, Melinda strains as she replies, "I can feel it. Here it comes."

"Take a deep breath and get ready to push when it's the most intense," the doctor advises. "Ready?"

A long, steady 'Ohh!' is heard, followed by a brief pause, a growing growl and 'Ahhhh!!"

The dull blue glow moves closer to the window, growing larger. It seems to be searching for entry.

The doctor says, "That's halfway, Melinda. If you give one more push whenever you're ready, I'll help you. Don't even wait for the next contraction. Just go when you're ready."

"Okay," Melinda murmurs with exhaustion. "Give me a few seconds." All is quiet until Melinda grunts, growls, and shouts "Ahhhh!!!" one more time.

The man says, "I think we've got it, Melinda."

"That's it!" the doctor exclaims. "Relax, don't push anymore! It's coming through!"

A few moments of silence and the nurse exclaims, "Oh, what a beautiful baby, Melinda."

The dull blue glow is now just outside the room. If it could be seen by anyone looking out, it would dominate the view through the window. Instantly, the glow zips down below the window and disappears completely.

The nurse states, "It's a baby boy, Mom and Dad." A baby's cry is heard.

"You did it, Melinda," the man says. "I'm so proud of you."

"I'm so tired," Melinda sighs.

The nurse says, "I'm almost done cleaning up this healthy, little baby boy. Do you have a name, yet?"

The man says, "We thought, if it's a boy, that we should name him after her father, Gordon."

The doctor says, "That's a nice name. I like that."

Melinda says, "Can I hold him? Can I hold my baby, now?"

"Here you are, Mama," the nurse says.

"Oh, he's looking up at you, honey," the man says, adding, "He looks content, doesn't he?"

"That he does," says the nurse. "And, look, he's closing his eyes. I'll bet he's tired."

"From a long journey," the man comments. "I'll bet every baby thinks it's a long journey."

"Well, so does Mama," the doctor says. "Take the baby, Kathy, and check all the vitals. We'll let Mom rest here for a while. Congratulations, Dad."

Closing Arguments

Manuel Rodriguez, in his fifties with graying hair short and well-groomed, drives to his next afternoon appointment when his cell phone rings. Attached to the hands-off option in his car, the dash reads "Rosita Schell," and he punches the answer button on the dash and yells, "What may I do for you this afternoon, Sweetie?"

Through his car speakers, a husky, sexy female voice replies, "I see you're still trying to soften me up for that inevitable courtroom clash we've been able to avoid to date." There's a short laugh, and Rosita adds, "It won't work. You know that, don't you?"

Manny laughs and advises, "Well, I'll use any means at my disposal in the interest of serving my clients, you know that." There's an awkward silence, which Manny breaks by asking, "What's on your mind today, hon?"

"Well, I've been thinking lately," Rosita's voice says through the speakers, "that I should leave the practice for a few months and take a long vacation visiting my children scattered all over. I think I need to see all those wonderful grandchildren they've given me before those kids forget they ever had a grandmother."

Suddenly, Manny is panic-stricken and nearly runs into the car ahead of him. Absent of his usual calm and persuasive demeanor, he nervously barks, "What was that you said, Rosita? Would you please repeat it?"

Not expecting that response, Rosita impatiently asks, "What's the matter with you, Rodriguez? Are you going deaf in your old age?"

Still somewhat panicky, Manny asks, again, "Rosita, just *please* repeat that last part that you said. Please!"

Skeptical and concerned, Rosita says, "What? About my grandchildren? That I want to see my grandchildren before those kids forget they ever had a grandmother?"

Rapidly, Manny states, "Yes, that's it. Thank you! When are you leaving?"

"Today," comes Rosita's response.

Even more panicked, Manny shouts, "What time? You *can't* leave before I see you."

"We're not leaving until about four this afternoon," Rosita assures him. "Maria will meet me at my office and we'll leave from here." She wonders what is going on with Manny and asks, "Listen, Manny, you sound worried about something. What's the matter?"

"Are you at your office, now?" Manny demands.

Rosita replies, "Yes, but—"

"Don't go anywhere!" Manny interrupts, his tone like a general delivering an order. "Stay right where you are. I'm coming right over and will explain everything!" Without waiting for her acknowledgment, he punches the button to disconnect the call, swerves into the left lane, barely avoiding a collision, and races across the opposing traffic lanes into a parking lot to quickly re-enter the street in the opposite direction. Barely under control, he rushes back to his office, calling his secretary to have her contact his next appointment and cancel it because of an emergency …

Barely an hour later, Manny races down a long hallway framed by mostly glass walls, his briefcase swinging wildly from his left hand. At the end of the hall, he reaches a glass door with lettering which reads "Rosita Schell and Associates," and below that, "Attorneys at Law." Manny comes to a nimble, quick halt, tests the door and when it opens, he immediately flings it wide with his free right hand and yells, "Rosita!"

From the near hidden recesses of the suite comes the answer, "Back here!"

Manny walks rapidly down the long hall to the last door on the left and steps through. Inside the room stands Rosita, her face a bit wrinkled but still youthful and vibrant and her hair still jet black, and Maria, older and graying but smiling as freely as always. Manny pants, almost out of breath, "Good. I caught you before you left."

"Rosita's pretty worried about you, Manny," Maria says, a twinkle in her eyes. "She was just telling me that she thinks you're losing it."

Rosita protests, "Now, that's not what I said, Maria."

"Look, I apologize for sounding a bit disconcerted," Manny explains, setting his briefcase on the floor. As he opens a side pocket, he adds, "but you'll understand why I was acting like I did. Here," he says, pulling out a letter-size envelope. He opens it and removes a sheet of paper and a smaller, unopened envelope. Handing the sheet to Rosita, he adds, "just read this and you'll know why."

Taking the sheet proffered by Manny, Rosita glances over it and comments, "My god, Manny, this is Gordon's handwriting, or printing. He always printed, and this is the date of his execution."

"Read it," Manny insists.

Rosita, in some initial shock, focuses on the paper before her and reads aloud, "Senor Manuel Rodriguez. Being my attorney of record, you have proven to be concerned only with my interests and those of my family. As evidence, your action in securing my will, strictly taken of your own account, will certainly protect and provide for my family. For this, you should receive my eternal gratitude and I trust that this letter serves as such.

"I ask of you one final act as my legal representative. As you may recall, you asked me once if I considered my wonderful wife—the only human being on this big blue spaceship who ever even attempted to truly understand me—if I considered her 'the love of my life.' While I responded that I did not, I have concluded that it is, indeed, true. In fact, she has been, is now, and was always meant to be with me in this life. I could not escape her desire for me any more than I could ignore my desire for her.

"Contained in this envelope are a few words that I want her to read at some point in the future, but at what point? If Rosita is truly the love of my life in this soon to be concluded existence, then I can state that I know her better than anyone else. I know her so well that I can predict her actions, even well into the future. So that you know when the 'point' has been reached, you will hear her speak of the need to visit her children, who will have scattered apart, successful in making their way in their lives, with children of their own. She will say that she needs to see her grandchildren before they forget they ever had a grandmother. Her children will be scattered; her grandchildren hardly know their grandmother. This will be her motivation for the next few months and you will recognize it when it occurs. Please deliver the envelope to her at that time and do not fail me.

"In all that has transpired, you still will maintain an obligation to me, if you are a man of honor and respect your responsibilities as an officer of the court. I do not hesitate in believing that you will act in accordance with these last requests. I will always be grateful for your cooperation and I remain, as always, Gordon R. Schell."

Maria hangs her head, looking at the floor as she walks around Rosita's desk to look out the window. Manny thrusts the sealed envelope in his left hand toward Rosita.

Rosita rubs her forehead as she sets the sheet down on her desk and takes the envelope from Manny. Confused, she asks, "Why didn't you share this with me earlier? Why did you wait twenty-two years, Manny?"

Manny shakes his head once as he replies, calmly, "It wasn't entrusted to you, Rosita. It was entrusted to me."

Frowning, Rosita slides the nail from her right thumb under the flap of the sealed envelope and opens it with little effort. She removes the sheet of paper folded three times in half and shakes it fully open. Glancing over it, she notices that it contains no date, but she recognizes the printing as that of her late husband. Reading aloud, she says, "There is no such thing as a coincidence. It is merely our humble effort to explain an event for which a reason has yet to be discovered or fully understood." Failing to understand any significance as to why she should receive this advice after such a long time has elapsed, she looks to Maria, but Maria continues to only stare out the window. She glances at the sheet and notices some more printing at the very bottom of the page. She reads, "PS I may have been imprisoned, but I heard you." Rosita's eyes begin to mist and she turns away from both to wipe her eyes with her free hand.

"That was it, Rosita," Manny says, trying to console her. "There was nothing else. That was delivered to me by the Department of Corrections a few days after his execution. Nothing more."

"I don't understand it," Rosita laments, discouraged. "It doesn't make any sense, after all this time. Though, to be honest, Gordon often didn't make a lot of sense."

Manny hesitates speaking, knowing what he wants to say but reluctant nevertheless. After a few moments, he softly offers, "Maybe, it's because he was involved in it all along."

"What?!" Rosita bristles, spinning around to confront Manny. "You better not be suggesting what I *think* you're suggesting!"

Manny bends down to his briefcase, opens the same side pocket and retrieves a yellowing, single sheet of paper, folded in half. He says, "I've been thinking about this a lot lately, ever since Johnny Morales granted that interview before he died."

"Johnny Morales?" Rosita spits, her tone unmistakable in its anger and resentment. "You would give credence to a man who killed the mother of his twin babies *and* the babies in a drug-induced haze, so fucked up from drugs that he could never remember exactly what he did?"

Manny shakes his head in disagreement. He calmly states, "You can't argue that the person who knew both Gordon and Gunther was Johnny Morales. He was on Death Row with Gordon for almost a year and he *did* spend three months on the run with Gunther. No one else can claim that much contact with both."

"Johnny Morales an expert on my dead husband?" Rosita belittles Manny's argument. "You have got to be kidding! That scum wasn't even an expert on himself, let alone anybody else!"

"Then, look at this," Manny insists, thrusting the folded paper at Rosita.

Angrily, Rosita snatches the paper from Manny's outstretched hand. Holding it with both hands, she unfolds it and reads the joke Gordon wrote for his psychiatrist visit with Angela. "Gordon wrote this," she comments, having read the paper's contents.

"That's right, Gordon wrote that," Manny declares. "Angela gave me that after his psychiatric exam, and even as I was going through everything for my book, even as I was looking through the few letters that he wrote to you from prison, I still didn't see it." He stops to walk right up to Rosita and waits until she finally looks at him. "*Until*, you told me just a few years ago, that Gordon's printing changed when he went to prison. Remember that? How you told me, *in passing*, Gordon's printing changed when he went to prison." When he pauses, Rosita looks down at the paper and lifts it to glance over it, again. "Except that!" Manny exclaims.

Rosita shakes the paper and drops it to her side, stating defiantly, "So what? Maybe he wrote it the old way to make some point. What's wrong with that?"

"What's wrong with that is Johnny Morales," Manny argues. "In that interview, he told *that* joke, almost word for word. So, who told him that joke? *Gunther Rankin* told him that joke while they were running after their escape!"

"How quickly you forget that Gordon and Morales sat across from each other on Death Row for several months," Rosita counters. "Morales probably heard it from Gordon and got the two confused. *That* wouldn't surprise me *one bit* with him!"

"Maybe Gordon didn't write it at all," Manny argues, pushing his face down to Rosita's. "Maybe Gunther Rankin wrote it and sent it to Gordon in prison."

"Now you're insane, Manny," Rosita scoffs.

Manny steps back from Rosita but still glares at her as he calmly states, "That's why I have quietly been securing samples of Rankin's printing over the last few years and showing them along with Gordon's samples to expert after expert. Sometimes I say they're by the same person. No disagreement. Sometimes I give them one from each and ask them to match the correct samples to the correct original piece. Usually, there is no match. *Experts* can't even tell their printing apart, that's how close they are."

Manny steps to his right to stand on the other side of Rosita's desk, while Rosita begins to appear disconsolate. He declares, "Further, Rankin said he followed Gordon for years, they never met, but that he would often be mistaken for Gordon. Well, I don't believe that they never met for a second! You can't convince me that Gordon was *never* mistaken for Gunther all that time and that they *never* ran into each other. I don't believe that in the slightest. I believe they *did* meet, they *did* have continuous contact, they *did* conspire with Simon Edwards to kill Darcy Rowland and only until the timing was *perfect* did they all agree on it. *And*, I believe that your husband was *twisted* enough that it was *his idea* to force the state to execute him, knowing that his own half-brother would confess and the state would be forced to pay the *big prize*, ten million dollars, like suckers. And *I* was suckered into it!"

Hearing that, Rosita seethes with uncontrollable anger and shouts, "Get out of my office, Rodriguez!" She points out the door and shouts in a higher volume, "Right now! Get out!"

"Shut up, both of you!" Maria shouts, still looking out the window. Both turn to Maria but are quiet, almost in shock. Slowly, they look at each other, knowing that Maria never raises her voice. Maria is always the calm, judicial, empathetic one.

No one makes a sound for what seems an eternity, but, in reality, is barely half a minute. Finally, still looking out the window, Maria states in a much calmer tone, "That's what I hate the most about both of you. Perhaps, it's your training and the way you must conduct yourselves in your profession, but when you're together, it always turns into an argument. *Now*, you're going to shut up and listen to me, because I have some things to tell both of you that neither of you know, so sit down."

Rosita obediently sits right down in the chair behind her and asks, softly, "What is it?"

Maria turns around without haste and immediately sees Rosita sitting but Manny still standing. She glowers at Manny and commands, "You too, counselor. Sit down."

Without hesitation, Manny pulls the near-by chair to him and immediately sits down. Timidly, he says, "Sorry."

Still glowering at Manny, Maria states with senior authority, "Having met Gordon long before either of you, I can safely say that I knew him best—"

"Maria!" Rosita interrupts, "I bore three children—"

"If I had had my say, I would never have allowed you, muchacha, to meet Gordon," Maria declares, glaring now at Rosita defiantly.

"What are you saying?" Rosita asks, feeling hurt and confused.

Maria's countenance softens and she says, sympathetically, "Be quiet, my child, and I will tell you." Concerned but attentive, Rosita simply stares at her oldest friend. Manny just stares quietly at Maria, a bit of wonder mixed with sudden admiration for the woman most people took for granted. Maria calmly begins, "Gordon lived next door to us for more than eighteen months and we knew him long before you met him. Jose liked him right from the start, maybe even thought of him as a little brother some. But, you should recall that when we sat in our kitchen and you talked about that 'hot' boy that lived next door, Jose thought you should meet but I said nothing, which is typical of our culture. The wife defers to the husband."

Rosita brightens a bit, though she's mildly confused as she responds, "I remember that night, but I thought you just agreed with Jose. You didn't?"

"No I didn't," Maria asserts, "because of what happened earlier. One evening, it was still light out, and Jose had come home from work. Gordon came over to say 'hi,' and we all were out on the patio in the back. I was tending my flowers, when Jose, dirty and sweaty, decided to take a shower. I didn't really think much of it, even though he was leaving me, his wife, alone with another man, but it was outside and, after all, it was just Gordon. I was making small talk when I remembered that his birthday was coming up, so I asked him what he wanted, not that we were going to get him anything." Maria looks down at the desk and frowns at the memory. "I thought I heard him struggle to talk, maybe even choking on the words, so I turned to face him, and I saw his eyes were watered. He was telling me that all he ever wanted in his life was to wake up one morning and know that everyone had finally rejected their impostor tribes, had returned to the one true tribe of human beings to become as one in peace and cooperation." Manny nods his head knowingly and Maria notices and says to him, "You've heard it before, haven't you?"

Manny continues nodding his head and replies softly, "Yes."

Maria turns her head from Manny to Rosita as she recalls, "He said he didn't want money, recognition or power. They held no value for him, but his billions of cousins won't give him what he really wants, to live in a home where everyone else lives in peace, not in this lifetime, maybe not *ever*. I could see tears running down his face, and, when he suddenly looked up at me, he could see the concern on my face, so he immediately got up and quickly walked around the patio back to his apartment and inside. He avoided me for several days or maybe I avoided him. I never told Jose about it, but can you see why I wouldn't have allowed you to see him, muchacha?"

Rosita hangs her head and replies softly, "A man who cries openly is considered weak and unworthy."

"I didn't think he was right for you, Rosita, for a long time," Maria confides.

Rosita looks up at her old friend and asks, "What changed your mind, Maria?"

Maria frowns at Rosita, replying, "You know when it was."

Rosita thinks for only a moment and offers, "The camping trip we took in the mountains."

"Yes," Maria simply says.

Manny looks from Maria to Rosita and back, uncertain what was meant by that reference, and when neither woman begins to explain, he asks, "What happened at the camping trip?"

"Gordon wanted to show us one of his favorite places in the mountains," Rosita says, turning to face Manny, "and JR offered to watch the kids, so off we went. That first afternoon, after we pitched the tents, Gordon and Jose took off for a long hike. They got about five miles until Jose slipped and fell and hurt his back. They started back, but Jose finally couldn't go any farther because his back hurt so much. Gordon stood him up, put him over his shoulder and carried him about two miles back, resting frequently, and mostly in the dark. We were in a panic because they didn't get back until after midnight, but I wouldn't let Maria get help." Rosita hangs her head for a moment, and looks up at Manny. "I didn't want any attention because I was here illegally."

"Jose said that he kept telling Gordon to leave him and go get help," Maria adds, "but Gordon said he couldn't do that. Rosita would be too scared and I would never forgive him for leaving Jose."

Rosita smiles at the memory and says, "He was so exhausted, that even though I tried to arouse him because I wanted to make love, he just fell asleep."

Maria smiles while looking at Rosita. She says, "He proposed the next week and you said, 'Yes.'"

Rosita nods her head and grins widely as she remarks, "I very much wanted to be his wife."

Maria looks at Rosita with a maternal compassion and says, "So, you see, muchacha, I kept quiet to give you two a chance, but I truly thought you would rip him apart, just like you did with most of your men."

Rosita smiles knowingly. "Gordon was unlike any other man I ever knew," Rosita confides. "I could never stay mad, even at him. He just knew how to make me smile and laugh, even when it was really bad."

It's quiet for a few seconds, until Maria looks at Manny and says, "As for you, Manny, I have this." She waits for Manny to look at him with attention. "I did read your book. I just didn't want to tell you, knowing that it would go to your ego-driven head." Manny smiles and starts to protest but Maria raises her hand to stop him. "Our district subscribes to many magazines with education themes, including some about innovative techniques or methods. Not long ago, I read about this village on one of the remote islands in the Phillipines. Over the years, this teacher, whose grandparents were from a different part of the island and had left for the U.S., had been building this computer network for all the villagers. He had scavenged, scoured and begged for microwave antennas, satellite antennas, routers, computers, generators driven by wind power, solar generators, and spare parts, all of it to be thrown away until he and some of the villagers he trained refurbished or rebuilt it back to working condition. They constructed water-tight buildings for every few families so that everyone had access to a computer and the Internet, connected by satellite. He obtained books and other materials and every child over ten could read and write English fluently. The village even made money with software applications, services and consulting. They had pictures and the setup was incredibly impressive."

Manny looks raptly at Maria, as she pauses to measure his interest. Finally, he asks, "What does this have to do with me?"

"Who do you think the teacher was?" Maria poses to both.

"Who?" Manny asks, impatiently.

"Barry," Maria answers, smiling contentedly.

Rosita and Manny both blurt out together, "Barry?"

Maria continues to smile broadly as she replies, "It pays to have a Masters in electrical engineering, I guess." She looks down at the desk before her and reaches into her purse. Removing a sheet of paper folded in half, she unfolds it, while Rosita and Manny look at each other quizzically. Looking up at Rosita, Maria says, "I was going to show this to you during our trip, but I want to share it with both of you, now."

Feeling a little tired on her feet, Maria pulls out the chair and sits down. Once she's comfortable, she holds the paper open before her and states, "There was an email address in the article, so I emailed Barry. For a while, I thought he must not have received it or he was, somehow, mad at me, at us, but, finally, after two months, I received an email with the subject reading, 'Hi, Maria! How have you been? I miss your cooking!' It was Barry and he wrote that he was so shocked to hear from someone in his past that it took him that long to compose a response.

Anyway, we've emailed back and forth ever since and I asked him once how he ended up where he did. This is what he wrote back."

Manny leans forward, resting his chin in his left fist, his left elbow set on his leg. Rosita wears a slight frown and leans back.

Maria reads from the paper, "Oh, how can I say it? After all that had happened, there came a time when I was lost. Gordon was gone. He was the friend I trusted the most. Rosita was so filled with misplaced anger about homosexuals, she made me uncomfortable—"

"I always considered Barry a friend," Rosita interrupts.

"Hush," Maria chides, looking up at Rosita, her eyelids narrowed. Rosita bows her head and Maria looks down at the paper and reads again. "You and your wonderful husband, Jose, were busy with school. Everyone, friends and family alike, seemed to be leaving me, moving away, and I was unsure of what to do, where to go, until one night I had a dream. In the dream, I was standing alone in some desolate, flat landscape, and everywhere I could see, there was nothing but dirt, miles and miles of dirt. I thought, *how do I get out of here? Which direction should I take?* Immediately, I heard a voice behind me say, 'Go back home, Barry.' When I turned around to see whose voice said that, Gordon was standing behind me, pointing forward. He looked at me with that half-smile of his—the one that when you saw it, you knew everything was all right—and he said, 'Your people want you, need you. You know the way.' I woke right up, thought about it for a while, and I knew what I had to do. I got my things in order the next day, made my way here the following day, and I've never looked back."

Maria stops reading, though she continues to look only at the paper. Both Manny and Rosita want to speak, but neither makes an attempt while Maria remains focused on the paper she holds. Instead, they glance at each other quizzically. After a few more seconds of silence, Maria reads, "Still, I was always uncertain why I was here and what my life means. That is, until I read Mr. Rodriguez' book." Manny smiles but Maria never looks up nor hesitates. "One of my old students found a copy and sent it to me from Manila. As I read it, I started remembering things about Gordon that I hadn't thought about for quite some time. When I finally got to the part where Mr. Rodriguez met Gordon the first time, there it was. Gordon told him, 'Death is not permanent,' and I remembered how many times he told me the same sentence. We live on, through our children, and our lifeblood becomes their lifeblood. We live on in the memories, even the dreams, of those we influence. We live on in the tangible works we leave behind for others to use. So, you see, Maria, he was right, as usual. Death is *not* permanent. I live on and all of this is my life, the one I forged and it has meaning. You live on. We all shall ..."

Maria glances from Rosita to Manny and says, "There's more, but that's enough for now." She folds the paper and rises from the chair. Her speech is soft, re-assuring. "You two argue, I suppose, because it's in your nature, but you can't convince me about Gordon's guilt or innocence, because I already know." She returns the paper to her purse and turns away from both. "And, to me it's pointless. If he's guilty, he paid for his crime." She walks to the window and glances about, stopping her focus on the trees, the people bustling below, the buildings, and the mountains in the distance. "If you feel somehow dirty from the settlement money, let me remind you that your endowment is one of the most successful at the university. Hundreds have completed their education only because of you two and contributions, mostly from those very graduates, have exceeded *forty million dollars*. No one's going to argue that you didn't give back."

Maria crosses her arms. "If Gordon was innocent, then he sacrificed himself for us. I would never have persevered through school if he were here to occasionally chastise me. I persevered to honor him, refusing to let him down, Jose, too."

Maria turns around and leans her back against the window, her arms still crossed. She stares ahead, not focusing on either of the other two occupants in the office. She says, "I remember how mad you used to get, muchacha, when Gordon would ask you to tell him who you are, and you would say, 'I'm a Mexican woman,' and he would stop you with that buzzing sound, and say, 'Tell me what I cannot see with my own eyes, what I cannot hear with my own ears.' But he taught you well, Rosita, and I hear you remind people of the human characteristics no one can control: gender, color, place of birth, and primary language. All of those are out of our control, so how can they possibly be a part of our identity? Because, if they *are*, just exactly who are you? Are you a human being out of control or a puppet whose strings are pulled by others?"

Maria pauses for only a moment and shifts her gaze to stare sympathetically at Rosita's face and Rosita stares back attentively, knowingly. Maria advises her oldest friend, "Gordon taught me well, too, and I learned from him. Only small bits and pieces are revealed by you and we must separate the relevant from the irrelevant, but time and experience allow us to 'see' the real you. We can never completely know you, but we *can* fill that gap in our knowledge of you with trust, belief, a leap of faith. One of the last things he said to you was, 'I believe in you.' Well, I believed in him and always will. In my heart, I know what happened, *know* it. I know what he did and didn't do, and he knew *exactly* what he was doing."

Manny sits quietly, looking intently from one woman to the other. When he hears the last of Maria's speech, he is suddenly shaken. He has heard that before.

Maria smiles warmly at Rosita and glances at Manny, still smiling. Suddenly, she lifts her right arm and notes the time on her watch and exclaims, "Rosita, it's getting late! I want to see my surrogate children and grandchildren. Let's get moving!"

Immediately, the office is a blur of movement as everyone gathers their respective items in preparation for departure. As Manny lifts his briefcase from the floor and out of Rosita's charge around the office, he remarks, "You know, there was a time when I wanted those children to be more than surrogates."

Maria and Rosita look at each other and burst out laughing. When Rosita can finally speak through her laughter, she asks, "And, would that time be around the endowment completion, Manny? When you followed me to the cemetery? When you and Angela were experiencing another of your misunderstandings?"

Manny blushes briefly and stammers, "You knew all along, huh?"

Rosita steps to Manny, pats his right arm below his shoulder with her right hand and consoles, "Yes, Manuel, but I've loved only one man in this life and I don't need another. You and Angela were always right for each other, and those wonderful children of yours are the proof."

"Say hello to your family for me, Manny," Maria says, smiling, her laughter subsided. "Send them my love." Maria turns to Rosita and advises, "I'm ready to go, Senora. Shall we?"

Rosita has stepped behind the desk, opened a drawer and removed her purse. She looks up at Maria, dangling the purse, and says, excitedly, "Ready. Let's get on the road!"

"To Melinda's?" asks Manny, leading the way out of the office, twisting his head slightly.

"Yes, my little baby," Rosita exclaims, now very excited. "I haven't seen her baby girl, yet, and her little boy is now five years old!"

"She's not a little baby any more, Rosita," Maria admonishes, smiling broadly.

"Gordon, isn't it?" Manny asks, "After his grandfather?"

"Yes," Rosita replies, "it was her husband's idea."

Manny stops at the door leading out of the law office and opens it wide for the women. Maria passes through first, followed by Rosita, and Manny steps through the entrance ...

As all three exit the building to the parking lot, they wave and say their good-byes. The two women move to their right and Manny separates from them, walking to his left toward his waiting car. During his short walk, he contemplates what Maria had said, especially that "he knew *exactly* what he was doing." Suddenly, he recalls when he heard it before and who said it: Adam! *Those two have so little in common, so why did they both say that?* Manny thinks. *What do they know that I don't?*

Manny can't shake his stubborn perception that Gunther and Gordon must have met, they must have known about each other. It's just too far-fetched to believe otherwise. As he reaches his car, he presses his remote entry to open the driver door and flings it open. Tossing his briefcase on the passenger seat, he sits down, pulls the door shut and sticks the key in the ignition. He twists the key and the car turns over. Quickly craning his neck to look behind, he hesitates to shift the car in reverse. His nagging consciousness tells him that he'll never know what happened with absolute certainty and he'll never know Gordon, either. It's the same conscious position he hasn't been able to escape for years, and he suddenly feels the need to vent his frustration and rage. Turning back to face forward, he raises his right hand in a fist and strikes the dash once, and fumes, "Dammit, Gordon! Who the hell were you!?" Manny studies the building grounds, shaking his head in abandon, as though confronted by an impossible obstacle …

Verdict

As they near the exit to Melinda's house, Rosita suggests to her friend sitting in the passenger seat that she should remove the CD and try to find something on the radio to listen to. Maria presses the eject button, removes the CD from its slot and turns on the FM section of the radio. She presses the seek button and they both listen for a few seconds, agree to try another and the process is repeated a few more times. Finally, the radio stops at a station playing a song that Rosita recognizes and she immediately tells Maria to leave it there.

"I haven't heard that song in a long time," Rosita comments, suddenly reminiscing. "Gordon liked that song a lot and I eventually grew to like it, too."

Maria turns to face her friend. "It fits our trip," she says, smiling. "We're almost there and you *are* going back to see your kids." They both nod to each other and settle back in their seats to listen to *Find Your Way Back* by Jefferson Starship as Rosita steers the car onto the exit ramp, now barely a few minutes from her youngest daughter's residence.

Rosita's car, just a typical, mid-size sedan, pulls into the driveway of a typical, middle class house in a typical middle class subdivision. It comes to a stop before the garage and the trunk pops open before the passenger doors open. Rosita emerges from the driver's side and Maria exits the front passenger side.

The front door of the house opens and Melinda, about twenty-five and beautiful despite bearing two children already, steps out and down the walk toward her guests. She says teasingly, "If it isn't my two favorite women of experience come to visit little old me."

Rosita pulls out her bag from the trunk and sets it on the gravel of the driveway to look at her daughter. "Now, be nice, baby girl," Rosita says, "especially to the one who carried you for nine months and brought you into this world."

Melinda stops at the front of the car and says, "I just miss you, Mom, and I'd like to see you more, that's all."

Rosita takes a step toward Melinda and says, "Then, come here and give me a big hug." Melinda steps up to her mother and they wrap their arms around each other and bury their heads on the other's shoulder. After a moment, they release each other and Melinda steps to Maria and hugs her, too.

Melinda stands up straight and, as the wind blows her dark blond, shoulder-length hair all around, she sweeps it from her face and crosses her arms. Her medium height accents her full feminine attributes and she smiles at her mother struggling with her bag.

"Can I help you with that, Mom?" she asks.

"I'll manage," Rosita advises, frowning, as she glances at her daughter and wheels the bag across the gravel and onto the walk. Melinda steps out of the way of both women and follows them up the walk to the front door.

Rosita steps into the house, followed by Maria and Melinda. Melinda says, as she closes the door behind her, "You can just set your bags to the side there and we'll help you put them away later. You probably want to rest after your trip, don't you, Mom?"

"I'm not decrepit, yet, Melinda," Rosita advises, wearing a frown but with her eyes twinkling. "Where are those beautiful babies?"

"Carol is napping and Gordon is out playing with the neighborhood kids," Melinda says.

"Well, then, I wouldn't mind sitting down and putting my feet up for a little while," Rosita says.

Rosita and Maria roll their bags to the side of the front hall and Melinda walks to the main hall of the house. She tells them, "Come with me into the living room. You can get comfortable there and I'll bring you something to drink, if you want." The senior women follow her as she turns left at the main hall, steps into the kitchen and turns right at the opening in the wall separating the kitchen from the living room.

Rosita sits down in an easy chair about six feet from a window to her right, facing the yard. Maria sits down on the sofa at the edge closest to Rosita, quickly pulls her feet from her sandals, leans back and puts her feet up on the sofa. Rosita pulls up the foot lever to lift her feet from the floor and sit back.

Melinda asks from the kitchen, "Can I bring you anything?"

"Not right now, hon," Rosita says, closing her eyes.

"I'm fine, Melinda," Maria says.

"I've got some things going on in the kitchen, so I hope you don't mind if I don't join you for a little bit," Melinda says.

Maria says, "You take care of what you need to, Melinda. We're fine. We can still take care of ourselves."

Melinda reaches for a radio on the kitchen counter and turns it on as she announces, "I'm going to listen to the radio while I putter around. If they play Mark's song, Mom, I'll call out."

Rosita opens her road-weary eyes and replies, "That would be nice. I haven't heard it in a while." She closes her eyes and begins to drift away into a nap, the low level of the music soothing her way.

Melinda leans against the counter, reading a cook book, when a timer goes off. She sets the book down, grabs an oven mitt, steps to the oven and opens it. She removes one tray of cookies and sets it on the open counter, reaches back into the oven and removes a second tray of cookies, setting it next to the first.

The door leading outside from the kitchen bursts open and a little boy about five leaps into the kitchen. He slams the door shut, takes two running steps, and stops dead in his tracks when Melinda admonishes, "Just hold it right there, buster."

Apologetically, the boy says, "Sorry, Mom."

"Your grandmother is sleeping in the living room so you need to be especially quiet, all right?" Melinda warns him.

Brushing back his thin, brown hair with his right hand, the little boy's eyes light up and he asks, "Can I go see her?"

"Sure," Melinda says, "but you have to be quiet."

"Okay," the little boy replies, grinning. He tiptoes quietly to the opening in the kitchen, stops to look through, and tiptoes into the living room. With great exaggeration, he tiptoes around the lifted foot section of the easy chair, and stands unmoving. His face is only a few inches from Rosita's face. He stares at her and grins, not making a sound.

Rosita suddenly opens her eyes, fixes her gaze upon the boy just inches from her face, smiles warmly and soothingly says, "Well, hello there, handsome."

Somewhat shyly, the little boy softly says, "Hi, Granma." Rosita lifts her right hand and rests it on the left side of his face. The little boy lifts his left arm and grabs Rosita's right forearm and both gaze unblinking at the other, smiling.

Melinda appears at the opening, leaning against the wall. Maria looks at the two to her right, young and old, and smiles happily. Rosita drops her arm to her side and the little boy lets his arm slide off hers to rest at his side.

Suddenly, his eyes widen, and he asks Rosita, "Can I show you something, Granma?"

Her smile widening, Rosita softly says, "You sure can."

"Okay," the little boy says, seeing if she's ready. "Watch," he adds and Rosita nods her acknowledgment. The little boy touches his chest at his heart with the index finger of his right hand. Lifting the same hand, he touches his nose with the same finger. He reaches to Rosita with his right hand and touches her nose gently with his finger and drops his hand to softly touch her chest, above her left breast. With a grand flair, he exclaims, "The nose knows all!" Instantly, he turns and runs out of the living room, past his mother and into the kitchen, stopping abruptly.

Rosita turns to Melinda, her eyes misting. Melinda shrugs her shoulders and remarks, "Yeah, he just started doing that a few days ago." She turns and steps into the kitchen, looking at the boy, and says, "What's on your mind, champ?"

"What's that I smell, Mom?" the little boy says with great curiosity.

Melinda walks past him, gently rubbing her hand over his head, and says, "I just baked some peanut butter cookies." She steps over to the counter.

"Oooh!" the boy says, excitedly. "Can I have one?"

"Yes," Melinda says. As she retrieves a spatula and slides it under one of the cookies, the boy steps up to his mother and wraps both arms around her right thigh and hugs her. She lifts the cookie and hands it to him, which he takes with his right hand while still squeezing her thigh with his left.

Maria, now with her feet on the floor and sitting up on the sofa, looks to her old friend, and, in Spanish, remarks, "Doesn't he remind you some of his grandfather?"

Rosita, with barely any emotion, simply says, "Si." She closes her eyes and a memory floods her consciousness …

Gordon and Rosita stand together on a hill before a huge sunset, young again. Rosita's arms are around his neck, his arms around her waist. Softly, Gordon asks, "Wouldn't it be beautiful to live here all the time? Is this not paradise?"

Rosita thinks for a moment and replies, "No, because paradise is not out there."

Looking confused, Gordon asks, "Where is it, then?"

She lifts her right hand from behind his head and taps the left side of his head once, saying, "In here."

Somewhat skeptically, he asks, "And love?"

She taps the side of his head again.

"Fear?" he asks.

Again, she taps the side of his head.

"Home?" he asks.

Once again, she taps the side of his head.

He demands, "What about my identity, who I am?"

Without hesitation, she taps the side of his head once more, smiling.

His expression changes to a grin of recognition and he says, "I couldn't agree more." Just as suddenly, his face grows serious and skeptical and he asks, "Say, where did you learn all that?"

Her arms wrap around his neck tightly and she turns her head to her right and rests it against his left shoulder. Softly, smiling warmly, she says, "I have a good teacher." He squeezes her tightly …

Rosita turns to Maria and softly adds, in Spanish, "Maybe more than we'll ever know."

Melinda says loudly so she can be heard in the living room, "Melanie was here about a month ago, Mom. Did you know that?" She puts her right hand across the boy's face and pushes him against her.

Rosita looks unfocused, dazed, as she replies, "What was that, baby? I'm sorry. Did you say, Melanie?"

"Yes," Melinda replies, patiently. "Melanie was here a month ago and she says little Gordon reminds her more and more of Dad." She pauses and looks out absentmindedly through the window above the kitchen sink. "You know, I can't remember Dad at all, Mom, try as I might."

"I know, baby girl," Rosita says with a slight wince, "but you two had a very special relationship, even if it was too short. He loved you very much and you loved him, too. Don't ever think otherwise."

A little softer, and looking down at the boy, Melinda says, "Thanks, Mom."

The boy, having finished the cookie, hugs his mother's thigh once more and darts to the door leading outside. As he holds the handle, he stops and turns back, yelling, "I'm gonna go play with my friends now, but I'll be back for you, Granma!" Immediately, he turns the handle, flings the door open, jumps outside and closes the door behind him with a slam.

Rosita turns to the window with the view of the yard, and smiles broadly watching her grandson join his friends. She laughs softly when he begins stomping, one-two with one leg, then one-two with the other and repeats. He puts his left arm out and swings his right wildly up and down, a born air guitarist. Under her breath, in Spanish, she mumbles, "Yes, I believe you shall." She smiles freely looking at the other kids touching their noses and hearts, while her little grandson plays rock star. In English, she adds, "Silly boy."

At that precise moment, the little boy turns in the direction of the window behind which sits his grandmother. His stomping and arm-flailing halts immediately, while the corner of his mouth lifts in the freakily similar half-smile of his grandfather. He forms his hands into little pistols, with the thumbs extended and index fingers pointed. Slowly, he raises his pistols flush with his face, fingers pointing up, holding them in that position for a brief moment. Twisting his hands to point to the window, he thrusts them forward a few inches, and, still wearing that half-smile, he winks his left eye, once.

978-0-595-41675-
0-595-41675-6

Printed in the United States
137420LV00004B/57/A